Heart of the World

Heart of the World

H. Rider Haggard

ÆGYPAN PRESS

Special thanks to John Bickers and Dagny.

This text, prepared from an 1896 edition published by Longmans, Green and Co., and printed from American plates by Spottiswoode and Co., New Street Square, London.

Heart of the World
A publication of
ÆGYPAN PRESS
www.aegypan.com

DEDICATION

I inscribe this story of the Golden City
"Heart of the World"
to my namesake and godchild
Henry Rider Haggard
of Butler, U.S.A.

Ditchingham,
Christmas Day, 1894.

Prologue

DON IGNATIO

The circumstances under which the following pages come to be printed are somewhat curious and worthy of record. Within the last few years a certain English gentleman, whom we will call Jones, because it was not his name, chanced to be employed as the manager of a mine not far from the Usumacinto River, the upper reaches of which divide the Mexican State of Chiapas from the Republic of Guatemala.

Now life at a mine in Chiapas, though doubtless it has some compensations, does not altogether fulfil a European's ideal of happiness. To begin with, the work is hard, desperately hard, and though the climate is healthy enough among the mountains, there are valleys where men may die of fever. Of sport, strictly speaking, there is none, for the forests are too dense to hunt in with any comfort, and, if they were not, the swarms of venomous insects of various degree, that haunt them, would make this particular relaxation impossible.

Society also, as we understand it, is conspicuous by its absence, and should a man chance even to be married, he could not well bring his wife into regions that are still very unsettled, across forest paths, through rivers, and along the brinks of precipices, dangerous and impassable enough to strike terror to the heart of the stoutest traveler.

When Mr. Jones had dwelt for a year at the mines of La Concepcion, the fact of his loneliness, and a desire for acquaintances more congenial than the American clerk of the stores and his Indian laborers, came home to him with some force. During the first months of his residence he had attempted to make friends with the owners of some neighboring *fincas* or farms. This attempt, however, he soon gave up in disgust, for these men proved to be half-breeds of the lowest class, living in an atmosphere of monotonous vice.

In this emergency, being a person of intelligence, Jones fell back upon intellectual resources, and devoted himself, so far as his time would allow, to the collection of antiquities, and to the study of such of the numerous ruins of pre-Aztec cities and temples as lay within his reach. The longer he pursued these researches, the more did they fascinate his imagination. Therefore, when he chanced to hear that, on the farther side of the mountain, at a *hacienda* called Santa Cruz, there dwelt an Indian, Don Ignatio by name, the owner of the *hacienda*, who was reported to have more knowledge of the *antiguos*, their history and relics, than anybody else in this part of Mexico, he determined to visit him upon the first opportunity.

This, indeed, he would have done before, for Don Ignatio boasted an excellent reputation, had it not been for the length of the journey to his home. Now, however, the difficulty was lessened by an Indian who offered to point out a practicable path over the mountain, which brought the *hacienda* of Santa Cruz to within a three-hours' ride on mule-back from La Concepcion, in place of the ten hours that were necessary to reach it by the more frequented road. Accordingly, one day in the dry season, when work was slack at the mine, owing to the water having fallen too low to turn the crushing-mill, Jones started. This was on a Saturday, for on the Monday previous he had dispatched a runner to Don Ignatio announcing his intended visit, and received in reply a most courteous and well-written letter, begging him to pass the next Sunday at the *hacienda*, "where any English gentleman would always be most welcome."

As he approached the *hacienda*, he was astonished to see the *façade* of an enormous white stone building of a semi-Moorish style of architecture, having towers and ornamented doorways at either end, and a large dome rising from the center of its flat roof. Riding through the *milpas*, or corn-fields, and groves of cocoa and coffee bushes, all in a perfect state of cultivation, which covered many acres on every side of the building, Jones came to the gateway of a large *patio*, or courtyard, where grew several gigantic *ceiba* trees, throwing their grateful shade over the mouth of a well. From under these trees an Indian appeared, who evidently had been watching for his arrival, and, taking the horse, informed him, with many salutations, that the Señor Ignatio was at even-song with his people in the chapel yonder, according to his habit, but that the prayers would soon be finished.

Leaving his horse in charge of the Indian, Jones went to the chapel, and, its great doors being open, he entered and sat down. So soon as his eyes became accustomed to the dim light, he perceived that the place was unusually beautiful, both in its proportions and its decorations.

The worshippers also were many — perhaps they numbered three hundred, clearly all of them Indians employed upon the estate; and so intent were they upon their devotions that his entry was not even noticed. To his mind, however, the most curious object in the building was a slab of white marble, let into the wall above the altar, whereon the following inscription was engraved in Spanish, in letters so large that he had no difficulty in reading it:

"Dedicated by Ignatio, the Indian, to the memory of his most beloved friend, James Strickland, an English gentleman, and Maya, Princess of the Heart, his wife, whom first he met upon this spot. Pray for their souls, of your charity, O passer-by."

While Jones was wondering who this James Strickland, and Maya, Princess of the Heart, might be, and whether it was his host who had set up the tablet to their memory, the priest pronounced his benediction, and the congregation began to leave the church.

The first to pass its doors was an Indian gentleman, whom Jones rightly took to be Don Ignatio himself. He was a man of about sixty years, but one who looked much older than his age, for sorrow, hardship, and suffering had left their marks upon him. In person he was tall and spare, nor did a slight lameness detract from the dignity of his bearing. His dress was very simple and quite innocent of the finery and silver buttons which have so much attraction for the Mexican mind, consisting as it did of a sombrero of Panama straw, with a black ribbon in place of the usual gilt cord, a clean white jacket and shirt, a black tie fastened in a bow, a pair of drab-colored trousers, and brown boots of European make.

Indeed, the only really remarkable thing about Don Ignatio was his face. Never, thought Jones, had he beheld so beautiful a countenance, or, to be more accurate, one that gave him such assurance of its owner's absolute goodness and purity of nature. The features were those of a highbred Indian, thin and delicately cut; the nose aquiline, the cheekbones and brow prominent, while beneath the latter shone a pair of large and soft black eyes, so tender and trustful in their expression that they seemed almost out of place in the face of a man.

He stood by the door of the chapel, in the light of the setting sun, leaning somewhat heavily on a stick, while the Indians filed past him. Every one of these, man, woman, and child, saluted him with the utmost reverence as they went, some of them, especially the children, kissing his long and finely-shaped hand when they bade him good-night in terms of affection, such as "father," and called on the Saints to guard him. Jones, watching them, reflected upon the difference of their attitude from that of the crouching servility which centuries of oppression have induced in their race towards any master of white blood, and wondered to what his host's influence over them was due. It was at this moment that Don Ignatio turned and saw him.

"A thousand pardons, señor," he said in Spanish, with a shy and singularly engaging smile as he lifted his sombrero, showing his long hair, which, like his pointed beard, was almost white. "You must indeed have thought me rude, but it is my custom at the end of the week's work to attend worship with the peons — do not press round the noble *Inglese,* my children — also I did not think that you would arrive before the sun was down."

"Pray don't apologize, señor," answered Jones; "I have been much interested in watching all your servants at their devotions. What a beautiful chapel this is! May I look at it before you shut the doors?"

"Certainly, señor. Like the rest of the house, it is fine. The old monks who designed it two hundred years ago — for this was a great monastery — knew how to build, and labor was forced in those days and cost nothing. Of course I have repaired it a great deal, for those who lived here before me did not trouble about such things.

"You would scarcely think, señor, that in the old days, twenty years ago, this place was a nest of highway robbers, smugglers, and man-slayers, and that these people whom you see tonight, or their fathers, were slaves with no more rights than a dog.

"But so it was. Many a traveler has lost his life in this house or its neighborhood. I, myself, was nearly murdered here once. Look at the carving of that altar-piece. It is fine, is it not? Those *sapote* wood columns date from the time of the old monks. Well, I have known Don Pedro Moreno, my predecessor, tie human beings to them in order to brand them with red-hot irons."

"To whom does that inscription refer?" asked Jones, pointing to the marble slab which has been described.

Don Ignatio's face grew very sad as he answered:

"It refers, señor, to the greatest friend I ever had, the man who saved my life at the risk of his own when I came by this limp, and one who was dear to me with a love passing the love of woman. But there was a woman who loved him also, an Indian woman too, and he cared for her more than he did for me, as was right, for has not God decreed that a man should leave his friends, yes, his father and mother even, and cleave unto his wife?"

"He married her then?" said Jones, who was growing interested.

"Oh, yes; he married her, and in a strange place and fashion. But it is an old story, señor, and with your permission I will not tell it; even to think of it revives too many painful memories, memories of death and loss, and disappointed ambition, and high hopes unfulfilled. Perhaps, one day, if I have the courage and live long enough, I will write it all down. Indeed, some years ago I made a beginning, and what I wrote seemed foolishness, so I gave up the task.

"I have lived a rough life, señor, and met with many adventures in it, though, thanks be to God, my last years have been spent in peace. Well, well, it is coming to an end now, and were it not for the thought that my people here may fall into evil hands when I am gone, that would not trouble me.

"But come, señor, you are hungry, and the good father, who has promised to eat with us, must ride tonight to celebrate a mass tomorrow at a village three leagues away, so I have ordered supper early. The porter with your bag arrived safely; it has been placed in your chamber, the Abbot's room it is called, and if you will follow me I will show you a short path to it from the chapel."

Then he led the way to a little door in the wall. Unlocking this door, they passed up some narrow stairs, at the head of which was a landing-place with a window, or rather *grille*, so arranged that, while it was invisible from below, an observer standing there could hear and see all that passed in the chapel.

"This was the place," said Don Ignatio, "whence the old abbots kept secret watch upon the monks, and it was here that once I saw a sight which I am not likely to forget."

Then he passed on through several long and intricate passages, till he came to a sitting room filled with handsome old Spanish furniture.

"Your sleeping-place lies beyond, señor," he said, opening another door that led into a large and dreary-looking chamber, lighted by heavily-barred windows, of which the sills were not less than ten feet from the ground.

On the walls were frescoes of the Last Judgment, and of scenes inspired by the bloody drama of the Inquisition, grim to look on and somewhat injured by damp, but executed with great power and vivid, if distorted, imagination. Below the center window, and reaching to within three feet of the floor, was an ancient full-length portrait of one of the abbots of the monastery, life-size and painted in oils upon a panel, representing a man of fierce and evil countenance, over whose tonsured head the Holy Spirit was shown hovering in the shape of a dove. For the rest, the room was well, if lightly, furnished, and boasted the luxury of squares of matting laid upon the brick floor.

"I fear that you will think this but a dismal apartment, señor," said Don Ignatio, "still it is our guest-chamber; moreover, there is a room attached which I thought might be useful to you to write in, should you wish to do so. The people here say that the place is haunted, but I know you Englishmen do not bother about such things. It is not wonderful, however, that they talk thus, seeing that murders were done in this chamber in the time of Don Pedro Moreno. Indeed, he laid a plot to kill me and my friend here, and, though he did not succeed in that instance, when I came into possession afterwards, I found several skeletons beneath the floor — two of them, I remember, just where the bed stands now — and gave them decent burial."

Jones, as in honor bound, declared himself to be totally indifferent to representations of tortures of the Inquisition, memories of departed abbots, skeletons of murdered men beneath the floor, ghosts, and *hoc genus omne.* Still, though he never confessed it to his host, his first night in the abbot's chamber, owing probably to the strong coffee which he had drunk, was not altogether a pleasant experience. In after days, however, he became well accustomed to the place, and, indeed, preferred it to any other room in the *hacienda.*

In contrast to the rude and ill-dressed fare with which Jones was fain to satisfy himself at the mine, Don Ignatio's supper was a feast worthy of Epicurus, especially as it was free from the horrible messes, compounded of oil and the inward parts of animals, that figure so largely in Mexican cookery.

After their meal, cigars and black coffee were handed round, of which the raw materials had been grown on the estate, and never in his life did Jones smoke better tobacco. When the *padre* — a gentle and well-informed man — had departed, Jones began to speak of the antiquities of the country. Soon he found that his host's knowledge of the subject had not been exaggerated, seeing that he was even able to decipher hieroglyphic writings of which the key was supposed to be lost, and to give an outline of the history of the races who built the great temples and palaces, whereof so many ruins are to be found in the Palenque district.

"It is sad to think," said Jones presently, "that nothing in which the breath of life remains is left of all this civilization. If only the old legend of the Golden City, hidden away somewhere in the unexplored recesses of Central America, were true, I think that I would give ten years of my existence to visit it. It would be a glorious thing to step back into the past, to see a system at work, and mingle with a people of which the world has lost all count and knowledge; for, let the imagination be active as it will, it is practically impossible to reconstruct these things from ruins and traditions. In fact, Don Ignatio, I do not understand how it is that you, who have never seen the *antiguos* in the flesh, can talk about them so certainly."

"If I had never seen them, señor," he answered, quietly, "it would be wonderful. Indeed, you might be justified in setting me down as a teller of tales, but it chances that I *have* seen the Golden City of fable and its civilization, and I can assure you that its wonders were far greater than any that have been told of in legend, or even by the Spanish romancers."

"What!" gasped Jones, "what! Have I been drinking too much of your excellent wine? Am I asleep, or did I hear you say that you, the gentleman sitting before me, with your own eyes had seen the secret city of the Indians?"

"You heard me say so, señor, though I did not in the least expect you to believe me. Indeed, it is because I cannot bear to be thought a liar, that I have never said anything of this story, and for this same reason I shall not repeat it to you, since I do not wish that one whom I hope will become my friend should hold me in contempt.

"In truth I am sorry that I have spoken so freely, but, in support of my veracity, I will beg you to remember that among the huge forests, wildernesses, and *sierras* of Central America, where no white man has set his foot, and whence the Indians vanished generations since, there is room for many ancient cities. Why, señor, within two hundred miles or less of where we sit tonight, there exist tribes of *Lacandones,* or unbaptised Indians, who have never seen a white man and who still follow their fathers' faiths. No, señor, that story shall never be told, at any rate in my lifetime, for I have nothing to show in proof of it, or at least only one thing —"

"What is it?" asked Jones, eagerly.

"You shall see if you wish, señor," his host answered, and left the room.

Presently he returned with a little leather bag from which he extracted a very curious and beautiful ornament. It was a great emerald, by far the largest that Jones had ever seen, uncut, but highly polished. This stone, which was set in pure gold, obviously had formed the clasp of a belt and could also be used as a seal; for on it, cut in *intaglio,* was the mask of a solemn and deathlike human face surrounded by a hiero-glyphic inscription, while on the reverse were other hieroglyphics.

"Can you read this writing?" asked Jones, when he had examined the ornament.

"Yes, señor. The words in front are: 'O Eyes and Mouth, look on me, plead for me.' And those on the back: 'Heart of Heaven, be thou my home.'"

"It is wonderful," said Jones, restoring the relic with a sigh, for he would have given everything that he had, down to his shoes, to possess it. "And now will you not make an exception in my favor, and tell me the story?"

"I fear that I cannot oblige you, señor," Don Ignatio answered, shaking his head.

"But," pleaded Jones, "having revealed so much, it is cruel to hide the rest."

"Señor," said his host, "will you take some more coffee? No. Then shall we walk a little on the roof and look at the view; it is pretty by moonlight, and the roofs here are wonderful, all built of solid stone; there is a tradition that the old monks used to dine on them in summer. They have a loopholed wall round them whence that abbot, whose portrait hangs in your sleeping-chamber, beat back a great attack of the Indians whom his oppression stirred into rebellion.

"Tomorrow I shall hope to show you round the lands, which have repaid me well for my twenty years of cultivation. Everybody in Mexico runs after mines, but its soil is the richest mine of all. I knew that, and, seeing the capacities of the place, I sold the other emeralds which went with this clasp — they were fine stones, but unengraved, and therefore of no particular interest — and bought it cheap enough. Now that the country is more settled, and I have planted so much, its value has become great, and will be greater still when all the young cocoa bushes are in full bearing a few years hence.

"There, thanks be to the Saints, the stair is done — of late my back hurts me when I climb up steps. The air is sweet, is it not, señor, and the prospect pleasing? Look, the river shines like silver. Ah! how beautiful is God's world! It makes me sad to think of leaving it, but doubtless He will provide still finer places for us to work and serve Him in, gardens where sin and grief cannot enter. Surely there is room enough yonder," and he nodded toward the sky.

*T*his was but the first of many nights that Jones spent under Don Ignatio's hospitable roof, where, as the months went by, he grew more and more welcome. Soon he conceived a great affection for the grave, sweet-natured, kindly old Indian gentleman, whose mind seemed to be incapable of any evil thought, and whose chief ambitions were to improve his land and do good to all about him, more especially to his Indian servants or peons.

In the beginning of their intimacy they made several expeditions together to inspect ruins in the neighborhood, and once Don Ignatio came to stay with him at the mine of La Concepcion, where his visit proved of the greatest use to Mr. Jones and the company he served. One of the difficulties in working this particular mine lay in the scarcity of labor. At a word from Don Ignatio this trouble vanished. He sent for a *cacique*, who lived in the mountains, and spoke to him, and lo! within a week, fifty stalwart Indians appeared to offer their services at the mine, thus affording one of many instances that came to Jones's knowledge, of his friend's extraordinary influence among the natives.

As time went on, however, these excursions ceased, since Don Ignatio's health grew too feeble to allow him to leave the *hacienda*.

At length, it was when they had been acquainted for nearly two years, a messenger arrived at the mine one morning, saying that he was instructed by his master, Don Ignatio, to tell the Señor Jones that he lay dying and would be glad to see him. He was to add, however, that if it should be in any way inconvenient, the Señor Jones must not trouble himself to come for so small a matter, as his master had written a letter which would be delivered to him after his death.

Needless to say the Señor Jones traveled across the mountains as fast as the best mule he owned would carry him. On arriving at the *hacienda* he found Don Ignatio lying in his room, almost paralyzed and very weak, but perfectly clear-headed and rejoiced to see him.

"I am about to make my last journey, friend," he said, "and I am glad, for of late I have suffered a great deal of pain in my back, the result of an ancient injury. Also it is time that a helpless old man should make room for a more active one." And he looked at his visitor strangely, and smiled.

Jones, whose feelings were touched, made the usual reply as to his having many months to live, but Don Ignatio cut him short.

"Don't waste time like that, friend," he said, "but listen. Ever since we knew each other you have been trying to extract from me the story of how I came to visit the city, Heart of the World, and of my friend, James Strickland, whom, thanks be to God, I so soon shall see again.

"Well, I never would tell it to you, though once or twice I nearly did, so when I saw how my silence chagrined you, partly because I pride myself upon being able to keep a secret when pressed to reveal it, and also because I am selfish and knew that so soon as you had heard my story, you would cease to interest yourself in a stupid, failing old man, for who is there that cares about the rind when he has sucked the orange?

"Also there were other reasons: for instance, I could not have related that history without displaying unseemly emotion, and I know that you Englishmen despise such exhibitions. Lastly, if I told it at all, I desired to tell it fully and carefully, keeping everything in proportion, and this it would have been difficult to do by word of mouth. Yet I have not wished to disappoint you altogether, and I have wished that some record of the curious things which I have seen in my life should be preserved, though this last desire alone would not have been sufficiently strong to move me to the task which I finished ten days ago, before the paralysis crept into my arm.

"May I trouble you to open that cupboard near the foot of the bed, and to give me the pile of writing that you will find in it. A thousand thanks. Here, señor, in these pages, if you care to take the trouble to read them, is set out an account of how I and my English friend came to visit the Golden City, of what we saw and suffered there, and of some other matters which you may think superfluous, but that are not without their bearing upon the tale. I fear that my skill in writing is small, still perhaps it may serve its turn, and if not, it matters nothing, seeing that you seek the spirit, not the letter, and are not sufficient of a Spanish scholar to be too critical.

"Now take the book and put it away, for the very sight of it wearies me, recalling the hours of labor that I have spent on it. Also I wish to talk of something more important. Tell me, friend, do you propose to stop in this country, or to return to England?"

"Return to England! Why, I should starve where there are no mines to manage. No, I am too poor."

"Then would you return if you were rich?" asked the dying man anxiously.

"I do not know; it depends. But I think that I have been too long away to go to live in England for good."

"I am glad to hear that, friend, for I may as well tell you at once that I have made you my heir, so that henceforth you will be a wealthy man as we understand wealth in this country."

"You have made me your heir!" stammered Jones.

"Yes. Why should I not? I like you well, and know you to be a good and honest man. I have no relations and no friends, and, above all, I am sure that you will deal justly and gently by my people here, for I have watched your bearing towards those who work under you at the mine. Moreover, I have conditions to make which will not be the less binding on you because they are not set out in the will, namely, that you should live here yourself and carry on the work that I have begun, for so long as may be possible, and that, if you are forced to sell the place by any unforeseen circumstance, or to leave it away by testament, you should do so to an Englishman only, and one of whom you know something. Do you accept?"

"Indeed, yes, and I know not how to thank you."

"Do not thank me at all, thank your own character and honest face which have led me to believe that I can make no better disposal of my property. And now go, for I am tired, but come to see me again tomorrow morning after the priest has left."

So Jones, who had entered that room possessed of a hard-earned eight hundred a year, departed from it the owner of a property which, before long, became worth as many thousands annually, as any who have visited him at Santa Cruz can testify. Three days later Don Ignatio passed away peacefully, and was laid to his rest in the chapel of the *hacienda.*

*T*his, then, was how the story of the city, Heart of the World, and of Don Ignatio and his friend, James Strickland, who saw it, came into the hands of him whom we have called Jones.

Here follows a translation of the manuscript.

Chapter I

HOW THE PLOT FAILED

I, Ignatio, the writer of this history, being now a man in my sixty-second year, was born in a village among the mountains that lie between the little towns of Pichaucalco and Tiapa. Of all that district my father was the hereditary *cacique*, and the Indians there loved him much.

When I was a lad, perhaps nine years old, troubles arose in the country. I never quite understood them, or I may have forgotten the circumstances, for such things were always happening, but I think that they were caused by some tax which the government at Mexico had imposed upon us unjustly. Anyhow, my father, a tall man with fiery eyes, refused to pay a tax, and, after a while, a body of soldiers arrived, mounted upon horses, who shot down a great number of the people, and took away some of the women and children.

Of my father they made a prisoner, and next day they led him out while my mother and I were forced to look on, and sat him by the edge of a hole that they had dug, holding guns to his head and threatening to shoot him unless he would tell them a secret which they were anxious to learn. All he said, however, was that he wished that they would kill him at once, and so free him from the torment of the mosquitoes which hummed around him.

But they did not kill him then, and that night they put him back in a prison, where I was brought to visit him by the *padre*, Ignatio, his cousin and my godfather. I remember that he was shut up in a dirty place, so hot that it was difficult even to breathe, and that there were some drunken Mexican soldiers outside the door, who now and again threatened to make an end of us Indian dogs.

My godfather, the priest Ignatio, confessed my father in a corner of the cell, and took something from his hand. Then my father called me to him and kissed me, and with his own fingers for a few moments he hung about my neck that thing which the priest had taken from him, only to remove it again and give it to Ignatio for safe-keeping, saying: "See that the boy has it, and its story with it, when he comes of age."

Now my father kissed me again, blessing me in the name of God, and as he did so great tears ran down his face. Then the priest Ignatio took me away, and I never saw my father anymore, for the soldiers shot him next morning, and threw his body into the hole that they had dug to receive it.

After this, my godfather, cousin, and namesake, Ignatio, took me and my mother to the little town of Tiapa, of which he was priest, but she soon died there of a broken heart.

In Tiapa we lived in the best house in the place, for it was built of stone and set upon a bank overhanging a beautiful rushing river with water that was always clear as glass, however much it rained, which river ran a hundred feet or more below the windows.

About Tiapa there is little to say, except that in those days the people were for the most part thieves, and such great sinners that my cousin, the *padre* would not shrive some of them, even on their deathbeds. There was a church, however, whereof the roof was overgrown with the most beautiful orchids. Also the roads were so bad that, except in the dry season, it was difficult to travel either to or from the town.

Here in this forgotten place I grew up, but not without education, as might have been expected, seeing that my cousin was a good scholar, and did all he could to keep me out of mischief.

When I was about fifteen years of age, of a sudden a desire took hold of me to become a priest. It was in this wise: One Sunday evening I sat in the church at Tiapa, looking now at the sprays of orchid flowers that swung to and fro in the breeze outside the window, and now at the votive pictures on the walls, offerings made by men and women who had called upon their patron saints in the hour of danger and had been rescued by them — here from fire, there from murderers, and here again from drowning; rude and superstitious daubs, but doubtless acceptable to God, who could see in them the piety and gratitude of those that out of their penury had caused them to be painted.

As I sat thus idly, my godfather, the good priest, began to preach. Now, it chanced that two nights before there had been a dreadful murder in Tiapa. Three travelers and a boy, the son of one of them, passing from San Christobel to the coast, stopped to spend the night at a house near our own. With them they brought a mule-load of dollars, the price of the merchandise that they had sold at San Christobel, which some of our fellow-townsmen, half-breeds of wicked life, determined to steal.

Accordingly, to the number of ten, these assassins broke into the house where the travelers lodged, and, meeting with resistance, they cut down the three of them with *machetes*, and possessed themselves of the silver. Just as they were leaving, one of the thieves perceived the boy hiding beneath a bed, and, dragging him out, they killed him also, lest he should bear witness against them.

Now, those who had done this deed of shame were well known in the town; still none were arrested, for they bribed the officers with part of their booty. But my godfather, seeing some of them present in the church, took for his text the commandment — "Thou shalt do no murder."

Never have I heard a finer sermon; indeed, before it was finished, two of the men rose and crept from the church conscience-stricken, and when the preacher described the slaughter of the lad whom their wicked hands had of a sudden hurled into eternity, many of the congregation burst into tears.

I tell this story because it was then for the first time, as I thought of the murdered boy, who some few days before had been as full of life as I was myself, that I came to know what death meant, and to understand that I also must die and depart forever either into heaven or hell. I shook as the thought struck me, and it seemed to me that I saw Death standing at my elbow, as he stands today, and then and there I determined that I would be a priest and do good all my life, in order that I might find peace at the last and escape the fate of the evil.

On the morrow I went into my godfather's room and told him of my desire. He listened to me attentively, and answered; "I would that it might be so, my son, holding as I do that the things of the world to come outweigh those of this present earth ten thousandfold, but it cannot be, for reasons that you shall learn when you are older. Then, when my trust is ended, you may make your choice, and, if you still wish it, become a priest."

* * * * *

Five more years passed away, during which time I grew strong and active, and skilled in all manly exercises. Also I studied much under the teaching of my godfather, who sent even to Spain to buy me books.

Among these books were many histories of my own race, the Indians, and of their conquest by the Spaniards, all that had been published indeed. Of such histories I never tired, although it maddened me to read of the misfortunes and cruel oppression of my people, who today were but a nation of slaves.

At length, on my twentieth birthday, my godfather, who now was grown very old and feeble, called me into his chamber, and, having locked the door, he spoke to me thus:

"My son, the time has come when I must deliver to you the last messages of your beloved father, my cousin and best friend, who was murdered by the soldiers when you were a little child, and tell you of your descent and other matters.

"First, then, you must know that you are of royal and ancient blood, for your forefather in the eleventh degree was none other than Guatemoc, the last of the Aztec emperors, whom the Spaniards murdered, which descent I can prove to you by means of old writings and pedigrees; also it is known and attested among the Indians, who even now do not forget the stock whence sprang their kings."

"Then by right I am Emperor of Mexico," I said proudly, for in my folly it seemed a fine thing to be sprung from men who once had worn a crown.

"Alas! my son," the old priest answered sadly, "in this world might is the only right, and the Spaniards ended that of your forefathers long ago by aid of torture and the noose. Save that it will earn you reverence among the Indians, it is but a barren honor which you inherit with your blood.

"Yet there is one thing that has come down to you from your ancestor, Guatemoc, and the monarchs who ruled before him. Perchance you remember that on the night previous to his death, your father set an amulet upon your neck, and, removing it again, gave it to me to keep. Here is that amulet."

Then he handed me a trinket made of the half of a heart-shaped emerald, smooth with wear, but unpolished, that, if joined to its missing section, would have been as large as a dove's egg. This stone was not broken, but cut from the top to the bottom, the line of separation being so cunningly sawn that no man, unless he had one half before him, could imitate the other. The charm was bored through so as to be worn upon a chain, and engraved upon its surface were some strange hieroglyphics and the outline of half a human face.

"What is it?" I asked.

The old priest shrugged his shoulders, and answered:

"A relic which had to do with their wicked heathen magic and rites, I suppose. I know little about it, except that your father told me it was the most valued possession of the Aztec kings, and that the natives believe that when the two halves of this stone come together, the men of white blood will be driven from Central America and an Indian emperor shall rule from sea to sea."

"And where is the other half, father?"

"How should I know," he answered testily, "who have no faith in such stories, or in stones with the heads of idols graven upon them? I am a priest, and therefore your father told me little of the matter, since it is not lawful that I should belong to secret societies. Still, some such society exists, and, in virtue of the ownership of that talisman, you will be head of it, as your ancestors were before you, though, so far as I can learn, the honor brought them but little luck.

"I know no more about it, but I will give you letters to a certain Indian who lives in the district of which your father was *cacique,* and, when you show him the stone, doubtless he will initiate you into its mysteries, though I counsel you to have nothing to do with them.

"Listen, Ignatio, my son, you are a rich man; how rich I cannot tell you, but for many generations your forefathers have hidden up treasure for an object which I must explain, and the gold will be handed over to you by those of your clan in whose keeping it is. It was because of this treasure that your father and your great-grandfather were done to death with many others, since the rumor of it came to the ears of those that ruled in Mexico, who, when they failed to force the secret from them, tormented and killed them in their rage.

"Now, this was the message of your father to you concerning the wealth which he and his ancestors had hidden:

"'Tell my son, Ignatio, should he live to grow up, that there has never departed from our family the desire to win back the crown that Guatemoc lost, or at least to drive out the accursed Spaniards and their spawn, and to establish an Indian Republic. To this end we have heaped up wealth for generations, that it might serve us when the hour was ripe; and because of this wealth, of which the whisper could not altogether be hid in a land which is full of spies, some of us have come to cruel deaths, as I am about to do tonight.

"'But I shall die keeping my secret, and when my son grows up others may rule at Mexico, or the matter may have been forgotten: at least the gold will be where I left it. Now, say to my son that it is my hope that he will use it in the cause to further which it has been amassed; that he will devote his life to the humbling of our white masters, and to the uplifting of the race which for centuries they have robbed, murdered, and enslaved.

"'Nevertheless, say to him that I lay no commands upon him as to these matters, seeing that he must follow his own will about them, for I cannot forget that, from generation to generation, those who went before him have reaped nothing but disaster in their struggle against the white devils, whom, because of the sins and idolatry of our forefathers, it has pleased God to set over us.'

"Those were your father's words, my son, which he spoke to me in the hour of his murder. And now you will understand why I said that you must wait before you determined to be a priest. If that is still your wish, it can be fulfilled, for your father left it to you to follow whatever life you might desire."

When he had finished speaking I thought for a while, and answered: "So long as my father's blood is unavenged I cannot become a priest."

"It is as I feared," said the old man with a sigh, "that cursed talisman which lies about your neck has begun its work with you, Ignatio, and you will tread the path that the others trod, perchance to die in blood as they died. Oh! why cannot man be content to leave the righting of wrongs and the destinies of nations in the hands of the Almighty and His angels?"

"Because for good or evil the Almighty chooses men to be His instruments," I answered.

W ithin a week from this day some Indians came to Tiapa disguised as porters, whose mission it was to lead me to the mountains among which my father had lived, and where his treasure still lay hidden.

Bidding farewell to my godparent, the priest, who wept when he parted from me, I started upon my journey, keeping my destination secret. As it chanced, I never saw him more, for a month later he was seized with some kind of *calentura*, or fever, and died suddenly. The best thing I can say of him is that, with one exception, there lives no man in heaven above whom I so greatly desire to meet again.

On the third day of my journey we reached a narrow pass in the mountains, beyond which lay an Indian village. Here my guides took me to the house of one Antonio, to whom the *padre* Ignatio had given me letters, an old man of venerable aspect, who greeted me warmly, and made me known to several *caciques* who were staying with him, I knew not why.

So soon as we were alone in the house, one of these *caciques*, after addressing me in words which I could not understand, asked me if I had a "Heart." To this I replied that I hoped so, whereat they all laughed. Then the man Antonio, coming to me, unbuttoned my shirt, revealing the talisman that had belonged to my father, and at the sight of it the company bowed.

Next the doors were locked, and, sentries having been posted before them, a ceremony began, which even now it is not lawful that I should describe in detail. On this solemn occasion I was first initiated into the mysteries of the Order of the Heart, and afterwards installed as its hereditary chief, thus becoming, while yet a boy, the absolute lord of a many thousand men, brethren of our Society, who were scattered far and wide about the land.

On the day after I had taken the final oaths, Antonio handed over to me the treasure that my ancestors hoarded in a secret place, which my father had left in his keeping, and it was a great treasure, amounting to more than a million dollars in value.

Now I was rich, both in men and money, still, following the counsel of Antonio, I abode for a while in the village, receiving those who came from every part of Mexico to visit me as Holder of the Heart, and as first in rank among the fallen peoples of the Indians.

It was during these months that I made the great error of my life. Some three miles from the village where I dwelt, lived two sisters, Indian ladies of noble blood, though poor, one of them a widow, and the other a very beautiful girl, younger than myself. It chanced that, riding past their house upon a certain Sunday evening, when most of the inhabitants of the valley were away at a *fiesta*, I heard screams coming from it.

Dismounting from my horse I ran in at the door, which was open, and saw one of the sisters, the widow, lying dead upon the ground, while two bandits, Mexicans, were attacking the younger woman. Drawing my *machete*, I cut down the first of them before he had time to turn, then I fell upon the second man with such fury that I drove him back against the wall. Seeing that his life was in danger, he called upon me not to kill him for the sake of a low Indian girl, which insult maddened me so that I slew him upon the spot, and caused his body, with that of his companion, to be buried secretly.

It happened that after this the girl whose life I had saved came to dwell in my village, where I saw much of her. So lovely was she and so clever, that soon she won my heart, and the end of it was that, being headstrong and in love, I married her, against the advice of Antonio and others of my brethren of the Order. It would have been better for the Indian people, and perhaps for me also, if I had died before I stood at the altar with this woman, though for a while she was a good wife, and, because of her cleverness, of great service to me at that time.

Now, it must be stated that during all these months I had not been idle. The more I thought on them, the more the wrongs of my countrymen, the real owners of the land, took hold of my mind, till at length they possessed it utterly, and I became an enthusiast and a dreamer. This was the object of my life — to form a great conspiracy, which should bring about a rising of the Indians in every province of Mexico upon a given day; then, when the Spaniards and their bastards, the Spanish Mexicans, had been stamped out, to re-establish the Empire of the Aztecs.

It was a madness, perhaps, but the madness lurked in my blood; my forefathers had suffered from and for it, and I think that it must have come down to us from our ancestor, Guatemoc, the greatest and most unfortunate Indian who ever lived. Where they failed I determined to succeed, and, strange to say, in the end I went near to success.

For years I labored, traveling to and fro about the land till there was no province where I was not known as the Holder of the Heart, and the chief by blood of the Indian tribes. Everywhere I strove to rouse the people from their sloth, and to win the *caciques,* or head men, to the cause, and I did not strive in vain. I used my great wealth to buy arms, to gain over the lukewarm with bribes, and in many other ways. When my fortune sank low I gathered more, for without gold nothing could be done. Treasures that were buried in the old days were given up to me as Lord of the Heart by those who had their secret; also many brought me money, each what he could spare, and I hoarded it against the hour of need.

For a year or more I was the greatest power in Mexico, and yet, though hundreds were privy to my plot, it was so well hidden that no whisper of it came to the ears of the Government. At length all was ready, and so carefully were my plans laid that success seemed certain; but the unforeseen happened, and I failed — thus:

That woman whose life I had saved, my own wife whom I loved and trusted, who was bound to my cause and that of my countrymen by every tie human and divine, betrayed me and it. Just before the time fixed for the rising, it was agreed that she should be placed, as one of whom we could be sure, to play the part of a servant in the house of the man who ruled Mexico in those days, that she might spy upon him.

Instead of so doing, she, my wife, fell in love with him. It is easy to guess the rest. One night, but a week before the appointed time, I and some five or six others, the leaders of our party, were seized. My companions were made away with secretly, but I was brought before the great man, who received me alone, holding a pistol in his hand.

"I know all your plans, friend," he said, "and I congratulate you on them, for they were cleverly managed. I know also that you have a great treasure in gold hidden away —" and he named the sum. "That wife of yours, whom you were fool enough to trust, has told me everything, but she cannot tell me where the money is hidden, for this you withheld from her, which shows that you are not altogether mad.

"Now, friend, I make you a fair offer — hand over this treasure, and you shall go free — of course when the day of vengeance is past and your sheep have found themselves without a shepherd — nor shall you be molested afterwards. Refuse to do so, and you will be brought to trial and die as you deserve."

"How can you promise for others?" I asked. "You are not the only white man who would have fallen."

"I can promise for others, first, because I am their master, and, secondly, because nobody but myself knows anything of this matter, since, if I told them, I must also share your wealth with them, and that, friend, I mean to keep. Give it up to me, and you may go and plot against my successors and the Government of Mexico as much as pleases you, and take your wife with you for aught I care; for, friend, having earned so comfortable a competence, I propose to leave a land where, as this business proves, people in authority are too apt to have their throats cut. Now choose, and be so good as to stand quite still while you are thinking the matter over, or I may be forced to shoot you."

"How about my associates?" I asked.

"I believe that three or four of them have been carried off — by typhus — within the last day or two, the prisons here are so unhealthy; but I am sure that if the gold is forthcoming, no more will sicken."

Then I chose, for I thought to myself that I might get more gold, but I could never get another life, and if I died many must suffer with me and all my hopes for the future of the Indian race would come to naught. Also I knew this villain to be a man of his word, and that what he promised he would fulfil.

Within ten days he had the money, and I was free to begin my life again, nor did any of those who were doomed to perish in it, learn the tale of the plot that had threatened them.

I was free; but what a freedom was this, when I had lost everything save the breath that God placed in my nostrils, and, perhaps, my honor. The great house that I had builded was fallen to the ground, the moneys I had amassed were stolen, the chief of my companions were dead, my credit as a deliverer of the people was gone, and my cause had become hopeless. All these things had come upon me because of a woman, a traitress, whom I had nurtured in my bosom.

At first I was dazed, but when I came to understand I swore a great oath before Heaven that, for her false sake, I would hate and renounce her sex; that, whatever might be the temptation, never again would I look kindly upon women, or have to do with one of them in word, or thought, or deed. That oath, so far as lay in my power, I have kept to this day, and I hope to keep through all eternity.

It may be asked what became of my wife. I do not know. I lifted no hand against her who was flesh of my flesh, but she perished. The story was known. I was forced to tell it to clear myself. After I escaped from the prison I lay ill for many weeks, and when I recovered she was gone. Others had been betrayed besides myself, and doubtless some of them had wreaked fitting vengeance on her. What it was I never asked.

For many years — twenty perhaps — I became a wanderer. Now as before the Indians loved me, and, as Lord of the heart and their hereditary *cacique*, in a sense I still was great, although but the shadow of power dwelt with me: the substance had departed, as it departs ever from those who fail. From time to time I strove to rebuild the plot; but, now that I was friendless and without fortune, few would follow me thus far.

So it came about that at length I abandoned the endeavor, and lived as best I could. I fought in three wars, and gained honors therein, and took my share in many adventures, all of which left me as poor as I had entered on them. At times I remembered my desire to become a priest, but now it was over late to study; also my hands were too much soiled with the affairs of the world.

Wearying of the struggle, I went back to my village in the mountains and dwelt there awhile, but this also wearied me, having nothing to do, and I turned my attention to the management of mines.

It was while I was thus employed, as a middle-aged man, that I made the acquaintance of James Strickland, who was destined to accompany me to the city, Heart of the World.

Chapter II

THE SEÑOR STRICKLAND

*T*wo-and-twenty years ago, I, Ignatio, visited a village in the State of Tamaulipas, named Cumarvo, a beautiful place, half-hidden in pine forests amongst the mountains. I came to this hamlet because a friend of mine, one of the brethren of the Order of the Heart, wrote to me saying that there was an Indian in the neighborhood who had in his possession an ancient Aztec scroll, which, being in picture-writing, neither he nor anyone else could read.

This scroll had descended to the Indian through many generations, and with it a tradition that it told of a very rich gold mine in the mountains whereof the site was lost, which had been closed to save it from the grip of Cortes, by the order of Guatemoc, my forefather, whom the Spaniards murdered — may their souls be accursed!

Now, I had been taught the secret of the picture-writing by old Antonio, my father's friend, when first I was initiated into the mysteries of the Heart, though it must die with me, for I believe that at this hour there is no other man living who can read it.

This writing the Indian was willing to give up to me as Lord of the Heart, and accordingly, having nothing better to do, I journeyed to Cumarvo to study it. In this matter, as in many others, I was destined to meet with disappointment, however — at any rate for a while; for, on my arrival at the house of my friend, I heard that the Indian had died of a sudden sickness, and that his son could not discover where the scroll was hidden.

Another thing I learnt also, namely, that a white man, an *Inglese*, the first who ever visited these parts, had come to the village about six months before, and was engaged in working some old silver mines on behalf of a company, a task that he found difficult, for the Mexican owners of land in the neighborhood, being jealous of him and angry because he paid his men a fair wage, were striving to prevent Indians from laboring in his mine.

Now the natives of this place, from Monday morning to Saturday night, were a gentle and industrious people, but they had this fault, that on the Saturday night many of them were accustomed to become drunk on *mescal*, the spirit that is distilled from the root of the aloe. Then their natures were changed, and fierce quarrels would spring up amongst them, for the most part about women, that ended often enough in bloodshed.

It chanced that such a fray arose on the night of my arrival at Cumarvo. On the morrow I saw the fruits of it as I walked down the little street which was bordered by white, flat-roofed houses and paved with cobble-stones, purposing to attend mass in the lime-washed church, where the bell rang night and day to scare evil spirits back to hell.

In the middle of the street, lying in the shade of a house, were two dead men. A handsome Indian girl, with a sullen and unmoved countenance, was engaged in winding a *serape*, or blanket, round one of the bodies; but the other lay untended, certain stains upon the clothing revealing the manner of its end. On a doorstep sat a third man, much wounded about the head and face, while the barber of the village, its only doctor, attempted to remove his hair with a pair of blunt scissors, so that he might dress the cuts.

The scene was dreadful, but no one took much notice of it, for Indian life is cheap, and in those days death by violence was even more common in Mexico than it is now. On the opposite side of the street an old woman chaffered with a passer-by about the price of her oranges, while some children with shouts and laughter strove to lasso and drag away a pig that haunted the place; and a girl on her way to mass stepped over the uncovered body which lay so quiet in the shade, and, recognizing it as that of a friend, crossed herself as she hurried on.

"What is the cause of this, señor?" I asked of the barber.

"I think that I have the honor of addressing Don Ignatio," the little man answered, and, lifting his hands from their work, he made a sign showing that he also was a member of our Brotherhood, though a humble one.

"Ah, I thought so," he went on as I gave the countersign; "we heard that you were going to visit us, and I am glad of it, for I weary of dressing wounds on Sundays, and perhaps you may be able to put a stop to these fights. The woman was the cause of it, of course, señor; these are not the first she has brought to their deaths," and he nodded at the girl who was wrapping the body in a blanket.

"You see, she was going to marry this man," and he tapped the Indian whose wounds he was dressing on the shoulder, "but she took up with that one," pointing to the nearest body, "whereon Number One here, being drunk with *mescal*, laid wait for Number Two and stabbed him dead. The girl who was with him ran for Number Three yonder, Number Two's brother, but Number One ambushed him, so he was killed also. Then, hearing the noise, the village guard came up and cut down our friend here with their *machetes*, but as you see, unfortunately, they did not kill him."

I heard, and anger took hold of me. Approaching the girl, I said:

"This is your doing, woman! Are you not afraid?"

"What of it?" she answered, sullenly; "can I help it if I am pretty, and men fight for me? Also, who are you who ask me whether I am afraid?"

"Fool!" cried the barber from the doorstep; "do you dare to speak thus to the Lord of the Heart?"

The girl started and replied:

"Why not? Is he then my lord?"

"Listen, girl!" I said; "others besides these have died through you."

"How do you know that?" she answered. "But what need to ask? If you are the Lord of the Heart you have the evil eye, and can read secrets without their being discovered to you."

"It is you that have the evil eye, woman, like many another of your sex!" I said. "Hear me, now: you will leave this place, and you will never return to it, for if you do, you die! Also, remember that if harm should come to anymore men on your account, wherever you go I shall know of it, and you will die there!"

"Whoever you are, you are not the Government, and have no right to kill me," she said, trying to hide the fear which crept into her dark eyes.

"No, woman, I am not the Government; but among our people I am more powerful than the Government. If you do not believe me, ask the doctor yonder, and he will tell you that I should be obeyed, even by people who had never seen me, where a troop of soldiers would be laughed at. If I say that you are to die, you will die in this way or in that, for my curse will be on you. Perhaps you may tumble over a precipice, or you may take a fever, or be drowned in crossing a river, *quien sabe!*"

"I know, lord, I know," she whispered, shivering, for now she was frightened. "Do not look so terribly at me; spare me this time for the love of God! I did not mean to do it, but when men put their hearts into a woman's hand, how can she help squeezing them, especially if she hates men? But I did not hate this one," and she touched the cheek of the dead Indian caressingly; "I really meant to marry him. It is that fellow whom I hate," pointing to her wounded lover, "and I hope that he will be shot, else I think that I shall poison him."

"You will not poison him, woman; and, though he deserves to die, you are worse than he. Now begone, and remember my words!"

Bending down, she touched the corpse's forehead with her lips, then, rising, said:

"I kiss your feet, Lord of the Heart," and went away without looking behind her, nor was she seen again in that village.

Then, with a sigh, I also was turning to go, for it saddened me to think that when drink got hold of them, a woman should have the power to change these men, who were my brethren, into savage beasts thirsting for each other's blood.

"Ah!" I mused, "had it not been for that other woman who destroyed me and my hope, by now I had begun to teach them better."

At this moment, looking up, I chanced to see a man such as I had never before beheld, standing by my side and gazing at me. Stories are told of how men and women, looking on each other for the first time, in certain cases are filled with a strange passion of love, of which, come what may, they can not again be rid.

Among many misfortunes, thanks be to my guardian angels, this fate has never overtaken me, yet at that moment I felt something that was akin to it — not love, indeed, but a great sense of friendship and sympathy for and with this man, which, mastering me then, is still growing to this hour, though its object has for many years been dead.

Perhaps it was the contrast between us that attracted me so much at first, since human beings are ever drawn towards their opposites in nature and appearance. I, as you, my friend, for whom I write this history, will remember, although you have only known me in my age, am tall, thin, and sallow, like all my race, with a sad expression reflecting the heart within, and melancholy eyes.

Very different were the mind and appearance of James Strickland, the Englishman. He was a fine man, over thirty years of age, short in proportion to his width, though somewhat spare in frame and slender in limb. His features were as clearly cut as those of an ancient god upon a marble wall; his eyes were blue as the sea, and, though just now they were troubled at the sight of death, merry like the eyes of a boy; his curling hair — for he had removed his hat in the presence of the dead — was yellow as mimosa bloom, darkening almost to red in the short beard and about the ears, where the weather had caught it; and beneath his shirt, which was open at the neck, his skin showed white like milk. For the rest, his hands were long and delicate, notwithstanding the hard work of which they bore traces; his glance was quick, and his smile the most pleasant that ever I had seen.

"Your pardon, señor," said this *Inglese,* in good Spanish, bowing to me as he spoke, "but unwittingly I have overheard some of your talk with yonder woman, and I cannot understand how it comes that you, a stranger, have so much authority over her. I wish that you would explain it to me in order that I might learn how to put a stop to such murders. These dead men were two of my best workmen, and I do not know where I shall look to replace them."

"I cannot explain it, señor," I answered, returning his bow, "further than to say that I have a certain rank among the Indians, on account of which they reverence me. Still, though I have no right to ask it of a stranger, I pray that you will forget any words of mine which may chance to have reached your ears, since of such authority the Government is jealous."

"By all means, señor; they are already forgotten. Well, *adios,* this sight is not so pleasant that I wish to study it," and replacing his hat upon his head, he passed on.

Although my journey proved to be in vain, seeing that the scroll I came to read had vanished, I lingered in the village of Cumarvo, alleging as the reason of my stay a hope that it might be discovered, but really, as I believe, because I desired to become friendly with this white man.

As it chanced, an opportunity was soon given to me to do him a signal service. I have stated that there dwelt men of position in this place, Mexicans who were jealous of the Englishman, and these people stirred up some discontented miners in his employ to make a plot to murder him, saying that, if they did so, they would win a great treasure which he kept hidden in his house.

This plot came to my ears through one of the Brotherhood, and I determined to frustrate it, to which end I collected together twenty good men and true, and, arming them with guns, bade them be silent about the matter, above all to the *Inglese,* whom I did not wish to alarm.

The plan of the murderers was at the hour of dawn to attack the house where the Señor Strickland slept with four or five servants only, and to put all within its walls to death. Accordingly, about one o'clock on the night fixed, I dispatched my men by twos and threes, instructing them to go round the hills at the back of the house, and, creeping into the garden, to hide themselves there among the trees till I appeared.

An hour later I followed them myself without being observed by the spies of the attacking party, for rain fell and the night was very dark. Arriving in the garden, I collected my men, and placed them in ambush under a low wall commanding the street, up which I knew the murderers must come. Here we waited patiently till the cocks crew and the dawn began to break in the east.

Presently we heard a stir in the village beneath, as of men marching, and in the gathering light we saw the murderers creeping stealthily up the street to the number of fifty or more. So great was their fear of the Englishman, that they thought it safer to bring many men to kill him, also each of the villains desired that his neighbor should be a sharer in the crime.

"Will you not wake up the *Inglese?*" asked the man next to me.

"No," I answered, "it will be time enough to wake him when the affair is settled. Let none of you fire till I give the word."

Now, the brigands in the street below — men without shame — after waiting a little time for the light to grow stronger, advanced towards the gate, looking like a procession of monks, for the air was chilly and each of them wore his *serape* wrapped about his head. In their hands they carried rifles and drawn *machetes.*

Within ten paces of the gate they paused for a minute to consult, and I heard their leader, a Mexican, direct half of them to creep round to the back of the house so as to cut off all escape. Then I whistled, which was the signal agreed upon, at the same time covering the Mexican with my rifle. Almost before the sound had left my lips, there followed a report of twenty guns, and some fifteen or sixteen of the enemy were stretched upon the ground.

For a moment they wavered, and I thought that the rest of them were going to fly, but this they dared not do, for they knew that they had been seen; therefore they rushed at the wall with a yell, firing as they came. As they climbed over it we met them with pistol shots and *machetes*, and for a few minutes the affair was sharp, for they were desperate, and outnumbered us.

Still they lost many men in scaling the wall and forcing the gate, and with the exception of fourteen who fled, and were for the most part caught afterwards, the rest of them we finished amongst the flowers and vegetables of the garden. Just as all was over, the Englishman, who was a sound sleeper, appeared yawning, dressed in white, and holding a pistol in his hand.

"What is this noise?" he asked, rubbing his eyes, "and why are you people fighting in my garden? Go away, all of you, or I shall shoot at you."

"I trust," I said, bowing, "that the señor will pardon us for disturbing him in his slumber, but this matter could not be settled without some noise. May I offer the señor my *serape?* The air is chilly, and he will catch cold in that dress."

"Thank you," he said, putting on the *serape*. "And now perhaps you will explain why you come to spoil my garden by making a battlefield of it."

Then I told him, and was astonished to see that as I went on he grew very angry.

"I suppose that I must thank you, gentlemen, for saving my life," he said at last, "though I never asked you to do it. But, all the same, I think it shameless that you should have had this fight in my own garden, without giving me the opportunity of sharing it. *Caramba!* am I a little girl that I should be treated in such a way?" And of a sudden he burst out laughing and shook me by the hand.

That day, when all the trouble was over, and the place had been made tidy, the Señor Strickland sent a man to ask if I would do him the pleasure to dine with him. I accepted, and as we sat smoking after dinner, having talked of the fight till we were tired of it, he spoke thus to me:

"Don Ignatio, I owe you my life, and, believe me, I am grateful, for I do not see why you should have risked so much for a foreign stranger."

"I did it because I like you, señor," I answered, "also because it is very pleasant to catch the wicked in their own toils. Those who perished this morning were villains, every one of them. They came in the hope of plunder, for such 'men without shame' will murder human beings for five dollars a head; but they were set on by others who hate you because you treat your Indian workmen fairly, and also because they do not wish foreigners here to compete with them, and think that you are but the first bird of the flock. Therefore they thought that it would be good policy to kill you so as to frighten away others who might follow. However, that danger has gone by, and you need have no more fear, for they have learnt a lesson which they will not forget."

"So much the better then," he answered, "for I have troubles enough to deal with here, without being bothered to protect my life against such contemptible vermin. And now, Don Ignatio, I hardly like to ask you, and I daresay that you will think the offer beneath contempt, but are you willing to accept an engagement? I am sadly in need of a sub-manager, one who could control the Indians, and to such a man I am prepared to pay a hundred dollars a month; the funds of the company I represent will not allow me to offer more."

I thought for a while and answered:

"Señor, the money is not enough to tempt me, though it will serve to buy food, lodging, and cigars, but I accept your offer for the same reason that I fought your battles this morning, because I like you, and will gladly do my best to serve you and your interests. Still, I must warn you, for aught I know, I may have to leave your service at short notice, for my time is not altogether my own. I also am the servant of a great company, señor, and though now I am on leave, as it were, and have been for these many years, I may be required at any moment."

*T*hus it was, then, that I entered the service of the Señor James Strickland, or rather of his company, in which I continued for something more than a year, working very hard, for the señor did not spare either me or himself. But as the records of those months of fruitless labor could have little interest for you, my friend, instead of writing of them, I will tell you in few words what was the history of this Englishman as he told it to me.

He was of noble blood, as might be seen in his face, for he had a right to be addressed as "honorable," which it would seem means more in England than it does here. Nevertheless, his father was a priest of the heretic church and quite poor, though, how this came about, you, being an Englishman, will understand better than I, seeing that in most countries it is the privilege of nobles to enrich themselves at the expense of others of less rank.

At any rate, when James Strickland's father died, his son, who was then a lad of twenty, found that he possessed in the world no more than five thousand dollars. This sum, being of adventurous mind and sanguine temperament, he invested in a ranch in Texas, where he endured much danger and hardship, and lost all his money.

After this experience, having nothing to live on and no friends, he was obliged to labor with his hands like a peon, and this he did in many ways. He broke horses, he herded cattle; once, even, for two months he sank so low — it makes me angry to write of it — as to be forced to wait upon the guests in an inn at Panama.

Thence he drifted to Nicaragua, and became mixed up in mining ventures, and when I first met him he had been a miner for ten years. Most of this time he spent managing a mine for an American, in the Chontales country, on the frontier of Honduras, where the fever is so bad that few white men can live. Here it was that he learned to speak Spanish and the Indian or Maya tongue. At length, after an attack of fever which nearly killed him, he left Honduras, and came to Mexico, where he accepted the management of this silver mine at Cumarvo. Hitherto it had been worked by a Mexican on behalf of its owners, who dismissed the rogue for stealing the ore and selling it.

This mine, though very rich, was hard to deal with profitably because of the water gathered in it, and all the months that the Señor Strickland had been its captain he was employed in driving a tunnel upwards from a lower level in the cliff, in order to drain the workings. Shortly after I came into his service this tunnel was finished, for now I was able to obtain plenty of labor, which before he had lacked, and we began to bring to bank ore running as high as two hundred ounces to the ton, so that for some months all went well.

Then of a sudden the ore body dipped straight downward, as though it had been bent over when hot, and we followed it till the water increased so much that we were unable to carry it out, for in those days there were no steam pumps in Mexico, such as are now used for the drying of mines. First we tried to strike another vein, but without success; then we attempted to pierce a second drainage tunnel at a still lower level, but, after more than three months' labor, the rock became so hard that we were obliged to abandon the task.

Now there was nothing to be done except to stop work at the tunnel, and report the matter by letter to the owners of the mine, employing ourselves meanwhile in the smelting of such ore as we had stacked. This, indeed, we needed to do in order to pay wages with the silver, seeing that after the first few months the owners ceased to remit us money.

One evening, on returning from the smelting-works to the house, I found the Señor Strickland, his chin resting on his hand and an unlighted cigar in his mouth, seated at a table, on which lay an open letter. All through our misfortunes and heavy labor he had never lost heart, or forgotten to smile and be merry, but now he looked sad as a man who has just buried his mother, and I asked him what evil thing had happened.

"Nothing particular, Ignatio," he answered; "but listen here." And he read the letter aloud.

It was from one of the owners of the mine, and this was the purport of it: that the shaft had become choked with water because of the incompetence and neglect of the señor; that they, the owners, hereby dismissed him summarily, refusing to pay him the salary due; and, lastly, that they held him responsible in his own person for such money as they had lost.

"Surely," I cried in wrath, when he had finished, "this letter was written by a man without shame, and I pray that he may find his grave in the stomachs of hogs and vultures!" for I forgot myself in my indignation against those that could speak thus of the señor, who had slaved day and night in their service, giving himself no rest.

"Do not trouble, Ignatio," he said, with a little smile, "it is the way of the world. I have failed, and must take the consequences. Had I succeeded, there would have been a different story. Still I think that, if ever I meet this man again, I will kick him for telling lies about me. Do you know, Ignatio, that, with the exception of one thousand dollars which remain to my credit in Mexico, I have spent all my own money that I had saved upon this mine, and of that thousand dollars, eight hundred are due to you for back pay, so, whatever trade I take to next, I shall not begin as a rich man."

"Be silent, I beg of you, señor," I answered, "for such words make my ears burn. What! am I also a thief that I should rob you, you who have already been plucked like a fowl for the good of others? Insult me once more by such thoughts and I will never pardon you."

And I left the house to calm myself by walking among the mountains, little knowing what I should hear before I entered it again.

Chapter III

THE SUMMONS

*A*s I walked down the street of the village I met my friend, with whom I had stayed when first I came to Cumarvo.

"Ah! lord," he said — for those who are initiated among the Indians give me this title when none are by — "I was seeking you. The scroll has been found."

"What scroll?"

"That picture-writing about the ancient mine which brought you here. You remember that he who owned the document died, and his son could not discover its whereabouts. Well, yesterday he found it by chance while he was hunting rats in the roof of his house, and brought it to me. Here it is," and he gave me a roll wrapped in yellow linen.

"Good," I answered, "I will study it tonight," and continued my walk, thinking little more about the matter, for my mind was full of other things.

The air was pleasant and the evening fine, so that I did not return to the house till the moon rose. As I passed up the path a man stepped so suddenly from the shelter of a bush in front of me, that I drew my *machete*, thinking that he meant to do me a mischief.

"Stay your hand, lord," said the man, saluting me humbly, and at the same time giving the sign of brotherhood. "It is many years since we met, so perchance you may have forgotten me; still, you will remember my name; I am Molas, your foster-brother."

Then I looked at him in the moonlight and knew him, though time had changed us both, and, putting my arms round him, I embraced him, seeing that he had been faithful when many deserted me, and I loved him as today I love his memory.

"What brings you here, Molas?" I asked; "when last I heard of you, you were dwelling far away in Chiapas."

"A strange matter: Business of the Heart, O Lord of the Heart, which I deemed so pressing that I have journeyed over land and sea to find you. Have you a place where I can speak with you alone?"

"Follow me," I said, wondering, and led him to my own chamber, where I gave him food and drink, for he was weary with travel.

"Now set out this business," I said.

"First show me the token, lord. I desire to see it once more for a purpose of my own."

I rose and closed the shutters of the window, then I bared my breast, revealing the ancient symbol. For a while he gazed upon it, and said, "It is enough. Tell me, lord, what is the saying that has descended with this trinket."

"The saying is, Molas, that when this half that I wear is reunited with the half that is wanting, then the Indians shall rule again from sea to sea, as they did when the Heart was whole."

"That is the saying, lord. We learn it in the ritual that is called 'Opening of the Heart,' do we not? and in this ritual that half which you wear is named 'Day' since it can be seen, and that half which is lost is named 'Night,' since, though present, it is not seen, and it is told to us that the 'Day' and the 'Night' together will make one perfect circle, whereof the center is named the 'Heart of Heaven,' of which these things are the symbol. Is it not so?"

"It is so, Molas."

"Good. Now listen. That which was lost is found, the half which is named 'Night' has appeared in the land, for I have seen it with my eyes, and it is to tell you of it that I have traveled hither."

"Speak on," I said.

"Lord, yonder in Chiapas there is a ruined temple that the *antiguos* built, and to that temple have come a man and a woman, his daughter. The man is old and fierce-eyed, a terrible man, and the girl is beautiful exceedingly. There in the ruins they have dwelt these four months and more, and the man practices the art of medicine, for he is a great doctor, and has wrought many cures, though he takes no money in payment for his skill, but food only.

"Now it chanced, lord, that my wife, whom I married but two years ago, was very sick — so sick that the village doctor could do nothing for her. Therefore the fame of the old Indian who dwelt in the ruined temple having reached me, I determined to visit him and seek his counsel, or, if possible, to bring him to my home.

"When my wife heard of it, she said it was of no use, as she saw Death sitting at the foot of her bed. Still I kissed her and went, leaving her in charge of the *padre* of the village and some women, her sisters. With me

I took a lock of her hair, and some fowls and eggs as a present to the *Lacandone,* for they said that, though of our race, this doctor was not a Christian.

"Starting before the dawn I traveled all day by the river and through the forest, till at evening I came to the ruined temple which I knew, and began to climb its broken stair. As I neared the top, a man appeared from beneath the leaning arch that is the gateway of the stair, and stood gazing at the ball of the setting sun. He was an aged man, clad in a linen robe only, very light in color, with long white beard and hair, a nose hooked like a hawk's beak, and fierce eyes that seemed to pierce those he looked upon and to read their most secret thoughts.

"'Greeting, brother,' he said, speaking in our own tongue, but with a strange accent, and using many words which are unknown to me, 'What brings you here?'

"Then he looked at me awhile, and asked slowly:

"'Say, brother, are you sick at heart?'

"Now, lord, when I heard those words whereof you know the meaning, I was so astounded that I almost fell backwards down the ruined stair, but, recovering myself, I tried him with a sign, and lo, he answered it. Then I tried him with the second sign, and the third, and the fourth, and so on up to the twelfth, and he answered them all, though not always as we use them. Then I paused, and he said:

"'You have passed the door of the Sanctuary, enter, brother, and draw on to the Altar.'

"But I shook my head, for I could not. Next he tried me with various signs and strange words that have to do with the inmost mysteries, but I was not able to answer them, though at times I saw their drift.

"'You have some knowledge,' he said, 'yet you do but stand at the foot of the pyramid, whereas I watch the stars from its crest, warming my hands at the eternal fire.'

"'None of my order have more, lord,' I answered, 'save the very highest.'

"'Then there are higher in the land?' he asked eagerly, but started suddenly, and, looking round, went on without waiting for an answer, 'You are in sorrow, Child of the Heart, and have come from one who was sick to the death; to your business, and perchance we will speak of these matters afterwards.'

"'First, lord,' I said, 'I have brought an offering,' and I set down the basket at his feet.

"'Gifts are good between brethren,' he replied; 'moreover, in this barren place food is welcome. Come hither, daughter, and take what this stranger brings.'

"As he spoke a lady came forward through the archway, dressed like her father, in a white robe of fine fabric, but somewhat worn. I looked at her, and it is truth, lord, that for the second time I went near to falling, for so great was the loveliness of this girl that my heart turned to water within me. Never before had I seen, or even dreamed of, such beauty in a woman."

"To your tale, Molas, to your tale. What has the fashion of a woman's beauty to do with the business of the Heart?" I broke in, angrily.

"I do not know, lord," he answered; "and yet I think that it has to do with all earthly things." Then he continued:

"The lady, whose name was Maya, looked at me carelessly, and took the basket. Following her through the archway to the terrace beyond, I set out the matter of my wife's illness to the doctor — or rather to him who passes as a doctor, and who is named Zibalbay, or Watcher — praying that he would come to the village and minister to her.

"He listened in silence, then took the lock of hair that I had brought with me, and, going to a fire that burned near by, he laid some of the hair upon an ember and watched it as it writhed and shrivelled away.

"'It would be of little use, brother,' he said, sadly, 'seeing that your wife is now dead. I felt her spirit pass us as we talked together in the gateway; still, until I burned the hair, I did not know whether it was she who went by, or another.'

"Here I may tell you, lord, that, as I found afterwards, my wife departed at that very hour of sunset, though whether the doctor, Zibalbay, guessed that she must die then from the symptoms which I described to him, or whether he has the spirit sight, and saw her, I do not know.

"Still, it seems natural that at that moment of her passing she should come to bid farewell to the husband whom she loved, though I think it is a bad omen for me, and I pray that I may never see that place again. At the least, when I heard him speak thus I did not doubt his truth, for something within me confirmed it, but I hid my face and groaned aloud in the bitterness of my grief.

"Then, taking my hand, Zibalbay, the Watcher, spoke great words to me in a solemn voice that seemed to soothe me as the song of a mother soothes a restless child, for he talked with certainty as one who has knowledge and vision of those who have gone beyond, telling me that this parting was not for long, and that soon I should find her whom I had lost made glorious and folded close to the Heart of Heaven. Then he laid his hand upon my head, and I slept awhile, to wake, sad, indeed, but filled with a strange peace.

"'Food is ready, my brother,' said Zibalbay. 'Eat and rest here this night; tomorrow you can return.'

"Now when we had eaten, Zibalbay spoke to me in the presence of his daughter, who, though a woman, is also of the Order, saying:

"'You are of our Brotherhood, therefore the words I speak will be repeated to none who are not brethren, for I speak upon the Heart.'

"'I hear with the Ears, lord,' I answered.

"'Listen!' he went on. 'I come from far with this maiden, my daughter, and we are not what we seem, but who and what we are now is not the hour to tell. This is the purpose of our coming — to find that which is one, but divided; that which is not lost, but hidden. Perchance, brother, you can point the path to it,' and he paused and looked at me with his piercing eyes.

"Now, lord, I understood to what his words had reference, for are they not part of the ritual of the service 'Opening of the Heart?' Still, because I desired to be sure, and not commit myself, I picked up a piece of burned wood, and, as though in idleness, bent down, and, by the light of the fire, I drew the half of a heart with a sawlike edge upon the pavement of the chamber where we sat. Then I handed the stick to Zibalbay, who took it and passed it on to his daughter, saying:

"'I have no skill at such arts; finish it, Maya.'

"She smiled, and, kneeling down, traced the half of a face within the outline that I had drawn, saying:

"'Is it enough, or do you need the writing also?'

"'It is enough,' I answered. 'Now, lord, what do you desire?'

"'I desire to know where that which is hidden can be brought to light, and if it dwells in this land, for I have journeyed far to seek it.'

"'It dwells here,' I answered, 'for I have beheld it with my eyes, and he guards it who is its keeper.'

"'Can you lead me to him, brother?'

"'No, for I have no such commands; but perhaps I can bring him to you, though I must journey by sea and land to find him — that is, if he wills to come. Say, what message shall I give? That a stranger whom I have met desires to look upon the holy symbol? It will scarcely bring him so far.'

"'Nay, tell him that the hour is come for "Night" and "Day" to be joined together, that a new sun may shine in a new sky.'

"'I can tell him this, but will he believe it, seeing that I have no proof? Will he not rather think that some cunning stranger and false brother lays a plot to trap him? Give me proofs, lord, or I do not start upon this errand.'

"'Will he believe that which you have seen with your eyes?'

"'He will believe it, for he has trusted me from childhood.'

"'Then look!' said the man, and, opening his robe at the neck, he kneeled down in the light of the fire.

"There, lord, upon his breast hung that which has been hidden from our sight since the sons of Quetzal, the god, ruled in the land, the counterpart of the severed symbol which is upon your breast. That is all my story, lord."

N<small>ow</small> I, Ignatio, listened amazed, for the thing was marvelous.

"Did the man send me no further message?" I asked.

"None. He said that if you were a true keeper of the mystery you would come to learn his mission from himself, or bring him to you."

"And did you tell him anything of me and my history, Molas?"

"Nothing; I had no such command. On the morrow at dawn I left to bury my wife, if she were dead, or to nurse her if she still were sick, saying that so soon as might be I would travel to the city of Mexico to seek out the Keeper of the Heart and give him this tidings, and that within eight weeks or less I trusted to report how I had fared. The old man asked me if I had money, and without waiting to be answered he gave me two handfuls of lumps of melted gold from a hide bag, whereof each lump was stamped with the symbol of the Heart."

"Let me see one," I said.

"Alas! my lord Ignatio, I have none. Not far from the ruined temple where this Zibalbay and his daughter sojourned, is the *hacienda* of Santa Cruz, and there, as you may have heard, dwell a gang of men under the leadership of one Don Pedro Moreno, who are by profession smugglers, highway robbers, and murderers, though they pretend to earn a living by the cultivation of coffee and cocoa.

"As it chanced, in journeying homewards, I fell into the hands of some of these men. They searched me, and, finding the lumps of gold in my pocket, handed them over to Don Pedro himself, who rode up when he saw that they had the fish in their net. He examined the gold closely, and asked me whence it came. At first I refused to answer, whereupon he said that I should be confined in a dungeon at the *hacienda* until such time as I chose to speak.

"Then, being mad to get back to my village and learn the fate of my wife, I found my tongue and spoke the truth, saying that the gold was given in exchange for food by an old Indian doctor, who dwelt with his daughter in a ruined temple in the forest.

"'Mother of Heaven!' said Don Pedro, 'I have heard of this man before; but now I know the kind of merchandise in which he trades, I think that I must pay him a visit and learn what mint it was stamped at.'

"Then, having plucked me bare as a fowl for the oven, they let me go without hurt, but often I have sorrowed because, in my hour of haste and need, I told them whence the gold came, since I fear lest I should have let loose these villains upon the old wanderer and his daughter, and in that case they may well be murdered before ever you can reach them."

"Doubtless Heaven will protect them," I answered, "though you acted foolishly. But tell me, Molas, how did you find me out and come here without money?"

"I had some money at home, lord, and when I had buried my wife I traveled to Frontera on the coast, where I found a ship bound for Vera Cruz, and in her I sailed, giving my service as a sailor, which is a trade that I have followed. From Vera Cruz I made my way to Mexico, and reported myself to the head of the Brotherhood in that city, who, as I expected, was able to give me tidings of you.

"Then I came on to this village, and arrived here tonight, having been a month and two days on my journey. And now, lord, if you can, give me a place to sleep in, since I am weary, who for three days have scarcely shut my eyes. Tomorrow you can let me know what answer I must bear to the old man, Zibalbay."

I, Ignatio, sat late that night pondering over these tidings, which filled me with a strange hope. Could it be that my hour of success was at hand after so many years of waiting? If there were truth in prophecies it would seem so, and yet my faith wavered. This traveler, whom Molas had seen, might be a madman, and his symbol might be forged. I could not tell, but at least I would put the matter to the proof, for tomorrow, or so soon as was possible, I would journey down to Chiapas and seek him out.

Thinking thus, I threw myself upon my bed and strove to sleep, but could not. Then, remembering the scroll that my friend had given me, I rose, purposing to change my thoughts in studying it and so win sleep. It was a hard task, but at length I mastered its meaning, and found that it dealt with a mine near Cumarvo, and described the exact position of the mouth of the tunnel.

This mouth, it would appear, had been closed up in the reign of Guatemoc, and the scroll was written by the *cacique* who had charge of the mine in those days, in order that a record might remain that would enable his descendants to reopen it, should a time come when the Spaniards were driven from the land. That the mine was very rich in free gold was shown by the weights of pure metal stated in this scroll to have been sent year by year to the Court of Montezuma by this *cacique*, and also by the fact that it was thought worth hiding from the Spaniards.

Early on the morrow I went to the room of the Señor Strickland and spoke to him with a heavy heart.

"Señor," I said, "you will remember that when I entered your service I told you that I might have to leave it at any moment. Now I am here to say that the time is come, for a messenger has arrived to summon me to the other end of Mexico upon business of which I may not speak, and tomorrow I must start upon the journey."

"I am sorry to hear it, Ignatio," he answered, "for you have been a good friend to me. Still, you do well to separate your fortunes from those of an unlucky man."

"And you, señor, do ill to speak thus to me," I answered with indignation; "still, I forgive you because I know that at times, when the heart is sore, the mouth utters words that are not meant. Listen, señor, when you have eaten your breakfast, will you take a ride with me?"

"Certainly, if you like. But whither do you wish to ride?"

"To another mine that is, or should be, about two hours on horseback from here, in a valley at the foot of yonder peak. I only heard of it last night, though I came to Cumarvo to seek it, and it would seem that it was very rich in Montezuma's day."

"In Montezuma's day?" he said.

"Yes, it was last worked then, and I propose that if we can find it, and it looks well, that you should 'denounce' it for yourself, giving a reward of a few dollars to the Indian from whom I had the information, who is a poor man."

"But if it is so good, why don't *you* denounce it, Ignatio; and how did you come to hear about it after all these years?"

"For two reasons, señor; first, because I wish to do you a service if it is in my humble power, and, secondly, because I cannot look after it and must leave you, though to do so will be a true grief to me, for, if you will permit me to say it, never have I met a man for whom I conceived a greater respect and affection. Perhaps, if I return again, you will give me a share in the profits, so that we may grow rich together. And now I will show you how I came to hear of the mine." And I fetched the scroll, with the translation which I had made, and read it to him.

He listened eagerly, for, like yourself, Señor Jones, your countryman, James Strickland, loved adventure and all things that have to do with the past of this ancient land.

"Let us go at once," he said when I had finished. "I will order the horses and a mule with the prospecting kit to be got ready. Shall we take men with us?"

"I think not, señor; the mine is not yet found, and the less talk there is about it the better, for if the matter is noised abroad somebody may be before you in denouncing it. The messenger who came to see me last night is a trusty man, but he is weary with journeying, and rests, so we will go alone."

An hour later we were riding among the mountains, I having left a message for Molas to say that I should return before dark. The trail which we were following was a difficult one, and ran for some miles along the edge of a precipice till it reached the crest of the range. Indeed, so bad was it in parts, that we were forced to dismount and drive the horses and mule before us, while we followed, clinging to the ferns and creepers on the rocks to keep ourselves from falling.

At length we came to the summit of the range, and turned downwards through a forest of oak and fir trees, heading for a valley that lay at the base of a solitary mountain peak, along which ran a stream. Down this stream we rode a mile or more, since I was searching for a certain pointed rock that was mentioned in the scroll as standing by itself on the slope of a mountain where no trees grew, beneath which should be the glen where in the days of Guatemoc was a great *ceiba* tree that, so said the writing, overshadowed the mouth of the mine.

Riding uphill through a dense grove of oaks, we came presently to the glen that lay just below the slope whereon stood the tall rock.

"This must be the place," I said, "but I see no *ceiba* tree."

"Doubtless it has fallen and rotted since those days," answered the Señor Strickland. "Let us tether the horses and search."

This we did, and the hunt was long, for here grasses and ferns grew thick, but at length I discovered a spot where the trunk of a very ancient tree had decayed in the ground, so that nothing remained except the outline of its circle and some of the larger roots.

Round about these roots we sought desperately for an hour or more, but without avail, till at length my companion grew weary of the sport, and went to pull up a small glossy-leaved palm that he had discovered, purposing to take it home and set it in his garden, for he was a great lover of plants and flowers.

While he was thus engaged, and I toiled amongst the grasses looking for the mouth of the mine, which, as I began to think, was lost forever, suddenly he called out, "Come here, Ignatio. Beneath the roots of this palm is refuse rock that has been broken with hammers. I believe that this must have been the platform in front of the mine. One can see that the ground was flat here."

I came to him, and together we renewed our search, till at length, by good luck, we discovered a hole immediately beneath a rock, large enough for a man to creep into.

"Was this made by a *coyote,* or is it the mouth of the mine?" the señor asked.

"That we can only find out by entering it," I answered. "Doubtless when they shut down the mine, the *antiguos* would have left some such place as this to ventilate the workings. Bring the pickaxe, señor, and we will soon see."

For ten minutes or more we labored, working in soft ground with pick and spade till we bared the side of a tunnel, which I examined.

"There is no need to trouble further," I said, "this rock has been cut with copper chisels, for here is the green of the copper. Without doubt we have found the mouth of the mine. Now give me the hammer and candles, and bring the leather bag for samples, and we will enter."

Chapter IV

THE LEGEND OF THE HEART

W hen I had gone a few paces down the hole, it widened suddenly, so that we were able to stand upright and light our candles. Now there was no doubt that we were in the tunnel of an old mine, a rudely-dug shaft that turned this way and that as it followed the windings of the ore body.

Along this tunnel we went for thirty or forty paces, creeping over the fallen boulders, and twisting ourselves between the brown stalactites that in the course of ages had formed upon the roof and floor, till presently we reached an obstacle that barred our further progress; a huge mass of rock which at some time or other had fallen from the roof of the tunnel and blocked it. I looked at it, and said:

"Now, señor, I think that we shall have to go back. You remember the writing tells us that this mine, although so rich, was unsafe because of the rottenness of the rock. Doubtless they propped it in the old days, but the timbers have decayed long ago."

"Yes," he answered, "we can do nothing here without help, and, Ignatio, I don't like the look of the roof, it is full of cracks."

As these last words left his lips a piece of stone, the size of a child's head, fell from above almost at his feet.

"Speak softly," I whispered, "the ring of your voice is bringing down the roof."

Then I stooped to pick up the fallen stone, thinking that it might show ore, and, as I did so, my hand touched something sharp, which I lifted and held to the candle. It was the jawbone of a man, yellow with age, and corroded by damp. I showed it to the señor, and, kneeling down, we examined the bed of the tunnel together, and not uselessly, for there we found the remainder of the skull and some fragments of an arm-bone, but the rest of the skeleton lay under the great boulder in front of us.

"He was coming out of the mine when the rock fell upon him, poor fellow," whispered the señor. "Look here," and he pointed to a little heap of something that gleamed in the candlelight.

It was free gold, six or seven ounces of it, almost pure, and for the most part in small nuggets, that once were contained in a bag which had long since rotted away.

Doubtless, after the mine was closed, some Aztec, who knew its secret, had made a practice of working there for his own benefit, till one day, as he was coming out, the rock fell upon him and crushed him, leaving his spirit to haunt the place forever.

"There is no doubt about this mine being rich," whispered the señor; "but all the same I think that we had better get out of it. I hear odd noises and rumblings which frighten me. Come, Ignatio," and he turned to lead the way towards the opening.

Two paces farther I saw him strike his ankle against a piece of rock that stood up some six or eight inches from the floor-bed of the tunnel, and the pain of the blow was so sharp that, forgetting where he was, he called out loudly. The next instant there was a curious sound above me as of something being torn, and, lo! I lay upon my face on the rock, and upon me rested a huge mass of stone.

I say that it rested upon me, but this is not altogether true, for, had it been so, that stone would have killed me at once, as a beetle is killed beneath the foot of a man, instead of taking more than two-and-twenty years to do it. The greater part of its weight was borne by the piece of rock against which the señor had struck his leg, a point of the fallen boulder only pressing into my back and grinding me against the ground. Now we were in darkness, for the señor had been knocked down also, and his candle extinguished, and, in the midst of my tortures, it came into my mind that he must be dead.

Presently, however, I heard his voice, saying, "Ignatio; do you live, Ignatio?"

Now I thought for a moment. Even in my pain I remembered that more of the roof would surely give ere long, and that if my friend stayed here he must die with me. Nothing could save me, I was doomed to a slow death beneath the stone; and yet if I told him this I knew that he would not go. Therefore I answered as strongly as I could:

"Fly, señor, I am safe, and do but stay to light a candle. I will follow you."

"You are lying to me," he answered; "your voice comes from the level of the floor." And as he spoke I heard the scratching sound of a match.

So soon as he had found his candle and lit it, he knelt down and looked at me. Then he examined the roof above, and, following his glance with difficulty, I saw that next to the hole whence the boulder had fallen, hung a huge block of stone, that, surrounded by great cracks from which water dropped, trembled like a leaf whenever he moved or spoke.

"For the love of God, fly," I whispered. "In a few hours it will be over with me, and you cannot help me. I am a dead man, do not stop here to share my fate."

For a moment he seemed to hesitate, then his courage came back to him, and he answered hoarsely:

"We entered this place together, friend, and we will go out together, or not at all. You must be fixed by the rock and not crushed, or you would not speak of living for hours. Let me look," and he lay upon his breast and examined the fallen rock by the light of the candle. "Thank God! there is hope," he said at last, "the boulder rests on the ground and upon the stone against which I struck my leg, for only one point of it is fixed in your back. Do you think that anything is broken, Ignatio?"

"I cannot say, señor, my pain is great, and I am being slowly crushed to death; but I believe that as yet my bones are whole. Fly, I beg of you."

"I will not," he answered sullenly, "I am going to roll this rock off you."

Then, lifting with all his strength, he strove to move the stone, but without avail, for it was beyond the power of mortal man to stir it, and all the while the black mass trembled above his head.

"I must go for help," he said, presently.

"Yes, yes, señor," I answered, "go for help;" for I knew well that before he could return with any, more of the roof would have fallen, shutting me in to perish by inches, or perhaps crushing the life out of me in mercy. Then I remembered, and added:

"Stay a moment before you go; you are noble, I will give you something. Feel here round my neck, there is a little chain — now, draw it over my head — so. You see a token hangs to it; if ever you are in trouble with the Indians, take their chief man apart and show him this, and he will die for you if need be.

"Englishman, by this gift I have made you heir to the empire of the Aztecs in the heart of every Indian, and the master of the great brotherhood of Mexico. Molas, the messenger, will tell you all and bring you to those who can initiate you. Bid him lead you whither he would have led me. Farewell, and God go with you. Tell the Indians how I died, that they may not think that you have murdered me."

To these words of mine the señor made no answer, but thrust the token into his pocket without looking at it, like one who dreams. Then, taking the candle with him, he crept forward down the tunnel and vanished, and my heart sank as I saw him go, leaving me to my dreadful fate without a word of farewell.

"Doubtless he is too frightened to speak," I thought, "and it is right that he should fly as quickly as possible to save his life."

Now, as I was soon to learn, I was doing the señor a bitter wrong in my mind, seeing that he never dreamed of deserting me, but went to find a means of rescue. As he told me afterwards, when he reached the mouth of the tunnel, he could think of no way by which I might be saved, since these mountains were uninhabited, and it would take several hours to bring men from Cumarvo.

Outside the mine he sat himself down to consider what could be done, but no thought came, for it was impossible to use the strength of the horses in that narrow place. Then he sprang up and looked round him in despair. Close to him was a little ravine hollowed by water, and on its very edge grew a small mimosa thorn of which the long roots had been washed almost bare by a flood. He saw it, and an inspiration entered into him. With the help of a lever he might be able to do a feat to which his unaided strength was not equal.

Springing at the little tree, that being of so tough a wood was the best possible for his purpose, he tore it from such root-hold as remained to it. A few strokes with his heavy hunting-knife trimmed off the branches and fibers, and soon he was creeping carefully up the tunnel, dragging the trunk after him. When he had gone some twenty paces he heard another fragment of the roof fall, and, so he said in his story, was minded to fly.

He had but just escaped from a horrible end, the end that generations ago overtook the poor Aztec, and it was awful to brave it again. He knew that his chances of being able to rescue me were few indeed, whereas those that he would perish miserably in the attempt were many. Then he remembered what my sufferings must be if I still lived, and how his own conscience would reproach him in the after years, should he leave me to my fate, and he went on.

Now he could see that the half-detached mass of the roof still hung; it was a smaller fragment which had fallen, one nearer to the entrance. He could see also that I lay in the same position beneath the rock, and he thought that I was dead, because I neither moved nor spoke, though, in fact, I had but swooned under the agony of my suffering.

"Are you dead?" he whispered, and I heard his voice through my sleep, and, lifting my head, looked up at him astonished, for I had never thought to see him again.

"Do I behold a spirit," I said, "or is it you come back?"

"It is I, Ignatio. and I have brought a lever. Now when I lift, struggle forward if you can."

Then he placed the trunk of the thorn tree in what seemed to him the best position, and put all his strength upon it. It was in vain; even so he could not stir the rock.

"Try a little more to the right," I said, faintly; "there is a better hold."

He shifted the lever and dragged at it till his muscles cracked, and I felt the stone tremble as its bulk began to rise.

"If you can help ever so little, it will come!" he gasped.

Then in my despair, though the anguish of it nearly killed me, I set my palms upon the ground, and, contracting myself like a snake that is held with a forked stick, thrust upwards with my back till the point of the stone was raised to the height of eight or ten inches from the ground.

For a moment, and one only, it hung there; next instant the lever slipped, and down it came again. But I had taken my chance, for, clinging to the floor with my fingers, so soon as my back was free, with a quick movement I dragged myself a foot or more forward. Then the point of rock that had been lifted from my spine fell again, but this time it struck the ground between my thighs.

Now he seized me by the arms and tore me free, though I left one of my long boots beneath the stone. I strove to rise, but could not because of the hurt to my back.

"You must carry me, señor," I said.

He glanced at the mass that trembled above us; then, giving me the candle, he lifted me from the ground like an infant and staggered forward down the tunnel. Perhaps we had gone some seven or eight paces, not more, when there was a dreadful crash behind us. The roof had fallen in, and the spot which we occupied some thirty seconds before was now piled high with rocks.

"Oh!" I said; "cracks are showing in the stone above us!" and he rushed forward till we found ourselves outside the mine.

Now I bowed my head and returned thanks for my escape; then, lifting it, I looked my preserver in the face and said:

"I swear by the name of God, señor, that He never made a man nobler than yourself!"

The next instant I fell forward and fainted there among the ferns.

*T*en days had passed since I was carried from the mouth of that accursed mine back to Cumarvo in a litter, and during all this time I had suffered much pain in my back, and been very ill — so ill, indeed, that I was scarcely allowed to speak with anyone. Now, however, I was much better, and one afternoon the Señor Strickland, assisted by my foster-brother Molas, lifted me from my bed into a hammock.

"By the way, Ignatio," said the señor when Molas had gone, "I never gave you back this charm of yours. What a strange trinket it is!" he added, taking it from his neck; "and what did you mean by your talk in the tunnel about its making me heir to the empire of the Aztecs in the heart of every Indian, and the rest of it? I suppose that you were delirious with pain, and did not know what you were saying."

"Is the door shut, señor?" I asked; "and are you sure that there is no one on the verandah? Good! Then draw your chair nearer and I will tell you something. I am not certain that I should take this talisman back again, still I will do so for reasons which you shall learn presently.

"Know, señor, that this broken gem is at once the foundation-stone and the secret symbol of a great order, of which, although you have not been initiated into it, you are now one of the lords, seeing that the crowning and vital ceremony of the creation of a Lord of the Heart consists in the hanging of the symbol about his neck for the space of a minute only by myself, who am the chief lord and Keeper of the Heart for life, and you have worn it for ten whole days.

"Before we part I will call a chapter of the order — for even among these mountains we have brethren — and you shall be initiated into its ritual and raised to the rank of a chief lord, as is your right. Meanwhile I will instruct you briefly in its mysteries, as it is my bounden duty to do.

"Understand, señor, that the first duty of the servant of the Heart is silence, and that silence I demand of you. Men have died ere now, señor; yes, they have died on the rack in the dungeons of the Inquisition, and shrivelled as wizards in the fires of the stake, sooner than reveal those things that have been told them upon the faith of the Heart, against which the confessional itself cannot prevail — no, not with the best of Catholics."

"But suppose that a man should not keep silence, Ignatio, what then?" he asked.

"There is a land, señor," I answered, "where the most talkative grow dumb, and its borders can be crossed by all, even by the Lords of the Heart, for fearful is the doom of a false brother!"

"You mean that if I repeat anything I may hear, I shall be murdered."

"Indeed, no, señor; but you may happen to die. I speak on the Heart; do you hear with the Ears?"

"I hear with the Ears," he answered, catching my meaning.

"Very well, señor, since you have now sworn secrecy to me by the most solemn oath that can pass the lips of man, I will speak to you openly. This is the tale of the Broken Heart, so far as I know it, though how much of it is truth and how much is legend I cannot say:

"You have heard the story of that white man, or god, sometimes called Quetzal by the Indians, and sometimes Cucumatz, who came to these lands in the far past and civilized their peoples? Afterwards he vanished away in a ship, promising that when many generations had passed he would return again.

"When he had gone, the empire which he created fell into the hands of two brothers, whose chief city was either at Palenque or in its neighborhood, and the citizens of this empire, like we Christians, worshipped one good god, the true God, under the name of the Heart of Heaven, and to Him they offered few sacrifices save those of fruit and flowers. Now one of these brothers married a wife from another country — a daughter of devils, very beautiful and a great witch.

"Soon this woman, as in the story of the wives of Solomon and their lord, drew away the king, her husband, from the true faith to the worship of the gods of her own land, and brought it about that he offered human sacrifice to them. Then there arose a great confusion in that country, and the end of it was that the people divided themselves into two parties, the worshippers of the Heart of Heaven and the worshippers of devils.

"They made war upon each other, till many of their chief men were killed; then they came to an agreement whereby the nation was sundered. Half of it, under that king who had married the woman, marched northwards, and became the fathers of the Aztecs and other tribes; and half, the faithful worshippers of the Heart, remained in the Tobasco country.

"Now from that day forward evil overtook both these peoples, for though the Aztecs flourished for a while, in the end Spaniards despoiled them. The worshippers of the Heart also were driven from their cities by hordes of barbarians who rolled down upon them, and their faith perished, or seemed to perish."

"But what has this history to do with the charm about your neck, Ignatio?" he asked.

"I will tell you. When Quetzal sailed away from his people, so says the legend, he left the stone, that once he had worn upon his brow, of which this is the half, to be a treasure to the kings who came after him. Also he set this fate upon it: that while the Heart remained unbroken, for so long should the people be one and whole; but if it came about that it was cut or shattered, they should be divided with it, to be no more one people until again the fragments were one stone.

"Now when these king-brethren quarreled and parted, they sawed the token asunder, as you see, each of them keeping a half, this half being that of him who married the woman. For generations it was worn by his descendants, and upon their deathbeds passed on by them to another, or at times taken from their bodies after they were dead.

"There are many stories told about the stone in the old days, and it is certain that he who had it was the real king of the country for the time being. At length it came into the hands of the great Guatemoc, last of the Aztec emperors, who, before the Spaniards hung him, found means to send it to his son, from whom it has come down to me."

"To you? What have you to do with Guatemoc?"

"I am his lineal descendant, señor, the eleventh in the male line."

"Then you ought to be Emperor of the Indians if every man had his rights, Ignatio."

"That is so, señor, but of my own story I will tell you presently. Now of this stone. Through all the ages it has never been lost, and it is known in the land from end to end; he who wears it for his life being called

'Keeper of the Heart,' and also 'Hope of those who wait,' since it may happen in his day that the two halves will come together again."

"And what if they do?"

"Then, so says the legend, the Indians will once more be a mighty nation, and drive those who oppress them into the sea, as the wind drives dust."

Now the señor rose from his chair and walked up and down the room.

"Do you believe all this?" he asked, suddenly.

"Yes," I answered, "or the greater part of it. Indeed, if what I hear is true, the lost half of the talisman that has been missing for so many generations is in Mexico at this moment, and, so soon as I am well enough, I go to seek him who bears it, and who has come from far to find me. That is why we must part, señor."

"Where has this man come from?" he asked, eagerly.

"I do not know for certain," I answered, "but I think that he has come from the sacred city of the Indians, the hidden Golden City which the Spaniards sought for but could not find, though it still exists among the mountains and deserts of the far interior, whither I hope to journey with him."

"That still exists! Ignatio, you must be mad. It never has existed except in the imagination."

"You say so, señor, but I think differently. At least, I knew a man whose grandfather had seen it. He, the grandfather, was a native of San Juan Batista, in Tobasco, and when he was young he committed some crime and fled inland to save his life.

"All that befell him I do not know, but at length he found himself wandering by the shores of a great lake, somewhere in or beyond the country that is now known as Guatemala, and, being exhausted, he laid himself down to die there and fell asleep.

"When he awoke, people were standing round him, like the Indians to look at, but very light in color, and beautifully dressed in white robes, with necklaces of emeralds and feather capes. These people put him on board a great canoe, and took him to a glorious city with a high pyramid in the center of it, which was named Heart of the World.

"Of this city he saw little, however, for its inhabitants kept him a prisoner, only from time to time he was brought before their king and elders, who sat in a hall filled with images of dead men fashioned in gold, and there was questioned as to the country whence he came, the tribes that dwelt in it, and more especially of the white men who ruled the land.

"In that hall alone, so he said, there were more gold and precious stones than are to be found in all Mexico. When he had nothing more to tell them, the people wished to kill him, fearing lest he should escape and bring upon them the white men who loved gold. The end of it was that he did escape by the help of a woman, who guided him back towards the sea, though she never came there, for she died upon the road.

"Afterwards this man went to live in a little village near Palenque, where he also died, having revealed nothing of what he had seen, since he feared lest the vengeance of the People of the Heart should follow him. When he was dying he told his son, who told his son, who told the tale to me. Señor, it has been the dream of my life to visit that city, and now at last I think that I have found the clue which will lead me to it."

"Why do you want to visit it, Ignatio?"

"To understand that, señor, you must know my history." And I told him of the failure of the great plot and the part that I had played in it, all of which I have already set out, also of the secret hopes and ambitions of my life.

"Señor," I added, "though I am beaten I am not yet crushed, and I still desire to build up a great Indian empire. I see by your face that you think me foolish. You may be right or I may be right. I may be pursuing truths or dreams, I may be sane and a redeemer, or insane and a fool. What does it matter? I follow the light that runs before me; will-o'-the-wisp or star, it leads to one end, and for me it is the light that I am born to follow. If you believe nothing else, at least believe this, señor, that I do not seek my own good or advancement, but rather that of my people. At the worst, I am not a knave, I am only a fool."

"But how will you help your cause by visiting this city, supposing it to exist, Ignatio?"

"Thus, señor: these people — among whom without doubt the old man of whom I have spoken, who is named Zibalbay, is a chief or king — are the true stock and head of all the Indian races, and when they learn my plans and whom I am, they will be glad to furnish me with means whereby I can bring them to their former empire."

"And if they take another view of the matter, Ignatio?"

"Then I fail, that is all, and among so many failures one more will scarcely matter. I am like a swimmer who sees, or thinks that he sees, a single plank that may bear him to safety. Maybe he cannot reach that plank, or, if he reach it, maybe it will sink beneath his weight. At least, he has no other hope.

"Señor, I have no other hope. There in the Golden City is untold wealth, for the man saw it, and without money, great sums of money, I am helpless, therefore I go thither to win the money. The ship has foundered under me, and with it the cargo of my ambitions and the work of my life; so, being desperate, I fall back upon a desperate expedient.

"First, I will seek this man, that the two halves of the Heart may come together, and the prophecy be fulfilled; then, if it may be, I will travel with him to the City, Heart of the World, careless whether I live or die, but determined, if there is need, to die fighting for the fulfillment of the dream of an Indian empire — Christian, regenerated, and stretching from sea to sea — that I have followed all my days."

"The dream, Ignatio? Perhaps you name it well, yet few have such noble dreams. And now, who goes with you on this journey?"

"Who goes with me? Molas, as far as the temple where the Indian is. After that, if I proceed, no one. Who would accompany a man grown old in failure, whom even those that love him deem a visionary, on such a desperate quest? Why, if I should dare to tell my projects even, men would mock me as children mock an idiot in the street. I go alone, señor, perhaps to die."

"As regards the dying, Ignatio, of course I can say nothing, since all men must die sooner or later, and the moment and manner of their end is in the hand of Providence. But for the rest you shall not make this journey alone, that is, if you care to have me for a companion, for I will accompany you."

"You, señor, *you.* Think what it means: the certainty of every sort of danger, the risk of every kind of death, and at the end, the probability of failure. It is folly, señor."

"Ignatio," he answered, "I will be frank with you. Notwithstanding all the prophecies about the wonders that are to follow the reuniting of the Heart, and the messages from the old man in the temple, I think your scheme of building up an Indian empire greater than that which Cortez destroyed, as impracticable as it is grand, since the time has gone by when it could have been done, or perhaps it has not yet returned.

"Before the Indians can rule again, they must forget the bitter lessons and the degradation of ages; in short, they must be educated, Ignatio. Still, if you think otherwise, that is your affair; you can only fail, and there are failures more glorious than most successes. Do you understand me?"

"Perfectly, señor."

"Very well. And now as regards the search for this Golden City. To me the matter seems very vague, since your hopes of finding it are based upon a traveler's tale, told by a man who died seventy or eighty years ago, and the chance that a certain person, whom you have not yet seen, has come from there, and is willing to guide you back to it.

"Still, the prospect of hunting for that city pleases me, for I am an adventurer in my heart. If ever we get further than the forest country in Tobasco, where your friend with the token is waiting for you, our search will probably end in the leaving of our bones to decorate some wilderness or mountain top in the unknown regions of Guatemala.

"But what of that? I have no chick or child; my death would matter nothing to any living soul; for years I have worked hard with small results; why should I not follow my natural bent and become an adventurer? I can scarcely do worse than I have done, and I think that the way of life would suit me.

"That mine you showed me is rich enough no doubt, but I have no capital to deal with it, and if I had, my experience of the place was such that I never wish to set foot in it again. In short, I am ready to start for Tobasco, and the Sacred City, and wherever else you like, so soon as you are fit to travel."

"Do you swear that on the Heart, señor?" I asked.

"By all means; but I should prefer to give you my hand upon it." And he stretched out his hand, which I took.

"Good. You swear on the Heart, and give me your hand — the oath is perfect. We are comrades henceforth, señor; for my part I ask no better one. I have nothing more to say. I cannot promise that you will find this City, or that, if you find it, it will advantage you. I am an unlucky man, and it is more likely that, by yoking yourself with me, you will bring my misfortunes upon your head. This I swear, however, that I will be a true comrade to you, as you were to me yonder in the mine, and for the rest, the adventure must be its own reward."

Chapter V

THE BEGINNING OF THE QUEST

Something more than a month from the day when the Señor Strickland and I made our compact to search for the secret city of the Indians, we found ourselves, together with Molas, at Vera Cruz, waiting for a ship to take us to Frontera, where we proposed to disembark. This port we had chosen in preference to Campeche, although the latter was nearer to the ruins where we hoped to find the Indian Zibalbay, because from it we could travel in canoes up the Grijalva and other rivers, unobserved by any save the natives.

Things are changed now in these parts, but in those days the white men who lived thereabouts beyond the circle of the towns were too often robbers, as Molas had found to his cost some few weeks before.

At Vera Cruz we purchased such articles as were necessary to our journey, not many, for we could not be sure of finding means to carry them. Among them were hammocks, three guns that would shoot either ball or shot, with ammunition, as many muzzle-loading Colt's revolvers, the best that were to be had twenty years ago, some medicines, blankets, boots, and spare clothes.

Also we took with us all the money that we possessed, amounting to something over fifteen hundred dollars in gold, which sum we divided between us, carrying it in belts about our middles. At Vera Cruz, where people are very curious about the business of others, we gave out that the Señor Strickland was one of those strange Englishmen who love to visit old ruins, for which purpose he was traveling to Yucatan; that I, Ignatio, was his guide and companion, and that Molas, my foster-brother, was our servant.

Now we purposed to leave Vera Cruz by a fine American vessel, a sailing ship, that, after touching at the ports along the coast, traded to Havana and New York. As it chanced, the departure of this ship was delayed for a week, so, being pressed for time and fearing lest we should catch the yellow fever that was raging in the town, unhappily for ourselves we took passage in a Mexican boat called the *Santa Maria.*

She was an old sailing vessel of not more than two hundred and fifty tons burden, that had been converted by her owners into a paddle-wheel steamer, with the result that, except in favorable weather, she could neither sail nor steam with any speed or safety. Her business was to trade with passengers and cargo between Vera Cruz and the ports of Frontera and Campeche.

"Where for?" asked the agent of the Señor Strickland, as he filled in the tickets.

"Frontera," he answered. "Your boat stops there, does she not?"

"Oh! certainly, señor," he said, as he pocketed the dollars, and yet all the while this shameless rogue knew that she had orders to touch at Campeche, which is the furthest port, first, and return to Frontera a week later. But of this more in its place.

That afternoon the *Santa Maria,* with us on board of her, was piloted out of the harbor of Vera Cruz, and we heard the pilot swearing because she would not answer properly to her helm. Standing by the engines we noticed also that, though they had not been working for more than half an hour, it was found necessary to keep a stream of water in constant play upon the bearings.

The señor asked the reason of this of the man who was mate and engineer of the boat, and he answered, with a shrug, that sand had got into the machinery when she was steaming over the bar of the Grijalva river, but that he thought the bearings, should it please the Saints, would last this voyage, unless they had the bad luck to run into a norther, as you English call *el Norte*; the fearful gales that in certain seasons of the year sweep over the Gulf of Mexico.

"And if we 'run into a norther'?" he asked — whereupon the man made a grimace, crossed himself to avert the omen, and vanished down the stoke-hole.

Now we began to feel sorry that we had not taken passage in the American ship, since of late northers had been frequent, but as, for good or ill, we were on board the *Santa Maria,* we amused ourselves by studying our fellow-passengers.

Of these there were several on board, perhaps twenty in all, Mexican landowners and officials returning to their *haciendas* and native towns after a visit to Vera Cruz, or the capital, some of them pleasant companions enough and others not so. Three or four of these gentlemen were accompanied by their wives, but the ladies had already retired to the bunks opening out of the cabin, where, although the sea was quite smooth, they could be heard suffering the pains of sickness.

Among the passengers was one, a man of not more than thirty years of age, who particularly attracted our attention because of the gorgeousness of his dress. In appearance he was large, handsome, and coarse, and he had Indian blood in his veins, as was shown by the darkness of his color and the thick black eyebrows that gave a truculent expression to his face. While I was wondering who he might be, Molas made a sign to me to come aside, and said:

"You see yonder man with the silver buttons on his coat: he is Don José Moreno, the son of that Don Pedro Moreno who waylaid and robbed me of the nuggets which the old Indian gave me for the cost of my journey to find you. I heard at the time that he was away from the *hacienda* in Vera Cruz or Mexico, and now doubtless he returns thither. Beware of him, lord, and bid the Englishman to do the same, for, like his father, he is a bad man —" and he told me certain things connected with him and his family.

While Molas was talking, a bell had rung for dinner, but I waited till he had finished before going down. At the door of the cabin I met the captain, a stout man with a face like a full moon and a bland smile.

"What do you seek, señor?" he asked.

"My dinner, señor," I answered.

"It shall be sent to you on the deck," he said, not without confusion. "I do not wish to be rude, señor, but you know that these Mexicans — I am a Spaniard myself and do not care — hate to sit at meat with an Indian, so, if you insist upon coming in, there will be trouble."

Now I heard, and though the insult was deep, it was one to which I was accustomed, for in this land, which belongs to them and where their fathers ruled, to be an Indian is to be an outcast.

Therefore, not wishing to make a stir, I bowed and turned away. Meanwhile, it seems that the Señor Strickland, missing me in the cabin, asked the captain where I was, saying that perhaps I did not know that the meal was ready.

"If you refer to your servant, the Indian," said the captain, "I met him at the door and sent him away. Surely the señor knows that we do not sit at table with these people."

"Captain," answered the Señor Strickland, "if my friend is an Indian, he is as good a gentleman as you or anybody else in this cabin; moreover, he has paid for a first-class fare and has a right to first-class accommodation. I insist upon a seat being provided for him at my side."

"As you wish," answered the captain, smiling, for he was a man of peace, "only if he comes there will be trouble." And he ordered the steward to fetch me.

Now this steward was an Indian who knew my rank. Therefore not wishing to offend me by repeating what had passed, he said simply that the captain sent his compliments and begged that I would come down to dinner. The end of it was that I went, though doubtfully, and, seeing me in the doorway the Señor Strickland called to me in a loud voice, saying:

"You are late for dinner, friend, but I have kept your place here by me. Sit down quickly or the food will be cold."

I bowed to the company and obeyed, and then the trouble commenced, for all present had heard this talk. As I took my seat the Mexicans began to murmur, and the passenger who was next to me insolently moved his plate and glass away. Now almost opposite to me sat Don José Moreno, that man of whom Molas had told me. As I took my seat he consulted hastily with a neighbor on his right, then, addressing the captain, said in a loud voice:

"There is some mistake; it is not usual that Indian dogs should sit at the same table with gentlemen."

The captain shrugged his shoulders and answered mildly:

"Perhaps the señor will settle the question with the English señor on my left. To me it does not matter; I am only a poor sailor, and accustomed to every sort of company."

"Señor Strickland," said Don José, "be so good as to order your servant to leave the cabin."

"Señor," he answered, for his temper was quick, "I will see you in hell before I do so."

"*Caramba,*" said the Mexican, laying a hand upon the knife in his belt, "you shall pay for that, Englishman."

"When and how you will, señor. I always pay my debts."

Then the captain broke in, in a strange way. First he put a hand behind him, and, drawing a large pistol from his pocket, he laid it by his plate.

"Señors, both," he said in a soft voice and with a gentle smile, "I am loth to interfere in a quarrel of two esteemed passengers, but though I am only a poor sailor, it is my duty to see that there is no bloodshed on board this vessel. Therefore, much as I regret it, I shall be obliged to shoot dead the first man who draws a weapon," and he cocked the pistol.

Now the Mexican scowled, and the Señor Strickland laughed outright, for it was a curious thing to hear a man with the face of a sheep growl and threaten like a wolf. Meanwhile I had risen, for this insult was more than I could bear.

"Señors," I said, speaking in Spanish, "as I see that my presence is unwelcome to the majority of those here, I hasten to withdraw myself.

But before I go I wish to say something, not by way of boasting, but to justify my friend, the English gentleman, in his action on my behalf. However well-born you may be, my descent is nobler and more ancient than yours, and therefore it should be no shame to you to sit at table with me. Least of all should the Don José Moreno, whose father is a murderer, a highway robber, and a man without shame, and whose mother was a half-bred *mestiza* slut, dare to be insolent to me who, as any Indian on board this ship can tell you, am a prince among my own people."

Now every eye was fixed upon Don José. His sallow complexion turned to a whitish green as he listened to my words, and for a moment he sank back in his chair overcome with rage. Then he sprung up, once more gripping at his knife.

"You dog!" he gasped, "let me but come at you and I'll cut your lying tongue out."

"You will do nothing of the sort, Don José Moreno," I answered, fixing my eyes upon his face; "what I have said of your father is true; more, there is a man on board this ship whom, not three months since, he robbed with violence. If the gentlemen your companions would like to hear the story I can tell it to them. For the rest, I am well able to defend myself. Moreover this vessel is manned by Indians who know me, and should any harm come to me or to my friend, the Señor Strickland, I warn you that you will not reach your home alive. Gentlemen, I salute you," and I bowed and left the cabin.

"Friend, I thank you," I said to the señor, when he came upon deck after the dinner was ended. "Knowing who I am and seeing how, in common with my race, I am accustomed to be treated by such hounds as these, can you wonder that I am not fond of Mexicans?"

"No, Ignatio," he answered; "but all the same I advise you to be careful of this Don José. He is not a man to kiss the stick that beats him, and he will make an end of you, and me too for the matter of that, if he can."

"Do not be afraid, señor," I answered, laughing; "besides the steward and Molas there are twenty Indians on board, most of them belonging to the tribe that dwells beyond Campeche, the finest race in Mexico. Two of these men are associates of the Heart, and all the rest know my rank, and will watch that man day and night so that he can never come near us without finding them ready for him. Only we shall do well to sleep on deck and not below."

That night we spent, wrapped in our *serapes*, upon two coils of rope on the forecastle of the *Santa Maria*, with Molas sleeping close behind us. It was a lovely night and we whiled away the hours in telling tales to each other of our adventures in past years, and in wonderings as to those that lay before us, till at length, fearing nothing, for we knew that our safety was watched over, we fell asleep, to be awakened by the sudden stoppage of the vessel.

The day was on the point of dawn; a beautiful and pearly light lay upon the quiet surface of the sea; above us the stars still shone faintly in the heavens, but to the east the cloud-banks were tinged with pink and violet. We sat up wondering what had happened, and saw the captain, wrapped in a dirty blanket, engaged in earnest conversation with the engineer, who wore a still dirtier shirt, and nothing else. Hearing that something was wrong, the Señor James went to the captain and asked him why we had stopped.

"Because the engines won't go anymore, and there is no wind to sail with," he answered politely. "But have no fear, my comrade says that he can mend them up. He has nursed them for years and knows their weak points."

"Certainly there is not much to fear in weather like this," said the señor, "except delay."

"Nothing, nothing," replied the captain, glancing anxiously at a narrow black band of cloud, that lay on the rim of the horizon beneath the fleecy masses in which the lights of dawn were burning.

"Do you think that we are likely to have a norther?" asked the señor in his blunt white man's way.

"No, no," exclaimed the captain, crossing himself at the name of that evil power — *el Norte,* "but *quien sabe!* God makes the weather, not we poor sailors." And with another glance at the threatening line of cloud, he hurried away as though to avoid further conversation.

Presently the engines began to work again, though haltingly, like a lame mule, and as the morning drew on the day became clear and the thin black cloud vanished from the horizon. Towards three o'clock in the afternoon Molas, pointing to a low coast-line, and a spot on the sea where the ocean swell showed tipped with white, told us that yonder was the bar of the Grijalva river, and that behind it lay the village of Frontera, our destination.

"Good," said the señor, "then I think that I will get my things on deck," and going to his cabin he brought up a sack containing some wraps and food.

"Why do you fetch your baggage?" asked the captain presently, "you may want it tonight."

"That is why I brought it up," he answered. "I do not wish to land at Frontera with nothing."

"Land at Frontera, señor? No one will land at Frontera from this ship for another six or seven days. We pass Frontera and run straight on to Campeche, which, by the blessing of the Saints, we shall reach tomorrow evening."

"But I have taken a ticket for Frontera," said the señor. "The agent gave them to me, and I insist upon being put on shore there."

"That is quite right, señor. All being well we shall call at Frontera this day week, and then you can go ashore without extra charge, but before this my orders are to put into no port except Campeche — that is, unless a norther forces me to do so."

"May the norther sink you, your ship, your agents, and everything you have to do with," answered the señor in so angry a voice, that the Mexican passengers who were listening began to laugh at the Englishman's discomfiture, though the more thoughtful of them crossed themselves to avert the evil omen.

Then followed a storm, for the señor — whose temper, as I have said, was not of the coolest — raged and swore in no measured terms; the captain shrugged his shoulders and apologized; the passengers smiled; and, seeing that there was no help for the matter, I looked on patiently after the manner of my race. At length the captain fled, wiping his brow and exclaiming:

"What manner of men are these English that they make such a trouble about a little time? Mother of Heaven! why are they always in a hurry? Is not tomorrow as good as today — and better?"

That evening we dined together upon deck; for neither of us were in any good mood to descend to the cabin and meet Don José Moreno, of whom we had seen nothing since the previous night. As we were finishing our meal the light faded and the sky grew curiously dark, while suddenly to the north there appeared a rim of cloud similar to that which we had seen upon the horizon at dawn, but now it was of an angry red and glowed like the smoke from a smelting-furnace at night.

"The sky looks very strange, Ignatio," said the señor to me, and at that moment we heard Molas and an Indian sailor speaking together in brief words.

"*El Norte,*' said Moras, pointing towards the red rim of light.

"*Si, el Norte,*" answered the sailor as he went towards the cabin.

Presently the captain hurried up the companion-ladder and studied the horizon, of which the aspect seemed to frighten him. In another minute the mate joined him, appearing from the engine hatch, and the two of them began to converse, or rather to dispute. I was sitting near, unobserved in the darkness, and, so far as I could gather, the mate was in favor of putting the ship about and running for Frontera, from which port we were now distant some forty miles.

On the other hand, the captain said that if they did so and the norther came up, it would catch them before they got there, and wreck them upon the bar of the Grijalva river; but he added that he did not believe there would be any norther, and if by ill-luck it should come, their best course was to stand for the open sea and ride it out.

The mate answered that this would be an excellent plan if the ship were staunch and the engines to be relied on, but he declared loudly that they might as well try to sail a boat with a mast made of cigarettes, as to attempt to lie head on to a norther with leaking boilers, worn-out engines, and a strained paddle-wheel.

After this the discussion grew fierce, and as full of oaths as a shark's mouth with teeth, but in the end the two sailors determined that their safest plan would be to hold on their present course, and, if necessary, round Point Xicalango and take shelter behind Carmen Island, or, if they could, in the mouth of the Usumacinto river. Then they parted, the captain adjuring the mate to say nothing of the state of the weather to the passengers, and above all to that accursed Englishman, who had called this misfortune upon them because he was not put off at Frontera, and whose evil eye brought bad luck.

Another two hours passed without much change, except that the night grew darker and darker, and stiller and yet more still. The Señor Strickland, who had been walking up and down the deck smoking a cigar, came and sat beside me on a coil of rope, and asked me if I thought the norther was coming.

"Yes, it is coming," I answered, "and I fear that it will sink us, at least so say the Indian sailors."

"You take the idea of being drowned like a puppy in a sack very coolly, Ignatio. How far are we from Point Xicalango?"

"About twelve miles, I believe, and I take it coolly because there is no use in making an outcry. God will protect us if He chooses, and if He chooses He will drown us. It is childish to struggle against destiny."

"A true Indian creed, Ignatio," he answered; "you people sit down and say — 'It is fate, let us accept it' — but one that I and the men of my nation do not believe in. If they had done so, instead of being the first country in the world today, England long ago would have ceased to exist, for many a time she has stood face to face with Fate and beaten her. For my part, if I must die, I prefer to die fighting. Tell me, are any of these people to be relied on if it comes to a pinch?"

"The Indian sailors are Campeche men and brave, also they know the coast, and if need be they will do anything that I tell them. For the rest I cannot say, but the captain seems to understand something of his business. Look and listen!"

As I spoke a vivid patch of lightning pierced the heavens above us, followed by a deafening peal of thunder. In its fierce and sudden glare we could see the coast some three or four miles away, and almost ahead of us the bolder outline of Point Xicalango. The water about our ship was dead calm, and slipped past her sides like oil; the smoke in the funnel rose almost straight into the air, where at a certain height it twisted round and round; and a sail that had been hoisted flapped to and fro for lack of wind to draw it.

A mile or so to windward, however, was a different sight, for there came the norther, rushing upon us like a thing alive; in front of it a line of white billows torn from the quiet surface of the sea, and behind it, fretted by little lightnings, a dense wall of black cloud stretching from the face of ocean to the arc of heaven.

Now the captain, who was on deck, saw his danger, for if those billows caught us broadside on we must surely founder. In the strange silence that followed the boom of the thunder, he shouted to the helmsman to bring the ship head on to the sea, and to the sailors to batten down the after-hatch, the only one that remained open, shutting the passengers, except ourselves and Molas, into the cabin.

His orders were obeyed well and quickly, the *Santa Maria* came round and began to paddle towards the open water and the advancing line of foam. It was terrible to see her, so small a thing, driving on thus into what appeared to be the very jaws of death. Now the unnatural quiet was broken, a low moaning noise thrilled through the air, the waters about the ship's side began to seethe and hiss, and spray flying ahead of the ship cut our faces like the lash of a whip.

A few more seconds and something white and enormous could be seen looking above our bows, and the sight of it caused the captain, whose face looked pale as death in the gleam of the lightnings, to shriek another order to his crew.

"Lie down and hold on tight to the rope," I said to the Señor Strickland and Molas, who were beside me, "here comes *el Norte*, and he brings death for many of us on board this ship."

Chapter VI

"EL NORTE"

*A*nother moment and *el Norte* had come in strength. First a sudden rush of wind struck the vessel, causing her to shiver, and with a sharp report rending from its fastenings the jib, which had not been furled. This gust went howling by, and after it rolled the storm.

To us it seemed that the *Santa Maria* dived head first into a huge wave, a level line of white illumined with lightnings and swept forward by the hurricane, for in an instant a foot of foaming water tore along her deck from stem to stem, sweeping away everything movable upon it, including two Indian sailors. We should have gone with the rest had we not clung with all our strength to the rope coiled about the foremast, but as it was we escaped with a wetting.

For a while the ship stood quite still, and it seemed as though she were being pressed into the deep by the weight of water on her decks, but as this fell from her in cataracts, she rose again and plowed forward. Fortunately the first burst of the tempest was also the most terrible, and it had not taken her broadside on, for one or two more such waves would have swamped us.

After it had passed shorewards, driven by the hurricane wind, for a little space there was what by comparison might be called a lull, then the *Santa Maria* met the full weight of the norther. For a while she forged again against the shrieking wind and vast succeeding seas, shipping such a quantity of water that presently the captain found it necessary to reduce her engines to half speed, which it was hoped would suffice to give her way without filling her.

Now less water came aboard, but on the other hand, as was soon evident, the vessel began to drift towards the Point Xicalango, and from this moment it became clear that only a miracle could save her. For an hour or more the *Santa Maria* kept up a gallant and unequal fight, being constantly pressed backwards by the might of the storm, till at length we could see in the glare of the lightning that the breakers of the Point were raging not two hundred paces from her stern. The captain saw them also and made a last effort. Shifting the vessel's bow a little, so that the seas struck her on the port quarter, he gave the order of "Full steam ahead," and once more we drove forward.

Before and since that day I have made many voyages across the Gulf of Mexico in all weathers, but never have I met with such an experience as that which followed. The ship plunged and strained and rocked, lifting now her bow and now her stern high above the waves, till it seemed as though she must fall to pieces, while water in tons rushed aboard of her at every dip, which, as she righted herself, streamed through the broken bulwarks.

Slowly, very slowly, we were forging away from the Point and out into the channel which lies between it and Carmen Island, but the effort was too fierce to last. Presently, after a succession of terrible pitchings, one paddle-wheel suddenly ceased to thrash the water, while the other broke to pieces, and a faint cry from below told those on deck that the worn-out machinery had collapsed.

Now we were in the mid-race or channel, through which the boiling current, driven by the fury of the gale and the push of the tide, tore at a speed of fifteen or sixteen knots, carrying the *Santa Maria* along with it as a chip of wood is carried down a flooded gutter. Twice she whirled right round, for now that her machinery had gone there was no power to keep her head to the waves, and on the second occasion, as she lay broadside to them, a green sea came aboard of her that swept her decks almost clean, taking away with it every boat except the cutter, which fortunately was slung upon davits to starboard and out of its reach.

Crouching under shelter of the mast, again the three of us clung to our ropes, nor did we leave go although the water ground us against the deck, covering us for so long that before our heads were clear of it we felt as though our lungs must burst. As it chanced, what remained of the starboard bulwarks was carried away by the rush, allowing the sea to escape, or the ship must have foundered at once. But it had done its work, for the engine-room hatchway and the cabin light were stove in, and the *Santa Maria* was half full of water.

Before a second sea could strike her, her nose swung round, and in this position she was washed along the race, her deck not standing more than four feet above the level of the waves.

Now from time to time the moon shone out between rifts in the storm clouds, revealing a dreadful scene. Fragments of the little bridge still remained, and to them was lashed the large body of the captain in an upright position, though, as he neither spoke nor stirred, we never learned whether he was only paralyzed by terror, or had been killed by a blow from the funnel as it fell.

You will remember, my friend, that he had ordered the passengers to be battened down, and there in the cabin they remained, twenty or more of them, until the hatchways were stove in. Then, with the exception of one or two, who were drowned by the water that poured down upon them, they rushed up the companion, men and women together, for they could no longer stay below, and, shrieking, praying, and blaspheming, clung to fragments of the bulwarks, shrouds of the mast, or anything which they thought could give them protection against the pitiless waves.

Awful were the wails of the women, who, clad only in their nightdresses, now quitted their bunks for the first time since they entered them in the harbor of Vera Cruz. Overcome by fear, and having no knowledge of the dangers of the deep, these poor creatures flung themselves at full length upon the deck, striving to keep a hold of the slippery boards, whence one by one they rolled into the ocean as the vessel lurched, or were carried away by the seas that pooped her.

Some of the men followed them to their watery grave, others, more self-possessed, crept forward, attempting to escape the waves that broke over the stern, but none made any effort to save them, and indeed it would have been impossible so to do.

Among those who crawled forward to where we and some of the Indian sailors were clinging to the rope that was coiled round the stump of the broken foremast, was Don José Moreno. Even in his terror, which was great, this man could still be ferocious, for, recognizing the señor, he yelled:

"Ah! *maldonado* — evil-gifted one — you called down the norther upon us. Well, at least you shall die with the rest," and, suddenly drawing his long knife, he rose to his knees, and, holding the rope with one hand, attempted to drive it into the señor's body with the other. Doubtless he would have succeeded in his wickedness had not an Indian boatswain, who was near, bent forward and struck him so sharply on the arm with his clenched fist that the knife flew from his hand. In trying to recover it Don José fell face downwards on the deck, where he lay making no further effort at aggression.

Afterwards the señor told me, such was the horror and confusion of the scene, that, at the time, he scarcely noticed this incident, though every detail came back to him on the morrow, and with it a great wonder that even when death was staring them in the face, the Indians did not forget their promise to watch over our safety.

Meanwhile, swept onward by the tide and gale, the *Santa Maria*, waterlogged and sinking, rushed swiftly to her doom. Our last hour was upon us, and for a space this knowledge seemed to benumb the mind of the Señor Strickland, who crouched at my side, as the wet and cold had benumbed his body. Nor was this strange, for it seemed terrible to perish thus.

"Can we do nothing?" he said to me at length. "Ask the Indians if there is any hope."

Putting my face close to the ear of the boatswain, I spoke to him, then shouted back:

"He says that the current is taking us round the point of the island, and if the ship weathers it, we shall come presently into calmer water, where a boat might live, if there is one left and it can be launched. He thinks, however, that we must sink."

When the señor heard this he hid his face in his hands, and doubtless began to say his prayers, as I did also. Soon, however, we ceased even from that effort, for we were rounding the point and once more the seas were breaking on and over the vessel's side.

For a few minutes there was a turmoil that cannot be described; then, although the wind still shrieked overhead, we felt that we were in water which seemed almost calm to us. The ship no longer pitched and rolled, she only rocked as she settled before sinking, while the moon, shining out between the clouds, showed that what had been her bulwarks were not more than two or three feet above the level of the sea.

Six Indians, our three selves, Don José, who seemed to be senseless, and the body of the captain lashed to the broken bridge, alone remained of the crew and passengers of the *Santa Maria*. The rest had been swept away, but there close to us the cutter still hung upon the davits.

The señor saw it, and I think that he remembered his saying of a few hours before, that he would die fighting; at least he cried:

"The ship is sinking. To the boat, quick!" and, running to the cutter, he climbed into her, as did I, Molas, and the six Indian sailors.

She was full of water almost to the thwarts, which could only be got rid of by pulling out the wooden plug in her bottom.

Happily the boatswain, that same man who had struck the knife from the hand of Don José, knew where to look for this plug, and, being a sailor of courage and resource, he was able to loose it, so that presently the water was pouring from her in a stream thick as a hawser. Meanwhile, urged to it by the hope of escape, the other Indians were employed in getting out the oars, and in loosening the tackles before slipping them altogether when enough water had run out to allow the boat to swim.

"Get the plug back," said the señor, "the vessel is sinking, you must bale the rest."

Half a minute more and it was done; then, at a word from the boatswain, the sailors lowered away — they had not far to go — and we were afloat, and, better still, quite clear of the ship.

Scarcely had they brought the head of the cutter round and pulled three or four strokes, when from the deck of the *Santa Maria* there came the sound of a man's voice crying for help, and by the light of the moon we discovered the figure of Don José Moreno clinging to the broken bulwarks, that now were almost awash.

"For the love of God, come back to me!" he screamed.

The oarsmen hesitated, but the boatswain said, with an Indian oath: "Pull on and let the dog drown."

It seemed as if Don José heard him, at least he raised so piteous a wailing that the señor's heart, which was always overtender, was touched by it.

"We cannot desert the man," he answered, "put back for him."

"He tried to murder you just now," shouted the boatswain, "and if we go near the ship, she will take us down with her."

Then he turned to me and asked, "Do you command us to put back, lord?"

"Since the señor wills it, I command you," I answered. "We must save the man and take our chance."

"He commands whom we must obey," shouted the boatswain again; "put back, my brothers."

Sullenly, but submissively, the Indians backed water till we lay almost beneath the counter of the vessel, that wallowed in the trough of the swell before she went down. On the deck, clinging to the stays of the mast, stood Don José — his straight oiled hair beat about his face, his gorgeous dress was soaked and disordered.

"Save me!" he yelled hoarsely, "save me!"

"Throw yourself into the sea, señor, and we will pick you up."

"I dare not," was the answer; "come aboard and fetch me."

"Does the señor still wish us to stay?" asked the boatswain, calmly.

"Listen, you cur," shouted the señor, "the ship is sinking and will take us with it. At the word 'three,' give way, men. Now will you come, or not? One, two —"

"I come," said the Mexican, and, driven to it by desperation, he cast himself into the sea.

With difficulty the señor, assisted by an Indian with a boathook, succeeded in getting hold of him as he was washed past on the swell. I confess that I would have no hand in the affair, since — may I be forgiven the sin — my charity was not true enough to make me wish to save this villain. There, however, the matter rested for the present, as they could not stop to pull him into the boat, for just then the deck of the *Santa Maria* burst with a rending sound, and she began to go down bodily.

"Row for your lives," shouted the boatswain, and they rowed, dragging Don José in the wake of the cutter.

Down went the *Santa Maria,* bow first, making a hollow in the sea that sucked us back towards her. For a moment the issue hung doubtful, for the whirlpool caused by the vanished vessel was strong and almost engulfed us, but in the end the stout arms of the Indians conquered and drew our boat clear.

So soon as this great danger had gone by, the sailors with much labor lifted Don José into the cutter, where he lay gasping but unharmed.

Then arose the question of what we could possibly do to save our lives.

We were lying under the lee of Carmen Island, which sheltered us somewhat from the fury of the norther, and we might either try to land upon this island, or to put about and run for the mouth of the Usumacinto river. There was a third course: to keep the boat's head to the seas, if that were possible, and let her drift till daylight. In the end this was what we determined to do.

Indeed, while we were discussing the question it was settled for us, for suddenly the rain began to fall in torrents, blotting out such moonlight as there was; and to land in this darkness would have been impossible, even if the nature of the beach allowed of it. Therefore we lay to and gave our thoughts and strength to the task of preventing the waves, which became more and more formidable as we drifted beyond the shelter of the island, from swamping or oversetting us.

It was a great struggle, and had it not been that the heavy rain beat down the seas, we could never have lived till morning. As it was we must have been swamped many times over but for the staunchness of the boat, which, fortunately, was a new one, and the seamanship and ceaseless vigilance of the Indian boatswain who commanded her. For hour after hour he crouched in the bow of the cutter, staring through the sheets of rain and the darkness with his hawklike eyes, and shouting directions to the crew as he heard or caught sight of a white-crested billow rolling down upon us, that presently would fling us upwards to sink deep into the trough on its further side, sometimes half filling the boat with water, which must be baled out before the next sea overtook us.

Afterwards the señor told me that, knowing it to be the nature of Indians to submit to evil rather than to struggle against it, he wondered how it came about that these men faced the fight so gallantly, instead of throwing down their oars and suffering themselves to be drowned. I also was somewhat astonished till presently the matter was explained, for once, when a larger sea than those that went before had almost filled us, the boatswain called out to his companions:

"Be brave, my brothers, and fear nothing. The Keeper of the Heart is with us, and death will flee him."

To the señor, however, this comfort seemed cold, since he did not believe that any talisman could save us from the powers of the sky and sea, nor indeed did I. Wet and half frozen as he was, his nerve broken by the terrible scenes that we had witnessed upon the lost ship, and by thoughts of the many who had gone down with her, his spirit, so he told me, failed him at last.

He gave no outward sign of his inward state indeed; he did not follow the example of the Mexican, who lay in the water at the bottom of the boat, groaning, weeping, and confessing his sins, which seemed to be many. Only he sat still and silent and surrendered himself to destiny, till by degrees his forces, mental and bodily, deserted him and he sank into a torpor. It was little wonder, for rarely have shipwrecked men been in a more hopeless position. The blinding rain, the bewildering darkness, the roaring wind and sea, all combined to destroy us while we drifted in our frail craft we knew not whither.

As minute after minute of that endless night went by, our escape seemed to become more impossible, for each took with it something of the strength and mental energy of those who fought so bravely against the doom that overshadowed us. For my part, I was sure that my hour had come, but this did not trouble me overmuch, since my life had not been so happy or successful that I grieved at the thought of losing it. Moreover, ever since I became a man it has been my daily endeavor to prepare my mind for Death, and so to live that I should not have to fear the hour of his coming.

In truth it seems to me that without such preparation the life of any man who thinks must be one long wretchedness, seeing that at the last, strive as he may, fate will overtake him, and that there is no event in our lives which can compare in importance with the inevitable end. We live not to escape from death, but in order that we may die; this is the great issue and object of our existence. Still, Death is terrible, more especially when we are called upon to await him hour after hour amid the horror and turmoil of a shipwreck.

Therefore I was very thankful when, having flung my *serape* about the form of my friend, at length I also was overcome by cold and exhaustion, and after a space of time, in which the present seemed to fade from me, taking with it all fears and hopes of the future, and the past alone possessed me, peopled by the dead, I sank into unconsciousness or swoon.

How long I remained in this merciful state of oblivion I do not know, but I was roused from it by Molas, who shook me and called into my ear with a voice that trembled with cold or joy, or both:

"Awake, awake, we are saved!"

"Saved?" I said, confusedly. "What from?"

"From death in the sea. Look, lord."

Then with much pain, for the salt spray had congealed upon my face like frost, I opened my eyes to find that the morning was an hour old, and though the skies were still leaden we were no longer at sea, but floated on the waters of a river, whereof the bar roared behind us.

"Where are we?" I asked.

"In the Usumacinto river, thanks be to God!" answered Molas. "We have been driven across the bay in the dark, and at the dawn found ourselves just outside the breakers. Somehow we passed them safely, and there before us is the blessed land."

I looked at the bank of the river clothed with reeds and grasses, and the noble palm trees that grew among them. Then I looked at my companions. The Señor Strickland lay as though he were dead beneath the *serape* that I had thrown over him, his head resting on the thwarts, but the Mexican, Don José, was sitting up in the bottom of the boat and staring wildly at the shore.

As for the Indians, the men to whom we owed our lives, they were utterly worn out. Two of them appeared to have swooned where they sat, and I saw that their hands were bleeding from the friction of the oars. Three others lay gasping beneath the seats, but Molas held the tiller at my side, and the boatswain still sat upright in the bow where he had faced death for so many dreadful hours.

"Say, lord," he asked, turning his face that was hollow with suspense and suffering, and white with encrusted salt, to speak to me, "can you row? If so, take the oars and pull us to the bank while Molas steers, for our arms will work no more."

Then I struggled from my seat, and with great efforts, for every moment caused me pain, I pulled the cutter to the bank, and as her bows struck against it, the sun broke through the thinning clouds.

So soon as the boat was made fast, Molas and I lifted the señor from her, and, laying him on the bank, we removed his clothes so that the sun might play upon his limbs, which were blue with cold. As the clouds melted and the warmth increased, I saw the blood begin to creep beneath the whiteness of his skin, which was drawn with the wet and wind, and rejoiced, for now I knew that he did but sleep, and that the tide of life was rising in his veins again, as in my own.

Whilst we sat thus warming ourselves in the sunlight, some Indians appeared, belonging to a *rancho*, or village, half a league away. On learning our misfortunes and who we were, these men hurried home to bring us food, having first pointed out to us a pool of sweet rain-water, of which we stood in great need, for our throats were dry. When they had been gone nearly an hour, the señor awoke and asked for drink, which I gave him in the baling-bowl. Next he inquired where we were and what had happened to us. When I had told him he hid his face in his hands for a while, then lifted it and said:

"I am a fool and a boaster, Ignatio. I said that I would die fighting, and it is these men who have fought and saved my life while I swooned like a child."

"I did the same, señor," I answered; "only those who were working at the oars could keep their senses, for labor warmed them somewhat. Come to the river and wash, for now your clothes are dry again," and throwing the *serape* over his shoulders, I led him to the water.

As we climbed down the bank we met the boatswain, and the señor said, holding out his hand to him:

"You are a brave man and you have saved all our lives."

"No, señor, not I," answered the Indian. "You forget that with us was the Keeper of the Heart, and the Heart that has endured so long, cannot be lost. This we knew, and therefore we labored on, well assured that our toil would not be in vain."

"I shall soon begin to believe in that talisman of yours myself, Ignatio," said the señor shrugging his shoulders; "certainly it did us good service last night."

Then he washed, and by the time he had dressed himself, women arrived from the *rancho* bearing with them baskets laden with *tortillas* or meal cakes, *frijole* beans, a roast kid, and a bottle of good *agua ardiente*, the brandy of this country. On these provisions we fell to thankfully, and, before we had finished our meal, the *alcalde*, or head man of the village, presented himself to pay his respects and to invite us to his house.

Now I whispered to Molas, who had some acquaintance with this man, to take him apart and discover my rank to him, and to learn if perchance he had any tidings of that stranger whom we came to visit, the doctor Zibalbay. He nodded and obeyed, and after a while I rose and followed him behind some trees, where the *alcalde*, who was of our brotherhood, greeted me with reverence.

"I have news, my lord," said Molas. "This man says that he has heard of the old Indian and his daughter, and that but this morning one who has traveled down the river told him how some five or six days ago they were both of them seized by Don Pedro Moreno, the father of Don José yonder, and imprisoned at the *hacienda* of Santa Cruz, where, dead or alive, they remain."

Now I thought a while, then, sending for the Señor James, I told him what we had learnt.

"But what can this villain want to do with an old Indian and his daughter?" he asked.

"The señor forgets," said Molas, "that Don Pedro robbed me of the gold which the doctor gave me, and that in my folly I told him from whom it came. Doubtless he thinks to win the secret of the mine whence it was dug, and of the mint where it was stamped with the sign of the Heart. Also there is the daughter, whom some men might value above all the gold in Mexico. Now, lord, I fear that your journey is fruitless, since those who become Don Pedro's guests are apt to stay with him forever."

"That, I think, we must take the risk of," said the señor.

"Yes," I answered: "having come so far to find this stranger, we cannot turn back now. At least we have lived through worse dangers than those which await us at Santa Cruz."

CHAPTER VII

"THE HACIENDA"

*R*eturning to the place where we had eaten, we found the *alcalde* talking with the sailors as to their plans. On seeing us the boatswain advanced, and said that, if it was our pleasure, he and his companions proposed to rest for a few days at the neighboring *rancho* and then to row the boat along the coast to Campeche, which they hoped in favorable weather to reach in sixty hours, adding that he trusted we would accompany them.

I answered that we wished for no more of the sea at present, and that we intended to pursue our journey to the town of Potrerillo, where we could refit before undertaking an expedition to the ruined cities of Yucatan. The boatswain said it was well, though he was sorry that they could not escort us so far, as it was their duty to report the loss of the ship to its owner, who lived at Campeche.

When we heard this the señor unbuckled the belt of money, which he wore about his waist, and, pouring out half a handful of gold pieces, he begged the boatswain to accept of them for division between himself and his companions. All this while Don José was sitting close to us, watching everything that passed, and I saw his eyes brighten at the sight of the belt of gold.

"You are fortunate to have saved so much," he said, speaking for the first time. "All that I had has gone down with the ship, yes, three thousand dollars or more."

"You should have followed our example," answered the señor; "we divided our cash between the three of us and secured it upon our persons, though perhaps you were wise after all, since such a weight of gold might have been awkward if, like you, we had been called upon to swim. By the way, señor, what are *your* plans?"

"If you will allow me," answered the Mexican, "I will walk with you towards Potrerillo, for my home lies on that road. Would you be offended, señor, if, on behalf of my father, I ventured to offer his hospitality to you and your companions?"

"To speak plainly, Don José," said the señor, "our past experience has not been such as to cause us to desire to have anything more to do with you. May I remind you, putting aside other matters, that last night you attempted to stab me?"

"Señor," answered the man with every sign of contrition, "if I did this it was because terror and madness possessed me, and most humbly do I beg your pardon for the deed, and for any angry and foolish words that I may have spoken before it. Señor, you saved my life, and my heart is filled with gratitude towards you, who have thus repaid evil with good. I know that you have heard an ill report of my father, and, to speak truth, at times when the liquor is in him, he is a bad and violent old man, yet he has this virtue, that he loves me, his son, and all those who are kind to me. Therefore, in his name and my own, I pray that you will forget the past and accept of our hospitality for some few days, or at least until you have recovered from your fatigue and we can furnish you with arms and horses to help you forward on your journey."

"Certainly we desire to buy mules and guns," answered the señor, "and if you think that your father will be able to supply these, we will avail ourselves of your kindness and pass a night or two at his *hacienda.*"

"Señor, the place is yours and all that it contains," Don José answered with much courtesy; but as he spoke I saw his eye gleam with an evil fire.

"Doubtless," I interrupted, "for I understand that Don Pedro Moreno is famed for his hospitality. Still, in accepting it, I venture to ask for a promise of safe-conduct, more especially as, save for our pistols and knives, we are unarmed."

"Do you wish to insult me, señor?" Don José asked angrily.

"Not in the least, señor, but I find it a little strange that you, who two nights ago refused to sit at meat with 'a dog of an Indian,' should now be anxious to receive that same dog into your home."

"Have I not said that I am sorry for what is past?" he answered, "and can a man do more? Gentlemen, if any evil is attempted towards you in my father's house, I will answer for it with my life."

"That is quite sufficient," broke in the señor, "especially as in such an event we should most certainly hold you to your bond. And now tell me how far is the *hacienda* from this spot?"

"If we start at once we should reach it at sundown," he answered, "that is on foot, though it is but three hours' ride from the house to the mouth of the river."

"Then let us go," he said, and ten minutes later we were on the road.

Before we went, however, we bade a warm farewell to the sailors, and also to the *alcalde* of the village, all of whom were somewhat disturbed on learning that we proposed to sleep at Santa Cruz.

"The place has an evil name," said the *alcalde,* "and it is a home of thieves and smugglers — only last week a cargo that never paid duty went up the river. They say that Don Pedro was fathered by the devil in person; may the Saints protect you from him, lord!"

"We have business that takes us to his house, friend," I answered; "but doubtless it will be easy for you to keep yourself informed of what chances in that neighborhood, and if we should not appear again within a few days, perhaps it may please you to advise the authorities at Campeche that we are missing."

"The authorities are afraid of Don Pedro," answered the *alcalde,* shaking his head, "also he bribes them so heavily that they grow blind when they look his way. Still I will do the best I can, be sure of that, and as an *Inglese* is with you, it is possible that I may be able to get help if necessary."

Our walk that day was long and hot, though we had nothing to carry except the clothes on our backs, all our possessions, having been lost in the ship. At noon we halted, and, the heat being great, ate some food that we had brought with us, and slept two hours in the shade, which sleep was most grateful, for we were weary. Then we rose and tramped on, till at length we came within sight of this *hacienda,* where, though I little guessed it at the time, I was fated to spend so many years of my life.

Walking through a large *milpa,* or corn field — that in front of the building which is now planted with coffee-bushes — we reached the gateway and entered the courtyard, where we were met by many fierce dogs which rushed upon us from all sides. Don José beat back the dogs, that knew him, and, leaving us under the charge of some half-breeds, he entered the house.

After a while he returned again and led us through the passages into the dining-hall, which, as you know, is the largest room in the *hacienda,* and in former days served as the refectory of the monks. Several lamps were hung upon its walls, for already it grew dark, and by their light we saw five or six people gathered round a long table waiting for supper, which was being laid by Indian girls. Of these men it is sufficient to say that they were of mixed nationality and villainous appearance. Turning from them we looked towards the far end of the chamber, where a hammock was slung from the beams in the roof, in which lay a man whom a handsome girl, also an Indian, was employed in rocking to and fro.

"Come and be introduced to my father, who expects you," said Don José, leading the way towards the hammock. "Father, here is that brave Englishman who saved my life last night, and with him the Indian gentleman, who — did not wish to save my life. As I told you, I have offered them hospitality on your behalf, feeling sure that they would be welcome here."

At the sound of his son's voice Don Pedro awoke, or pretended to awake, from his doze, and bade the girl cease swinging the hammock. Then he sat up and looked at us. He was a short stout man of about sixty years of age — so short indeed that, although the hammock was slung low, his legs did not touch the floor. Notwithstanding this lack of stature, Don Pedro's appearance was striking, while his long, carefully brushed white hair gave him a venerable aspect.

Other beauties he had none, however, for his cheeks were flabby and wrinkled, his mouth was cruel and sensuous; and his dull eyes, which were small, half opened, and protected from the glare of the lamps by spectacles of tinted glass, can best be described as horrible, like those of a snake. Looking at him we could well believe that his reputation was not exaggerated, for he bore the stamp of evil on his face. Still he bowed with much courtesy and addressed the señor in Spanish.

"So you are the Englishman who saved my son here from the sinking ship," he said in a slow, powerful voice, peering at us with his fishlike eyes from beneath the colored glasses. "He tells me that you rowed back to the side of the foundering vessel merely in order to fetch him. Well, it was a brave deed and one that I should not have dared myself, for I have always found it hard enough to keep my own breath in me without attempting to preserve that of other people. But as I have seen several times, you Englishmen are peculiar in these matters, foolhardy indeed. Señor, I am grateful to you, and this house and all within it is at your disposal and that of your companions," and he glanced with genuine affection at the coarse beetle-browed man beside him, who was gnawing one end of his moustache and staring at us out of the corners of his eyes.

"Tell me," he added, "to what do I owe the honor of your presence?"

"To an accident, Don Pedro," the señor answered. "As it chances, the ruins of this ancient land interest me much, and I was traveling to Palenque with my Indian friend, Don Ignatio, when we were so unfortunate as to be wrecked near your hospitable house. In our dilemma we accepted the invitation of your son to visit you, in the hope that you may be able to sell us some guns and mules."

"Ruins, Señor Strickland! Decidedly you Englishmen are strange. What pleasure can you find in hunting about among old walls, built by men long dead, unless indeed you seek for treasure there. For my part I hate the name of ruins, for I have always suffered from a presentiment that I should meet my end among them, and that is bad to think of. Bah!" — and he spat upon the floor — "there, it comes upon me again, suddenly as a fit of the ague."

"Well," he went on, "you are lucky to have saved your lives and your money, and tomorrow we will see about the things that you desire to buy. Meanwhile, you are travel-stained and doubtless will wish to cleanse yourself before you eat. José, conduct the señor and his Indian friend, since he is so fond of his company, to their room, the abbot's chamber. Supper will be served shortly, till then, *adios.* Girl, go with them," he added, addressing the woman who had been engaged in swinging the hammock, "water may be wanted and other things."

The woman bowed and went away, and at the door we found her standing, lamp in hand, to light us down the passage.

Now, Señor Jones, you, for whom I write my history, have so often slept in the abbot's chamber in this house that it is needless for me to stop to describe it. Except for the furniture, the room is just as it was in those days. Then it was empty save for a few chairs, a rough washing-stand, and two truckle bedsteads of American make, which were placed at a little distance from each other on either side of the picture of the abbot.

"I fear that you will think this a poor place, after the luxury of Mexico, gentlemen," said Don José, "but it is our guest-chamber, the best that we have."

"Thank you," answered the señor, "it will do very well, though perhaps your visitors suffer sometimes from nightmare," and he glanced at the awful and life-sized picture on the south wall of an Indian being burned at an *auto-da-fé*, while devils hanging above his head dragged the soul from his tortured and expiring body.

"Pretty, are they not?" said Don José; "I would have them white-washed over, but my father likes them. You see all the victims are Indians, there isn't a white man among them, and the old man never could bear Indians. Well, when you are ready, will you come to supper? You will not lose the way, for you can follow the smell of the food," and he left the room.

"One moment," I said addressing the girl, who was about to accompany him, "perhaps you will see that our servant," and I pointed to Molas, "has some meat brought to him here, since your masters will not wish him to sit at table."

"*Sí,*" answered the girl, whose name was Luisa, searching my face with her eyes.

By this time Don José was through the door, which the draft pushed to behind him. I watched it close, then a thought struck me, for I remembered that among our Order there are women, associates of the outer circle, and I whispered some words into Luisa's ear and made a sign with my hand. She started and gave the ancient answer, which is taught even to children, whereto I replied with another sign, that of the Presence of the Heart. "*Where?*" she asked glancing at each of us in turn.

"*Here,*" I answered, and, drawing out the symbol, I held it before her eyes.

She saw and made obeisance, and at that moment we heard Don José calling her from the further side of the door.

"I come," she cried in answer, then added in a whisper: "Lord, you are in danger in this house. I cannot tell you now, but if possible I will return. The wine is safe, but drink no coffee, and do not sleep when you lie down. Search the floor and you will understand the reason. I come, señor! I come!" and she fled from the room.

So soon as the girl was gone, the Señor James went to the door and locked it, then he returned and said:

"What does all this mean, Ignatio?"

I did not answer, but, pushing aside one of the beds, I searched the floor beneath it. It was discolored in several places. Next I pulled the blankets off the beds and examined the webbing that formed the mattresses, to discover that this also was stained, though slightly, for it had been washed. Then I said:

"Men have died in these beds, señor, and yonder stains were made by their blood. It would seem that the guests of Don Pedro sleep well; first they are drugged, then they are murdered; and it is for this purpose that we have been lured to the house. Well, we expected nothing else."

"That is a pleasing prospect," he answered, "we are this man's guests, surely therefore he will not –" and he drew his hand across his throat.

"Certainly he will, señor, and it is to this end that we have been brought here by Don José. If others have been murdered, it is not likely that we shall escape, since Don Pedro will be sure that an *Inglese* would not travel without a large sum of money. Moreover, we have a quarrel with the son, and I know too much about the father."

"Again I say that the prospect is a pleasant one," answered the señor. "On the whole it would have been better to be drowned than to live on to be butchered by those villains in this awful place. What an end!"

"Do not despair," I answered. "We were warned in time and therefore, I think, shall escape by the help of that girl and the other Indians in the place, since in an hour every one of them will have learned who we are, and be prepared to venture their lives to save us. Also we came for a purpose, knowing our risk. Now let us make ready and go among these men with a bold face; for of this you may be sure, that nothing will be attempted till late at night when they think us sleeping. Have you understood, Molas?"

"Yes," answered the Indian.

"Then watch here, or in the outer room, till we return, and should the girl come, learn all you can from her as to the whereabouts of the old doctor and his daughter, and other matters, for when she knows you to be of the Order she will speak. Have you been recognized by anyone?"

"I think not, señor. When we entered it was too dark for them to see."

"Good. Then keep out of their way if possible, do the best you can with the girl, and take note of all that passes. Farewell."

When we reached the dining-hall, nine of the company were already seated at the table impatient for their food, but Don Pedro was still sitting in his hammock engaged in earnest conversation with his son José. Of those at the table but one was a white man, a lanky, withered-looking person with a broken nose, whose general appearance filled us with disgust. The rest were half-breeds, the refuse of revolutions, villains who had escaped the hand of justice and who lived by robbery and murder.

Looking at these outcasts it became clear to us that, if once we fell into their power, we could expect little mercy at their hands, for they would think no more of butchering us in cold blood than does a sportsman of shooting a deer.

When Don Pedro perceived us, he slid from his hammock to the ground, and, taking the señor by the hand, he said:

"Let me introduce you to my overseer, the Señor Smith, from Texas. He is an American, and will be glad to meet one who can speak English, for, notwithstanding much practice, his Spanish is none of the best."

The señor bowed, and the American desperado spoke to him in English, wearing a grin on his face like that of a wicked dog as he did so, though I do not know what he said. Then Don Pedro conducted his guest to a place of honor at the head of the table, that beside his own seat, while I was led to another table at a little distance, where my meat was served to me alone, since, as an Indian of pure blood, I was not thought fit for the company of these cross-bred curs. Don José having taken his place at the further end of the board with the *Americano*, the meal began, and an excellent one it was.

Now, in the conversation that ensued I took no part, except when members of the gang called to me to drink wine with them, for they desired to make me drunk; but while I pretended to be occupied with my meat, I thought much and watched more. The talk that passed I set down as I overheard it and as it was reported to me by the señor.

"Try some more of this Burgundy," said Don Pedro when the dishes had been removed, filling his tumbler for the seventh or eighth time, "it is the right stuff, straight from France, though it never paid duty," and he winked his leaden eye.

"Your health, señor, and may you live to do many such brave deeds as that of yesterday, when you saved my son from the sea. By the way, do you know that on board the *Santa Maria* they said that you had the evil eye and brought her to wreck; — yes, and your long-faced companion, the Indian, also?"

"Indeed, I never heard of it before," answered the señor with a laugh; "but if so, our evil eyes shall not trouble you for long, as we propose to continue our journey tomorrow."

"Nonsense, friend, nonsense, you don't suppose that I believe in that sort of rubbish, do you? We say many things that we do not believe just for a joke; thus," and he raised his voice so that I could hear him at my table, "your companion there — is he not named Ignatio? — told a story to my disadvantage on board the ship, which I am sure that he did not believe," and suddenly he stared at me and added insolently: "Is it not so, Indian?"

"If you seek my opinion, Don Pedro," I answered, leaning forward and speaking very clearly, "I say that it is unprofitable to repeat words that are said, or to remember deeds that are done with. If I spoke certain words, or if in the past you did certain deeds, here beneath your hospitable roof is not the place to recall them."

"Quite so, Indian, quite so, you talk like an oracle, as Montezuma used to talk to Cortes till the Conqueror found a way to teach him plain speaking — a great man, Cortes, he understood how to deal with Indians." Then he spat upon the floor and, having looked down the table, spoke to the señor in a somewhat anxious voice.

"Tell me," he said, "for your sight is better than mine, how many are there present here tonight?"

"Counting my friend, thirteen," he answered.

"I thought so," said our host, with an oath, "and it is too late to mend matters now. Well, may the Saints, and they should be thick about a monastery, avert the omen. I see you think me a fool."

"Not at all," he replied; "I am rather superstitious myself and dislike sitting down thirteen to table."

"So do I, so do I, Señor Strickland. Listen; last time we dined thirteen in this room, there were two travelers here, *Americanos,* friends of Don Smith, who were trying to open up a trade in these parts. They drank more than was good for them, and the end of it was that in the night they quarreled and killed each other, yonder in the abbot's chamber, where you are sleeping — poor men, poor men! There was trouble about the matter at the time, but Don Smith explained to his countrymen and it came to nothing."

"Indeed," answered the señor; "it was strange that two drunken men should kill each other."

"So I say, señor. In truth for a while I thought that Indians must have got into their rooms and murdered them, but it was proved beyond a doubt that this was not so. Ah! they are a wicked people, the Indians; I have seen much of them and I should know. Now the Government wishes to treat them too well. Our fathers knew better how to deal with them, but luckily the arm of the Government scarcely reaches here, and no whining *padres* or officials come prying about my house, though once we had some soldiers," and he cursed at the recollection and drank another glass of Burgundy.

"I tell you that they are a wicked people," he went on, "the *demonios* their fathers worshipped still possess them, also they are secret and dangerous; there are Indians now who know where vast treasures are buried, but they will tell nothing.

"Yes" — and suddenly growing excited under the influence of the strong drink, he leaned over and whispered into his guest's ear — "I have one such in the house at this moment, an old *Lacandone*, that is, an unbaptised Indian, not that I think him any the worse for that, and with him his daughter, a woman more beautiful than the night — perhaps if I go on liking you, Englishman, I will show her to you tomorrow, only then I should have to keep you, for you would never go away. Beautiful! yes, she is beautiful, though a devil at heart. I have not dared to let these little ones see her," and he winked and nodded towards the villains at the table, "but José is to pay her and her papa a visit tonight, and he won't mind her tempers, though they frighten me.

"Well, would you believe it? this girl and her old father have the secret of enough treasure to make every man of us here rich as the Queen of England. How do I know that? I know it because I heard it from their own lips, but fill your glass and take a cigar and I will tell you the story."

Chapter VIII

THE SUPPER AND AFTER

"*L*isten, señor; if you are interested in old ruins and the Indians, you must have heard tales of races living away in the forest country, where no white man has set his foot, and of their wonderful cities that are said to be full of gold. Many say that these tales are lies, that no such people and no such cities exist, and they say this because nobody has found them; but I, for my part, have always believed there was something in the story, seeing that otherwise it would not have lasted so long.

"Well, a few months back, I heard that a strange old Indian doctor, who was said to have traveled from the far interior, was dwelling somewhere in the forest together with a woman, but where he dwelt exactly I could not learn, nor, indeed, did I trouble myself to do so. About eight weeks ago, however, it happened that an Indian, being asked for the toll, which I charge all passers-by — to recoup me for my expense in making roads, señor — paid it with a little lump of pure gold having a heart stamped on either side of the metal.

"Now, you may not know, though I do, that the heart is a sacred symbol among these Indians, and has been for many generations, for it is to be seen cut upon the walls of their ruins, though what it means only Satan, their master, can tell.

"Therefore, when I saw the lump of gold with the token on it, I asked the Indian whence he had it, and he told me readily enough that it came from this old doctor, who gave it to him in payment for some food. He told me also where I might find him, and went upon his way, but, his heart being full of deceit, he lied as to the place, so that I searched in vain. Well, to shorten a long story, although to this hour I do not know where the Indian was hiding, I set a trap for him and caught him — aye, and his daughter too.

"It was a simple one, a man in my pay knew another man who visited the doctor in the forest to get medicine from him, but who would not reveal his hiding place. Still, my servant drew it out of him thus: he sent piteous messages through his friend, begging the doctor to come and save the life of his dying child, which lay in a house near here, and could not be moved.

"The end of it was that the doctor came, and his daughter with him. Yes, they walked at night straight to the snare, into this very house, señor, and only discovered their mistake when they found the doors locked upon them, and that the dying child was none other than your humble servant, Don Pedro Moreno.

"I can tell you, señor, that I laughed till I nearly cried at the sight of their faces, when they found out the trick, though there was nothing to laugh at in them, for the man looked like an old king, and the girl like a queen, quite different from the Indians in these parts; moreover, they were two such *serapes* as I had never seen, made of green feathers fastened to a foundation of linen.

"When the old man found himself caged, he asked what it meant and where he was, speaking in a dialect so like the Maya tongue that I could understand him quite well. I told him that he was to be my guest for a while, and with the help of two men who were with me I proceeded to secure him and his daughter in a safe place, whereat he flew into a fearful rage, and cursed all of us most dreadfully, and more especially that man who had betrayed him. So awful were his curses and the vengeance that he conjured upon us from heaven, that my hair stood straight upon my head, and as for the man who lured him here under pretence of visiting his child, it came about that within two days he died of a sudden sickness bred of his own fears. When the second man heard of his companion's death, he in turn fled from the place, dreading lest a like fate should overtake him, and has been no more heard of.

"Thus it comes about, señor, that I alone know where these birds are caged, though I hope to introduce my son to them tonight, for I dare not trust the others, and wish to keep them in the family, nor will I let any Indians near them.

"Well, when they had calmed down a little, I spoke to my prisoners through a grating, telling them that I wished to know whence they had obtained those lumps of gold stamped with a heart, to which the old man answered that he had no knowledge of any such gold. Now, I was sure that he lied, and took refuge in another trick. The cell they were shut up is that in which the old monks imprisoned such as were suspected of heresy, and others, and close to it is a secret place — there are many such in this house, señor — where a spy may be hid, and both see and hear all that passes in the cell.

"In this place I ensconced myself, and lay there for hours, with the rats running over me, so anxious was I to get at the truth. In the end I was not disappointed, for they began to talk. A great deal of their conversation I could make nothing of, but at length the girl said, after examining an old gilt crucifix that hung upon the wall:

"'Look, father, here also they have gold.'

"'It is gilt, not gold,' he answered, 'I know the art of it, though with us it is not practiced, except to keep from corruption the spears and arrowheads that fowlers use upon the lake.' Then he added:

"'I wonder what that leaden-faced, greedy-eyed white thief would say if he knew that in a single temple we could show him enough of the metal he covets to fill this place five times over from floor to ceiling.'

"'Hush!' she said, 'ears may be listening even in these walls; let us risk nothing, seeing that by seeming to be ignorant alone we can hope to escape.'"

"Well," asked the señor eagerly, "and what did Zibalbay answer? I think that you said the old man's name was Zibalbay," he added, trying to recover the slip.

"Zibalbay! No, I never mentioned that name," Don Pedro replied suspiciously, and with a sudden change of manner. "He answered nothing at all. Next morning, when I came to question them, the birds had flown. It is a pity, for otherwise I might have asked the old man — if his name is Zibalbay. I suppose that the Indians had let them out, but I could not discover."

"Why, Don Pedro, you said just now that they were still in the house."

"Did I? Then I made a mistake, as you did about the name; this wine is strong, it must have gone to my head; sometimes it does — a weakness, and a bad one. It is an odd tale, but there it ended so far as I am concerned. Come, señor, take a cup of coffee, it is good."

"Thank you, no," answered the señor, "I never drink coffee at night, it keeps me awake."

"Still, I beg you to try ours, friend, we grow it ourselves and are proud of its flavor."

"It is poison to me, I dare not," he said. "But pray tell me, do the gentlemen whom I have the honor to see at table cultivate your plantations?"

"Yes, yes, they cultivate the coffee and the cocoa, and other things also when they have a mind. I daresay you think them a rough-looking lot, but they are kind-hearted, ah! so kind-hearted; feeble as I am they treat me like a father. Bah! señor, what is the good of hiding the truth from one of your discernment? We do business of all sorts here, but the staple of it is smuggling rather than agriculture.

"The trade is not what it was, those sharks of customs officers down on the coast there want so much to hold their tongues, but still there are a few pickings. In the old times, when they did not ask questions, it was otherwise, for then men of pluck were ready for anything from revolution down to the stringing up of a coach-load of fat merchants, but now is the day of small profits, and we must be thankful for whatever trifles Providence sends us."

"Such as the two Americans who got drunk and killed each other," suggested the señor, whose tongue was never of the most cautious.

Instantly Don Pedro's face changed, the sham geniality born of drink went out of it, and was replaced by a hard and cunning look.

"I am tired, señor," he said, "as you must be also, and, if you will excuse me, I will light another cigar and take a nap in my hammock. Perhaps you will amuse yourself with the others, señor, till you wish to go to rest." Then rising, he bowed and walked somewhat unsteadily to the far end of the room.

When Don Pedro had retired to his hammock, whither the Indian girl, Luisa, was summoned to swing him to sleep, I saw his son José and the Texan outcast, Smith, both of whom, like the rest of the company, were more or less drunk, come to the señor and ask him to join in a game of cards. Guessing that their object was to make him show what cash he had about him, he also affected to be in liquor, and replied noisily that he had lost most of his money in the shipwreck, and was, moreover, too full of wine to play.

"Then you must have lost it on the road, friend," said Don José, "for you forget that you made those sailors a present from a belt of gold which you wore about your middle. However, no gentleman shall be forced to gamble in this house, so come and talk while the others have their little game."

"Yes, that will be better," answered the señor, and he staggered to an empty chair, placed not far from the table at which I remained, and was served with spirits and cigars. Here he sat watching the play, which was high, although the counters looked innocent enough — they were cocoa beans — and listened to the conversation of the gamblers, in which he joined from time to time.

The talk was not good to hear, for as these wretches grew more drunken, they began to boast of their past exploits in various parts of the country. One man told how he had kidnapped and tortured an Indian who had offended him; another, how he had murdered a woman of who he was jealous; and the third, of the successful robbing of a coach-load of travelers, and their subsequent butchery by the driving of the coach over the edge of a precipice. All these stories, however, were as milk to brandy compared to those that Don Smith, the *Americano,* growing confidential in his cups, poured forth one after the other, till the señor, unable to bear them any longer, affected to sink into a tipsy doze.

All this while I sat at the little table where my dinner had been served, saying nothing, for none spoke to me, but within hearing of everything that passed. There I sat quiet, my arms folded on my breast, listening attentively to the tales of outrage, wrong, and murder practiced by these wicked ones upon my countrymen.

To them I was only a member of a despised and hated race, admitted to their company on sufferance in order that I might be robbed and murdered in due course, but in my heart I looked on them with loathing and contempt, and felt far above them as the stars, while I watched and wondered how long the great God would suffer his world to be outraged by their presence.

Some such thoughts seemed to strike others of that company, for presently Don Smith called out —

"Look at that Indian rascal, friend, he is proud as a turkey-cock in springtime: why, he reminds me of the figure of the king in that ruin where we laid up last year waiting for the señora and her party. You remember the señora, don't you, José? I can hear her squeaks now" — and he laughed brutally, and added, "Come, king, have a drink."

"*Gracias*, señor," I answered, "I have drunk."

"Then smoke a cigar, O king."

"*Gracias*, señor, I do not smoke tonight."

"My lord *cacique* of all the Indians won't drink and won't smoke," said Don Smith, "so we will offer him incense" — and, taking a plate, he filled it with dry tobacco and cigarette-paper, to which he set fire. Then he placed the plate on the table before me, so that the fumes of the tobacco rose into the air about my head.

"There, now he looks like a real god," said the *Americano*, clapping his hands; "I say, José, let us make a sacrifice to him. There is the girl who ran away last week, and whom we caught with the dogs —"

"No, no, comrade," broke in José, "none of your jokes tonight, you forget that we have a visitor. Not but what I should like to sacrifice this old *demonio* of an Indian to himself," he added, in an outburst of drunken fury. "Curse him! he insulted me and my father and mother, yonder on board the ship."

"And are you going to put up with that from this wooden Indian god? Why, if I were in your place, by now I would have filled him as full of holes as a coffee-roaster, just to let the lies out."

"That's what I want to do," said José, gnashing his teeth, "he has insulted me and threatened me, and ought to pay for it, the black thief," and, drawing a large knife, he flourished it in my face.

I did not shrink from it; I did not so much as suffer my eyelids to tremble, though the steel flashed within an inch of them, for I knew that if once I showed fear he would strike. Therefore I said calmly:

"You are pleased to jest, señor, and your jests are somewhat rude, but I pass them by, for I know that you cannot harm me because I am your guest, and those who kill a guest are not gentlemen, but murderers, which the highborn Don José Moreno could never be."

"Stick the pig, José," said Smith, "he is insulting you again. It will save you trouble afterwards."

Then, as Don José again advanced upon me with the knife, of a sudden the señor sprang up from his chair and stood between us.

"Come, friend," he said, "a joke is a joke, but you are carrying this too far, according to your custom," and, seizing the man by the shoulders, he put out all his great strength, and swung him back with such force that, striking against the long table with his thighs, he rolled on to and over it, falling heavily to the ground upon the farther side, whence he rose cursing with rage.

By now, Don Pedro, who had wakened or affected to waken from his sleep, thought that the time had come to interfere.

"Peace, little ones, peace!" he cried sleepily from his hammock. "Remember that the men are guests, and cease brawling. Let them go to bed, it is time for them to go to bed, and they need rest; by tomorrow your differences will be healed up forever."

"I take the hint," said the señor, with forced gaiety. "Come, Ignatio, let us sleep off our host's good wine. Gentlemen, sweet dreams to you," and he walked across the hall, followed by myself.

At the door I turned my head and looked back. Every man in the room was watching us intently, and it seemed to me that the drunkenness had passed from their faces, scared away by a sense of some great wickedness about to be worked. Don Smith was whispering into the ear of José, who still held the knife in his hand, but the rest were staring at us as people stare at men passing to the scaffold.

Even Don Pedro, wide awake now, sat up in his hammock and peered with his horny eyes, while the Indian girl, Luisa, her hand upon the cord, watched our departure with some such face as mourners watch the out-bearing of a corpse. All this I noted in a moment as I crossed the threshold and went forward down the passage, and as I went I shivered, for the scene was uncanny and fateful.

Presently we were in the abbot's chamber, our sleeping-place, and had locked the door behind us. Near the washstand, on which burned a single candle set in the neck of a bottle, sat Molas, his face buried in his hands.

"Have they brought you no supper, that you look so sad?" asked the señor.

"The woman, Luisa, gave me to eat," he whispered. "Listen, lord, and you, Señor Strickland, our fears are well founded; there is a plot to murder us tonight, of this the woman is sure, for she heard some words pass between Don Pedro and a white man called Smith; also she saw one of the half-breeds fetch spades from the garden and place them in readiness, which spades are to be used in the hollowing of our graves beneath this floor."

Now when we heard this our hearts sank, for it was terrible to think that we were doomed within a few hours to lie beneath the ground whereon our living feet were resting. Yet, if these assassins were deter-mined upon our slaughter, our fate seemed certain, seeing that we had only knives wherewith to defend ourselves, for, though we had saved the pistols and some powder in a flask, the damp had reached the latter during the shipwreck, so that it could not be relied upon.

"I am afraid that we have been too venturesome in coming here," I said, "and that unless we can escape at once we must be prepared to pay the price of our folly with our lives."

"Do not be downcast, lord," answered Molas, "for you have not heard all the tale. The woman has shown me a means whereby you can save yourselves from death, at any rate for tonight. Come here," and, leading us across the room, he knelt upon the floor at a spot almost opposite the picture of the abbot, and pressed on a panel in the low wainscoting of cedar wood with which the wall was clothed to a height of about three feet.

The panel slid aside, leaving a space barely large enough for a man to pass. Through this opening we crept one by one, and descended four narrow steps, to find ourselves in a chamber hollowed out of the foundations of the wall, so small that there was only just room for the three of us to stand in it, our heads being some inches above the level of the floor.

And here I may tell you, Señor Jones, that, though I have never shown it to you, this place still exists, as you may discover by searching the wainscoting. For many years I have used it for the safe keeping of papers and valuables. There, by the way, you will find that emerald which I showed you on the first night of our meeting. What the purpose of this chamber was in the time of the abbots I do not know, and perhaps it is as well not to inquire, though they also may have used it to store their wealth.

"How can we save ourselves by crouching here like rats in a drain?" I asked of Molas. "Doubtless the secret of the hiding place is known to those who live in the house, and they will drag us out and butcher us."

"The woman Luisa says that it is known to none except herself, lord, for she declares that not two months ago she discovered it for the first time by the accident of the broom with which she was sweeping the floor striking against the springs of the panel. Now let us come out for a while, for it is not yet eleven o'clock, and she says that there will be no danger till after midnight."

"Has she any plan for our escape?" I asked.

"She has a plan, though she is doubtful of its success. When the murderers have been, and found us gone, they will think either that we are wizards or that we have made our way out of the house, and will search no more till dawn. Meanwhile, if she can, Luisa will return, and, entering the chamber by the secret entrance, will lead us to the chapel, whence she thinks that we may fly into the forest."

"Where is this secret entrance, Molas?"

"I do not know, lord; she had no time to tell me, but the murderers will come by it. She did tell me, however, that she believes that a man and a woman are imprisoned near the chapel, though she knows nothing of them and never visits the place, because the Indians deem it to be haunted. Doubtless these two are Zibalbay and his daughter, so that if you live to come so far, you may find them there and speak with them."

"Why do you say 'if *you* live,' Molas?"

"Because I think, lord, that then I shall be already dead; at least, death waits on me."

"What do you mean?" asked the señor.

"I will tell you. After the woman Luisa had gone I ate the food she brought me and drank some wine. Then I think that I fell asleep, for when I awoke the candle had burned out and I was in darkness. Hastily I turned to search for another candle that I had placed by the bottle, and was about to make fire when something drew my eyes, causing me to look up.

"This was what I saw: at the far end of the chamber, enclosed in a film of such pale light as is given by the glow-fly, stood the figure of a man, and that man myself, dressed as I am now. There I stood surrounded by faint fire; and though the face was the face of a dead man, yet the hand was not dead, for it beckoned towards me through the darkness.

"Now I saw, and the cold sweat of fear broke out upon me, so that I could scarcely light the candle which I held. At length, however, it burned brightly, and, holding it over my head, I walked towards the spot where I had seen the shadow, only to find that it was gone."

"Or in other words, that you had slept off your indigestion," said the señor. "I congratulate you on getting rid of it so soon."

"It is easy to mock," answered Molas, "but that which I have seen, I have seen, and I know that it portends my death. Well, so be it; I am not yet old, but I have lived long enough and now it is time to go. May Heaven have mercy on my sins, and thus let it be."

After this the señor and I strove to reason him out of his folly, but in vain, nor, in fact, was it altogether a folly, seeing that Molas was doomed to die upon the morrow; though whether the vision that he saw came to warn him of his fate, or was but a dream, it is not for me to say.

Presently we ceased talking of ghosts and omens, for we must look to our own bodies and the necessities of the hour. Some minutes before midnight we extinguished the light, and, creeping one by one through the hole in the paneling, we closed it behind us and took our stand in the little dungeon. Here the darkness was awful, and as the warmth of the wine that we had drunk passed from our veins, fears gathered thick upon us and oppressed our souls. Those hours on the sinking ship had been evil, but what were they compared to this?

Deep as was the silence, yet there were noises in it, strange creaks and flutterings that thrilled our marrows. We prayed till we were weary, then for my part I tried to doze, only to find that at such a time sleep was worse than waking, for my imagination peopled it with visions till it seemed to me that all the painted horrors on the walls of the chamber took life, and enacted themselves before my eyes.

I heard the groaning of the martyrs, and the cruel jeers of those who watched their agony, urged on by the hard-faced abbot, whose picture hung above us. Then the vision changed and I seemed to see the tragedy of the two Americans, of whose fate the señor had told me and whose blood still stained the floor. The darkness opened as it were, and I saw the beds on which they were sleeping heavily, stalwart men in the prime of life.

Then appeared figures standing over them, Don Pedro, Don José, and others, while from the shadows behind peeped the wicked face of their countryman, Don Smith. The bed-clothes were twitched away and once more all was black, but in the darkness I heard a sound of blows and groaning, of the hurrying feet of murderers, and the clinking of bags of money stolen from the dead men. Now the señor touched me and I woke with a start.

"Hark," he whispered into my ear, "I hear men creeping about the room."

"For the love of God, be silent," I answered, gripping his hand.

Chapter IX

THE DUEL

Now we placed our ears against the paneling and listened. First we heard creaks that were loud in the stillness, then soft heavy noises such as are made by a cat when it jumps from a height to the ground, and a gentle rubbing as of stockinged feet upon the floor. After this for some seconds came silence that presently was broken by the clink of steel, and the sound of heavy blows delivered upon a soft substance with swords and knives. The murderers were driving their weapons through the bed-clothes, thinking that we slept beneath them. Next we heard whisperings and muttered oaths, then a voice, Don José's, said:

"Be careful, the beds are empty."

Another instant and candles were lit, for their light reached us through small peep-holes in the panel, and by putting our eyes to these we could see what passed in the room. There before us we beheld Don José, Don Smith, and four of their companions, all armed with knives or *machetes,* while, framed, as it were in the wall, in the place that had been occupied by the picture of the abbot, stood our host, Don Pedro, holding a candle above his head, and glaring with his fishlike eyes into every corner of the room.

"Where are they?" he said. "Where are the wizards? Find them quick and kill them."

Now the men ran to and fro about the chamber, dragging aside the beds and staring at the pictures on the walls as though they expected to see us there.

"They are gone," said José at length, "that Indian, Ignatio, has conjured them away. He is a *demonio* and not a man; I thought it from the first."

"Impossible!" cried Don Pedro, who was white with rage and fear. "The door has been watched ever since they entered it, and no living thing could force those bars. Search, search, they must be hidden."

"Search yourself," answered Don Smith sullenly, "they are not here. Perhaps they discovered the trick of the picture and escaped down the passages to the chapel."

"It cannot be," said Don Pedro again, "for just now I was in the chapel and saw no signs of them. We have some traitor among us who has led them from the house; by Heaven, if I find him out —" and he uttered a fearful oath.

"Shall we bring the dogs?" asked José — and I trembled at his words: "they might smell their footing."

"Fool, what is the use of dogs in a place where all of you have been tramping?" answered the father. "Tomorrow at dawn we will try them outside, for these men must be found and killed, or we are ruined. Already the authorities suspect us because of the disappearance of the two *Americanos*, and they will send soldiers from Vera Cruz to shoot us down, for without doubt this *Inglese* is rich and powerful. It is certain that they are not here, but perhaps they are hidden elsewhere in the building. Come, let us search the passages and the roof," and he vanished into the wall, followed by the others, leaving the chamber as dark and silent as it had been before their coming.

For a while the danger had passed, and we pressed each other's hands in gratitude, for to speak or even to whisper we did not dare. Ten minutes or more went by, when once again we heard sounds, and a light appeared in the room, borne in the hand of Don Pedro, who was accompanied by his son, Don José.

"They have vanished," said the old man, "the devil their master knows how. Well, tomorrow we must hunt them out if possible, till then nothing can be done. You were a fool to bring them here, José. Have I not told you that no money should tempt me to have more to do with the death of white men?"

"I did it for revenge, not money," answered José.

"A nice revenge," said his father, "a revenge that is likely to cost us all our lives, even in this country. I tell you that, if they are not found tomorrow and silenced, I shall leave this place and travel into the interior, where no law can follow us, for I do not wish to be shot down like a dog.

"Listen, José, bid those rascals to give up the search and go to bed, it is useless. Then do you come quietly to my room, and we will visit the Indian and his daughter. If we are to screw their secret out of them, it must be done tonight, for, like a fool, I told that Englishman the story when the wine was in me, thinking that he would never live to repeat it."

"Yes, yes, it must be tonight, for tomorrow we may have to fly. But what if the brutes won't speak, father?"

"We will find means to make them," answered the old man with a hideous chuckle; "but whether they speak or not, they must be silenced afterwards —" and he drew his hand across his throat, adding, "Come."

*A*n hour passed while we stood in the hole trembling with excitement, hope, and fear, and then once more we heard footfalls, followed presently by the sound of a voice whispering on the further side of the panel.

"Are you there, lord?" the whisper said. "It is I, Luisa."

"Yes," I answered.

Now she touched the spring and opened the panel.

"Listen," she said, "they have gone to sleep all of them, but before dawn they will be up again to search for you far and wide. Therefore you must do one of two things; lie hid here, perhaps for days, or take your chance of escape at once."

"How can we escape?" I asked.

"There is but one way, lord, through the chapel. The door into it is locked, but I can show you a place from which the priests used to watch those below, and thence, if you are brave, you can drop to the ground beneath, for the height is not great. Once there, you can escape into the garden through the window over the altar, which is broken, as I have seen from without, though to do so, perhaps, you will have to climb upon each other's shoulders. Then you must fly as swiftly as you can by the light of the moon, which has risen. The dogs have been gorged and tied up, so, if the Heart is your friend, you may yet go unharmed."

Now I spoke to the señor, saying:

"Although the woman does not know it, I think it likely that we shall find company in this chapel, seeing that the Indian and his daughter are imprisoned there, where Don Pedro and José have gone to visit them. The risk is great, shall we take it?"

"Yes," answered the señor after a moment's thought, "for it is better to take a risk than to perish by inches in this hole of starvation, or perhaps to be discovered and murdered in cold blood. Also we have traveled far and undergone much to find this Indian, and if we lose our chance of doing so, we may get no other."

"What do you say, Molas?" I asked.

"I say that the words of the señor are wise, also that it matters little to me what we do, since whether I turn to left or right death waits me on my path."

Now one by one we climbed through the false panel, and by the light of the moon Luisa led us across the chamber to the spot between the beds, where hangs the picture of the abbot, which picture, that is painted on a slab of wood, proved to be only a cunningly devised door constructed to swing upon a pivot.

Placing her knee on the threshold of the secret door, Luisa scrambled into the passage beyond. When the rest of us stood by her side, she closed the panel, and, bidding us cling to one another and be silent, she took me by the hand and guided us through some passages till at length she whispered:

"Be cautious now, for we come to the place whence you must drop into the chapel, and there is a stairway to your right."

We passed the stairway and turned a corner, Luisa still leading.

Next instant she staggered back into my arms, murmuring, "Mother of Heaven! the ghosts! the ghosts!" Indeed, had I not held her she would have fled. Still grasping her hand, I pushed forward to find myself standing in a small recess — the one I showed you, Señor Jones — that was placed about ten feet above the floor of the chapel, and, like other places in this house, so arranged that the abbot or monk in authority, without being seen himself, could see and hear all that passed beneath him.

Of one thing I am sure, that during all the generations that are gone no monk watching here ever saw a stranger sight than that which met my eyes. The chancel of the chapel was lit up by shafts of brilliant moonlight that poured through the broken window, and by a lamp which stood upon the stone altar. Within the circle of strong light thrown by this lamp were four people, namely, Don Pedro, his son Don José, an old Indian, and a girl.

On either side of the altar then, as now, rose two carven pillars of *sapote* wood, the tops of which were fashioned into the figures of angels, and to these columns the old Indian and the woman were tied, one to each column, their hands being joined together at the back of the pillars in such a manner as to render them absolutely helpless. My eyes rested first upon the woman, who was nearest to me, and seeing her, even as she was then, disheveled, worn with pain and hunger, her proud face distorted by agony of mind and impotent rage, I no longer wondered that both Molas and Don Pedro had raved about her beauty.

She was an Indian, but such an Indian as I had never known before, for in color she was almost white, and her dark and waving hair hung in masses to her knees. Her face was oval and small-featured, and in it shone a pair of wonderful dark-blue eyes, while the clinging white robe she wore revealed the loveliness of her tall and delicate shape.

Bad as was the girl's plight, that of the old man her father, who was none other than the Zibalbay we had come to seek, seemed even worse. As Molas had described him, he was thin and very tall, with white hair and beard, wild and hawklike eyes, and aquiline features, nor had Don Pedro spoken more than the truth when he said that he looked like a king. His robe had been torn from him, leaving him half naked, and on his forehead, breast, and arms were blood and bruises which clearly had been caused by a riding-whip that lay broken at his feet.

It was not difficult to guess who had broken it, for in front of the old man, breathing heavily and wiping the perspiration from his brow, stood Don José.

"This mule won't stir," he said to his father in Spanish; "ask the girl, it must wake her up to see the old man knocked about."

Then Don Pedro slipped off the altar rail upon which he had been seated, and, advancing to the woman, he peered at her with his leaden eyes:

"My dear," he said to her in the Maya language, "this sight must grieve you. Put an end to it then by telling us of that place where so much gold is hidden."

"As with my last breath, daughter," broke in Zibalbay, "I command you to say nothing, no, not if you see them murder me by inches before your eyes."

"Silence, you dog," said Don José, striking him across the lips with his hand.

"Oh! that I were free to avenge you!" gasped the girl as she strained and tore at the ropes which held her.

"Don't be in a hurry, my love," sneered Don José, "wait a while and you will have yourself to avenge as well as your father. If he won't speak I think we can find a way to make you talk, only I do not want to be rough with you unless I am forced to it. You are too pretty, much too pretty."

The girl shivered, gasping with fear and hate, and was silent.

"What shall we try him with now?" he went on, addressing Don Pedro; "hot steel or cold? Make up your mind, for I am growing tired. Well, if you won't, just hand me that *machete*, will you? Now, friend," he said, addressing the Indian, "for the last time I ask you to tell us where is that temple full of gold, of which you spoke to your daughter in my father's hearing?"

"There is no such place, white man," he answered sullenly.

"Indeed, friend! Then will you explain where you found those little ingots, which we captured from the Indian who had been visiting you, and whence came this *machete?*" and he pointed to the weapon in his hand.

It was a sword of great beauty, as I could see even from where we stood, made not of steel, but of hardened copper, and having for a handle a female figure with outstretched arms fashioned in solid gold.

"The *machete* was given to me by a friend," said the Indian, "I do not know where he got it."

"Really," answered José with a brutal laugh, "perhaps you will remember presently. Here, father, warm the point of the *machete* in the lamp, will you, while I tell our guest how we are going to serve him and his daughter."

Don Pedro nodded, and, taking the sword, he held the tip of it over the flame, while José bending forward whispered into the Indian's ear, pointing from time to time to the girl, who, overcome with faintness or horror, had sunk to the ground, where she was huddled in a heap half hidden by the masses of her hair.

"Are you white men then devils?" said the old man at length, with a groan that seemed to burst from the bottom of his heart, "and is there no law or justice among you?"

"Not at all, friend," answered José, "we are good fellows enough, but times are hard and we must live. As for the rest, we don't trouble over much about law in these parts, and I never heard that unbaptised Indian dogs have any right to justice. Now, once more, will you guide us to the place whence that gold came, leaving your daughter here as hostage for our safety?"

"Never!" cried the Indian, "better that we two should perish a hundred times, than that the ancient secrets of my people should pass to such as you."

"So you have secrets after all! Father, is the sword hot?" asked José.

"One minute more, son," said the old man, quietly turning the point in the flame.

*T*his was the scene that we witnessed, and these were the words that astonished our ears.

"It is time to interfere," muttered the señor, and, placing his hand upon the rail, he prepared to drop into the church.

Now a thought struck me, and I drew him back to the passage.

"Perhaps the door is open," I said.

"Are you going in there?" asked the girl Luisa.

"Certainly," I replied; "we must rescue those people, or die with them."

"Then, señors, farewell, I have done all I can for you, and now the saints must be your guide, for if I am seen they will kill me, and I have a child for whose sake I desire to live. Again, farewell," and she glided away like a shadow.

We crept forward down the stair. At the foot of it was a little door, which, as we had hoped, stood ajar. For a moment we consulted together, then we crawled on through the gloom towards the ring of light about the altar. Now José had the heated sword in his hand.

"Look up, my dear, look up," he said to the girl, patting her on the cheek. "I am about to baptise your excellent father according to the rites of the Christian religion, by marking him with a cross upon the forehead," and he advanced the glowing point of the sword towards the Indian's face.

At that instant Molas pinned him from behind, causing him to drop the weapon, while I did the same office by Don Pedro, holding him so that, struggle as he might, he could not stir.

"Make a sound, either of you, and you are dead," said the señor, picking up the *machete* and placing its hot point against José's breast, where it slowly burned its way through his clothes.

"What are we to do with these men?" he asked.

"Kill them as they would have killed us," answered Molas; "or, if you fear the task, cut loose the old man yonder and let him avenge his own and his daughter's wrongs."

"What say you, Ignatio?"

"I seek no man's blood, but for our own safety it is well that these wretches should die. Away with them!"

Now Don Pedro began to bleat inarticulately in his terror, and that hero, José, burst into tears and pleaded for his life, writhing with pain the while, for the point of the sword scorched him.

"You are an English gentleman," he groaned, "you cannot butcher a helpless man as though he were an ox."

"As you tried to butcher us in the chamber yonder — us, who saved your life," answered the señor. "Still, you are right, I cannot do it because, as you say, I am a gentleman. Molas, loose this dog, and if he tries to run, put your knife through him. José Moreno, you have a sword by your side and I hold one in my hand; I will not murder you, but we have a quarrel, and we will settle it here and now."

"You are mad, señor," I said, "to risk your life thus, I myself will kill him rather than it should be so."

"Will you fight if I loose you, José Moreno?" he asked, making me no answer, "or will you be killed where you stand?"

"I will fight," he replied.

"Good. Let him free, Molas, and be ready with your knife."

"I command you," I began, but already the man was loose and the señor stood waiting for him, his back to the door, and grasping the Indian *machete* handled with the golden woman.

Now José glanced round as though he sought a means of escape, but there was none, for in front was the *machete* and behind was the knife of Molas. For some seconds — ten perhaps — they stood facing each other in the ring of the lamp-light, whilst the moonbeams played faintly about their heads. We watched in utter silence, the Indian girl shaking the long hair from her face, and leaning forward as far as her bonds would allow, that she might see this battle to the death between him who had insulted and tormented her, and the noble-looking white man who had appeared out of the gloom to bring her deliverance.

It was a strange scene, for the contrast of light and darkness, or of good and evil, is not greater than was that of these two men, and what made it stranger were the place and hour. Behind them was the half-lit emptiness of the deserted chapel, before them stood the holy crucifix and the desecrated altar of God, and beneath their feet lay the bones of the forgotten dead, whose spirits mayhap were watching them from the shadows as earnestly as did our living eyes. Yes, that midnight scene of death and vengeance enacted in the House of Peace was very strange, and even now it thrills my blood to think of it.

From the moment that I saw them fronting each other, my fears for the issue vanished. Victory was written in the calm features of the señor, and more especially in his large blue eyes, that of a sudden had grown stern as those of an avenging angel, while the face of José told only of baffled fury struggling with bottomless despair. He was about to die, and the terror of approaching death unnerved him.

Still it was he who struck the first, for, stepping forward, he aimed a desperate blow at the señor's head, who, springing aside, avoided it, and in return ran him through the left arm. With a cry of pain, the Mexican sprang back, followed by the señor, at whom he cut from time to time, but without result, for every blow was parried.

Now they were within the altar rails, and now his back was against one of the carved pillars of *sapote* wood — that to which the girl was tied. Further he could not fly, but stayed there, laying about him wildly, so that the woman at the other side of the pillar crouched upon the ground to avoid the sweep of his sword.

Then the end came, for the señor, who was waiting his chance, drew suddenly within reach, only to step back so that the furious blow aimed at his head struck with a ringing sound upon the marble floor, where the mark of it may yet be seen. Before Don José, whose arm was numbed by the shock, could lift the sword again, the señor ran in, and for the second time thrust with all his strength. But now the aim was truer, for his *machete* pierced the Mexican through the heart, so that he fell down and died there upon the altar step.

Now I must tell of my own folly that went near to bringing us all to death. You will remember that I was holding Don Pedro, and how it came about I know not, but in my joy and agitation I slackened by grip, so that with a sudden twist he was able to tear himself from my hands, and in a twinkling of an eye was gone.

I bounded after him, but too late, for as I reached the door it was slammed in my face, nor could I open it, for on the chapel side were neither key nor handle.

"Fly," I cried, rushing back to the altar, "he has escaped, and will presently be here with the rest."

The señor had seen, and already was engaged in severing with his sword the rope that bound the girl, while Molas cut loose her father. Now I leapt upon the altar — may the sacrilege be forgiven to my need — and, springing at the stonework of the broken window, I made shift to pull myself up with the help of Molas pushing from below. Seated upon the window ledge I leaned down, and catching the Indian Zibalbay by the wrists, for he was too stiff to leap, with great efforts I dragged him to me, and bade him drop without fear to the ground, which was not more than ten feet below us. Next came his daughter, then the Señor, and last of all, Molas, so that within three minutes from the escape of Don Pedro we stood unhurt outside the chapel among the bushes of a garden.

"Where to now?" I asked, for the place was strange to me.

The girl, Maya, looked round her, then she glanced up at the heavens.

"Follow me," she said, "I know a way," and started down the garden at a run.

Presently we came to a wall the height of a man, beyond which was a thick hedge of aloes. Over the wall we climbed, and through the aloes we burst a path, not without doing ourselves some hurt — for the thorns were sharp — to find ourselves in a *milpa* or corn-field. Here the girl stopped, again searching the stars, and at that moment we heard sounds of shouting, and, looking back, saw lights moving to and fro in the *hacienda*.

"We must go forward or perish," I said. "Don Pedro has aroused his men."

Then she dashed into the *milpa,* and we followed her. There was no path, and the cornstalks, that stood high above us, caught our feet and shook the dew in showers upon our heads, till our clothes were filled with water like a sponge. Still we struggled on, one following the other, for fifteen minutes or more, till at length we were clear of the cultivated land and standing on the borders of the forest.

"Halt," I said, "where do we run to? The road lies to the right, and by following it we may reach a town."

"To be arrested as murderers," broke in the señor. "You forget that José Moreno is dead at my hands, and his father will swear our lives away, or that at the best we shall be thrown into prison. No, no, we must hide in the bush."

"Sirs," said the old Indian, speaking for the first time, "I know a secret place in the forest, an ancient and ruined building, where we may take refuge for a while if we can reach it. But first I ask, who are you?"

"You should know me, Zibalbay," said Molas, "seeing that I am the messenger whom you sent to search for him that you desire to find, the Lord and Keeper of the Heart," and he pointed to me.

"Are you that man?" asked the Indian.

"I am," I answered, "and I have suffered much to find you, but now is no time for talk; guide us to this hiding place of yours, for our danger is great."

Then once more the girl took the lead, and we plunged forward into the forest, often stumbling and falling in the darkness, till the dawn broke in the east, and the shoutings of our pursuers died away.

Chapter X

HOW MOLAS DIED

*F*or some few minutes we rested to recover our breath, then we started forward again. In front went the girl, Maya, our guide, whom the señor led by the hand, while behind followed Zibalbay supported by Molas and myself. At first these two had run as quickly as the rest of us, but now all the fatigues and terrors that they had undergone took hold of them, so that from time to time they were forced to stop and rest. This was little to be wondered at, indeed, seeing that during five days they had eaten no solid food, for it had been Don Pedro's purpose to starve their secret out of them. Doubtless he would have succeeded in this design, or in doing them to death, had it not been for a quantity of a certain preparation of the *cuca* leaf, mixed with pounded meat and other ingredients, which they carried with them. Zibalbay had the secret of this Indian food, and by the help of it he and his daughter had journeyed far across unpopulated wastes, for so wonderful are its properties that a piece no larger than a bullet will serve to stay a man's stomach for twenty-four hours, even when his power is taxed by work or travel. On this nutriment they had sustained themselves to the amazement of their captor, who could not discover whence they drew their strength; still it is a stimulant rather than a food, and so great was their craving to fill themselves, that as they ran they plucked cobs of the Indian corn and devoured them.

Our path lay through a tropical forest so dense that, even when the sun shone, the gloom was that of twilight. Many sorts of huge and uncouth trees grew in it, whereof the boughs were starred with orchids and hung with trailing ferns, or in places with long festoons of grey Spanish moss that gave them a very strange and unnatural appearance. Up these trees climbed creepers, some of them thicker than a man's thigh, and beneath them the ground was clothed with soft-wooded bush, or with vast brakes of a plant that in Mexico attains a height of from ten to twelve feet, which the señor told me is cultivated in English gardens under the name of Indian Shot. Slowly and with much toil we forced a path through this mass of vegetation. Now we were creeping over the rotten trunks of fallen and fern-encumbered trees, now foot by foot we must make our way between the stout stems of the Indian Shot, and now our clothes were caught and our flesh was torn by the hooklike thorns and brambles, or our feet tripped in the roots of climbing plants. No breath of air penetrated that measureless thicket, whereof the stagnant atmosphere, laden with the decay of ages, choked and almost overpowered us, causing the sweat to start from every pore. Above us, hiding the sky, hung masses of deep green foliage, beneath which we struggled on in the solemn gloom and the silence that was broken only from time to time by the grunting of an ape, or by a distant crash, as some great tree, after centuries of life, fell with a noise like thunder to the earth from whence it sprang.

This forest that seemed so destitute of life was peopled by millions of insects, all of them venomous. *Garrapatas,* tiny grey flies, wood-wasps, and ants black and red, tormented us with their bites and stings till we groaned aloud in misery, then, remembering our danger, pushed on again.

Thus two hours and more passed, till, reaching a little stream that ran through a ravine in the forest, we paused to drink and to cool our fevered feet and hands. Zibalbay sank exhausted upon the bank, where I brought him water in my sombrero, while his daughter sat herself down on a stone in the stream, suffering it to flow over her feet and ankles, that by now were swollen with ant-bites and bleeding from the cuts of thorns and grasses. Presently she looked up, and, seeing the señor, who stood upon a bank talking to me, she invited him with a motion of her hand to seat himself beside her.

"What is your name, white man?" she asked.

"James Strickland, lady."

"James Strickland," she repeated with some difficulty. "I thank you, James Strickland, for rescuing my father from torment and me from insult; and because of that deed, I, Maya of the Heart, whom many have served, am your servant forever."

"You should thank my friend, Don Ignatio," he said, pointing to me.

For a few moments she looked at me searchingly, then replied, "I thank him also, but you I thank the most, for your hand rid me of that hateful man and saved us."

"It is early to return thanks, lady," he said; "we are not out of danger yet."

"I have little fear now that we have escaped from that dreadful house," she answered almost indifferently, "since our hiding place is at hand. Also how can they find us in this forest? Hark! what was that?"

As she spoke a faint and distant sound fell upon our ears — such a sound as might have been made by a bell struck far away at night.

"That is how they will find us," he said, springing to his feet. "Do you hear, Ignatio? The dogs have hit our trail. Which way does our road run now, lady?"

"Along the banks of this stream."

"Then we must go forward in the water," said the señor, "it is our only chance, for the hounds cannot track us there."

Now we began to scramble down the bed of the stream as fast as the boulders and the weariness of Zibalbay would allow. Fortunately it was not a broad river, nor very deep, still sometimes we could hardly stand in the rapids, and twice, not daring to set foot upon the bank, we were forced to swim the length of the pools, which we did in terror fearing lest they should be haunted by alligators. For something over an hour we followed the stream thus, till suddenly Maya halted, saying that if we would gain the building where they had dwelt, we must leave the water and plunge into the forest. By now we were exhausted — indeed, unless he were carried, the old Indian Zibalbay could not have gone another mile; so, notwithstanding the danger of setting foot upon the land, on learning that the place was near and that food was to be found in it, we hesitated no longer, but once more began to thread the bush. Not more than three hundred paces from the banks of the river we came upon a high mound densely overgrown with trees, between the boles of which appeared masses of cut stone.

"This is the place," gasped Zibalbay. "Look, yonder above us are the walls of the temple, and here is the stairway that led to it," and he pointed to a long flight of crumbling stone, almost hidden in ferns and bushes, which stretched from the base of the pyramid to the ancient Indian fane on its crest. Up these steps we went with caution, for the climb was dangerous, Molas carrying Zibalbay upon his broad back, since so weary was he that the old Indian could mount them in no other fashion.

This staircase was built in three flights, the top flight, now almost entirely broken away, emerging on what once had been a broad and splendid terrace, but today was a chaos of stonework, in the crevices of which grew bushes and even large trees. Over the head of the stairway still stood a colossal arch sculptured with the figures of gods and beasts. This arch was in the last stage of decay — indeed the crown of it, a mass of masonry that must have weighed between one and two hundred tons, had been nearly separated from its supports by the action of time and rain, aided perhaps by a shock of earthquake, and hung threateningly over the top steps of the stair. In truth so slight were the attachments which remained between it and its supporting side columns and buttresses, that at first sight it seemed as though it must fall at once. A closer examination showed, however, that it was held in place by three or four great roots, which, springing from trees that grew upon the crown of the arch, in the course of years had thrust themselves deep into the crevices of the masonry of the massive pillars, and through their foundations into the soil beneath. Beyond the arch, on the further side of the terrace, rose the ruined temple, a long single-storied building with a flat roof whereon grew many shrubs and palms.

Passing through the central doorway of this temple, Maya led us into a chamber decorated everywhere with serpents carved in stone, which had been occupied, and recently, for it was clean, and upon the floor were ashes and bits of burned wood. In the corner also lay a little pile of articles covered over with a *serape* that Maya hastened to remove, revealing amongst other things an earthen cooking-pot, a copper axe of similar workmanship to the *machete* with which the señor had killed Don José, two curiously fashioned blow-pipes with a supply of poisoned darts, and, lastly, bags containing dried flesh, beans, and *cuca* paste.

"All is safe," she said; "now let us eat that we may be strong to meet danger."

While we were filling ourselves thankfully with the dried meat, the señor spoke to me, saying he hoped that our pursuit had been abandoned.

"You can know little of these men to speak thus," I answered; "they must hunt us down for their own sakes, also Don Pedro will certainly seek to avenge the blood of his son. Our only hope is that the water will baffle the hounds, or that, if they strike the place where we left it, the heat of the day may have killed our scent. But I fear that this will not be so, since the ground is damp beneath the trees."

"Then what do you propose to do?" he asked. "Start on again, or stop here?"

"Señor, we must stop here because we cannot travel farther, unless you would abandon the old man and his daughter. Moreover in the forest it would be easy to overwhelm us, but this place is hard to climb, and here at least we may die fighting. Let us make ready for the worst, señor."

"How are we to make ready," he asked, "when we have nothing to fight with except *machetes* and Indian blow-pipes? The powder in the pistol flasks is damp and the caps will miss fire, so that if we are attacked our death is certain."

"It seems so," I answered, "yet if it pleases God we may live. Yonder lie stones in plenty; let us pile them up beneath the archway, perhaps we can kill some of our foes by rolling them down the steps."

This we did, then, while Maya watched us. At length the task was finished, and as we turned to leave the heaps of stones, of a sudden we heard a dog baying down by the river, followed by a sound of men and horses forcing a path through the bush. For a while we stared at each other in silence, then Molas said, "They are coming."

"If so I wish they would come quickly," answered the señor.

"Why, White Man? Are you afraid?" asked Maya.

"Yes, very much," he answered, with a little laugh, "for the odds are heavy, and probably we shall soon be killed, that is, all the men among us will be killed. Does not the prospect frighten you?"

"Why should it," she answered, with a shrug and a smile, "seeing that if it comes to the worst, I shall be killed also and spared a long journey home?"

"How can you be sure of that, Lady?"

"So," she answered, holding a tiny blow-pipe dart before his eyes. "If I prick myself with this here —" and she touched the large vein in her neck, "in one minute I shall be asleep, and in two I shall be dead."

"I understand; but you talk of death very easily for one so young and beautiful."

"If so, señor, it is because I have not found life too soft, nor" — she added with a sigh — "do I know what destiny awaits me in the future; but I do know that when we sleep upon the Heart of Heaven, we shall find peace if nothing more."

"I hope so," said the señor. "Look, here they come," and as he spoke a party of seven or eight men, three of them riding on mules, appeared at the foot of the mound, and, dismounting, picketed their animals to trees.

"Now for it," said the señor, rising and shaking himself like a dog that leaves the water. "I wonder how many of us will be left alive when this sun sets."

As he spoke one of the men reached the foot of the stairway holding a great hound in a leash. For a moment the dog sniffed the stones, then, lifting his head, he bayed aloud, whereat the band shouted, for they knew that they had trapped us. Still for a while they did not advance, but, gathering themselves in a knot, they consulted together earnestly. We looked at each other in despair, for truly our case was desperate. Fly we could not, and we had no arms wherewith to fight, therefore it seemed certain that within some few minutes we must lose our lives at the hands of these murderers, if indeed they chose to kill us outright in mercy.

The señor hid his face in his hands for awhile, then he looked up and said,

"Can we bargain with them, Ignatio?"

"Impossible," I answered, "what have we to give that they cannot take?"

"Then there is nothing for it except to die as bravely as we may," he answered. "This is the end of our quest for the Golden City. The quest has not been a lucky one, Ignatio."

Now the old Indian, Zibalbay, who was crouched upon the ground beside us, spoke for the first time, saying,

"Friends, why do you not fly? Doubtless you can find a path down the further side of the pyramid, and in the forest you may hide from these men."

"How can we fly," answered the señor, "when you have no strength to walk a step?"

"I am old and ready to die," he answered; "leave me here, and be sure that when the time comes I shall know how to slip through the grasp of these villains. My daughter, go you with them. You have the holy symbol, and should you escape and prove this stranger to be the man whom we seek, lead him to our home that things may befall as they are fated."

"Peace, my father," said Maya, throwing her arms about his neck, "together we will live or perish. These señors may go if it pleases them, but here I stay with you."

"And so do I," said Molas, "for I weary of flying from the death that dogs me. Also it is too late to talk of flight, for look, they are coming up the stair, the eight of them with Don Pedro and the *Americano* at their head."

I looked; it was true. Already they had climbed half the steps of the first flight.

"Oh for some rifles!" groaned the señor.

"It is useless to cry for what we have not," I answered. "God can help us if He wishes, and if He does not, we must bow us to His will."

Then there was silence, broken only by the voice of Zibalbay, who, standing behind us, lifted his hands to heaven and prayed aloud to his gods to bring a vengeance upon our foes. Now we could see through the trees and bushes that the men were beginning to climb the second flight.

"Come, let us do something," said the señor, and, running to the piles of stones which we had prepared, he called to us to help him roll the heaviest of them upon the enemy. This we did for awhile, but without effect, for the tree-trunks turned our missiles; moreover those against whom they were directed, taking cover at the sides of the stairway, opened so sharp a fire on us with their rifles, that in a few minutes we were driven from the stone heaps and forced to retreat behind the shelter of the arch.

Now they came on again, till presently they reached the foot of the third flight, and paused to take breath. Then it was that Molas, seizing one of the Indian blow-pipes, ran out on to the terrace, followed by the señor, though why the latter went I do not know, for he could not use this weapon. Before the men beneath were aware of their presence, Molas had set the blow-pipe to his lips and discharged the poisoned dart among them. As it chanced it struck the Texan Smith full in the throat. Watching round the corner of the arch, I saw him lift his hand to pull out the dart, then of a sudden he fell to the ground, and in that instant a storm of bullets swept through the archway, aimed at Molas and the señor as they fled back for refuge. I saw Molas fall and the señor stop to lift him to his feet, and, as he was in the very act, a patch of red appear upon his face. Another moment and they were under cover.

"Are you hurt?" I asked of the señor.

"No, no," he answered; "my cheek was grazed by a bullet, that is all. Look to Molas, he is shot in the side."

"Leave me," said Molas, "it is nothing."

Then we were silent, only Maya sobbed a little as she strove to staunch the blood that flowed from the señor's wound with cobwebs which she gathered from among the stones.

"Do not trouble, lady," he said, with a sad smile, "for soon there will be other wounds that cannot be dressed. What shall you do?"

By way of answer she showed him the poisoned dart which she held in the hollow of her hand.

"I cannot advise you otherwise," he said. "Farewell, I am glad to have met you and I hope that we may meet again yonder," and he glanced towards the sky. "Now you had best say good-bye to your father, for our time is short." She nodded, went to the old man, Zibalbay, who stood silent, stroking his grey beard, and, putting her arms about his neck, she kissed him tenderly.

Looking out carefully we saw that the men had dragged Don Smith to the side of the stairway, where some of them supported him while he died of the poison, and others watched for a chance to shoot us should we show ourselves upon the terrace. Presently he was dead, and, cursing us aloud, his companions commenced to mount the third flight with great caution, for they feared a snare.

"Is there nothing to be done to save our lives?" asked the señor, in a heavy voice.

There was no answer, but of a sudden Molas, who was standing with one hand pressed upon the wound in his side and the other before his eyes, turned and ran into the chamber behind us, whence he reappeared carrying the copper axe. Then, without speaking, he climbed the masonry of the archway with great swiftness, till he stood with his feet in the crack beneath the crown of the arch, which you will remember was held in place only by the tough tree-roots, that grew from it into the stonework of the buttresses. Supporting himself by a creeper with his left hand, with his right he struck blow after blow at the biggest of these roots, severing them one by one. Now we saw his purpose — to send two hundred tons of stonework thundering down the stairway upon the heads of the murderers.

"By heaven! that is an answer to my question," said the señor; then he paused and added, "Come down, Molas; if the arch falls, you will fall with it and be crushed."

"It matters little," he answered; "this is my doom day, that bullet has cut me inside and I bleed to death, and on this spot, as I have long feared, it is fated that I should die. Pray for my soul, and farewell."

"Fare you well, you gallant man," said the señor. "I have no axe or I would come with you."

"Farewell, Molas, my brother, true servant of the Heart," I echoed; "of this I am sure, that you shall not lose your reward."

Now three of the roots were severed, but the fourth and largest, which was thicker than a man's leg, remained, and at this Molas began to hew despairingly.

"Are they near?" he gasped, as the white chips flew.

We peeped round the corner of the arch and saw that some seventy feet below us the band had halted on the slippery face of the pyramid, fearing they knew not what, for they heard the dull sound of the axe blows, but could not guess what it portended. One of their number was talking to Don Pedro, apparently urging something upon him to which he did not agree, and in this way they wasted two minutes before at last the order was given to rush up the remaining steps and take the temple by storm.

Two minutes — it was but a short time, yet it meant much, for only a third of the root remained unsevered, and the bark crackling and peeling showed how great was the strain upon it.

"Quick," whispered the señor, "they come" — and as he spoke the handle of the axe broke and its head fell to the ground.

"Now if the root holds we are lost," I said.

But it was not to be, for Molas still had his heavy hunting-knife, and with this he hewed frantically at the wood. At the third cut it began to part, torn slowly asunder as though by the strength of a giant, and while it gave, the vast superincumbent mass of masonry, which it had helped to support for so many years, shifted a little with a grinding sound, then hung again.

"Come down, Molas, come down!" cried the señor.

But Molas would not. He struck one more blow, severing the root, then with a shout of farewell, either through faintness or by design, he cast himself forward with outstretched arms against the face of the wall. His weight was little indeed, yet it seemed that it sufficed to turn the balance as dust turns a scale, for again the trembling mass moved perceptibly and the tall trees upon the top of it began to nod as though beneath the sudden pressure of wind. Now it slid forward faster and faster, while sharp sounds like pistol-shots came from the heart of it, and the trees above bent like a rod beneath the rush of a fish. Now also for the first time the villains on the slope below perceived the doom that threatened them, and uttered such a yell as I had never heard. Some stood still and some flung themselves down the stair, one only, Don Pedro himself, rushed forward. It was too late; the mass of stonework, sixty feet long by twenty in breadth, was falling. It was falling — it fell, taking Molas with it. With a roar like that of thunder it struck upon the stairway, and, bursting into fragments, swept it from end to end. No discharge of grape-shot could have been so terrible in its effects as this hurricane of stones that nothing could withstand, for even the big trees which stood in its path were snapped like sticks and borne away upon its crest, as the carved masonry that had been carried up the pyramid by the long labor of the Indians of a bygone age, rushed downward to its foot.

In less than a minute it was done, the sounds had died away, and nothing was left to tell of what had happened except a little dust and some remains that had been men. Of all those who stood upon the stairway only one survived, Don Pedro, who had run forward in the hope of escaping the fall of the arch. As it chanced he was too late, for though the mass had missed him, a single stone struck him across the middle, breaking his bones and sweeping him to the foot of the first flight, but leaving him alive.

*W*hen all was finished, and the dust had fallen to the earth again, the señor spoke, saying, "Let us go and search for the body of our deliverer."

So we went, the three of us, leaving Zibalbay in the temple, but we could not find it; doubtless to this day Molas lies buried beneath some of the larger blocks of masonry. There were other bodies indeed, from which we did not scruple to take the rifles and whatever else was likely to be of value to us. Better still, tied among some trees near the foot of the pyramid, we found four good mules, one of them laden with ammunition and provisions, for Don Pedro had come out determined to hunt us down, even if he must follow us for days.

Having picketed the mules where they could graze, we returned to the temple, bearing with us food and drink, of which we stood in sore need. On our way up the steps, Don Pedro called to us from where he lay broken and bleeding against an uprooted tree.

"Water," he cried, "give me water."

The señor gave him some mixed with brandy that we had found upon the sumpter mule.

"Your heart is merciful," said Maya gravely; "I am not cruel, yet I think that I should suffer that dog to die untended."

"We all of us have sins to pay for, Lady, and the thought of them should teach us charity, especially now when it has pleased God to spare us," answered the señor.

"I am dying," moaned the wretch; "my presentiment has come true, and death finds me amongst ruins. How dare I die who have been a murderer and a thief from my boyhood?"

The señor shrugged his shoulders, for he could not answer this question.

"Give me absolution," he went on, "for the love of Christ, give me absolution."

"I cannot," said the señor; "I have no authority. Pray to Heaven to shrive you, for your time is short."

Then he turned and went, but for a long time we were troubled by the last cries and blasphemies of this most evil man; indeed they did not cease till sunset, when the devil came to claim his own.

Chapter XI

ZIBALBAY TELLS HIS MISSION

*W*hen we reached the ruins of the temple we ate and drank, then, knowing that we could travel no farther that night, I spoke, saying:

"Some two months since, Zibalbay, you sent a message to Molas, my foster-brother, that man who died to save us this day, to him who among the Indians is known as Lord of the Heart. Your messenger traveled fast and far, by sea and by land, till he found him and delivered the message."

"To whom did he deliver it?" asked Zibalbay.

"To me, for I am the man you seek, and with my companion I have journeyed here to find you, suffering many dangers and evils on the path."

"Prove that you are the man" — and he asked me certain, secret questions, to all of which I returned answers.

"You are instructed," he said at length, "yet something is lacking; if, indeed, you are the Lord of the Heart, reveal its mystery to my eyes."

"Nay," I answered, "it is you who seek me, not I you. To Molas, your messenger, you showed a certain symbol; let me see that symbol, for then and not till then will I reveal the mystery."

Now he looked round him doubtfully, and said, "You I have proved, and this woman is my daughter and knows all; but what of the white man? Is it lawful that I should unveil the Heart before him?"

"It is lawful," I answered, "for this white man is my brother, and we are one till death. Also he is sworn of our brotherhood, and himself, for a while, was Lord and Holder of the Heart, for I passed it on to him when I thought that I lay dying, and to him cling its virtues and prerogatives. So it comes about that we have no secrets from each other; that his ears are my ears, and his mouth is my mouth. Speak to us, then, as though we were one man, or be silent to both, for I vouch for him and he for me."

"Are these things so, White Man?" asked Zibalbay, making the sign of the brotherhood.

"They are so," replied the señor, giving the countersign.

"Then I speak," said Zibalbay, "I speak in the name of the Heart, and woe be to him who betrays the secrets that he learns under cover of this name. Come hither, daughter, and give me that which is hidden about you."

Now Maya put her hands to her head, and drawing forth something from the dense masses of her hair, she passed it to her father.

"Is this what you would see?" he asked, holding the talisman in the light of the setting sun.

I looked, and lo! there before me was the very counterpart of that which had descended to me from my forefathers, and which I wore about my neck.

"It would seem so, unless my sight deceives me," I answered; "and is this what you have come so far to seek, Zibalbay?" and I drew forth the ancient symbol of the Broken Heart.

Now he leaned forward, and examined first the one half and then the other, searching them both with his eyes. Then he clasped his hands and, looking to the heavens, said:

"I thank thee, O Nameless One, god of my fathers, that thou hast led my feet aright, and given it to mine eyes to see their desire. As thou hast prospered the beginning, so prosper thou the end, I beseech thee."

Then he turned to me and continued as in an ecstasy:

"Now have Day and Night come together, and soon shall the new sun rise, the sun of our glory, for already the dawn is breaking. Take that which is in your keeping, and I will take that which is in mine, for not here must they be joined, but far away. Listen, brethren, to my tale, which shall be brief, seeing that if it be the will of Heaven, your eyes shall prove my words where all things can be made clear to you, and if not, that of which little is told is the more easily forgotten. Perchance, my brethren, you have heard legends of that ancient undiscovered city, the last home of our race which is undefiled by the foot of the white conqueror, and the secret sanctuary of the pure faith given to our forefathers by the divine Cucumatz, who is of some named Quetzal."

"We have heard of it and greatly desire to see it," I answered.

"If this be so," went on Zibalbay, "in us you have found those who can guide you to that city, of which I am the *cacique* and hereditary high priest, and my only child here is the heiress and lady. You wonder how it comes then that we, being of this condition, are found unguarded and alone, wandering like beggars in the land of the white man. Listen: The City of the Heart, as it is called, is of all cities the most beautiful and ancient, and once in the far past she ruled these lands from sea to sea, for her walls were built by one of those brethren whom the holy

Cucumatz, the white god, left to share his throne, after there had been war between the brethren and they separated, each becoming the father of a nation. So great was her power in the early days that all the cities whose ruins may be found buried in these forests were her tributaries, but as the years went by, hordes of barbarians rolled down upon her frontier towns so that they were lost to her. Still no enemies came near her gates, and she remained the richest and most powerful of the cities of the world.

"Now the City of the Heart is built upon an island in the center of a lake, but many thousands of her children lived upon the mainland, where they cultivated fields and dug in the earth for gold and gems. So she flourished, and her children with her, till twelve generations since, when there came tidings to the king of that day that a nation of white men had conquered the empires near the sea, putting their inhabitants to the sword and possessing themselves of their wealth. Tidings came also that these white men, having learned the tale of the City of the Heart and of the measureless treasures of gold with which it is adorned, purposed to seek it out to sack it. When the ruling *cacique* was sure that these things were true, he took counsel with his wise men and with the oracle of the god which is in the Sanctuary, and issued a decree that all those who lived upon the mainland should be brought within the walls of the city, so that the white men might find none to guide them thither. This was done then, and the spoilers sought in vain for many years, till it was reported among them that this legend of a town filled with gold was but a fable. Now, however, great sickness took hold of those who lived in the City of the Heart, because it was over full of men — so great a sickness, indeed, that soon there was space and to spare for all who remained within its walls. The sickness went away, but as the generations passed a new and a worse trouble fell upon our forefathers. The blood of the people grew old, and but few children were born to them. There were none left upon the mainland to replenish the race, and this is our law, a law which cannot be broken under pain of death, that no man or woman may leave our territories to seek a husband or a wife of different blood.

"Thus, then, has it come about that the people have grown less and less, wasting away like snow upon a mountain top in summer, till at length they are dwindled to a few thousands, who in bygone days could count their number by tens and twenties of thousands. Now I, Zibalbay, have ruled this city since I was young, and bitterly has it grieved me to know that before another hundred years have been added to the past, the city, Heart of the World, must become nothing but a waste and a home for the dead, though of that those who live therein today reck but little, for the people have no thought for the morrow, and the hearts of its nobles have become gross and their eyes blind.

"But an ancient prophecy has come to us from our forefathers, and it is, that when once more the two halves of the symbol of the Heart are laid side by side in their place upon the altar in the Sanctuary of the holy city, then from that hour she shall grow great again. Over this saying I brooded long, and long and often did I pray to that god whom I worship and whose high priest I am, the Nameless god, Heart of Heaven and Lord of all the earth, that it would please him to give me light and wisdom whereby I might find that which was lost, and save the people from perishing as, in a season of drought, flowers perish for lack of rain, bringing forth no seed. At length upon a certain night it came about that a voice spoke to me in a dream answering my prayer, bidding me to wander forth from the country of the Heart and follow the ancient road towards the sea, for there near to the eastern shore I should find that which was lost.

"Then I summoned the Council of the Heart and opened my mind to them, telling them of my dream, and that I purposed to obey it. But they made a mock of me, for they thought me mad, and said that I might go if I wished, for being their ruler they had no power to stay me, but that no man of the people should accompany me across the mountains, for that was against the ancient law.

"I answered that it was well, and I would go alone since go I must, whereon my daughter rose in her place and said that she would journey with me, as she had a right to do, and to this they must consent, though one of their number spoke bitterly against it, for he was my nephew, and affianced to my daughter. Was it not so, Maya?"

"It was so," she answered with a smile.

"To be short," went on Zibalbay, "since my heart was set upon this mission, and my daughter yonder, who is willful, would not be gain-sayed of her desire to accompany me, Tikal, my nephew, was placed over the city to rule as *cacique* in my stead until I should return again. Then I left the city with this my daughter, many of the nobles and of the common people accompanying us across the lake and a day's journey beyond it to the mountain pass, where they bid us farewell with tears, for they were certain that we were mad and went to our deaths.

"Alone we crossed the mountains, and alone, following the traces of the ancient road, we traveled through the desert and the forest that lies beyond it, till at length we reached this secret place and stayed here, for, though we were unharmed, danger, toil, and hunger had worn us out, moreover we were afraid to venture among the white people. Brethren, there is no need to tell the rest of the tale, for it is known to you. That power which sent me on my mission has guided me through all its troubles, and after much hardship and suffering has caused me to triumph, seeing that tonight we are still alive, having found that which we came forth to seek. Such is my story, brother; now, if it pleases you, let us hear yours, and learn what purpose led you and your companion here in time to save us from the group of that white devil who lies dead upon the stairway."

Then I spoke, telling to Zibalbay and his daughter the story of my life, whereof I have written already, and of my great scheme to build up again that empire which fell in the day of Montezuma.

"Now you speak words that are after my own heart," said the old chief; "but tell me, how is it to be done?"

"By your help," I answered. "Men are here in plenty, but to use them I must have gold, whereas yonder it seems you have gold but no men. Therefore I ask of you some portion of your useless wealth that by its help I may lift up your people and my own."

"Follow me to the city, and if I can bring it about you shall have all that you desire," he answered. "Brother, our ends are one, and fate has brought us together from far away, in order that they may be accomplished. The prophecy is true, and truly have I dreamed; soon shall the severed symbol be brought together in the Sanctuary and the will of Heaven be made clear. Oh! not in vain have I lived and prayed, enduring the mockery of men, for Day and Night have met, and already the light of the new dawn is shining in the sky. Place your hand in mine, and let us swear an oath upon the Heart that we, its guardians, will be true to each other and to our purpose until death chooses us. So, it is sworn. Now, daughter, lead me to my rest, for I am overwhelmed, not with toil and suffering, but with too much joy. O Heart of Heaven, I thank thee!" and lifting his hands above his head, as though in adoration, Zibalbay turned, and, followed by the girl, Maya, he tottered rather than walked into the chamber.

When he had gone the señor spoke to me.

"This is very well, Ignatio," he said, "and most interesting, but just now, as I may remind you, there are things more pressing than the regeneration of the Indian race; for instance, our own safety. Tomorrow, at the latest, men will come to seek these villains who lie yonder, and if we are found here it seems likely that we shall be shot down as murderers. Say, then, what do you propose to do?"

"I propose, señor, that at the first light of dawn we should take the mules and ride away. The forest is dense, and it will be difficult to find us in it, moreover two days' journey will place us beyond the reach of white men. Tell me, Lady," I added to Maya, who had returned from the chamber, "do you know the road?"

"I know the road," she answered, "but, sirs, before you take it, it is right that I should tell you something, seeing that not to do so would be to make an ill return for all the nobleness which you have shown towards my father and myself, saving us from death and shame. You have heard my father's words, and they are true, every one of them, but they are not all the truth. He rules that city of which he has spoken to you, but the nobles there are weary of his rule, which at times is somewhat harsh; also they deem him mad. It was for this reason that they suffered him to wander forth, seeking the fulfillment of a prophecy in which none of them have faith, for they were certain that he would perish in the wilderness and return no more to trouble them."

"Then why did they allow you, who are his heiress, to accompany him, Lady?"

"Because I would have it so. I love my father, and if he was doomed to die because of his folly, it was my wish to die with him. Moreover, if you would know the truth, I hate that city where I was born, and the man in it to whom I am destined to be married, and desired to escape from it if only for a while."

"And does that man hate you, Lady?"

"No," she answered, turning her head aside; "but if he loves me, I believe that he loves power more. Had I stayed, although I am a woman, my father must have appointed me to rule in his place, and Tikal, my cousin, would have been next the throne, not on it; therefore it was that he consented to my going, or at the least I think so. Sirs, I learn now that you are to accompany us to the City of the Heart, should we live to reach it, and for my own part I rejoice at this, though I should be glad if our faces were set towards some other land. But I learn also that you have entered into a compact with my father, under which he is to give you the gold you need, and many great things are to happen, having for their end the setting up of the Indian people above the white men, and the raising of the City of the Heart to the place and power that she has lost, which according to the prophecy shall come about after the two halves of the broken symbol are set once more in the place that is prepared for them."

"Do you not believe, then, in the prophecy?" asked the señor quickly.

"I did not say so," she answered. "Certainly it is strange that by following a dream my father should have found that which he sought so eagerly, the trinket that your companion bears upon his breast. And yet I will say this; that I have no great faith in priests and visions and gods, for of these it seems there have been many" — and she glanced at the walls of the temple, that were sculptured over with the demons which our forefathers worshipped, then added — "indeed, if I understand aright, you, sire, follow a faith that is unknown to us."

"We follow the true faith," I answered, "all the rest are false."

"It may be so," she said, "but I know not how this saying will sound in the ears of the servants of the Heart of Heaven. Come if you will, but be warned; my people are a jealous people, and the name of a stranger is hateful to them. Few such have ever reached the City of the Heart for many generations, and of those, save for one or two, none have escaped from it alive. They do not desire new things, they have little knowledge of the world beyond their walls, and seek for none; they wish to live as their forefathers lived, careless of a future which they will never see, and I think that it must go very ill with any who come among them bringing new faiths and doctrines, seeking to take power from their hands and to awake them from their narrow sloth. Now, sirs, choose whether you will accompany us in our march towards the City of Waters, or whether you will set your face to the sea again and forget that you chanced to hear a certain story from a wandering doctor, whose misfortunes had made him mad, and an Indian girl who tended him."

Now I listened to these words which the Lady Maya spoke very earnestly and with power, and understood that they meant much; they meant that in going to the City of the Heart we were, as she believed, going to our doom.

"Lady," I said, "it may well chance that Death waits me yonder, but I have looked too often in his eyes of late to shun them now. Death is everywhere, lady, and, did men stop to let him pass, little work would be done in the world. I have my task to do, or to attempt, and it seems that it lies yonder in the Secret City, therefore thither I shall go if my strength does not fail me and fate will suffer it. Come what may, I travel with your father towards the City of the Heart. For the señor here it is different. Weeks ago I told him that no good could come to him from this journey, and what I said then I say now. He has heard your words, and if he will hearken to them and to mine, he will bid us farewell tomorrow, and go his ways, leaving us to go ours."

She listened, and, turning towards him, said, "You hear. What say you, White Man?" and it seemed to me, who was watching her, that she awaited his answer anxiously.

"Yes, Lady, I hear," he replied, with a laugh, "and doubtless it is all true enough, and I shall leave my bones yonder among your country-men. Well, so be it, I have determined to go, not in order to regenerate the race of Indians or any other race, but that I may see this city; and go I will, since, other things apart, I am too idle to change my mind.

Also it seems to me that after this day's business there is more danger in staying here than in pushing forward."

"I am glad that you are going, since you go of your own free will," she said, smiling. "May our fears be confounded, and your journey and ours prove prosperous. And now let us rest, for you must be very weary, as I am, and we should be stirring before the dawn."

Next morning, at the first break of light, we started upon our journey, riding on three of the mules that we had captured, and leading the fourth laden with our goods and water-skins. Very glad were all of us to see the last of that ruined temple, and yet it was sad to me to leave it, for there, hidden beneath some of the masses of the fallen masonry, lay all that was left of my friend and foster-brother, Molas, he whose bravery and wit had saved our lives at the cost of his own.

Our plan was to avoid villages where we might be seen by men, and to keep ourselves hidden in the forest, for we feared lest we should be followed and brought to judgment because of the death of Don Pedro and his companions. This, as it chanced, we were able to do, since, having guns and ammunition in plenty, we shot birds and deer for our daily food. Traveling thus on mule-back, soon our strength returned to us, even to the old man Zibalbay, who had suffered the most from fatigue and from ill-treatment at the hands of the Mexicans.

In something less than a week we had passed through the inhabited districts of Yucatan and far out of reach of the white man, and now were journeying through the forest towards the great *sierra* that lies beyond it. To find a way in this thick and almost endless forest appeared impossible; indeed, it would have been so but for the knowledge that Zibalbay and his daughter had gathered on their path seaward, and for an ancient map which they brought with them. On this map were traced the lines of the roads that in the days of Indian civilization pierced the country in every direction. One of these roads, the largest, ran from the mountain range which surrounds the lake of the City of the Heart, straight across *sierras* and through woodlands to the ruined town of Palenque, and thence to the coast. This road, or rather causeway, was in many places utterly overgrown by trees, and in others sunk in swamps or hidden by the dust and sand of the *sierras*. Sometimes for two or three days' journey there was nothing to show us that it had ever existed, still, by following the line traced upon the map, and from time to time taking our position by the ruins of cities marked thereon, we never failed to find it again.

The number of these old cities and temples was wonderful, and astonished the señor beyond measure, which is not strange, seeing that he was the first white man who had ever looked upon them. Often, as we rode, he would talk to me about them, and strive to paint in words a picture of this country, now but desert plains or tangled bush, as it must have been five hundred years or more before our day, when cities and villages, palaces and temples, crowded with tens of thousands of inhabitants, were to be seen everywhere, and the fertile face of the earth was hidden in the green of crops. What histories lay buried in those jungles, and what scenes must have been enacted on the crumbling pyramids which confronted us day by day, before the sword of the conqueror or the breath of pestilence, or both, made the land desolate. Then it would have been a sight worth seeing; and our hearts beat at the thought that if things went well with us it might be our fortune to witness that sight; that *our* eyes might behold the greatest of these cities, sought for many generations but as yet unfound, the very navel of this ancient and mysterious civilization, dying indeed, but still existent.

I had other hopes to draw me onward, but, as I believe, it was this desire that sustained the señor in many a difficulty and danger of our march. It was with him while he was hacking a mule-path through the scrub with his *machete,* when we toiled along hour after hour beneath the burning sun, and even at night as he lay overtired and sleepless, tormented by insects, and aching with fever. Filled with this thought he was never weary of questioning the silent Zibalbay as to the history, or rather the legend, of the land through which we journeyed, or of listening to the Lady Maya's descriptions of the City of the Heart, till even she grew tired, and begged him to speak, instead, of the country across the water where he was born, of its ceaseless busy life, and the wonders of civilization. Strange as it may seem, I, who watched them both from day to day, know it to be true that she was in mind the more modern of the two — so much so, indeed, that, in listening to their talk, I might have fancied that Maya was the child of the New World, filled with the spirit of today, and he the heir of a proud and secret race dying beneath its weight of years.

"I cannot understand you," she would say to him; "why do you so love histories and ruins and stories of people that have long been dead? I hate them. Once they lived, and doubtless were well enough in their place and time, but now they are past and done with, and it is we who live, live, live!" and she stretched out her arms as though she would clasp the sunshine to her breast.

"I tell you," she went on, "that this home of mine, of which you are so fond of talking, is nothing but a great burying-place, and those who dwell in it are like ghosts who wander to and fro thinking of the things that they did, or did not do, a thousand years before. It was their ancestors who did the things, not they, for they do nothing except plot against each other, eat, sleep, drink, and mumble prayers to a god in whom they do not believe. Did my father but know it, he wastes time and trouble in making plans for the redemption of the People of the Heart, who think him mad for his pains. They cannot be redeemed. Were it otherwise, do you suppose that they would have been content to sit still all these hundreds of years, knowing nothing of the great world outside of them, and day by day watching their numbers dwindle, till life but flickers in the race as in a dying lamp? So it is also, if in a less degree, with those Indians whom Don Ignatio here seeks to lift out of the mire into which the Spanish trod them. Sirs, I believe that our blood has had its day. There is no more growth in us, we are corn ripe for the sickle of Death — that is, most of us are. Therefore, if I could have my will, while I am still young I would turn my back upon this city which you so desire to see, taking with me the wealth that is useless there, but which, it seems, would bring me many good things in other lands, and live out my time among people who have a present and a future as well as a past."

Then the señor would laugh, and argue that the past is more than the present, and that it is better to be dead than alive, and many other such follies; and I would grow angry and reprove Maya for her words, which shocked me, whereat she would yawn, and talk of something else, for I and my discourses wearied her. Only Zibalbay took no heed, for his mind was set upon other things, even if he heard us, which I doubt.

But all this while, notwithstanding her light talk and careless manner, the Lady Maya was learning — yes, even from me — when the señor was not at hand, for she would inquire into everything and forget nothing that she heard. The history of the countries of the world, their modes of government and religions, the manners, customs, and appearance of their inhabitants — he told her of them all from day to day. Nor did she weary of listening, till at length the señor met with an adventure that went near to separating him from her forever, and showed me, although I had no great love for her or any of her sex, that, whatever might be her faults, this woman's heart was true and bold.

Chapter XII

MAYA DESCENDS THE CUEVA

One evening — it was after we had left the forest country, and with much toil climbed the *sierra* till we reached the desert beyond, a desert that seemed to be boundless — we set our camp amongst a clump of great aloes that grew at the foot of a stony hill. This hill was marked on Zibalbay's map as being the site of an underground reservoir, known as a *cueva*, whence in the old days, when this place was inhabited, the Indians drew their supply of water in the dry season from deep down in the bowels of the earth. That this particular *cueva* existed was proved by the fact that the ancient road, which here was plainly visible, ran through the ruins of a large town whereof the population must once have been supplied by it; but when Zibalbay and his daughter slept at the spot on their downward journey, they were spared the necessity of looking for it by the discovery of a rain-pool in the hollow of a rock. Now, however, no rain having fallen for weeks, after we had eaten, and drunk such water as remained in the water-skins, we determined to seek for the *cueva* in order to refill the skins and give drink to the thirsty mules.

Accordingly we began to examine the rocky hill, and presently found a stone archway, now nearly filled up with soil and half hidden by thorn bushes, which from its appearance and position we judged to be the entrance to the *cueva*. Having provided ourselves with an armful of torches made from the dead stems of a variety of aloe that grew around in plenty, we lit four of them, and I led the way through the hole to find myself in a cave where a great and mysterious wind blew and sighed in sudden gusts that almost extinguished our lights. Following this cave we came to a pit or shaft at the end of it, which evidently led to the springs of water. This shaft, of unknown depth, was almost if not quite as smooth and perpendicular as though it had been hollowed by the hand of man, but the strangest thing about it was the terrible stairway that the ancients had used to approach the water, consisting, as it did,

of a double row of notches eight or ten inches deep, cut in the surface
of the shaft. Up and down these notches the water-carriers must have
passed for generations, for they were much worn, and a groove made by
the feet of men ran to the top of this awful ladder. The señor, finding
a fragment of rock, let it fall over the edge of the pit, and several seconds
passed before a faint sound told us that it had touched the bottom.

"What a dreadful place!" he said. "I think that I had rather die of
thirst than attempt to go down it."

"Still people have gone down in the past," answered Maya, "for look,
this is where they stepped off the edge."

"Perhaps they had a rope to hold by, lady," I suggested. "When I was
a young man I have descended mines almost as steep, with no other
ladder than one made of tree-trunks — monkey-poles they are called —
notched after this fashion, and set from side to side of the shaft, but
now it would be my death to try, for such heights make me dizzy."

"Come away," said Zibalbay; "none of us here could take that road
and live. The mules must go thirsty; five hours' journey away there is a
pool where they can drink tomorrow."

Then we turned and left this cave of the winds and were glad to be
outside of it, for the place had an unholy look, and, all the draft
notwithstanding, was hot to suffocation.

Zibalbay walked to the camp, but we stayed to pluck some forage for
the mules. Soon the others grew weary of this task and fell to talking as
they watched the sunset, which was very beautiful on these lonely plains.
Presently I heard the Lady Maya say:

"Pick me that flower, friend, to wear upon my breast," and she
pointed to a snow-white cactus-bloom that grew amongst some rocks.

The señor climbed to the place and stretched out his hand to cut the
flower, when of a sudden I heard him utter an exclamation and saw him
start.

"What is it?" I said, "have you pricked yourself or cut your hand?"
He made no answer, but his eyes grew wide with horror, and he pointed
at something grey that was gliding away among the stones, and as he
pointed I saw a spot of blood appear upon his wrist. Maya saw it also.

"A snake has bitten you!" she cried in a voice of agony, and, springing
at him before I guessed what she was about to do, she seized his arm
with both hands and set her lips to the wound.

He tried to wrench it free, but she clung to him fiercely, then, calling
to me to bring a stick, she tore a strip off her robe and made it fast
round his wrist above the puncture. By now I was there with the stick,
and, setting it in the loop of linen, I twisted it till the hand turned blue
from the pressure.

"What snake was it?" I asked.

"The deadly grey sort," he answered, adding: "Don't look so frightened, Maya, I know a cure. Come to the camp, quick!"

In two minutes we reached it, and the señor had snatched a sharp knife and a powder-flask.

"Now, friend," he said, handing me the knife, "cut deep, since it is life or death for me and there are no arteries in the top of the wrist."

Seeing what had come about, Zibalbay held the señor's hand and I cut twice. He never winced, but at each slash Maya groaned. Then, having let the blood fall till it would run no more, we poured powder into the wound, as much as will lie on a twenty cent piece, and fired it. It went off in a puff of white smoke, leaving the flesh beneath black and charred.

"Now, as we have no brandy, there is nothing more to be done except to wait," said the señor, with an attempt at a smile; but Zibalbay, going to a bag, produced from it some *cuca* paste.

"Eat this," he said, "it is better than any fire-water."

The señor took the stuff and began to swallow it, till presently I saw that he could force no more down, for a paralysis seemed to be creeping over him; his throat contracted, and his eyelids fell as though weighed upon by irresistible sleep. Now, notwithstanding our remedies, seeing that the poison had got hold of him, we seized him by the arms and began to walk him to and fro, encouraging him at the same time to keep a brave heart and fight against death.

"I am doing my best," he answered feebly; then his mind began to wander, and at length he fell down and his eyes shut.

A great fear and horror seized me, for I thought that he was about to die, and with them a kind of rage because I was impotent to save him. Already, to tell the truth, I was jealous of the Lady Maya, and now my jealousy broke out in bitter and unjust words.

"This is your fault," I said.

"You are cruel," she answered, "and you speak thus because you hate me."

"Perhaps I am cruel, lady. Would not you be cruel if you saw the friend you love perishing through a woman's folly?"

"Are you the only one that can love?" she whispered.

"Unless we can rouse him the white man will die," said Zibalbay.

"Oh! awake," cried Maya despairingly, placing her lips close to the señor's ear. "They say that I have killed you, awake, awake!"

He seemed to hear her, for, though his eyes did not open, he smiled faintly and murmured, "I will try." Then with our help he struggled from the ground and began to walk once more, but like a man who is drunk. Thrice he staggered backwards and forwards along the path our feet had worn. Then he fell again, and, putting our hands upon his breast, we could feel the contractions of his heart growing weaker every moment, till at last they seemed to die away. But of a sudden, when we had already abandoned hope, it pulsed violently, and from every pore of his skin, which till now had been parched and dry, there burst so profuse a perspiration that in the light of the rising moon we could see it running down his face.

"I think that the white man will live now; he has conquered the poison," said Zibalbay quietly, and hearing his words I returned thanks to God in my heart.

Then we laid him in a hammock, piling blankets and *serapes* over him till at length the perspiration ceased, all the fluid in his body having evaporated, taking the venom with it.

For an hour or more he slept, then awoke and asked for water in a faint voice. We, who were watching, looked at each other in dismay, for we had not a single drop to give, and this we were obliged to tell him. He groaned and was silent for a while, then said:

"It would have been kinder to let me die of the poison, for this torment of thirst is more than I can bear."

"Can we try the *cueva?*" faltered Maya.

"It is impossible," answered her father. "We should all be killed."

"Yes, yes," repeated the señor, "it is impossible. Better that one should die than four."

"Father," said Maya, "you must take the best mule and ride forward to the pool where we should camp tomorrow. The moon shines, and with good fortune you may be back in eight or nine hours."

"It is useless," murmured the señor, "I can never live so long without drink, my throat is hot like a coal."

Zibalbay shrugged his shoulders, he also thought that it was useless, but his daughter turned upon him fiercely and said:

"Are you going, or shall I ride myself?"

Then he went, muttering in his beard, and in a few minutes we heard the footsteps of the mule as it shambled forward into the desert.

"Fear not," I said to the señor, "it is the poison that has dried you up, but thirst will not kill you so soon, and presently you will feel it less. Oh! that we had medicine here to make you sleep!"

He lay quiet for a space, giving no answer, but from the workings of his hands and face we could see that he suffered much.

"Maya," he said at length, "can you find me a cool stone to put in my mouth?"

She searched and found a pebble which he sucked, but after a time it fell from his lips, and we saw that it was as dry as when it entered them. Then of a sudden his brain gave way, and he began to rave huskily in many languages.

"Are you devils," he asked, "that you suffer me to die in torment for the want of a drink of water? Why do you stand there and mock me? Oh! have pity and give me water."

For a while we bore it, though perhaps our agonies were greater than his own — then Maya rose and looked at his face. It was sunken as with a heavy illness, thick black rings had appeared beneath his blue eyes, and his lips were flecked with blood.

"I can endure this no more," she said, in a dry voice; "watch your friend, Don Ignatio."

"You are right," I answered, "this is no place for a woman. Go and sleep yonder, so that I can wake you if there is need."

She looked at me reproachfully, but went without answering, and sat down behind a bush about thirty yards away. Here it seems — for all this story she told me afterwards, and for the most part I do but repeat her words — she began to think. She was sure that without water the señor could not live through the night, and it was impossible that her father should return before dawn at the earliest. He was dying, and she felt as though her life were ebbing with his own, for now she knew that she loved him. Unless something could be done he must soon be dead, and her heart would be broken. Only one thing could save him — and her — water. In the depths of yonder hill, within a few paces of her, doubtless it lay in plenty, but who would venture to seek it there? And yet the descent of the *cueva* must be possible, since the ancients used it daily, and why could she not do what they had done? She was young and active, and from childhood it had been a delight to her to climb in dangerous places about the walls and pyramids of the City of the Heart, nor had her head failed her however lofty they might chance to be. Why, then, should it fail her now when the life of the man she loved was at stake? And what would it matter if it did fail her, seeing that if he died she wished to die also?

Yes, she would try it!

When once she had made up her mind Maya set about the task swiftly. I was standing by the hammock praying to heaven to spare the life of my friend, who lay there beating his hands to and fro and moaning in misery, when I saw her creep up and look at him.

"You think you love him," she said to me suddenly, "but I tell you that you do not know what love is. If I live, I, whom you despise, will teach you, Don Ignatio."

I took no heed of her words, for I thought them foolish.

Then, unseen by me, Maya glided away to where the mules were picketed and provided herself with flint, steel, tinder, a rope, and a small water-skin of untanned hind, which she strapped upon her shoulders. In another minute she was running across the desert like a deer. At the entrance to the *cueva* she paused to gather up the aloe torches which had been thrown down there, and also to look for one moment at the familiar face of night, the night that she might never see again. Then she lit a torch and crept through the narrow opening.

The place had been awful in the evening when she visited it in the company of the rest of us. Now, alone and at night, it appalled her. Great winds roared round its vast recesses, sucked thither from the hollows of the earth, and in them could be heard sounds like to those of human voices, sobbing and making moan. Myra shivered, for she thought that these were the ghosts of dead *antiguos* bewailing their eternal griefs in this unearthly place, but she pressed forward boldly, notwithstanding her fears, till she stood on the brink of the pit. Here she halted to strip herself so that there might be as little as possible to impede her movements in climbing the stair, and twisted her hair into a knot. Next she tied the cord about her middle, and the water-skin, to which she fastened the flint and steel, upon her shoulders. Lighting two of the largest torches she fixed them slantingwise in crevices of the rock, so that their flame shone over the mouth of the shaft, down which she threw, first, a bundle of unlit torches, and, lastly, one on fire. This torch did not go out, as she half expected that it would, for presently, looking down the pit, she saw a spark of light shining a hundred and fifty feet or more beneath her.

Now all her preparations were complete, and nothing remained to be done except to descend and search for the water. For a moment Maya hesitated, looking at the spark of fire that gleamed so far below, and at the narrow niches cut in the smooth surface of the rock. Then, feeling that if she stood longer thus, her terrors would master her, she knelt down, and, holding to the rock with her hands, she thrust her leg over the edge of the pit, feeling at its side with her foot till she found the first niche. Resting her weight on this foot, she dropped the other till she reached the second niche, which was about eighteen inches lower and ten inches to the left of the first, for these niches were cut in a zigzag fashion, No. 1 being above No. 3, No. 2 above No. 4 and so on. Now she must face one of the most terrible risks of the descent, for it was impossible for her to reach No. 3 niche without leaving go of the edge of the pit, nor could she get a hold of No. 1 with her hand until her foot was in No. 4, so that there was no alternative except to balance herself on one leg, and, placing her palms against the smooth rock, slide them down it till her foot rested on No. 4, and her fingers in No. 1.

Clinging thus like a fly to the rock, she stepped into No. 3, and, not daring to pause, began at once to feel for No. 4. In her anxiety she dropped her leg too low, and while drawing it back almost overbalanced herself. A thrill of horrible fear struck her, causing her spine to creep, but, resting her face against the rock, by a desperate effort she retained her presence of mind, and in another second was standing in No. 4 and holding to No. 1. Thenceforward the descent was easier, since all she had to do was to shift the grip of her hands from hole to hole and remember in which line she must search with her foot for the succeeding niche. So far from hindering her, the darkness proved a boon, since it prevented her from beholding the horror of the place.

By the time that she was a third of the way down the shaft her courage returned to her, and the only fear she felt was lest some of the niches should be broken. Fortunately this was not the case, although one of them was so much worn that her toes slipped out of it and for a second or two she hung by her hands. Recovering herself, she went on from step to step till at length she stood at the bottom of the shaft.

After a minute's pause to get her breath, Maya found one of the dry aloe stems, and lit it at the embers of the torch which she had thrown down the pit. Then she looked round her, to find herself in a large natural cavern of no great height, which sloped gently downwards further than she could see. Turning her eyes to the floor, she searched for and discovered the path that had been hollowed out by the feet of the ancients, but now was half hidden in sand and dust. It ran straight down the cave, and she followed it for fifty paces or more, holding the light in one hand, and some spare torches under her arm. Here in this cave the atmosphere was so hot and still, that she was scarcely able to breathe, though even at a distance she could hear a strange eddying wind roaring in the shaft down which she had come. Presently the cavern began to decrease in size till it narrowed into a small passage, and Maya sighed aloud, fearing lest she should be coming to the mouth of a second shaft, for she had heard me say that the water in these *cuevas* was sometimes found at a depth of five or six hundred feet, whereas she had not descended more than two hundred.

When she had walked another ten or fifteen paces, however, the passage took a sudden turn and her doubts were set at rest, for there in the center of a wonderful place, such as she had never seen before, gleamed the water which she had risked her life to reach.

How large the place where she found herself might be Maya never knew, since the feeble light of her torch did not pierce far into the gloom. All that she could see was a number of white columns — without doubt stalactites, though she imagined them to have been fashioned by man — rising from the floor of the cavern to its roof, and in the midst of them a circular pit, thirty feet or more across, in which lay the water. This water, though clear as crystal, was not still, for once in every few seconds a great bubble three or four feet in diameter rose in the center of the pool, to burst on its surface and send a ring of ripples to the rocky sides. So beautiful was this bubble and so regular its appearance that for some minutes Maya watched it; then, remembering that she had no time to spare, she set herself to get the water, only to learn that she was confronted by a new difficulty and one which but for her foresight might have proved insuperable. The rock bank of the pool was so smooth, and sloped so steeply to the water, that it was quite impossible for anyone to keep a footing on it. The ancients had overcome the trouble by means of a wooden staircase, as was evident from the places hollowed in the rock to receive the uprights, but this structure had long since rotted away. At the head of where this staircase had stood, a hole was bored in the rock, doubtless to receive a rope by which the water-bearers supported themselves while they filled their jars, and the sight of this hole gave Maya a thought. Untying the cord which she had brought with her, she made it fast through the hole, and, having fixed the torch into one of the spaces hollowed to hold the timbers of the stairway, she slid down the bank till she stood breast high in the water.

For a minute or more she remained thus, drinking her fill and enjoying the coolness of her bath, which was pleasing after the stupefying heat of the caves, then, first having taken care to remove the tinder that was tied to it, she slipped the water-skin from her shoulder, washed it out, filled and replaced it. Next she dragged herself up the bank, and by the light of a new torch started for the foot of the shaft.

Here Maya rested awhile, gathering up her energies, then, feeling that once more she began to grow afraid, she commenced the ascent. There were a hundred and one of the notches, for she had counted them as she came down, and now again she began to count, so that she might know her exact position in the shaft, of which she could see nothing because of the intense darkness. Before she had ascended fifty steps she was dismayed to find a feeling of weariness taking possession of her, which forced her to pause awhile hanging to the face of the pit. Then she went on again and with great efforts reached the seventy-fifth step, where once more she was obliged to hang, gaining breath, till a pain in her right leg, upon which most of her weight rested, warned her that she must stay no longer. For the third time she struggled upwards, desperately and despairingly dragging her feet from niche to niche. Her breath came in gasps, the straps of the heavy water-skin cut into her tender flesh, and her brain began to reel.

Now there were but ten more steps. It came into her mind that she might save herself by loosing the burden of water from her shoulders, to fall to the bottom of the pit, but this she would not do. Now only three niches remained and the goal would be won, but now also her brain was giving. Darker and more bewildered it grew, yet by a desperate effort she kept some fragment of her sense. Her foot was in the topmost hole, her body was balanced upon the edge of the pit, and, pulled down by the choking weight of the water, she was like to fall backwards. Then it seemed that a voice called her, and for the last time she struggled, writhing forward as does a wounded snake, till darkness closed in upon her mind.

When Maya recovered a while later, she found that she was lying on the edge of the shaft, over which her feet still hung. Instantly she remembered all, and, with a little scream of terror, drew herself along the floor. Then with difficulty, for she was still breathless, and her muscles seemed to have no strength, she rose to her feet, and having felt for and picked up her linen robe, she crept towards the spot of light which marked the entrance to the cave. Presently she was through it, and with a sigh of thankfulness sank to the earth and put on her garment, then, rising, she walked slowly towards the camp, bearing the precious water with her.

Meanwhile, knowing nothing of all this, I, Ignatio, also had been thinking. I remembered how, when I lay crushed beneath the rock, the señor had ventured his life to save me. Should I not then venture mine to save his? It seemed so. Without water he would certainly die, and greatly as I dreaded to attempt the descent of the *cueva*, yet it must be done. Leaving the hammock, I searched for the Lady Maya, but could not find her, so I called aloud — "Señora, señora. Where are you, señora?"

"Here," she answered. "What is it? Is he dead?"

"No," I said, "but I am sure that unless he has water he will die within little more than an hour. Therefore I have made up my mind to try to descend the *cueva*. Will you be so good as to watch the señor till I return, and if I return no more, as is probable, to tell your father what has happened. He will find the talisman of the Broken Heart lying with my clothes at the mouth of the pit. I pray that he will take it, and I pray also that he should travel back to Mexico, bearing with him some of the wealth of his city, there to continue the great work that I have begun, of which I have spoken to him. Farewell, señora."

"Stop, Don Ignatio," said Maya in a hoarse voice, "there is no need for you to descend the *cueva*."

"Why not, Lady? I should be glad to escape the task, but this is a question of life or death."

"Yes," she answered, "and because it is a question of life or death, Don Ignatio, I have already climbed that hideous place, and — here is the water" — and she fell forward and swooned upon the ground.

I said nothing. I was too much amazed, and, indeed, too much ashamed, to speak. Lifting Maya's senseless form, I placed her in a hammock that was slung close by. Then I took the water-skin and a leather cup, and ran with it to my friend's side. By now the señor was lost in a coma and lay still, only moaning from time to time. Undoing the mouth of the skin, I poured out a cupful of water, with which I began to sprinkle his brow and to moisten his cracked lips. At the touch and smell of the fluid a change came over the face of the dying man, the empty look left it, and the eyes opened.

"That was water," he muttered, "I can taste it." Then he saw the cup, and the sight seemed to give him a sudden strength, for he stretched out his arms and, snatching it from my hand, he drained it in three gulps.

"More," he gasped, "more."

But as yet I would give him no more, though he prayed for it piteously, and when I did allow him to drink again it was in sips only. For an hour he sipped thus till at length even his thirst was partially satisfied, and the shrunken cheeks began to fill out and the dull eyes to brighten.

"That water has saved my life," he whispered; "where did it come from?"

"I will tell you tomorrow," I answered; "sleep now if you can."

Chapter XIII

IGNATIO'S OATH

At sunrise on the following day I lit a fire by which to prepare soup for the señor, who still slept, and as I was engaged thus I saw the Lady Maya walking towards me, and noticed that her hands and feet were swollen.

"Señora," I said, bowing before her, "I humbly congratulate you upon your courage and your escape from great dangers. Last night I said words to you in my grief that should not have been spoken, for it is my fault that I am apt to be unjust to women. I crave your pardon, and I will add that if, in atonement for my past injustice, I can serve you in any way now and afterwards, I pray you to command me."

She listened and answered:

"I thank you for your kind words, Don Ignatio, and I forget other words that were not kind which you have spoken to me from time to time. If in truth you wish to show yourself my friend, it is in your power to do so. You have guessed my secret, therefore I am not ashamed to repeat that the señor yonder has become everything to me, though as yet I may be little to him. I ask you, then, to swear upon the Heart that you will do nothing to turn him from me, or to separate us should he ever learn to love me, but rather, should this come about, that whatever may be our need, you will help us by all means in your reach."

"You ask me to swear a large oath, señora, and one that deals with the future, of which we have no knowledge," I answered, hesitating.

"I do, señor, but remember that were it not for me at this moment your friend, who sleeps yonder like a child, would be stiff in death. Remember also that you have ends to gain in the City of the Heart, where it will be well for you to keep me as a friend should we ever live to reach it. Still, do not swear unless you wish, only then I shall know that you are my secret enemy and I shall be yours."

"There is no need to threaten me, señora," I answered, "nor am I to be moved thus, but I promise that I will not stand between you and the señor. Why should I? His will is his own, and, as you say, you saved his life. But see, he awakes, and his soup is ready."

She took the pot off the fire, skimmed it, and poured the contents into a gourd.

"Shall I take it, or will you?" she asked.

"I think that you had better take it," I answered.

Then she walked to the hammock and said, "Señor, here is your soup."

He was but newly awakened, and looked at her vacantly.

"Tell me, Maya," he asked, "what has happened?"

"Last evening," she began, "in picking a flower for me you were bitten by a snake, and very nearly died."

"I know," he answered. "Without doubt I should have died had you not sucked the wound and tied a bandage round my wrist, for that grey snake is the deadliest in the country. Go on."

"After the danger of the poison was past you became thirsty, so thirsty that you were dying of it, and there was no water to give you."

"Yes, yes," he said, "it was agony; I pray that I may never suffer so again. But I drank water and lived. Who brought it to me?"

"My father started on to the next camping-place, where there is a pool," she answered.

"Has he returned?"

"No, not yet."

"Then he cannot have brought the water. Where did it come from?"

"It came from the *cueva*, that cave which we examined before you were bitten."

"Who went down the *cueva* to get it? The place is unclimbable."

"I went down."

"You!" he said, in amazement. "*You!* It is not possible. Do not jest. Tell me the truth quickly. I am tired."

"I am not jesting. Listen, señor. You were dying for want of water, dying before our eyes; it was horrible to see. I could not bear it, and I knew that my father would not be back in time, so I took the water-skin and some torches and went without saying anything to Ignatio. The shaft was hard to climb, and the adventure strange. I will tell you of that by and by, but as it chanced I came through it safely to find Ignatio about to start on the same errand."

The señor heard and understood, but he made no answer; he only stretched out his arms towards her, and there and thus in the wilderness did they plight their troth.

"Remember that I am but an Indian girl," she murmured presently, "and you are one of the white lords of the earth. Is it well that you should love me?"

"It is well," he answered, "for you are the noblest woman that I have known, and you have saved my life."

Zibalbay did not return till past midday, when he appeared with the water, leading the mule, which had set its foot upon a sharp stone in the desert and gone lame.

"Does he still live?" he asked of Maya.

"Yes, father."

"He must be strong, then," he whispered; "I thought that thirst would have killed him ere now."

"He has had water, father. I descended the *cueva* and fetched it," she added, after a moment's pause.

The old man looked at her amazed.

"How came it that you found courage to go down that place, daughter?" he asked at length.

"The desire to save a friend gave me courage," she answered, letting her eyes fall beneath his gaze. "I knew that you could not be back in time, so I went."

Zibalbay pondered awhile, then said:

"I think that you would have done better to let him die, daughter, for I believe that this white man will bring trouble upon us. It has pleased the gods to preserve you alive; remember, then, that your life belongs to them, and that you must follow the path which they have chosen, not that which you would choose for yourself. Remember also that one waits you in the city yonder who may have a word to say as to your friendship with this wanderer." And he passed on with the mule.

That same evening Maya told me of her father's words and said:

"I think that before all is done I shall need the help that you have sworn to give me, señor, for I can see well that my father will be against me unless my wish runs with his purpose. Of one thing I am sure, that my life is my own and not a possession of the gods; for in such gods as my father worships and I was brought up to serve, I have lost faith, if indeed I ever had any."

"You speak rashly," I answered, "and if you are wise you will not let your father hear such words."

"Lest by and by my life should be forfeit to the gods whom I blaspheme!" she broke in. "Say, then, do you believe in these gods, Don Ignatio?"

"No, Lady, I am a Christian and have no part with idols or those who worship them."

"I understand; it is only in their wealth that you would have part. Well, and why should I not become a Christian also? I have learned something of your faith from the señor yonder, and see that it is great and pure, and full of comfort for us mortals."

"May grace be given to you to follow in that road, Lady, but it is not Christian to taunt me about the wealth which I come to seek for the advantage of our race, seeing that you know I ask nothing for myself."

"Forgive me," she answered, "my tongue is sharp — as yours has been at times, Don Ignatio. Hark! the señor calls me."

*F*or two more days we rested there by the *cueva* till the señor was fit to travel, then we started on again. Ten days we journeyed across the wilderness, following the line of the ancient road, and meeting with no traces of man save such as were furnished by the familiar sight of ruined pyramids and temples. On the eleventh we began to ascend the slope of a lofty range of mountains that pushed its flanks far out into the desert-land, and on the twelfth we reached the snow-line, where we were obliged to abandon the three mules which remained to us, seeing that no green food was to be found higher up, and the path became too steep for them to find a footing in it. That night we slept, with little to eat, in a hole dug in the snow, wrapped in our *serapes,* or, rather, we tried to sleep, for our rest was broken by the cold, and the moaning of bitter and mysterious winds which sprang up and passed away suddenly beneath a clear sky; also, from time to time, by the thunder of distant avalanches rushing from the peaks above.

"How far must we travel up this snow?" I asked of Zibalbay, as we stood shivering in the ashy light of the dawn.

"Look yonder," he answered, pointing to where the first ray of the sun shone upon a surface of black rock far above us; "there is the highest point, and we should reach it before nightfall."

Thus encouraged we pushed forward for hour after hour, Zibalbay marching ahead in silence, until our sight was bewildered with snow-blindness, and I was seized with a fit of mountain sickness. Fortunately the climbing was not difficult, so that by four in the afternoon we found ourselves beneath the shadow of the wall of black rock.

"Must we scale that precipice?" I asked of Zibalbay.

"No," he answered, "it would not be possible without wings. There is a way through it. Twice in the old days bodies of white men searching for the Golden City to sack it, came to this spot, but, finding no path through the cliff, they went home again, though their hands were on the door."

"Does the wall of rock encircle all the valley of the city?" asked the señor.

"No, White Man, it ends many days' journey away to the west, but he who would travel round it must wade through a great swamp. Also the mountains may be crossed to the east by journeying for three days through snows and down precipices; but so far as I have learned only one man lived to pass them, a wandering Indian, who found his way to the banks of the Holy Waters in the days of my grandfather. Now, stay here while I search."

"Are you glad to see the gateway of your home, Maya?" asked the señor.

"No," she answered, almost fiercely, "for here in the wilderness I have been happy, but there sorrow awaits me and you. Oh! if indeed I am dear to you, let us turn even now and fly together back to the lands where your people live," and she clasped his hand and looked earnestly into his eyes.

"What," he answered, "and leave your father and Ignatio to finish the journey by themselves?"

"You are more to me than my father, though perhaps the solemn Ignatio is more to you than I am."

"No, Maya, but having come so far I wish to see the sacred city."

"As you will," she said, letting fall his hand. "See, my father has found the place and calls us."

We walked on for about a hundred paces, threading our path through piles of boulders that lay at the foot of the precipice till we came to where Zibalbay stood, leaning against the wall of rock in which we could see no break or opening.

"Although I trust you, and, as I believe, heaven has brought us together for its own purposes," said the old *cacique,* "yet I must follow the ancient custom and obey my oath to suffer no stranger to see the entrance to this mountain gate. Come hither, daughter, and blindfold these foreigners."

She obeyed, and as she tied the handkerchief about the señor's face I heard her whisper,

"Fear not, I will be your eyes."

Then we were taken by the hand, and led this way and that till we were confused. After we had walked some paces, we were halted and left while, as we judged from the sounds, our guides moved something heavy. Next we were conducted down a steep incline, through a passage so narrow and low that our shoulders rubbed the sides of it, and in parts we were obliged to bend our heads. At length, after taking many sharp turns, the passage grew wider and the path smooth and level.

"Loose the bandages," said the voice of Zibalbay.

Maya did so, and, when our eyes were accustomed to the light, we looked round us curiously to find that we stood at the bottom of a deep cleft or volcanic rift in the rock, made not by the hand of man but by that of Nature working with her tools of fire and water. This cleft — along which ran a road so solidly built and drained that, save here and there where snowdrifts blocked it, it was still easily passable after centuries of disuse — did not measure more than forty paces from wall to wall. On either side of it towered sheer black cliffs, honeycombed with doorways that could only have been reached by ladders.

"What are those?" I asked of Zibalbay. "Burying-places?"

"No," he answered, "dwelling-houses. They were there, so say the records, before our forefathers founded the City of the Heart, and in them dwelt cave-men, barbarians who fed on little and did not feel the cold. It was by following some of these cave-men through that passage which we have passed that the founder of the ancient city discovered this cleft and the good country and great lake that lie beyond it, where the rock-dwellers, whom our forefathers killed out, used to live in the winter season. Once, when I was young, with some companions I entered these caves by means of ropes and ladders, and found many strange things there, such as stone axes and rude ornaments of gold, relics of the barbarians. But let us press on, or night will overtake us in the pass."

By degrees the great cleft, that had widened as we walked, began to narrow again till it appeared to end in a second wall of rock.

Passing round a boulder that lay at the foot of this wall, Zibalbay led the way into a tunnel behind it.

"Do not fear the darkness," he said, "the passage is short and there are no pitfalls."

So we followed the sound of his footsteps through the gloom, till presently a spot of light appeared before us, and in another minute we stood on the further side of the mountain, though we could see nothing of the place because of the falling shadows.

Without pausing, Zibalbay pushed on down the hill, and, suddenly turning to the right, stopped before the door of a house built of hewn stone.

"Enter," he said, "and welcome to the country of the People of the Heart."

As the door was thrown open, light from the fire within streamed through it, and a man's voice was heard asking, "Who is there?"

Without answering, Zibalbay walked into the room. It was a low vaulted apartment, and at a table placed before the great fire which burned upon the hearth sat a man and a woman eating.

"Is this the way that you watch for my return?" he asked in a stern voice. "Haste now and make food ready for we are starved with cold and hunger."

The man, who had risen, stood hesitating, but the woman, whose position enabled her to see the face of the speaker, caught him by the arm, saying,

"Down to your knees, husband. It is the *cacique* come back."

"Pardon," cried the man, taking the hint; "but to be frank, O lord, it has been so dinned in my ears down in the city yonder, that neither you nor the Lady of the Heart would ever return again, that I thought you must be ghosts. Yes, and so they will think in the city, where I have heard that Tikal rules in your place."

"Peace," said Zibalbay, frowning heavily. "We left robes here, did we not? Go, lay them out in the sleeping-chambers, and with them others for these my guests, while the woman prepares our meat."

The man bowed, stretching out his arms till the backs of his hands touched the ground. Then, taking an earthenware lamp from a side table, he lit it and disappeared behind a curtain, an example which the woman followed after she had rapidly removed the dishes that were upon the table, and fed the fire with wood.

When they were gone we gathered round the hearth to bask in the luxury of its warmth.

"What is this place?" asked the señor.

Zibalbay, who was wrapped in his own thoughts, did not seem to hear him, and Maya answered,

"A poor hovel that is used as a rest-house and by hunters of game, no more. These people are its keepers, and were charged to watch for our return, but they seem to have fulfilled their task ill. Pardon me, I go to help them. Come, father."

They went, and presently the señor awoke from a doze induced by the delightful warmth of the fire, to see the custodian of the place standing before him staring at him in amazement not unmixed with awe.

"What is the matter with the man, and what does he want, Ignatio?" he asked in Spanish.

"He wonders at your white skin and fair hair, señor, and says that he does not dare to speak to you because you must be one of the Heaven-born of whom their legends tell, wherefore he asks me to say that water to wash in and raiment to put on have been made ready for us if we will come with him."

Accordingly we followed the Indian, who led us into a passage at the back of the sitting-chamber, and thence to a small sleeping-room, one of several to which the passage gave access. In this room, which was lit by an oil lamp, were two bedsteads covered with blankets of deerskin and cotton sheets, and laid upon them were fine linen robes, and *serapes* made in alternate bands of grey and black feathers, worked on to a foundation of stout linen. Standing upon wooden stools in a corner of the room, and half-filled with steaming water, were two basins, which the señor noticed with astonishment were of hammered silver.

"These people must be rich," he said to me so soon as the keeper of the place had gone, "if they fashion the utensils of their rest-houses of silver. Till now this story of the Sacred City of which Zibalbay was *cacique,* and Maya heiress apparent, has always sounded like a fairy tale to me, but it seems that it is true after all, for the man's manner shows that Zibalbay is a very important person."

Then we put on the robes that had been provided for our use, not without difficulty, since their make was strange to us, and returned to the eating-room. Presently the curtain was drawn, and the Lady Maya joined us — the Lady Maya, but so changed that we started in astonishment.

Different, indeed, was she to the ill-clad and travel-stained girl who had been our companion for so many weeks. Now she was dressed in a robe of snowy white, bordered with embroidery of the royal green, and having the image of the Heart traced in gold thread upon the breast. On her feet were sandals, also worked in green, while round her throat, wrists, waist, and ankles shone circlets of dead gold. Her dark hair no longer fell loose about her, but was twisted into a simple knot and confined in a little golden net, and from her shoulders hung a cloak of pure white feathers, relieved here and there by the delicate yellow plumes of the greater egret.

"Like you I have changed my garments," she said in explanation. "Is the dress ugly, that you look astonished?"

"Ugly!" answered the señor, "I think it is the most beautiful that I ever saw."

"This is the most beautiful dress that you ever saw! Why, friend, it is the simplest that I have. Wait till you see me in my royal robes, wearing the great emeralds of the Heart; what will you say then, I wonder?"

"I cannot tell, but I say now that I don't know which is the most lovely, you or your dress."

"Hush!" she said, laughing, yet with a note of earnestness in her voice. "You must not speak thus freely to me. Yonder in the pass, friend, I was the Indian girl your fellow-traveler; here I am the Lady of the Heart."

"Then I wish that you had remained the Indian girl in the pass," he answered, after a pause, "but perhaps you jest."

"I was not altogether jesting," she answered, with a sigh, "you must be careful now, or it might be ill for you or me, or both of us, since by rank I am the greatest lady in this land, and doubtless my cousin, Tikal, will watch me closely. See! here comes my father."

As she spoke Zibalbay entered, followed by the two Indians bearing food. He was simply dressed in a white togalike robe similar to that which had been given to the señor and myself. A cloak of black feathers covered his shoulders, and round his neck was hung a massive gold chain to which was attached the emblem of the Heart, also fashioned in plain gold.

We noticed that, as he came, his daughter, Maya, made a courtesy to him, which he acknowledged with a nod, and that whenever they passed him the two Indians crouched almost to the ground.

Evidently the friendship of our desert journeying was done with, and the person of whom we had hitherto thought and spoken as an equal must henceforth be treated with respect. Indeed the proud-faced, white-bearded chief seemed so royal in his changed surroundings that we were almost moved to follow the example of the others, and bow whenever he looked at us.

"The food is ready," said Zibalbay, "such as it is. Be seated, I beg of you. Nay, daughter, you need not stand before me. We are still fellow-wanderers, all of us, and ceremony can stay till we are come to the City of the Heart."

Then we sat down and the Indians waited on us. What the dishes consisted of we did not know, but after our long privations it seemed to us that we had never eaten so excellent a meal, or drunk anything so good as the native wine which was served with it. Still, notwithstanding our present comfort, I think the señor's heart misgave him, and that he had presentiments of evil. Maya and he still loved one another, but he felt that things were utterly changed, as she herself had shown him. While they wandered, in some sense he had been the head of the party, as, to speak truth, among companions of a colored race a white man is always acknowledged to be by right of blood. Now things were changed, and he must take his place as an alien wanderer, admitted to the country upon sufferance, and already this difference could be seen in Zibalbay's manner and mode of address. Formerly he had called him "señor," or even "friend;" tonight, when speaking to him, he used a word which meant "foreigner," or "unknown one," and even myself he addressed by name without adding any title of respect.

One good thing, however, we found in this place, who had lacked tobacco for six weeks and more, for presently the Indian entered bearing cigarettes made by rolling the herb in the thin sheath that grows about the cobs of Indian corn.

"Come hither, you," said Zibalbay to the Indian, when he had handed us the cigarettes. "Start now to the borders of the lake and advise the captain of the village of the corn-growers that his lord is returned again, commanding him in my name to furnish four traveling litters to be here within five hours after sunrise. Warn him also to have canoes in readiness to bear us across the lake, but, as he values his life, to send no word of our coming to the city. Go now and swiftly."

The man bowed, and, snatching a spear and a feather cloak from a peg near the door, vanished into the night, heedless of the howling wind and the sleet that thrashed upon the roof.

"How far is it to the village?" asked the señor.

"Ten leagues or more," Zibalbay answered, "and the road is not good, still if he does not fall from a precipice or lose his life in a snowdrift, he will be there within six hours. Come, daughter, it is time for us to rest, our journey has been long, and you must be weary. Good-night to you, my guests, tomorrow I shall hope to house you better." Then, bowing to us, he left the room.

Maya rose to follow his example, and, going to the señor, gave him her hand, which he touched with his lips.

"How good it is to taste tobacco again," he said as Maya went. "No, don't go to bed yet, Ignatio, take a cigarette and another glass of this *agua ardiente*, and let us talk. Do you know, friend, it seems to me that Zibalbay has changed. I never was a great admirer of his character, but perhaps I do not understand it."

"Do you not, señor? I think that I do. Like some Christian priests the man is a fanatic, and like myself, a dreamer. Also he is full of ambition and tyrannical, one who will spare neither himself nor others where he has an end to gain, or thinks that he can promote the welfare of his country and the glory of his gods. Think how brave and earnest the man must have been who, at the bidding of a voice or a vision, dared in his old age, unaccompanied save by his only child, to lay down his state and travel almost without food through hundreds of leagues of bush and desert, that none of his race had crossed for generations. Think what it must have been to him who for many years has been treated almost as divine, to play the part of a medicine-man in the forests of Yucatan, and to suffer, in his own person and in that of his daughter, insults and torment at the hands of low white thieves. Yet all this and more Zibalbay has borne without a murmur because, as he believes, the object of his mission is attained."

"But, Ignatio, what is the object of his mission, and what have we to do with it? To this hour I do not quite know."

"The object of his mission, and indeed of his life, is to build up the fallen empire of the City of the Heart. In short, señor, though I do not believe in his gods, in Zibalbay's visions I do believe, seeing that they have led him to me, whose aim is his aim, and that neither of us can succeed without the other."

"Why not?"

"Because I need wealth and he needs men; and if he will give me the wealth, I can give him men in thousands."

"I hear," answered the señor. "It sounds simple enough, but perhaps you will both of you find that there are difficulties in the way. What I do not understand, however, is what part Maya and I are to play in this affair, who are not anxious to regenerate a race or to build up an empire. I suppose that we are only spectators of the game."

"How can that be, señor, when she is Lady of the Heart and heiress to her father, and when," I added, dropping my voice, "you and she have grown so dear to one another?"

"I did not know that you had noticed anything of that, Ignatio. You never seemed to observe our affection, and, as you hate women so much, I did not speak of it," he answered, coloring.

"I am not altogether blind, señor. Also, is it possible for a man not to know when a woman comes between him and the friend he loves? But of that I will say nothing, for it is as it should be; besides, you might scarcely understand me if I did. No, no, señor, you cannot be left out of this game, you are too deep in it already, though what part you will play I cannot tell. It depends, perhaps, upon what the gods reveal to Zibalbay, or what he guesses that they reveal. At present he is well disposed towards you because he thinks that the oracle may declare you to be the son of Quetzal through whom his people shall be redeemed, since it seems that here there is some such prophecy, and for this reason it is that he has not forbidden the friendship between you and his daughter, or so he hinted to me. But be warned, señor; for if he comes to know that you are not the man, then he will sweep you aside as of small account, and you may bid farewell to the Lady of the Heart."

"I will not do that while I live," he answered quietly.

"No, señor, perhaps not while you live, but those who stand in the path of priests and kings do not live long. Still, though there is cause to be cautious, there is no cause to be down-hearted, seeing that if you are not the man, I may be, in which case I shall be able to help you, as I have sworn to the Lady Maya that I will do, or perhaps you will be able to help me."

"At any rate, we will stand together," said the señor. "And now, as there is no use in talking of the future, I think that we had better go to sleep. Of one thing, however, you may be certain — unless she dies, or I die, I mean to marry Maya."

Chapter XIV

THE CITY OF THE HEART

*W*hile it was yet dark on the following morning we were awakened by the voice of Zibalbay calling us.

"Arise," he said; "it is time to start upon our road."

"Are the litters here?" I asked.

"No, nor can be for some hours. I desire to reach the city this night, therefore we must push forward on foot to meet them."

Then we rose, and, having no choice, dressed ourselves as best we could in the garments of the country that had been given to us, for our own were but rags, in which we were ashamed to be seen. In the common room we found Zibalbay and the Lady Maya.

"Eat," said the old man, pointing to food that was ready, "and let us be going."

Ten minutes later we were outside the house. There was no wind, but at this great height the air is of so piercing a quality that we were glad to fold our *serapes* round us and walk briskly forward, Zibalbay leading the way. At first a grey gloom reigned, but presently snowy peaks shone through it, everywhere radiant with the hues of the unrisen sun, although the mountain sides beneath us were still wrapped in night. By degrees, as the light grew, we saw that the country at our feet was shaped like a bowl, whereof the mountain range upon which we stood formed the rim, and at the bottom of the bowl, fed by numberless streams that had their sources among the surrounding snows, lay the lake, the Holy Waters of this people. Of all this, however, we could as yet see little, since the vast expanse beneath us lay hidden in volumes of mist that moved and rolled like the face of ocean. Never before had we looked upon anything so strange as this dense garment of vapor while the light of heaven gathered upon its surface, tingeing it with lines and patches of color. It seemed as though a map of the world was unrolled before us — continents, seas, islands, and cities formed themselves, only to disappear in quick succession, and assume new and endless shapes.

"It is beautiful, is it not?" said Maya. "But wait until the mist breaks. Look, it is beginning!"

As she spoke, of a sudden the sea of mist grew thin and opened in its center, and through the gap thus formed showed first the pyramids and temple tops, and then the entire panorama of the city Heart of the World, floating, as it were, upon the face of the Holy Waters. It was far away, but, now that the night fog no longer thickened the air, so clear was the atmosphere and so high were we above it, that it seemed to be almost at our feet. The city, which appeared to be surrounded by a wall, was built of marble or some other snow-white stone, whereon the light gleamed and flashed. It stood upon a heart-shaped island, and round about the shores of this island, stretching further than the eye could reach, sparkled the blue waters of the Holy Lake. By degrees the ring of mist rolled up the sides of the mountains and vanished, and in place of it the round bowl of the valley was filled with the clear light of day. Now we could see the shores of the lake, with their green fringe of reeds; and above them grass lands threaded by silver streams; and above these again, upon the flanks of the mountains, great forests of oak and cedars rising almost to the snow line. To the right and left of us the huge, round-shouldered mountains stretched in a majestic sweep till they melted into the blue of the horizon, while here and there some tall, snow-robed peak, the cone of an extinct volcano, towered above us like a sentinel.

"There lies my country," said Maya, with a proud wave of her hand; "does it please you, white man?"

"It pleases me so well, Maya," he answered, "that now less than ever can I understand why you wish to leave it."

"Because, though lakes and mountains and cities full of wealth are fine things, it is not to these, but to the men and women among whom we live, that we must look for happiness."

"Some people might think otherwise, Maya. They might say that happiness must be sought for in ourselves. At least I could be happy in such a land as this."

"You think so now," she answered, meaningly, "but when you have been awhile in the city yonder, you will think otherwise. Oh!" she went on, passionately, "if, indeed, you care for me, we should never have crossed that mountain behind us. But you do not care for me — not truly; for all this time you have been half ashamed of your affection for an Indian girl whom you were obliged to become fond of, because she was pretty and you were so much with her, and she chanced to save your life. Yes, you would have been ashamed to marry me according to your customs, and to show me as your wife among the white people — me, the wandering Indian with a mad father whom you found in the hands of thieves. Here it will be different, for here at least I am a great lady, and you will see the people in the streets bow themselves to the ground before me; and if I say that a man shall die, you will see that man killed. Also here I have wealth more than any white woman, and you will be fond of me for that —"

"You are very unjust," he broke in, angrily; "it is shameful that you should speak to me thus for no cause."

"Perhaps I am unjust," she answered with a sob, "but there are so many troubles before us. First there is Tikal —"

"What does Tikal want?" asked the señor.

"He wants to marry me, or to become *cacique* of the city in my right, which is the same thing; at least he will not give me up without a struggle. Then there is my father, who serves two masters only — his gods and his country — and who will use me like a piece in a game if it suits his purpose — yes, and you too. Our good days are done with, the evil ones have to come, and after them — the night. Henceforward we shall find few opportunities of speaking, even, for I shall be surrounded by officers and waiting-ladies who will watch my every action and hear my every word, and my father will watch me also."

"Now I begin to be sorry that I did not take your advice and stop on the further side of the mountain," answered the señor. "Do you think that we could escape there?"

"No, it is too late — they would track us down; we must go on now and meet our fate, whatever it may be. Only swear to me by my gods, or your own, or whatever you hold dear, that you will cleave to me till I am dead, as I will cleave to you." And, taking his hand in hers, she looked up appealingly into his face.

At this moment Zibalbay, who was walking in front, lost in his own thoughts, chanced to turn and see them.

"Come hither, daughter, and you, White Man," he said, in a stern voice. "Listen, both of you — I am old, but my sight and hearing are still keen, though yonder in the wilderness I took no heed of much that I saw and heard. Here in my own land it is otherwise. Learn, White Man, that the Lady of the Heart is set far above you, and there I think she will remain. Do you understand my meaning?"

"Perfectly," answered the señor, striving to control his anger; "but, Chief, it is a pity that you did not see well to tell me this before. Had it not been for what we and one dead were able to do to save you, today your bones would have been whitening in the forest. Why did you not tell me there that I was no fit company for your daughter?"

"Because you were sent by the gods to do me service, and because there I had need of you, White Man," answered Zibalbay quietly, "as may be I shall have need of you again. Had it not been for that chance, we should have parted company on the further side of the mountain."

"In truth I wish that we had!" exclaimed the señor.

"I may come to wish it, too," said the old man grimly. "But you are here and not there, perhaps for so long as you shall live, and I would have you remember that you are in my power. A word from me will set you high or lay you low beneath the earth; therefore be warned and take with gratitude that which it shall please me to give you. No, do not look behind you — escape is impossible. Submit yourself to my will in this and everything, and all shall be well with you; struggle against it and I will crush you. I have spoken: be pleased to walk in front of me, and do you, my daughter, walk behind."

Now I saw that the señor's rage was great, and that he was about to answer angrily, and lifted my hand in warning, while Maya looked at him entreatingly. He saw, and checked himself.

"I hear your words, Chief," he said, in a forced voice. "You are right, I am in your power, and it is useless for me to answer you," and he took his place in front as he had been commanded, while Maya fell behind.

As I walked on, side by side with Zibalbay, I spoke to him, saying:

"You use sharp words towards him who is my brother, Chief, and therefore towards me."

"I speak as I must," he answered, coldly. "Many troubles await me at the city. Did you not hear what that knave said last night — that Tikal, my nephew, whom I left in charge, rules in my stead? Well, this girl of mine, who is affianced to him, and through whom he hopes to govern in after years, may be the only bait that will tempt him from his place, for he looks upon me as one dead, and it will not please him to lay down the rod of power. How should it please him then, and those who follow him, to see a white stranger holding that daughter's hand, and whispering in her ear. Ignatio, I tell you that such a sight would provoke a war against me, and therefore it is that I spoke sharply while there is yet time, and therefore you will do well to drive the nail home, seeing that if I fall your plans will come to nothing, and your life be forfeit."

I made no answer, for at that moment we turned a corner, and came face to face with the bearers of the litters whom Zibalbay had summoned to meet us.

There were forty of these men or more; for the most part they were tall and well shaped, with regular features, and, like Zibalbay and Maya, very fair for Indians, but the look upon their faces was different from any that I have seen among my people. It was not stupid or brutal, or even empty; rather did it suggest great weariness. The youngest man there, notwithstanding his rounded cheeks and eyes full of health, seemed as though he were weighed down by the memories of many years. Weariness was the master, not of their bodies, for they were very strong and active, but of their minds; and, looking at them, I could understand what Zibalbay meant when he said that his race was out-worn. Even the sight of the white face of the señor, strange as it must have been to them, did not seem to move them. They stared indeed, muttering something to each other as to the length and color of his beard, and that was all.

But to Zibalbay they said, in low, guttural tones, "Father, we salute you," then, at a signal given by their captain, they cast themselves on the ground before him, and lay there with outstretched arms as though they were dead.

"Rise, my children," said Zibalbay. Then, summoning the captain of the bearers, he talked to him while his companions ate food that they had brought with them, and I noted that what he heard seemed to give him little pleasure. Next he ordered us to enter the litters, which were of rude make, being constructed of chairs without curtains, lashed between two poles, and carried, each of them, by eight bearers, for the road was very steep and rough.

We started forward down the mountain, and in an hour we had left the region of snow behind, and entered the cedar forests. These great trees grew in groups, which were separated by glades of turf, the home of herds of deer. So thick was their foliage that a twilight reigned beneath them, while from each branch hung a fringe of grey Spanish moss that swayed to and fro in the draft of the mountain breeze. Everywhere stretched vistas that brought to my mind memories of the dimly-lighted nave of the great cathedral at Mexico, roofed by the impenetrable boughs of these cedars, whereof the trunks might have been supporting columns and the scent of their leaves the odor of incense.

After the cedar belt came the oak groves, and then miles of beautiful turf slopes, clothed in rich grass starred with flowers. Truly it was a lovely land. It was late in the afternoon before we descended the last of these slopes and entered the tract of alluvial soil that lay between them and the lake, where the climate was much warmer. It was easy to see by the irrigation ditches and other signs that this belt of country had always supplied the inhabitants of the City of the Heart with corn and all necessary crops. Here grew great groves of sugar-cane, and cocoa-bushes laden with their purple pods, together with many varieties of fruit trees planted in separate orchards. Soon it became clear to us that the greater part of these ancient orchards were untended, since their fruit rotted in heaps upon the ground. Evidently they had been planted in more prosperous days, and now their supply exceeded the wants of the population.

At length, as the evening began to fall, we entered the village of corn-growers, a half-ruined place of which the houses were for the most part built of *adobe* or mud bricks, and roofed with a concrete of white lime. In the center of the village was a *plaza*, planted round with trees, and having in its midst a fountain, near to which stood a simple altar, piled with fruit and flowers. Close to this altar the inhabitants of the village, to the number of a hundred or so, were gathered to meet us. Most of the men had but just come in from their labors, for their garments and feet were stained with fresh earth, and they held copper hoes and reaping-hooks in their hands. All these men wore upon their faces the same look of weariness of mind which we had noticed in the bearers. So monotonous were their countenances, indeed, that I turned my eyes impatiently to the group of women who were standing behind them. Like their husbands and brothers, these women were very fair for Indians, and handsome in person, but they also had been stamped with melancholy. The sight of the señor's white skin and chestnut-colored beard seemed for some few moments to rouse them from their attitude of listless indifference. Soon, however, they fell into it again, and began to chat idly, or to play with and pull to pieces the flowers that every one of them wore at her girdle. There were hardly any children among the crowd, and it was strange to observe how great was the resemblance of the individuals composing it to each other. Indeed, had they all been members of a single family it would not have been more marked, seeing that it was difficult for a stranger to distinguish one woman from another of about the same age.

When Zibalbay descended from his litter, all those present prostrated themselves, and remained thus till, followed by some of the headmen, he had passed into a house which was made ready for his use, leaving us without.

"Do all your people look so sad?" I asked the Lady Maya.

"Yes," she answered, "that is, all the common people who labor. It is otherwise with the nobles, who are of a different blood. Here, Don Ignatio, there are two classes, the lords and the people, and of the people each family is forced to work for three months in the year, the other nine being given to them for rest. The fruits of their labor are gathered into storehouses and distributed among all the Children of the Heart, but the temples, the *cacique*, and many of the nobles have their own serfs who have served them from father to son."

"And what happens if they will not work?" asked the señor.

"Then they must starve, for nothing is served out to them or their families from the common store, and when they grow hungry they are set to the heaviest tasks."

Now we understood why these people looked so weary and listless. What could be expected from men and women without ambition or responsibility, the gain of whose toil was placed to the public credit and doled out to them in rations? In my old age I have heard that there are teachers who advocate such a system for all mankind, but of this I am sure, that had they dwelt among the People of the Heart, where it had been in force for many centuries, they would cease to preach this doctrine, for there, at least, it did not promote the welfare of the race.

Presently a messenger came from Zibalbay to summon us into the house, where we found an ample meal prepared, consisting chiefly of fish from the lake, baked wild-fowl, and many sorts of fruit. By the time we had finished eating and had drunk the chocolate that was served to us in cups of hammered silver, the night had fallen completely. I asked Zibalbay if we should sleep there, to which he replied shortly that we were about to start for the city. Accordingly we set out by the light of the moon and were guided to a little harbor in the shore of the lake, where a large canoe, fitted with a mast and sail, and manned by ten Indians, was waiting for us. We embarked, and, the wind being off land, hoisted the sail and started towards the Island of the Heart, which stood at a distance of about fifteen miles from the mainland.

The breeze was light, but after the cold of the mountains the air was so soft and balmy, and the scene so new and strange, that I, for one, did not regret our slow progress. Nobody spoke in the boat, for all of us were lost in our own reflections, and the Indians were awed to silence by the presence of their lord, who alone seemed impatient, since from time to time he pulled his beard and muttered to himself. So we glided across the blue lake, whose quiet was broken only by the whistling wings of the wild-fowl traveling to their feeding grounds, by the sudden leaps of great fish rising in pursuit of some night-fly, and by the lapping of the water against the wooden sides of the canoe. Before us, luminous and unearthly in the perfect moonlight, shone the walls and temples of the mysterious city which we had traveled so far to reach. We watched them growing more and more distinct minute by minute, and, as we watched, strange hopes and fears took possession of our hearts. This was no dream: before us lay the fabled golden town we had so longed to see; soon our feet would pass its white walls and our eyes behold its ancient civilization.

"What waits us there?" whispered the señor, and he looked at Maya. She heard his words and shook her head sadly. There was no hope in her eyes, which were dimmed with tears. Then he turned to me as though for comfort, and the easy fires of enthusiasm burned up within me and I answered:

"Fear not, the goal is won, and we shall overcome all difficulty and danger. The useless wealth of yonder Golden City will be ours, and by its help I shall wreak the stored-up vengeance of ages upon the oppressors of my race, and create a great Indian Dominion stretching from sea to sea, whereof this city shall be the heart."

He heard and smiled, answering:

"It may be so; for your sake, I trust that it will be so; but we seek different ends, Ignatio," and he looked again at the Lady Maya.

On we glided, through the moonlight and the silence, for from the town came no sound, save the cry of the watchmen, calling the hours, as they kept their guard along the ancient walls, till at length we entered the shadow of the Holy City lying dark upon the waters, and the Indians, getting out their paddles (for the wind no longer served us), rowed the canoe up a stone-embanked canal that led to a watergate.

Now we halted in front of the gate, where there was no man to be seen. In an impatient voice, Zibalbay bade the captain hail the guardian of the gate, and presently a man came down the steps yawning, and inquired who was there.

"I, the *cacique*," said Zibalbay. "Open."

"Indeed! That is strange," answered the man, "seeing that this night the *cacique* holds his marriage-feast at the palace yonder, and there is but one *cacique* of the People of the Heart! Get back to the mainland, wanderers, and return in the day-time, when the gates stand wide."

Now when Zibalbay heard these words, he cursed aloud in his anger, but Maya started as though with joy.

"I tell you that I am Zibalbay, come home again, your lord, and no other," he cried, "and you will be wise to do my bidding."

The man stared, and hesitated, till the captain of the boat spoke to him, saying:

"Fool, would you become food for fishes? This is the Lord Zibalbay, returned from the dead."

Then he hastened to open the gate, as fast as his fear would let him.

"Pardon, father, pardon," he cried, prostrating himself, "but the Lord Tikal, who rules in your place, has given it out that you were dead in the wilderness, and commanded that your name should be spoken no more in the city."

Zibalbay swept by him without a word. When he had passed up the marble steps, and through the water-way, pierced in the thickness of the frowning walls, he halted, and, addressing the captain of the boatmen, said:

"Let that man be scourged tomorrow at noon in the marketplace, that henceforth he may learn not to sleep at his post!"

On the further side of the wall ran a wide street, bordered by splendid homes built of white stone, which led to the central square of the city, a mile or more away. Up this street we walked swiftly and in silence, and as we went I noticed that much of it was grass-grown, and that many of the great houses seemed to be deserted; indeed, though light came from some of the latticed window-places, I could see no sign of any human being.

"Here is the city," whispered the señor to me, "but where are the people?"

"Doubtless they celebrate the wedding-feast in the great square," I answered. "Hark, I hear them."

As I spoke the wind turned a little, and a sound of singing floated down it, that grew momentarily clearer as we approached the square. Another five minutes passed and we were entering it. It was a wide place, covering not less than thirty acres of ground, and in its center, rising three hundred feet into the air, gleamed the pyramid of the Temple of the Heart, crowned by the star of holy fire that flickered eternally upon its summit. In the open space between the walls of the enclosure of this pyramid and the great buildings that formed the sides of the square, the inhabitants of the city were gathered for their midnight feast. All were dressed in white robes, while many wore glittering feather capes upon their shoulders and were crowned with wreaths of flowers. Some of them were dancing, some of them were singing, while others watched the tricks of jugglers and buffoons. But the most of their number were seated round little tables eating, drinking, smoking, and making love, and we noticed that at these tables the children seemed the most honorable guests, and that everybody petted them and waited on their words.

Nothing could be more beautiful or stranger to our eyes than this innocent festival celebrated beneath the open sky and lighted by the moon. Yet the sight of it did not please Zibalbay.

Along the side of the square ran an avenue of trees bearing white flowers with a heavy scent, and Zibalbay motioned to us to follow him into their shadow. Many of the tables were placed just beyond the spread of these trees, so that he was able to stop from time to time and, unseen himself, to listen to the talk that was passing at them. Presently he halted thus opposite to a table at which sat a man of middle age and a woman young and pretty. What they said interested him, and we who were close by his side understood it, for the difference between the dialect of these people and the Maya tongue is so small that even the señor had little difficulty in following their talk.

"The feast is merry tonight," said the man.

"Yes, husband," answered his companion, "and so it should be, seeing that yesterday the Lord Tikal was elected *cacique* by the Council of the Heart, and today he was wedded in the presence of the people to Nahua the Beautiful, child of the Lord Mattai."

"It was a fine sight," said the man, "though for my part I think it early to proclaim him *cacique*. Zibalbay might yet come back, and then —"

"Zibalbay will never come back, husband, or the Lady Maya either. They have perished in the wilderness long ago. For her I am sorry, because she was so lovely and different from other great ladies; but I do not grieve much for him, for he was a hard taskmaster to us common people; also he was stingy. Why, Tikal has given more feasts during the last ten months than Zibalbay gave in as many years; moreover, he has relaxed the laws so that we poor women may now wear ornaments like our betters;" and she glanced at a gold bracelet upon her wrist.

"It is easy to be generous with the goods of others," answered the man. "Zibalbay was the bee who stored; Tikal is the wasp who eats. They say that the old fellow was mad, but I do not believe it. I think that he was a greater man than the rest of us, that is all, who saw the wasting of the people and desired to find a means to stop it."

"Certainly he was mad," answered the woman. "How could he stop the wasting of the people by taking his daughter to wander in the wilderness till they died of starvation, both of them. If anybody dwells out yonder it is a folk of white devils of whom we have heard, who kill and enslave the Indians, that they may rob them of their wealth, and we do not desire that such should be shown the way to our city. Also, what does it matter to us if the people do waste away? We have all things that we wish, those who come after must see to it."

"Yet, wife, I have heard you say that you desired children."

Suddenly the woman's face grew sad.

"Ah!" she answered, "if Zibalbay will give me a child I will take back all my words about him, and proclaim him the wisest of men, instead of what he is, or rather was — an old fool gone crazy with vanity and too much praying. But he is dead, and if he were not he could never do this; that is beyond the power of the gods themselves, if indeed the gods are anything but a dream. So what is the use of talking about him; let me enjoy the feast that Tikal gives us, husband, and do not speak of children, lest I should weep, and learn to hate those of my sisters who have been blest with them."

Then at a sign from Zibalbay we moved on, but Maya, hanging back for a moment, whispered:

"Look at my father's face. Never have I seen him so angry. Yet these tidings are not altogether ill," and she glanced at the señor.

Now Zibalbay walked on swiftly, pulling at his beard and muttering to himself, till we came to a great archway where two soldiers armed with copper spears stood on guard, chatting with women in the crowd that gathered round the open door, and eating sweetmeats which they offered them. Zibalbay covered his face with the corner of his robe, and, bidding us do likewise, began to walk through the archway, whereupon the two soldiers, crossing their spears, demanded his name and title.

"By whose orders do you ask?" said Zibalbay.

"By order of our lord, the *cacique*, who celebrates his marriage-feast with the nobles his guests," answered one of them. "Say, are you of their number who come so late?"

Then Zibalbay uncovered his face and said:

"Look at me, man. Did I command you to shut my own doors against me?"

He looked and gasped: "It is the *cacique* come home again!"

"How, then, do you say that you keep the doors by order of the *cacique*? Can there be two *caciques* in the City of the Heart?" asked Zibalbay in a bitter voice, and, without waiting for an answer, he walked on, followed by the three of us, into the *plaza* or courtyard of the palace, where many fountains splashed upon the marble pavement.

Passing beneath a colonnade and through an open doorway whence light flowed, of a sudden we found ourselves in a great and wonderful chamber, a hundred feet or more in length, having a roof of paneled cedar, supported by a double row of wooden columns exquisitely carved, between which were set tables laden with fruit and flowers, drinking-vessels, and other ornaments of gold. The walls also were cedar-paneled, and hung over with tapestries worked in silver, and ranged along them stood grotesque images of dwarfs and monkeys, fashioned in solid gold, each of which held in its hand a silver lamp. At the far end of this place was a small table, and behind it, seated upon thronelike chairs, were a man and a woman, having an armed guard on either side of them.

The man was magnificently dressed in a white robe, broidered with the symbol of the Heart, and a glittering feather cloak. Upon his brow was a circlet of gold, from which rose a *panache,* or plume, of green feathers, and in his hand he held a little golden scepter tipped with an emerald. He was of middle height, very stoutly built, and about five-and-thirty years of age, having straight black hair that hung down upon his shoulders. In face he was handsome, but forbidding, for his dark eyes shone with a strange fire beneath the beetling brows, and his powerful mouth and chin wore a sullen look that did not leave them even when he smiled. The lady at his side was also beautifully attired in white bridal robes, broidered with silver, and having the royal Heart worked upon her breast, while on her brow, arms, and bosom shone strings of emeralds. She was young and tall, with splendid eyes and a proud, handsome face, somewhat marred, however, by the heaviness of the mouth, and it was easy to see that she loved the husband at her side, for all her looks were towards him.

Between us and this royal pair stretched the length of the great hall, filled with people – for the most of the feasters had left their seats – so splendidly attired and so bright with the flash of gems and gold that for a few moments our eyes were dazzled. The company, who may have numbered two or three hundred, stood in groups with their backs towards us, leaving a clear space at the far end of the chamber, where beautiful women, in filmy, silken robes adorned with flowers and turquoises, were singing and dancing to the sound of pipes before the bride and bridegroom on the throne.

Chapter XV

HOW ZIBALBAY CAME HOME

*F*or a while we stood unnoticed in the shadow of the doorway, observing this strange and beautiful scene, till, as Zibalbay was about to advance towards the throne, the Lord Tikal held up his scepter as a signal, and suddenly the women ceased from their dance and song. At the sight of the uplifted scepter, Zibalbay halted again and drew back further into the shadow, motioning us to do likewise. Then Tikal began to speak in a rich, deep voice that filled the hall:

"Councilors and Nobles of the Heart," he said, "and you, highborn ladies, wives and daughters of the nobles, hear me. But yesterday, as you know, I took upon myself the place and power of my forefathers, and by your wish and will I was proclaimed the sole chief and ruler of the People of the Heart. Now I have bidden you to my marriage feast, that you may grace my nuptials and share my joy. For be it known to you that tonight I have taken in marriage Nahua the Beautiful, daughter of the High Lord Mattai, Chief of the Astronomers, Keeper of the Sanctuary, and President of the Council of the Heart. Her, in the presence of you all, I name as my first and lawful wife, the sharer of my power, and your ruler under me, who, whate'er betide, cannot be put away from my bed and throne, and as such I call upon you to salute her."

Then, ceasing from his address, he turned and kissed the woman at his side, saying:

"Hail! to you, Lady of the Heart, whom it has pleased the gods to lift up and bless. May children be given to you, and with them happiness and power for many years."

Thereon the whole company bowed themselves before Nahua, whose fair face flushed with pride and joy, and repeated, as with one voice:

"Hail! to you, Lady of the Heart, whom it has pleased the gods to lift up and bless. May children be given to you, and with them happiness and power for many years."

"Nobles," went on Tikal, when this ceremony was finished, "it has come to my ears that there are some who murmur against me, saying that I have no right to the ancient scepter of *cacique* which I hold in my hand this night. Nobles, I have somewhat to say to you of this matter, that tomorrow, after the sacrifice, I shall repeat in the ears of the common people, and I say it having consulted with my Council, the masters of the mysteries of the Heart. Tomorrow a year will have gone by since Zibalbay, my uncle, who was *cacique* before me, and his only child and heiress of his rank and power, the Lady Maya, my affianced bride, left the city upon a certain mission. Before they departed upon this mission, it was agreed between Zibalbay, Maya, the Lady of the Heart, myself, and the Council, the Brotherhood of the Heart, that I should rule as next heir during the absence of Zibalbay and his daughter, and that if they should not return within two years, then their heritage should be mine forever. To this agreement I set my name with sorrow, for then, as now, I held that my uncle was mad, and in his madness went to doom, taking with him his daughter whom I loved. Yet when they were gone I fulfilled it to the letter; but trouble arose among the people, for they will not listen to the voice of one who is not their anointed lord, but say, 'We will wait until Zibalbay comes again and hear his command upon these matters.'

"Also, Zibalbay being absent, there was no high priest left in the land, so that until a successor was raised up to him, certain of the inmost mysteries of our worship must go uncelebrated, thus bringing down upon us the anger of the Nameless god. So it came about that many pressed it on me that for the sake of the people and the welfare of the city, I should shorten the period of my regency and suffer myself to be anointed. But, remembering my promise, I answered them sharply, saying that I would not depart from it by a hair's breadth, and that, come what might, two full years must be completed before I sat me down in the place of my fathers.

"To this mind, then, I held till three days since, when those of the people to whose lot it fell in turn to pass to the mainland, there to cultivate the fields that are apportioned to the service of the temple, refused to get them to their labor, declaring that the high priest alone had authority over them, and there was no high priest in the city. Then in my perplexity I took counsel with the Lord Mattai, Master of the Stars, and he consulted the stars on my behalf. All night long he searched the heavens, and he read in them that Zibalbay, who, led by a lying dream, broke the laws of the land and wandered across the mountains, has paid the price of his folly, and is dead in the wilderness, together with his daughter that was my affianced and the Lady of the Heart. Is it not so, Mattai?"

Now the person addressed, a stout man with a bald head, quick, shifting eyes, and a thick and grizzled beard, stepped forward and said, bowing,

"If my wisdom is not at fault, such was the message of the stars, O lord."

"Nobles," went on Tikal, "you have heard my testimony and the testimony of Mattai, whose voice is the voice of truth. For these reasons I have suffered myself to be anointed and set over you as your ruler, seeing that I am the heir of Zibalbay by law and by descent. For these reasons also — she to whom I was affianced being dead — I have taken to wife Nahua the daughter of Mattai. Say, do you accept us?"

Some few of the company were silent, but the rest cried:

"We accept you, Tikal and Nahua, and long may you rule over us according to the ancient customs of the land."

"It is well, my brethren," answered Tikal. "Now, before we drink the parting-cup, have any of you ought to say to me?"

"I have something to say to you," cried Zibalbay in a loud voice from the shadows wherein we stood at the far end of the hall.

At the sound of his voice, the tones of which he seemed to know, Tikal started and rose in fear, but, recovering himself, said:

"Advance from the shadow, whoever you are, and say your say where men may see you."

Turning to his daughter and to us, Zibalbay bade us follow him, and do as he did. Then, veiling his face with a corner of his robe, he walked up the hall, the crowd of nobles and ladies opening a path till we stood before the throne. Here he uncovered himself, as we did also, and standing sideways, so that he could be seen both by Tikal and all that company, he opened his lips to speak. Before a word could pass them a cry of astonishment broke from the nobles, and of a sudden the scepter fell from the hand of Tikal and rolled along the floor.

"Zibalbay!" said the cry. "It is Zibalbay come back, or the ghost of him, and with him the Lady of the Heart!"

"Aye, nobles," he said, in a quiet voice, although his hand shook with rage, "it is I, Zibalbay, your lord, come home, and not too soon, as it would seem. What, my nephew, were you so hungry for my place and power, that you must break the oath you swore upon the Heart, and seize them before the appointed time? And you, Mattai, have you lost your skill, or have the gods smitten you with a curse, that you prophesy falsely, saying that it was written in the stars that we who are alive were dead, thereby lifting up your daughter to the seat of the Lady of the

Heart. Nay, do not answer me. Standing yonder I have heard all your story. I say to you, Tikal, that you are a foresworn traitor, and to you, Mattai, that you are a charlatan and a liar, who have dared to use the holy art for your own ends, and the advancement of your house. On both of you will I be avenged — aye, and on all those who have abetted you in your crimes. Guards, seize that man, and the Lord Mattai with him, and let them be held fast till I shall judge them."

Now the soldiers that stood on either side of the thrones hesitated for a moment, and then advanced towards Tikal as though to lay hands upon him in obedience to Zibalbay's order. But Nahua rose and waved them off, saying:

"What! dare you to touch your anointed lord? Back, I say to you, if you would save yourselves from the doom of sacrilege. Living or dead, the day of Zibalbay is done, for the Council of the Heart has set his crown upon the brow of Tikal, and, whether for good or ill, their decree cannot be changed."

"Aye!" said Tikal, whose courage had come back to him. "The Lady Nahua speaks truth. Touch me not if you would live to look upon the sun."

But all the while he spoke his eyes were fixed upon Maya, whose beautiful face he watched as though it were that of some lost love risen from the dead.

Now, as Zibalbay was about to speak again, Mattai the astronomer bowed before him and said:

"Be not angry, but hear me, my lord. You have traveled far, and you are weary, and a weary man is apt at wrath. You think that you have been wronged, and, doubtless, all this that has chanced is strange to you, but now is not the time for us to give count of our acts and stewardship, or for you to hearken. Rest this night; and tomorrow on the pyramid, in the presence of the people, all things shall be made clear to you, and justice be done to all. Welcome to you, Zibalbay, and to you also, Daughter of the Heart — and say, who are these strangers that you bring with you from the desert lands across the mountains?"

Zibalbay paused awhile, looking round him out of the corners of his eyes, like a wolf in a trap, for he sought to discover the temper of the nobles. Then, finding that there were but few present whom he could trust to help him, he lifted his head and answered:

"You are right, Mattai, I am weary; for age, travel, and the faithlessness of men have worn me out. Tomorrow these matters shall be dealt with in the presence of the people, and there, before the altar, it shall be made known whether I am their lord, or you, Tikal. There, too, I will tell you who these strangers are, and why I have brought them across the mountains. Until then I leave them in your keeping, for your own sake charging you to keep them well. Nay, here I will neither eat nor drink. Do you come with me," and he called to certain lords by name whom he knew to be faithful to him.

Then, without more words, he turned and left the hall, followed by a number of the nobles.

"It seems that my father has forgotten me," said Maya, with a laugh, when he had gone. "Greeting to you all, friends, and to you, my cousin Tikal, and greeting also to your wife, Nahua, who, once my waiting-lady, by the gift of fortune has now been lifted up to take my place and title. Whatever may be the issue of these broils, may you be happy in each other's love, Tikal and Nahua."

Now Tikal descended from the throne and bowed before her, saying, "I swear to you, Maya —"

"No, do not swear," she broke in, "but give me and my friends here a cup of wine and some fragments from your wedding-feast, for we are hungry. I thank you. How beautiful is that bride's robe which Nahua wears, and — surely — those emeralds were once my own. Well, let her take them from me as a wedding-gift. Make room, I pray you, Tikal, and suffer these ladies to tell me of their tidings, for remember that I have wandered far, and it is pleasant to see faces that are dear to me."

For a while we sat and ate, or made pretence to eat, while Maya talked thus lightly and all that company watched us, for we were wonderful in their eyes, who never till now had seen a white man. Indeed, the sight of the señor, auburn-haired, long-bearded, and white-skinned, was so marvelous to them, that, unlike the common people, they forgot their courtesy and crowded round him in their amazement. Still, there were two who took small note of the señor or of me, and these were Tikal, who gazed at Maya as he stood behind her chair serving her like some waiting slave, and Nahua his wife, who sat silent and neglected on her throne, sullenly noting his every word and gesture. At length she could bear this play no longer, but, rising from her seat, began to move down the chamber.

"Make room for the bride, ladies," said Maya. "Cousin, good-night, it grows late, and your wife awaits you."

Then, muttering I know not what, Tikal turned and went, and side by side the pair walked down the great hall, followed by their guard of soldiers.

"How beautiful is the bride, and how brave the groom!" said Maya, as she watched them go, "and yet I have seen couples that looked happier on their wedding-day. Well, it is time to rest. Friends, good-night. Mattai, I leave these strangers in your keeping. Guard them well — and, stay, bring them to my apartments tomorrow after they have eaten, for if it is my father's will, I would show them something of the city before the hour of noon, when we meet upon the temple-top."

When she had gone, Mattai bowed to us with much ceremony, and begged us to follow him, which we did, across the courtyard and through many passages, to a beautiful chamber, dimly lighted with silver lamps, that had been made ready for us. Here were beds covered with silken wrappings, and on a table in the center of the room cool drinks and many sorts of fruits, but so tired were we that we took little note of these things.

Bidding good-night to Mattai, who looked at us curiously and announced that he would visit us early in the morning, we made fast the copper bolts upon the door and threw ourselves upon the beds.

Weary as I was, I could not sleep in this strange place, and when, from time to time, my eyes closed, the sound of feet passing without our chamber door roused me again to wakefulness. Of one thing I was sure, that Zibalbay was not wanted here in his own city, and that there would be trouble on the morrow when he told his tale to the people, for certainly Tikal would not suffer himself easily to be thrust from the place he had usurped, and he had many friends. Doubtless it was their feet that I heard outside the door as they hurried to and fro from the chamber where Mattai sat taking counsel with them. What would be our fate, I wondered, in this struggle for power that must come? These people feared strangers — so much I could read in their faces — and doubtless they would be rid of us if they might. Well, we had a good friend in Maya, and the rest we must leave to Providence.

Thinking thus, at length I fell asleep, to be awakened by the voice of the señor, who was sitting upon the edge of his bed, singing a song and looking round the chamber, for now the daylight streamed through the lattice. I wished him good-morrow, and asked him why he sang.

"Because of the lightness of my heart," he answered. "We have reached the city at last, and it is far more splendid and wonderful than anything I dreamed of. Also the luck is with us, for this Tikal has taken another woman in marriage, who, to judge from the look of her, will not readily let him go, and therefore Maya has no more to fear from him. Thirdly, there is enough treasure in this town, if what we saw last night may be taken as a sample, to enable you to establish three Indian Empires, if you wish, and doubtless Zibalbay will give you as much of it as you may want. Therefore, friend Ignatio, you should sing, as I do, instead of looking as gloomy as though you saw your own coffin being brought in at the door."

I shook my head, and answered:

"I fear you speak lightly. There is trouble brewing in this city, and we shall be drawn into it, for the struggle between Tikal and Zibalbay will be to the death. As for the Lady Maya, of this I am certain, that — wife or no wife — Tikal still loves her and will strive to take her; I saw it in his eyes last night. Lastly, it is true enough that here there is boundless wealth; but whether its owners will suffer me to have any portion of it, to forward my great purposes — useless though it be to them — is another matter."

"There was a man in the Bible called Job, and he had a friend named Eliphaz — I think you are that friend come to life again, Ignatio," answered the señor, laughing. "For my part, I mean to make the best of the present, and not to trouble myself about the future or the politics of this benighted people. But hark, there is someone knocking at the door."

I rose, and undid the bolt, whereon attendants entered bearing goblets of chocolate, and little cakes upon a tray. After we had eaten, they led us to the baths, which were of marble and very beautiful, one of them being filled with water from a warm spring, and then to a chamber, where breakfast was made ready for us. While we sat at table, Mattai came to us, and I saw that he had not slept that night, for his eyes were heavy.

"I trust that you have rested well, strangers," he said courteously.

"Yes, lord," I answered.

"Well, it is more than I have done, for it is my business to watch the stars, especially my own star, which just now is somewhat obscured," and he smiled. "If you have finished your meal, my commands are to lead you to the apartments of the Lady Maya, who wishes to show you something of our city, which, being strangers, may interest you. By the way, if I do not ask too much, perhaps you will tell me to what race you belong," and he bowed towards the señor. "We have heard of white men here, though we have learned no good of them, and tradition tells us that our first ruler, Cucumatz, was of this race. Are you of his blood, stranger?"

"I do not know," answered the señor, laughing. "I come from a cold country far beyond the sea, where all the men are as I am."

"Then the inhabitants of that country must be goodly to behold," answered Mattai gravely. "I thank you for your courtesy, Son of the Sea, in answering my question so readily. I did not ask it from curiosity alone, since the people in this city are terrified of strangers, and clamor for some account of you."

"Doubtless our friend Zibalbay will satisfy them," I said.

"Good. Now be pleased to follow me" — and Mattai led us across courts and through passages till we reached a little anteroom filled with ancient carvings and decorated with flowers, where some girls stood chatting.

"Tell the Lady Maya that her guests await her," said Mattai, then turned to take his departure, adding, in a low voice, "doubtless we shall meet at noon upon the pyramid, and there you will see I know not what; but, whatever befalls, be sure of this, strangers, that I will protect you if I can. Farewell."

One of the girls vanished through a doorway at the further end of the chamber, and, having offered us seats, the others stood together at a little distance, watching us out of the corners of their eyes. Presently the door opened, and through it came Maya, wearing a silken *serape* that covered her head and shoulders, and looking very sweet and beautiful in the shaded light of the room.

"Greetings, friends," she said, as we bowed before her. "I have my father's leave to show you something of this city that you longed so much to see. These ladies here will accompany us, and a guard, but we shall want no litters until we have ascended the great temple, for I desire that you should see the view from thence before the place is cumbered with the multitude. Come, if you are ready."

Accordingly we set out, Maya walking between us, while her guards and ladies followed after. Crossing the square, which had been the scene of the festival of the previous night, but now in the early morning was almost deserted, we came to the enclosure of the courtyard of the pyramid, a limestone wall worked with sculptures of hunting scenes, relieved by a border of writhing snakes, and at intervals by emblems of the Heart. At the gateway of this wall we paused to contemplate the mighty mass of the pyramid that towered above us. There is one in the land of Egypt that is bigger, so said the señor, although he believed this to be a more wonderful sight because of its glittering slopes of limestone, whose expanse was broken only by the vast stair that ran up its eastern face from base to summit.

"It is a great building," said Maya, noting our astonishment, "and one that could not be reared in these days. Tradition says that five-and-twenty thousand men worked on it for fifty years — twenty thousand of them cutting and carrying the stone, and five thousand laying the blocks."

"Where did the material come from, then?" asked the señor.

"Some of it was hewn from beneath the base of the temple itself," she answered, "but the most was borne in big canoes from quarries on the mainland, for these quarries can still be seen."

"Is the pyramid hollow, then?" I asked.

"Yes, in it are many chambers, for the most part store and treasure houses, and beneath its base lie crypts, the burying-place of the *caciques*, their wives, and children. There also is the Holy Sanctuary of the Heart, which you, being of the Brotherhood, may perhaps be permitted to visit. Come, let us climb the stair" — and she led us across the courtyard to the foot of a stairway forty feet or more in breadth, which ran to the platform of the pyramid in six flights, each of fifty steps, and linked together by resting-places.

Up these flights we toiled slowly, followed by the ladies and the guard, till at length our labor was rewarded, and we stood upon the dizzy edge of the pyramid. Before us was a platform bordered by a low wall, large enough to give standing room to several thousand people. On the western side of this platform stood a small marble house, used as a place to store fuel, and as a watchtower by the priests, who were on duty day and night, tending the sacred fire which flared in a brazier from its roof. Sitting in front of it, was a small altar wreathed with flowers, but for the rest the area was empty.

"Look," said Maya.

The city beneath us was built upon a low, heart-shaped island, so hollow in its center that once it might have been the crater of some volcano, or perhaps a mere ridge of land enclosing a lagoon. This island measured about ten miles in length by six across at its widest, and seemed to float like a huge green leaf upon the lake, the Holy Waters of these Indians, of which the circumference is so great that even from the summit of the pyramid, a few small and rocky islets excepted, land was only visible to the north, whence we had sailed on the previous night. Elsewhere the eye met nothing but blue expanses of inland sea, limitless and desolate, unrelieved by any sail or sign of life. Amidst these waters the island gleamed like an emerald. Here were gardens filled with gorgeous flowers and clumps of beautiful palms and willows, framed by banks of dense green reeds that grew in the shallows around the shores. So luxuriant was the vegetation, fertilized year by year with the rich mud of the lake, and so lovely were the trees and flowers in the soft light of the morning, that the place seemed like a paradise rather than a home of men; and as was the island, so was the city that was built upon one end of it.

Following the lines of the land upon which it stood, it was heart-shaped — a heart of cold, white marble lying within a heart of glowing green. All about it ran a moat filled with water from the lake, and on the hither side of this moat stood a wall fifty feet or more in height, built of great blocks of white limestone that formed the bed-rock of the island, which wall was everywhere sculptured with allegorical devices and designs, and the gigantic figures of gods. Within the oblong of this wall lay the city; a city of palaces, pyramids, and temples, or rather the remains of it, for we could see at a glance that the population was unable to keep so many streets and edifices in repair. Thus palm trees were to be found growing through the flat roofs of houses, and in crevices of the temple-pyramids, while many of the streets and avenues were green with grass and ferns, a narrow pathway in the center of them showing how few were the feet of the passers-by. Even in the great square beneath us the signs of traffic were rare, and there was little of the bustle of a people engaged in the business of life, although this very place had been the scene of last night's feast, and would again soon be filled with men and women flocking to the pyramid. Now and again some graceful, languid girl, a reed basket in her hand, might be seen visiting the booths, where rations of fish from the lake, or of meal, fruit, dried venison, and cocoa, were distributed according to the wants of each family. Or perhaps a party of men, on their way to labor in the gardens, stopped to smoke and talk together in a fashion that showed time to be of little value to them. Here and there also a few — a very few — children played together with flowers for toys in the shadow of the palaces, barracks, and store-houses which bordered the central square; but this was all, for the rest the place seemed empty and asleep.

Chapter XVI

ON THE PYRAMID

"Does not the city lie very low?" I asked of Maya, when we had studied the prospect on every side. "To my eye its houses seem almost upon a level with the waters of the lake."

"I believe that is so," she answered. "Moreover, during those months of the year that are coming, the surface of the lake rises many feet, so that the greater portion of the island is submerged, and the water stands about the wall."

"How, then, do you prevent the town from being flooded?" asked the señor. "If once the water flowed in, the place would vanish and every soul be drowned."

"Yes, friend, but the waters never rise beyond a certain height, and they are kept from flooding the city by the great sluice-gate. If that gate were to be opened in the time of inundation, then we should perish, everyone. But it never is opened during those months, for if any would leave or enter the city they do so by means of ladders leading from the summit of the wall to floating landing-stages on the moat beneath. Also night and day the gate is guarded; moreover, it can be moved from one place only by those that know its secret, who are few."

"It seems a strange place to build a city," answered the señor. "I do not think that I should ever sleep sound during the months of inundation, knowing that my life depended upon a single gate."

"Yet men have slept safely here for a thousand years or more," she said. "Legend tells us that our ancestors who came up from the coast in ancient days settled on the island and by command of their gods, choosing this hollow bed of land to build in, so that rather than submit themselves to foes, as their fathers were forced to do in the country beyond the mountain, they could, if need were, flood the place and perish in the water. For this reason it is that the holy sanctuary of the Nameless god, the Heart of Heaven, is hollowed deep in the rock beneath us, for the waters of the lake would flow in upon it at a touch, burying it and all its treasures from the sight of man forever. Now, if you have seen enough, I will take you to visit the public workshops where fish is dried, linen woven, and all other industries carried on that are necessary to our comfort" — and, turning, she led the way with her ladies towards the head of the stairs.

As we drew near to it, however, three men appeared upon the platform, in one of whom I knew Tikal. Seeing Maya he advanced toward her, bowing as he came.

"Lady," he said, "learning that you were here with these strangers, I have followed you to beg that you will speak with me alone for some few minutes."

"That I cannot do, cousin," she answered coldly, "for who knows what color might afterwards be put upon my words. If you have anything to say to me, say it before us all."

"That *I* cannot do," he replied, "for what I have to say is secret. Still, for your father's sake, and perhaps for your own, you will do well to hear it."

"Without a witness I will not listen to you, Tikal."

"Then, Lady, farewell," he said, and turned to go.

"Stay, cousin. If you fear to speak before our own people, let this stranger —" and she pointed to me, Ignatio — "be present at our talk. He is of our blood, and can understand our tongue, a discreet man, moreover, one of the Brethren of the Heart."

"One of the Brethren of the Heart? How can a stranger be a Brother of the Heart? Prove it to me, wanderer."

And, drawing me aside, he said certain words, which I answered, giving him the signs.

"Do you agree?" asked Maya.

"Yes, Lady, since I must, though it pleases me little to open my mind before a stranger. Let us step apart" — and he walked to the center of the platform, followed by Maya and myself.

"Lady," he began, "my business with you is not easy to tell. For many years we were affianced, and both you and your father promised that we should be wed when you returned from this journey —"

"Surely, as things are, cousin, it is needless to discuss the matter of our betrothal," she broke in with sarcasm.

"Not altogether needless, Lady," he answered. "I have much to ask your pardon for, yet I make bold to ask it. Maya, you know well that I have loved and love you dearly, and that no other woman has ever been near my heart."

"Indeed," she said with a laugh, "these words sound strange in the mouth of the new-made husband of Nahua."

"Perhaps, Lady, and yet they are true. I am married to Nahua, but I do not love her, though she loves me. It is you whom I love, and when I saw you yesterday all my heart went out to you, so that I almost hated the fair bride at my side."

"Why, then, did you marry her?"

"Because I must, and because I believed you dead, and your father with you, as did every man in the city. You and Zibalbay being dead, as I thought, was it wonderful that I should wish to keep the place that many were plotting to take from me? This could be done in one way only, by the help of Mattai, the most clever and the most powerful man in the city, and this was Mattai's price, that his daughter should become the Lady of the Heart. Well, she loved me, she is beautiful, and she has her father's strength and foresight, so that among all the ladies in the land there was none more fitted to be my wife."

"Well, and you married her, and there's an end. You ask my forgiveness, and you have it, seeing that it does not befit me to play the part of a jealous woman. Doubtless time will soften the blow to me, Tikal," she added, mockingly.

"There is not an end, Maya, and I come to ask you today to renew your promise that you will be my wife."

"What, cousin! Having broken your troth, would you now offer me insult? Do you then propose that I, the Daughter of the Heart, should be Nahua's handmaid?"

"No, I propose that when Nahua is put away you should take her place and your own."

"How can this be, seeing that the Lady of the Heart cannot be divorced?"

"If she ceases to be the Lady of the Heart she can be divorced like any other woman; at the least, love has no laws, and I will find a way."

"The way of death, perhaps. No, I will have none of you. Honor has laws, Tikal, if love has none. Go back to your wife, and pray that she may never learn how you would have treated her."

"Is that your last word, Lady?"

"Why do you ask?"

"Because more hangs on it than you know. Listen: Very soon all the men in the city will be gathered on this place to hear your father's words, and to decide whether he or I shall rule. See, already they assemble in the temple square. Promise to be my wife, and in return I will yield to your father and he shall be master for his life's days and have his way in all things. Refuse, and I will cling to power, and matters may go badly for him, for you, and —" he added threateningly, "for these strangers, your friends."

"All this must befall as it chances," she answered proudly, "I do not meddle with such questions, nor do your threats move me. If you are so base as to plot mischief against an old man who has poured benefits upon you, plot on, and in due time meet with your reward, but for myself I tell you that I have done with you, and that, come what may, I will never be your wife."

"Perhaps you may yet live to take back those words, Lady," he said in a quiet voice; then, with a bow of obeisance, he turned and went.

"You have made a dangerous enemy, Lady," I said, when he was out of earshot.

"I do not fear him, Ignatio."

"That is well," I answered, "but for my part I do. I think that his plans are ready, and that before this day is done there will be trouble. Indeed, I shall be thankful if we live to see tomorrow's light."

By this time we had reached the others.

"Are you weary of waiting?" she said to the señor, giving him a sweet look as she spoke. "Well, I should have been happier here than I was yonder. Give me your hand and lead me down the stair, for I am tired. Ah, friend, did you but know it, I have just dared more for your sake than I should have done for my own."

"What have you dared?" he asked.

"That you will learn in due time, if we live long enough, friend," she answered, "but, oh! I would that we had never set foot within this city."

*T*wo hours had passed, and, following in the train of Zibalbay and Maya, who walked beside him, once more we found ourselves upon the summit of the pyramid. Now, however, it was no longer empty, for on it were collected men to the number of some thousands; indeed, all the adult male population of the city. On one side of the altar were seated Tikal, his bride Nahua, who was the only woman there, and some hundreds of nobles, all of whom, I noted, were armed and guarded by a body of soldiers that stood behind them. On the other side were many vacant places; and as Zibalbay, with Maya and all the great company of followers that he had gathered, advanced to take them, Tikal and every man present on the pyramid uncovered their heads and bowed in greeting to him.

After a few moments' pause, two priests came forward from the watch-house behind the altar, and, having laid upon it an offering of fresh flowers, the elder of them, who was robed in pure white, uttered a short prayer to the Nameless god, the Heart of Heaven, asking that he would be pleased to accept the gift, and to send a blessing upon the deliberations of his people here assembled. Then Zibalbay rose to address the multitude, and I noted that his fierce face was pale and anxious, and that his hand shook, although his eyes flashed angrily:

"Nobles and people of the City of the Heart," he began, "on this day a year ago, I, your hereditary ruler and *cacique,* and the high priest of the Heart of Heaven, left this city on a certain mission. This was my mission: To find the severed portion of the sacred symbol that lies in the sanctuary of the temple, the portion that is called Day, which has been lost for many an age. You know that our race has fallen upon evil times, and that, year by year, our numbers dwindle, till at length the end of the people is in sight, seeing that within some few generations they must die out and be forgotten. You know also the ancient prophecy, that when once more the two halves of the Symbol of the Heart, Day and Night, are laid side by side, in their place upon the altar in the sanctuary, then, from that hour, this people shall grow great again; and you know how a voice spoke to me, in answer to my prayers, bidding me, Zibalbay, to wander forth from the country of the Heart, following the road to the sea, for there I should find that which was lost.

"Thither, then, having won the permission of my Council, the Brotherhood of the Heart, I have wandered alone with my daughter, the Lady Maya, suffering much hardship and danger in my journeyings, and lo! I have found that which was lost, and brought it back to you, for here it hangs upon the neck of this Ignatio, who has accompanied me from the lands beyond the desert."

Now a murmur of astonishment went up from the multitude, and Zibalbay paused awhile.

"Of this matter of the finding of the symbol," he continued, "I will speak more fully at the proper time, and to those who have a right to hear it, namely, to the elected Brotherhood of the Heart, in the holy Sanctuary, on the day of the Rising of Waters, being one of the eight days in each year on which it is lawful for the Council of the Heart to meet in the Sanctuary. But first in this hour I will deal with other questions.

"It is known to you that, when I went upon my mission, I left my nephew Tikal to sit in my place, it being agreed between us and the Council that if I should return no more within two years he should become *cacique* of the people. I have returned within one year, and I find this: That already he has allowed himself to be anointed *cacique,* and more, that he, who was affianced to my daughter, has taken another woman to be his wife. Last night with my own ears I heard him proclaim his treachery in the hall of the palace, and when I spoke out the bitterness that was in my heart, I, your lord, was met with threats, and told that Tikal, having been anointed, could not now be deposed. I use the saying against him. Nobles, have I not been anointed, and can I then be deposed — I, who am not a traitor to my master, nor a forswearer of my oaths, as is my nephew yonder?"

Again he paused, and some of the audience, with those who had accompanied Zibalbay, shouted "No;" but the most of them looked towards Tikal and were silent. Now Mattai rose from his place behind Tikal and spoke, saying:

"As one who had to do with the anointing of Tikal to be *cacique* when we believed you and the Lady Maya to be dead, I would ask you, Zibalbay, before we on this side of the altar answer you, to tell us openly what is the meaning of this journey that you have undertaken, and for what purpose you have brought these two strangers, who are named Ignatio and Son of the Sea, with you, in defiance of the ancient law, which says that he who brings a stranger across the mountains into the land of the City of the Heart shall die, together with the stranger."

Now, when Zibalbay heard this question he started, for he had forgotten this law, and saw the cunning trap that Mattai had spread for his feet. Nevertheless he answered boldly, since it was his nature to be outspoken and straightforward.

"It becomes you ill, Mattai, to question me — you who have proved yourself a plotter and a lying prophet, reading in the stars that I and my daughter were dead, while we still draw the breath of life beneath them. Yet I will answer you, and, scorning subterfuge or falsehood, set out the whole matter in the hearing of the people, that they may judge between me, your party, and your master. First, I will say that I had forgotten the law of which you speak, whereof I have broken the letter, or, if at any time I remembered it, my necessities caused me to disregard it. Learn, then, that the stranger Ignatio is of royal Indian blood, and the holder of that symbol which I went forth to seek, and that the white man whom you call Son of the Sea is as a brother to him, and that both of them are of the fellowship of the Heart, the Lord Ignatio being no less a man than the master of the order in yonder lands, as I am here. This Lord Ignatio I summoned to me, and he came. He came, and with his companion, Son of the Sea, saved me and my daughter from shame and death at the hands of certain murderers, white men. Then, when we had escaped, we tried each other, and laid the symbols side by side, and, lo! Day and Night came together and they were one. Then, also, I told him the story of how it happened that I was wandering far from my own place, and he told me what was his purpose and the desire of his life.

"This is his purpose — to break the yoke that the white man has set upon the neck of the Indians in the far lands, and to build up a mighty Indian nation stretching from sea to sea, whereof this city, Heart of the World, shall be the center and the capital. Then we made a compact together, a compact that cannot be broken, and it was this: That the Lord Ignatio, with the white man, his companion, from whom he will not be separated, should accompany us here, where the symbols should be set in the appointed place, that the prophecy may be fulfilled and fortune return to us: That I should give to him so much as he may need of the treasures which lie useless in our storehouses, wherewith he may arm troops and bring about his ends, and that in return he should bring to us what we need far more than gold and gems — men and women with whom we may intermarry, so that our race, ceasing to dwindle, may once again multiply and grow great.

"Such, nobles, is our compact, and this is the path which the god who rules us has pointed out for our feet to tread. Accept it and grow great — refuse it and perish. For know that not for myself do I speak, who am old and near to death, but for you and your posterity forever. Be not bewildered or amazed, for, though these things are new to you, it may well chance that after the Council of the Heart has been celebrated in the Sanctuary on the night of the Rising of Waters, the god whom we worship, the Nameless god under whose guidance all these things have come about, will reveal his purpose by the mouth of his oracle, and show what part these strangers and each of us shall play in the fate that is to be. Oh! nobles, and my people, let not your sight be dimmed nor your heart hardened, and put not away the fortune and the future that lies before you. I have dared much for your sake; dare a little for your own. Shut your ears and your gates and rise in rebellion against me, and I tell you that soon there shall remain of you and of your glorious home scarcely a memory; but be gentle and be guided by my wisdom and the will of your gods, and your fame and power shall cover the world; aye! you shall be to what you were as is the sun in all its glory to some faint and fading star. I have spoken — now choose."

He ceased, and for a while there was silence, the silence of amaze, for the nobles stared each on each, and such of the common people as were within earshot stood gaping at him with open mouths, since to them who did not meddle in matters of polity, and, indeed, thought little for themselves, his words had small meaning. Presently it was broken, and by Tikal, who sprang from his seat and cried aloud:

"Of a truth they were wise who said that this old man was mad. Have you heard and understood, O people of the Heart? This is what you must do to fulfil the will of Zibalbay: First, you must set him in his place again, giving him all power, and me you must condemn to death or chains; next, you must pardon him his breaches of the law — the law that he of all men was bound to keep. Then you must hand over your treasures — the treasures hoarded by your forefathers for many a generation — to these wandering thieves whom he has brought with him; and, lastly, you must open your gates, which have been kept secret for a thousand years, to other thieves that they shall lead here, to whom, forsooth, you must give your women in marriage that the race may be increased. Say, will you do these things, children of the Heart?"

Now all the nobles who stood behind Tikal shouted "Never!" and the people beyond took up the cry with a voice of thunder, though the most of them understood little of what was passing.

Tikal held up his hand, and there was silence.

"You will not do them," he said, "and base indeed were you had you answered otherwise. What, then, will you do? Tell me, first, whom do you choose as your ruler, my uncle, who now is mad and would bring you to shame and ruin; or me, who have sworn to preserve your ancient laws?"

"We choose you, Tikal, Tikal!" came the answer.

"I thank you," he cried, "but what then shall be done with this old man, and those whom he has brought with him to spy out our secrets and to rob us?"

"Kill them before the altar!" they shouted, waving their swords.

Tikal thought for a moment, then pointed towards us and said, "Seize those men."

At his word a hundred or more of the nobles, who evidently had been instructed to execute his orders, rushed at us suddenly. As they came across the open space I saw the señor put his hand to his belt, and said to him:

"For the love of God! do not strike, for should you touch one of them they will certainly kill us."

"That they will do in any case — but as you wish," he answered.

Then they broke on us. As they came, all those nobles who had followed Zibalbay to the crest of the pyramid gave way before their rush, leaving the three of us and the Lady Maya standing alone.

"Cowards!" said Zibalbay, glancing behind him. Then he drew his *machete* and with a great shout cut down the foremost of those who assailed us — a great noble. In another instant the weapon was struck from him, and the señor and I were being dragged towards the altar, followed by Zibalbay and the Lady Maya, upon whom, however, our assailants laid no hand.

"What shall we do with these men?" cried Tikal again.

And again the nobles answered, "Kill them!"

So they threw us down, and men came at us with swords to make an end of us, which indeed they would have done quickly, had not the Lady Maya sprung forward, and, standing over the señor, cried "Hold!" in so piercing a voice that they stayed their hands.

"Listen, people of the Heart," she said, "would you do murder upon your own holy altar, staining it with the blood of innocent men? You talk of broken laws. Is there not a law in the city that none can be put to death except after trial before the *cacique* and his Council? Have these men been tried, and if so, by whom? You say that my father, your lawful ruler, is deposed. If that is so, not Tikal, but I, who am his heir, rule in his stead, and I have passed no judgment on them."

Now at her words there was a murmur of mingled doubt and applause, but Tikal answered her, saying:

"Lady, the law you quote holds good for you, for your father, and for every citizen of the Heart, however humble; but in the case of these men it does not hold, for they are wandering strangers and spies, who can claim no protection from our justice, and therefore it is right that they should die."

"It is not right that they should die," she answered passionately. "You, Tikal, have usurped my father's place, and now you would celebrate the beginning of your rule by a deed of the foulest murder. I tell you that these men are innocent of all offence. If any are guilty it is my father and I, and if any should suffer we should suffer. More," she went on, with flashing eyes, "if these men to whom we have sworn safe-conduct must die, then for my part I will die with them, and whether I pass by your hands or by my own, may the curse of my blood rest upon you forever and forever."

As she spoke she snatched a knife from her jeweled girdle, and stood before them, its bare blade glittering in the sunlight, looking so beautiful and fierce that the nobles fell back from her, and hundreds of the people applauded, saying:

"Hear the Lady Maya, and obey her. She is *cacique*, and no other."

Now Zibalbay, who had covered his eyes with his hands, looked up and said:

"You are right, daughter. Since the people reject us, and we cannot even protect our guests, it is best that we should die with them," and once more he covered his eyes with his hands.

Then there came a pause and a sound of whispering. I looked up between the sword-blades which were pointed at my throat, and saw that Nahua was standing at the side of her lord, and pleading with him. They were so close to me that my hearing, always keen, being sharpened moreover by the fear of instant death, enabled me to catch some of their talk.

"She will do what she says," said Nahua, "and that will be your ruin; for if her father is hated, she is beloved, and many will arise to avenge her."

"Why should she kill herself because of a white wanderer?" he asked.

Nahua shrugged her shoulders, and smiled darkly, as she answered:

"Who can tell; he is her friend, and women have been known to give their lives for their friends. Do as you will, but if Maya dies I do not think that we shall live to see another dawn," and, leaving his side, she sought her chair again.

Now Tikal looked at the señor, who was stretched upon the ground beside me, and seeing that there was hate in his eyes I trembled, thinking that the end had come, then turned my head aside, and began to commend my soul to the care of Heaven. As I prayed he spoke, addressing himself to Maya:

"Lady," he said, "you have appealed to the law on behalf of these wanderers, of your father, and of yourself, and by the law you shall be dealt with. Tomorrow the judges shall be chosen, and hold their court here before the people."

"It cannot be, Tikal," she answered calmly, "there is but one court which can try us four, all of whom are Brethren of the Heart, and that is the Council of the Heart sitting in the Sanctuary, which assembles on the eighth day from now, on the night of the Rising of Waters. Is it not so, nobles?"

"If you are of the number of the Brethren of the Heart, all of you, it is so," they answered.

"So be it," said Tikal; "but till then I must hold you in safe-keeping. Will it please you to follow Mattai, Lady, and you, my Lord Zibalbay. Guards, bring these men to the watch-house yonder, and keep them there till I come to you."

Maya bowed, and, turning to the audience, she said in a clear voice, "Farewell, my people. If we are seen no more you will know that my father and I have been done to death by Tikal, who has usurped our place, and to you I leave it to take vengeance for our blood."

Chapter XVII

THE CURSE OF ZIBALBAY

*T*hankful enough was I to rise from the ground feeling my life whole in me.

"Death has been near to us," said the señor with something between a sob and a laugh, as we followed Zibalbay and Maya into the guard-house.

"He is near to us still," I answered, "but at least, unless Tikal changes his mind, we have won some days of respite."

"Thanks to her," he said, nodding to Maya, and as he spoke we entered the guard-house, a small chamber with a massive door, somewhat roughly furnished.

So soon as we were in, the door was shut upon us, and we found ourselves alone. Zibalbay sat himself down, and, fixing his eyes upon the wall, stared at it as though it offered no hindrance to his sight, but the rest of us stood together near the door, listening to the turmoil of the multitude without. Clearly argument ran high among them, for we could hear the sound of angry voices, of shouting, and of the hurrying footfalls of the people leaving the pyramid by way of the great stair.

"You have saved our lives for a while, for which we owe you thanks," said the señor to Maya presently, "but tell me, what will they do with us now?"

"I cannot say," she answered, "but in this pyramid are chambers where we shall be hidden away until our day of trial. At the least I think so, for they dare not let us out among the people, lest we should cause a tumult in the city."

Before the words had left her lips the door was opened, and through it came Tikal, Mattai, and other of the great lords who were hostile to Zibalbay.

"What is your pleasure with us?" asked Zibalbay, awaking from his dream.

"That you should follow me," answered Tikal sternly, "you and the others" — adding, with a low bow to Maya, "forgive me, Lady, that I must exercise this violence towards you and your father, but I have no other choice if I would save you from the vengeance of the people."

"It is not the vengeance of the people that we have to fear, Tikal," she answered quietly, "but rather your hate."

"Which it is in your power to appease, lady," he said in a low voice.

"It may be in my power, but it is not in my will," she answered, setting her lips. "Come, cousin, take us to the dungeon that you have prepared for us."

"As you wish," he said; "follow me." And he led the way across the guard-house, through a sleeping-chamber of the priests that lay behind it, to the further wall that was hidden by a curtain.

This curtain, on being drawn, revealed a small stone door, which Mattai, having first lit some lamps that stood ready in the chamber, unlocked with a key which hung at his girdle. One by one we passed through the door, Tikal preceding us, and Mattai, with others of the great lords, to the number of six, following after us. Beyond the door lay a flight of twenty steps, then came a gate of copper bars. On the further side of this gate were flight upon flight of steps, joined together by landings, and running, now in this direction now in that, into the bowels of the mighty pyramid. At length, when my limbs were weary of descending so many stairs, we found ourselves in front of other gates, larger and more beautifully worked than those that we had already passed. Presently they clanged behind us, and we stood in a vast apartment or hall that was built in the heart of the pyramid. It would seem that this hall had been made ready for our coming, for it was lighted with many silver lamps, and in one part of it rugs were laid and on them stood tables and seats. So great was the place that the light of the lamps shone in it only as stars shine in the sky, still, as we passed down it, we saw that its roof was vaulted, and that its walls and floor were of white marble finely polished. Once, as we learned afterwards, it had served as the assembly-rooms for the priests of the temple, but now that they were so few it was not used, except from time to time as a prison for offenders of high rank. At intervals along its length were doors leading to sleeping and other chambers. Some of the doors were open, and as we passed them Mattai told us that these were to be our bedchambers. Then, having announced that food would be brought to us, the nobles, headed by Tikal, withdrew, and we heard the copper gates clash and the echo of their footsteps into nothingness upon the endless stairs.

For a while we stood staring at each other in silence. It was Zibalbay who broke it, and his voice rang strangely in the vaulted place.

"It is his hour now," he said, shaking his fist towards the stair by which Tikal had left us, "but let him pray that mine may never come," and suddenly he turned and, walking to a couch, flung himself upon it and buried his face in his hands.

Maya followed him and, bending down, strove to comfort him, but he waved her away and she came back to us.

"This is a gloomy place," said the señor, in a half whisper, for here one scarcely dared to speak aloud because of the echoes that ran about the walls, "but, dark though it is, it seems safer than the summit of the pyramid, where sword-points are so many," and he pointed to a little cut upon his throat.

"It is safe enough," Maya answered, with a bitter laugh, "and safely will it keep our bones till the world's end, for through those gates and the men that guard them there is no escape, and the death that threatened us in the sunshine shall overtake us in the shadow. Did I not warn you against this mad quest and the seeking of the city of my people? I warned you both, and you would not listen, and now the trouble is at hand and your lives will pay the forfeit for your folly and my father's."

"What must be, must be," answered the señor with a sigh, "but for my part I hope that the worst is past and that they will not kill us. It was your father's rashness which brought these evils on us, and perhaps misfortune may teach him wisdom."

"Never," she answered, shaking her head, "for they are right; on this matter he is mad, as you, Ignatio, are mad also. Come, let us look at our prison, for I have not seen it till this hour," and, taking one of the hand-lamps that stood near, she walked down the length of the hall. At its further end were gates similar to those by which we had entered, and through them came a draft of air.

"Where do they lead?" I asked.

"I do not know," she answered, "perhaps to the Sanctuary by a secret way. At least the pyramid is full of these chambers, that in old days were used for many things, such as the storage of corn and weapons, and the burying-places of priests, thousands of whom are at rest within it. Now they are empty and deserted."

As we walked back again I stopped before a wooden door that stood ajar, leading into one of the chambers of which I have spoken.

"Let us go in," said Maya, pushing it open, and we entered, to find ourselves in a small room lined with shelves. On these shelves, each of which was numbered, lay hundreds of rolls thickly covered with dust. Maya took up one of them at a hazard and unrolled the parchment, revealing a manuscript beautifully executed in the picture-painting of the Indians.

"This must be nearly a thousand years old," she said; "I know it by the style of the painting. Well, we shall not lack history to read while we sojourn here," and she threw the priceless roll back on to its shelf and left the chamber.

A few steps further on we came to another room of which the door was closed, but so rotten was the woodwork with age that a push freed it from its fastenings, and we entered. Here also there were shelves, packed some of them with yellow and some with white bars of metal.

"Copper and lead," said the señor glancing at them.

"Not so," answered Maya with a laugh, "but that which you white men covet, gold and silver. Look what is painted upon the shelves," and she held up the lamp and read: "Pure metal from the southern mines, set apart for the services of the Temple of the Heart, and of the Temples of the East and West. Of gold — such a weight; of silver — such a weight."

I stared and my eyes grew greedy, for here in this one room, neglected and forgotten, was enough wealth to carry out my purpose three times over, stored there by the forefathers of this strange rust-eaten race. Ah, if only I could see one half of it safe across the mountains, how great might be my future and that of the people which I lived to serve.

"Perhaps you may win it after all, Ignatio," said Maya, interpreting my thoughts, "but, to be frank, I fear that you will gain nothing except a sepulcher in these gloomy vaults."

After this we visited several chambers that were empty, or filled only with the wreck of moth-eaten tapestries and curious furnitures, till at length we came to a room, or rather a large cupboard, piled from floor to ceiling with golden vessels of the most quaint and ancient workmanship, which had been discarded by the priests and cast aside as worthless – why, I do not know. In front of this gleaming pile stood a chest, unlocked, that the señor opened. It was packed with priestly ornaments of gold, set with great emeralds. Maya picked out a belt from the box and gave it to me, saying:

"Take it, Ignatio, since you love such trinkets. It will set off that robe of yours."

I took it and put it on, not over my robe, but beneath it. My friend, it is the clasp of that belt, which now is yours, that I showed you a while ago, and with the price of the other gems in it I bought this *hacienda* and all its lands.

Wearied at length by the sight of so much useless treasure, we returned to Zibalbay, who was seated as we had left him, lost in thought.

At this moment the gates of our prison were opened, and men came through them, escorted by captains of the guard, bringing with them food in plenty, which they set upon the table, waiting on us while we ate, but speaking no word, good or bad. Our meal finished, they cleared away the fragments, and, having replenished the lamps and prepared the chambers for us to sleep in, they bowed and left us. For a while we sat round the table, Zibalbay and I in silence, and Maya and the señor talking together in a low voice, till at length the dreariness of the place overcame us, and, as though by a common impulse, we rose and sought the sleeping-vaults, there to rest, if we might.

We slept, and woke, and rose again, though whether it was night or day here, where no light came, we could not tell; indeed, as time went on, our only means of distinguishing the one from the other was by the visits of those who brought our food and waited on us.

I think it must have been in the early afternoon of the day following that on which we were imprisoned, that Tikal visited us, accompanied only by four guards.

"A small band," said the señor as he watched them advance, "but enough to put us to death, who are unarmed" (for all our weapons had been taken from us), "if such should be their will."

"Have no fear, friend," said Maya, "they will not do murder so openly."

By now Tikal stood before us, bowing, and Zibalbay, who as usual was seated brooding at the table, looked up and saw him.

"What do you seek, traitor?" he asked angrily, the blood flushing beneath his withered skin. "Would you kill us? If so, slay on, for thus shall I come the sooner to the bosom of that god whose vengeance I call down upon you."

"I am no murderer, Zibalbay," answered Tikal with dignity. "If you die, it will be by command of the law that you have broken, and not by mine. I am here to speak with you, if you will come apart with me."

"Then speak on before these others, or leave your words unsaid," he answered, "for not one step will I stir with you, who doubtless seek some opportunity to stab me in the back."

"Yet it is necessary that you should hear what I have to say, Zibalbay."

"Say on then, traitor, or go."

Tikal thought for a while, looking doubtfully at Maya, from whose fair face, indeed, he rarely took his eyes.

"Is it your wish that I should withdraw?" she asked shortly.

"It is not mine," said Zibalbay; "stay where you are, daughter."

Now Tikal hesitated no longer, but, bidding the guards who had accompanied him to fall back out of earshot, he said:

"Listen, Zibalbay; yesterday, before the gathering on the pyramid, I saw your daughter, the Lady Maya, and spoke with her, telling her that now, as always, I loved her, although believing her to be dead, for reasons of state I had taken another woman to be my wife. Then I made her this offer: That if she would consent to become my wife I would put away Nahua, whom I had married. Moreover, I added this, that I would give up my place as *cacique* to you, Zibalbay, whose it is by right, to hold for so long as you should live, and would not oppose you or your policy in any matter. I told her, on the other hand, that if she refused to become my wife, I would surrender nothing, but would put out my strength to crush you and her and these strangers, your friends. She answered me with contempt, saying that I might do my worst, but she would have naught to say to me. What happened afterwards you know, Zibalbay, and you know also the danger in which you stand today, now that power has left you, and your very life trembles in the balance."

He paused, and Zibalbay, who had been listening to his words amazed, turned to Maya and said sternly:

"Does this man speak lies, daughter?"

As she was about to answer — though what she meant to say, I do not know — Tikal broke in:

"What is the use of asking her, Zibalbay? Is it to be thought that she will answer you truly, though that I speak truth this wanderer who stands at your side can bear witness, for he was present and heard my words. This offer I made to her, and, that it may be put beyond a doubt, now I make it to her and to you again. If she will take me in marriage, for her sake I will put away Nahua; I will lay down my rule and set you in your place again, with liberty, so long as you shall live, to work such follies as the gods may suffer. All these things I will do because I love her to whom I have been affianced from my youth up, better than them all, because she is as the light to mine eyes and the breath to my nostrils, and without her I have no joy in life, as I have had none since I believed her to be dead."

Zibalbay heard, and, rising, lifted his hand to the vault above him, and said:

"I thank thee, O god, who, in answer to my prayers, hast shown me a way of escape from the troubles that beset me. Tikal, it shall be as you wish, and we will swear our peace upon the altar of the Heart. Doubtless there will be trouble with Mattai and some of his following, but if we stand together they can be overcome. Rejoice with me, Ignatio, my friend, for now the seed that we have planted with so much labor shall bring forth golden fruit."

Here I heard the señor groan with doubt and wrath behind me, and knew that, like so many others, this vision which filled my mind with glory must be brought to nothing because of the fancy of a woman.

"Your pardon, Zibalbay," I interrupted, "the Lady Maya has not spoken."

"Spoken!" he exclaimed. "Why, what should she say?"

"What I said to my cousin Tikal yesterday," she answered, setting her lips and speaking very low — "that I will have nothing to do with him."

"Nothing to do with him, girl! Nothing to do with him! Why he is your affianced; you do not understand?"

"I understand well, father, but for naught that can be offered to me upon the earth will I give myself in marriage to a man who has treated you and me as my cousin Tikal has done — a man who could not keep his oath to you, or wait for me one single year."

"Cease to be foolish," said Zibalbay. "Tikal has erred, no doubt; but now he would make atonement for his error, and if I can forgive him, so can you. Think no more of the girl's folly, Tikal, but send for ink and parchment and let us set down our contract, for I am old and have little time to lose; and perhaps, before another year is gone, that which you would have snatched by force shall come to you by right."

"I have the paper here, lord," said Tikal, drawing a roll from his breast; "but, pardon me, does the Lady Maya consent?"

"Aye, aye, she consents."

"I do *not* consent, father, and if you drag me to the altar with yonder man, I will cry out to the people to protect me, or, failing their aid, I will seek refuge in death — by my own hand if need be."

Now Zibalbay turned upon his daughter, trembling with rage, but, checking himself of a sudden, he said:

"Tikal, for the moment this girl of mine is mad; leave us, and come back in some few hours, when you shall find her of another mind. Go now, I pray, before words are said that cannot be forgotten."

Tikal turned and went, and, until the gates at the far end of the hall had clashed behind him and his guards, there was silence.

Then Zibalbay spoke to his daughter.

"Girl," he said, "I know your heart and that your lips spoke a lie, when you told us that it was because of Tikal's forgetfulness of his vow and troth that you will not marry him. There is another reason of which you have not spoken. This white man, who in his own country is named James Strickland, is the reason. You have suffered yourself to look on him with longing, and you cannot pluck his image from your breast. Do I not speak truth?"

"You speak truth, father," she answered, placing her hand in that of the señor as she said the words. "To you, at least, I will not lie."

"I thank you, daughter. Now, hear me; I am sorry for your plight and for that of the white man, if indeed he would make of you anything more than his toy, but here your wishes must give way to the common good. Who and what are you that your whims should stand between me and the fulfillment of my lifelong desire, between your people and their redemption? Must all these things come to nothing because of the fancies of a love-sick girl, whose poor beauty, as it chances by favor of the gods, can avail to bring them about?"

"It seems so, father," she said, "seeing that in this matter my duty to myself and to him who loves me, and whom I love, is higher than my duty to you and to your scheme. Everything else you, who are my father, may require of me, even to my life, but my honor is my own."

"What shall I say to this headstrong girl?" gasped Zibalbay. "Speak, White Man, and tell me that you renounce her, for surely your heart is not so wicked that it will lead you to consent to this folly, and to your own undoing to stand between her and her destiny."

Now all eyes were fixed upon the señor, who turned pale in the lamplight and answered slowly:

"Zibalbay, I grieve to vex you, but your daughter's destiny and mine are one, nor can I command her to forsake me and give herself in marriage to a man she hates."

"Yet it seems that you could command her to break her plighted troth for your sake, O most honorable White Man," said Zibalbay with a bitter laugh. "Hearken, friend Ignatio, for you at least are not in love, tell your brother there and this rebellious girl which way their duty lies. Teach them that we are sent here to dwell upon the earth for higher ends than the satisfying of our own desires. Stay, before you speak, remember that with this matter your own fate is interwoven. Remember how you have suffered and striven for many years, remember all you have undergone to win what today lies in your grasp, the wealth that shall enable you to carry out your purposes. There, in those vaults, it lies to your hand, and if that be not enough I will give you more. Take it, Ignatio, take it to bribe your enemies and pay your armies, and become a king, a righteous king, crowned by heaven to complete the destinies of our race. Say such words as shall bend this girl and her lover to our will, and triumph; or fail to say them, and some few days hence meet the end of a thief at the hands of Tikal. Now speak."

I heard him, and my heart stood still within me. Alas! his words were true, and now was the turning-point of my fate. If the girl would give herself to Tikal, who was mad with love of her, all would be well, and within three years the dream of my race might be fulfilled, and the vengeance of generations accomplished upon the spawn of the accursed Spaniard. There in those vaults, useless and forgotten, lay the treasures that I needed, and yonder in Mexico were men in thousands who by their means might be armed and led; but between me and them stood the desire of this woman and the folly of my friend. Oh! truly had my heart warned me against her when first I learned to know her lovely face, having foreknowledge of the evil that she should bring upon me. With her I could do nothing, for who can turn a woman from her love or hate? But with my friend it was otherwise; he would listen to me if I pleaded with him, seeing that not only my hopes but my very life hung upon his answer, and no true man has the right to bring others to their death in order that he may fulfil the wishes of his heart. Also, it would be better that he should be separated from this girl, who was not of his blood and color, and whose love soon or late would be his undoing. Surely I should do well to pray him to let her go to the man whose affianced she had been, and he would do well to hearken to me. Almost the entreaty was upon my lips when Maya, reading my thought, touched me on the arm and whispered:

"Remember your oath, Ignatio." Then I called to mind what I had promised yonder in the desert, when by her courage she had saved her lover's life, and knew that once again a woman must be my ruin, since it is better to lose all than to break such vows as this.

"Zibalbay," I said, "I cannot plead your cause and mine, though not to do so be our destruction, seeing that I have sworn that, come what may, I will not stand between these two. Today, for the second time in my life, my plans are brought to nothing by the passion of a woman. Well, so it is fated, and so let it be!"

Zibalbay did not answer me, but, turning to the señor, he said:

"White Man, you have heard from your friend words that should touch you more deeply than any prayer. Will you still cling to your purpose, and take advantage of my daughter's madness? If so, know that your triumph shall be short, for when, in some few hours, Tikal comes again, I will tell him all and give you over to his keeping to deal with as he wishes. Then Heaven help you, wanderer, for he is vengeful by nature, nor is that life likely to be long which bars the way between a ruler of men and the woman he would wed. Answer then, and for the last time: Do you choose life or death?"

"I choose death," he said, boldly, "if the price of life be the breaking of my troth and the surrender of my bride to another man. I am sorry for you, Zibalbay; and for you, Ignatio, my friend, I am still more sorry: but it is fate and not I that has brought these evils on you. If Ignatio here cannot forget his oath, how much less can I forget mine, which I have sworn with this lady. Moreover, worse fortune even than today's would come upon us if I did, seeing that such cowardice could breed no luck. Therefore, till the Lady Maya renounces me, for good or for evil, in death or in life, I will cleave to her."

"And in death or in life I will cleave to you, beloved," she said. "Take such vengeance as you wish upon us, my father, yes, if you wish, give over this man, to whom my heart drew me across the mountains and the desert, to die at the hands of Tikal; but know that he will hold me faster dead than he did while he was alive, for into the valley of death I shall follow him swiftly."

Now at last the rage of Zibalbay broke loose, and it was terrible. Rising from his seat he shook his clenched hands above his daughter's head and cursed her, till in her fear she shrank away from him to her lover's breast.

"As with my last breath," he cried, "I pray that the curse of your gods, of your country, of your ancestors, and of me, your father, may rest upon you and your children. May your desire turn to ashes in your mouth, and may death rob you of its fruit; may your heart break by inches for remorse and sorrow, and your name become a hissing and a shame. Oh! I seem to see the future, and I tell you, daughter, that you shall win him for whose sake you brought your father to death and ruin. By fraud shall you win him, and for a while he shall lie at your side, and this is the price that shall be asked of you, and that you shall pay – the doom of your race, and its destruction at your hands –"

He paused, gasping for breath, and Maya fell at his knees, sobbing:

"Oh! father, unsay those words and spare me. Have you no pity for a woman's heart?"

"Aye!" he said, "so much pity as you have for my sorrows and grey hair. Why should I spare you, girl, who have not spared me, your father. My curse is spoken, and I will add to it, that it shall break your heart at last, aye! and the heart of that man who has robbed me of your duty and your love."

Then suddenly he ceased speaking, his eyes grew empty, he stretched out his arms and fell heavily to the floor.

Chapter XVIII

THE PLOT

Springing forward, but too late to save him, the señor and I lifted Zibalbay from the ground and laid him on a couch. Peeping over our shoulders, Maya caught sight of his ghastly face and the foam upon his lips.

"Oh, he is dead," she moaned; "my father is dead, and he died cursing me."

"No," said the señor, "he is not dead, for his heart stirs. Bring water, Maya."

She obeyed, and for hard upon two hours we struggled to restore his sense, but in vain; life lingered indeed, but we could not stir him from his stupor. At length, as we were resting, wearied with our fruitless labor, the gates opened and Tikal came again.

"What now?" he asked, seeing the form of Zibalbay stretched upon the couch. "Does the old man sleep?"

"Yes, he sleeps," answered the señor, "and I think that he will wake no more. The words he spoke to you today are coming true, and that which you took from him by force will soon be yours by right."

"No," answered Tikal, "by right it will be the Lady Maya's yonder, though by force it may remain mine, unless, indeed, she gives it to me of her own free will. But say, how did this come about?"

Now I broke in hastily, fearing lest the señor should tell too much, and thus bring some swift and awful fate upon himself.

"He was worn out with the fatigue of our journey and the excitement of yesterday. After you had left he began to talk of your proposals, and suddenly was taken with this fit. These matters are not for me to speak of, who am but a prisoner in a strange land; still, lord, it will not look well if he who once was *cacique* of this city dies here and unattended, for then people may say that you have murdered him. Have you no doctors who can be summoned to minister to him, for, without drugs, or even a bleeding-knife, we have done all we can do."

"Murdered him! That they will say in any case. Yes, there are doctors here, and the best and greatest of them is Mattai, my father-in-law. I will send him. But, Maya, before I go, have you no word for me?"

Maya, who was seated by the table, her face buried in her hands, looked up and said:

"Is your heart stone that you can trouble me in such an hour? When my father is recovered, or dead, I will answer you, and not before."

"So be it, Lady," he said, "till then I wait. And now I must get hence, for there may be trouble in the city when this news reaches it."

A while passed, and Mattai appeared before us, followed by one who carried his scales and medicines. Without speaking, he came to where Zibalbay lay, and examined him by the light of a lamp. Then he poured medicine down his throat, and waited as though he expected to see him rise, but he neither rose nor stirred.

"A bad case," he said. "I fear that he will awake no more. How came he thus?"

"Do you wish to know?" asked Maya, speaking for the first time. "Then bid your attendant stand back, and I will tell you. My father yonder was smitten down while he cursed me in his rage."

"And why did he curse you, Lady?"

"For this reason: While we wandered in the wilderness, Tikal, my cousin and my betrothed, took a wife, your daughter Nahua, who was crowned with him as Lady of the Heart. But it seems, Mattai, that though he gave your daughter place and power, he gave her no love, for today this son-in-law of yours came to my father, and in the presence of us all offered to set him in his lawful place again and to suffer him to carry out his schemes, whatever they might be, if I would but consent to become his wife."

"To become his wife!" said Mattai, in amazement. "How could you become his wife when he is married? Can there then be two Ladies of the Heart?"

"No," answered Maya quietly, "but the proposal of Tikal, my cousin, is, that he should either put away or kill your daughter — and you with her, Mattai — in order that he may set me in her place."

Now when Mattai heard this his quick eyes flashed, and his very beard seemed to bristle with rage.

"He proposed that! He dared to propose that!" he gasped. "Oh! let him have a care. I set him up, and perchance I can pull him down again. Continue, Lady."

"He proposed it, and my father agreed to the offer, for, knowing that you have plotted against him, he had little care for the honor and safety of you or of your house, Mattai. But if my father accepted, I refused, seeing that it is not my wish to have more to do with Tikal. Then my father cursed me, and while he cursed was stricken down."

"You say it is not your wish to marry Tikal, Lady. Is it, then, your wish to marry any other man?"

"Yes," she answered, letting her eyes fall, "I love this white lord here, whom you name Son of the Sea, and I would become his wife. I would become his wife," she went on after a pause, "but, Mattai, Tikal is very strong, and it may be, unless I can find help elsewhere, that in order to save the life of the man I love, of his friend and mine, Ignatio, and my own, I shall be forced into the arms of Tikal. But now Tikal has asked me for my answer, and I have told him that I will give it when my father is recovered or dead. Perhaps it will be for you to say what the answer shall be, for alone and in prison I am not strong enough to stand against Tikal. Say, now, do the people love me well enough to depose Tikal and set me in my father's place, should he die?"

"I cannot say, Lady," he answered shortly, "but at the least you will scarcely ask me thus to bring about my own and my daughter's ruin. I will be open with you. I gained over the Council of the Heart to Tikal's cause, and my price was that he should marry my daughter, thereby satisfying her love and my ambition. Yes, I have plotted to set Nahua on high, both for her sake and for my own, seeing that after the *cacique* I sought to be the chief man in the city. Can I, then, turn round and depose him, and my daughter and myself with him? And if I did, what would be my fate at your hands in the days to come? No, I seek to be revenged on Tikal, indeed, who has offered so deadly an affront to me and mine, but it must be in some other way than this. Tell me now, lady, what is it that you desire most — to be *cacique* of this city by your right of birth, or to marry the man you love?"

"I desire to marry the man I love," she answered, "and to escape from this place with him back to those lands where white men live. I desire also that my friend and my lord's friend, Ignatio, should be given as much gold as he needs to enable him to carry out his purposes in the coast country yonder. If things can be brought about thus, Tikal and Nahua and their descendants, for aught I care, may rule in the City of the Heart till the world's end."

"You ask little enough, Lady," said Matti, "and it shall go hard if I cannot get it for you. Now I will leave you, for I must have time to think; but, if Tikal returns, say him neither yea nor nay till we have spoken again. And as for you, strangers, remember that your lives depend upon your caution. Farewell."

*T*wo more days passed, or so we reckoned by the number of meals that were brought to us, but neither Tikal nor Mattai returned to visit us. Other doctors came, indeed, and saw Zibalbay, who lay upon his bed like one plunged in a deep sleep, but though they tried many remedies they were of no avail. On the night of the second day we were gathered round his couch, watching him and talking together sadly enough, for the solitude, and the darkness, and the fear of impending death had broken our spirits, so that even the señor ceased to be merry, and the presence of her beloved to give comfort to Maya.

"Alas!" she said, "it was an evil day when we met yonder in the land of Yucatan, and, friend, no gift could have been more unlucky than that of my love to you, for which, being worth so little, you are doomed to pay so dear. Fortune has gone hardly with you also, Ignatio, who are fated thus for the second time to see a woman wreck your hopes. Say, now, friend" — and she caught the señor by the arm — "would it not be best that we should make an end of all this folly, and that I should give myself to Tikal? Then I could bargain for you both that before I pass to him I should, with my own eyes, see you safe across the mountains, taking that with you which would make you rich for life. Nor need you trouble for me, or think that you left me to dishonor, for, so soon as you were gone, I should seek the arms of another lord whose name is Death, and there take my rest, till in some day unborn you came to join me."

"Cease to talk thus, Maya," said the señor, drawing her to his breast; "whatever there is to bear we will undergo together, since, even if I could be so base as to buy safety at such a price, without you my life would be worth nothing to me, and, indeed, I had rather die at your side than live on alone. It is my fault that ever we came to this pass, seeing that, if I had taken your counsel, we should not have set foot within the City of the Heart. But curiosity conquered me, for I longed to see the place, as now I long to see the last of it; also, had we turned back, I must have left Ignatio to go on alone. Keep your courage, sweetheart, for though your father is dying and our danger is great, I am sure that we shall escape from these dungeons and be happy with each other beneath the sunlight."

Then he kissed her upon the lips and comforted her, wiping away the tears that ran from her blue eyes.

It was at this moment that I looked up and saw Mattai standing in the doorway, — for we were gathered, not in the hall, but in Zibalbay's chamber — watching the scene curiously and with a softened face.

"Greeting," he said, "and forgive me that I come so late, but my business is secret and such as is best done at night. How goes it with Zibalbay?"

"He lives," I answered; "I can say no more, for he is senseless, and, without doubt, soon must die. But come, see for yourself."

Mattai walked to the bed and examined the old man, lifting the eyelids and feeling his heart.

"He cannot live long," he said. "Well, death is his best friend. Now to my business. There is trouble in the city, and strange rumors pass from mouth to mouth among the people, many of whom declare that Tikal has murdered Zibalbay, and demand that you, Lady, should be brought before them, that you may be named *cacique* in his place. Things being so, it has been urged upon Tikal by the chiefs of his party that as, do what he will, he can never clear himself of the death of Zibalbay, it would be well that he should make away with you also, Lady, and, of course, with these two strangers, your friends, seeing that then there will be none to dispute his rights. The matter was laid before him strongly at a secret council held this afternoon, and once he issued the order for your deaths, only to recall it before the messenger left the palace; for at the last I saw that his heart overcame his reason, and he could not bear thus to divorce himself from you, Lady, though what he said was that he would not stain his hands with the blood of one so innocent and fair. Still, I will not hide from you, Lady, or from you, strangers, that your danger is very great, that you go, indeed, in jeopardy of your life from one hour to the next."

Now he paused, and Maya asked in a low voice:

"Have you no plan to save us, Mattai?"

"Why should I have a plan, Lady, who with my house would benefit so greatly by your death?"

"I do not know why you should have a plan, old man," broke in the señor; "but I tell you that you will do well to make one, else you do not leave this place alive" — and as he spoke, with a sudden movement, he sprang between Mattai and the door.

"If we are to be murdered like birds in a cage," he went on, "at least your neck shall be twisted first. Do you understand?"

"I understand, Son of the Sea," answered Mattai, flinching a little before the señor's fierce face and hand outstretched as though to grip him. "But I would have you understand something also; namely, that if I do not return presently, there are some without who will come to seek me, and then —"

"And then they will find your carcase," broke in the señor, "and what will all your plots and schemes advantage you when you are a lump of senseless clay?"

"Little indeed, I confess," he answered. "Still, my daughter, whom I love better than myself, will reap some profit, and with that, in this sad case, I must be content. But, do not be so hasty, white man. I asked why I should have a plan? I did not say that I had none."

"Then if you have one, let us hear it without more ado," said the señor.

Mattai bowed, as he answered:

"Your will is mine: but I know not how my plan will please the Lady Maya yonder, and therefore, before I unfold it, I will make it clear to you that there is but one alternative — the death of all of you by tomorrow's light. Your lives lie in my hand, and if I must do so to save my daughter and myself, I shall not hesitate to take them."

"Anymore than I shall hesitate to take yours, old man," said the señor, grimly; "for remember always that if you do not make your plan such as we can accept, you will leave this chamber feet first with a broken neck."

Again Mattai bowed, and continued;

"In one way only has Tikal been able to pacify the tumult among the people, by declaring that the Lady Maya shall be produced before the Council of the Heart, in the Sanctuary of the Nameless god, upon the

night of Rising of Waters, being the first day when it is lawful for the
Council to sit in the Sanctuary, and afterwards at dawn in the eyes of
the whole city. The words of Zibalbay have taken a strange hold of the
people, although they cried him down as he spoke them; and they desire
to know what will happen when the prophecy is fulfilled, and once more
the severed halves of the symbol of the Heart are laid side by side in
their place upon the altar. Zibalbay told them that he believed that then
the god would reveal his purpose, and show what part each of you should
play in the fate that is to be, and therefore the people — aye! and many
among the nobles, and even the Council of the Heart — look to see
some sign or wonder when Day and Night are come together, and that
which was parted is made one, for they begin to hold that the madness
of Zibalbay is from heaven, and that the voice of heaven sent him on
his journey."

Now Mattai thought for a while and went on:

"Lady, I am old, and for many years I have followed the worship of
the gods, doing sacrifice to them, and importuning them with prayers,
yet never have I known the gods to make answer to their votaries, or
heard the voices of the immortals speaking into human ears. It seems
that gods are many: thus, perchance these strangers have their own; and,
Lady, thus it comes that in my age I ask myself if there are any gods
other than those that the mind of man has shaped from nothingness,
or fashioned in the likeness of its own passions. I cannot tell, but I think
that were I in so sore a strait as you find yourselves tonight, I should
not hesitate to give a voice to these dumb gods."

"What is your meaning?" asked Maya.

"This: When the severed halves of the Heart are set in their place
upon the altar, if there be any gods they should give a sign. Thus, as I
who am the keeper of the Sanctuary know, the ancient symbol on the
altar is hollow, and if it were to chance to open, it might be that a writing
would be found within it — an ancient writing of the gods, prepared
against the present time — that shall be to us as a lantern to one
wandering in the dark; or it might be that nothing would be found.
Now, as it happens, in searching through the earliest records of the
temple, I have discovered a certain writing, and it seems to me that your
fortune would be great if this writing should lie within the symbol on
the night of the Rising of Waters. Here it is —"

And from his robe he produced a small plate of dull gold, covered
over with hieroglyphics.

"Read it," said Maya.

Then Mattai read:

"This is the voice of the Nameless god that his prophet heard in the year of the building of the Sanctuary, and graved upon a tablet of gold which he set in a secret place in the symbol of the Sanctuary, to be declared in that far-off hour when the lost is found and the signs of the Day and the Night are come together. To thee it speaks, unborn daughter of a chief to be, whose name is the name of a nation. When my people have grown old and their numbers are lessened, and their heart is faint, then, maiden, take to thyself as a husband a man of the race of the white god, a son of the sea-foam, whom thou shalt lead hither across the desert, for so my people shall once more prosper and grow strong, and the land shall be to thy child and the child of the god, east and west, and north and south, further than my eagles wing between sunrise and sunset."

He finished reading, and there was silence as we looked on each other, amazed at the boldness and cunning of this old priest and plotter. It was Maya who spoke first.

"You have forged this writing, Mattai," she said coldly, "and now you desire that I should set it in the symbol, for you are mindful of that curse which is written in the ritual Opening of the Heart against him who shall profane its mysteries and token, or who should are to tell a lie within the Sanctuary, or to swear falsely by the symbol. In short, if you do not fear the vengeance of the god, you fear the vengeance of the Order."

"To speak truth, lady, I fear both, for, in offering insult to the Nameless god, who knows what he offends? Still, you must make your choice — and swiftly, seeing that if you refuse the deed, by tomorrow you will have learned, or, perhaps — remembering the words of the white lord — I should say *we* shall have learned what virtue there is in the religions."

Now she turned to us, saying:

"Advise me, friends, for I know not what to answer. In the faith of my people I have lost faith, and it is to yours that I look for comfort; and yet the deed seems awful, for if we are not worshippers of the Nameless god, still we are all of us brethren of the ancient mysteries of the Heart, and to do this thing would be to break our solemn oaths. Come, let us put it to the vote, and do you who are the oldest and the wisest among us, vote first, Ignatio."

"So be it," I answered. "For my part I give my vote against the trick. Of the gods of your people I know nothing and think less, but I am the Master of our Order in my own land, and I will not offend against it.

To do this thing would be to act the greatest of lies and a lie is a sin in the face of heaven. All men must die, but I wish to pass to doom with my hands unstained by fraud. Still, in this matter your lives are at stake as well as mine; therefore, if, of the three of us, two are in favor of the act, I will be bound by their decision. But if only one is in favor, then he must be bound by ours."

"Good, let it be so," said Maya. "And now, beloved, speak and tell us whether you choose death and a clean conscience, or life and my love to gladden it" — and she looked into his face with her beautiful eyes, and half stretched out her arms as though she would clasp him to her breast.

Now, although the señor did not answer at once, when I saw this and heard her words, I, Ignatio, knew that it was finished, since it could not be in the heart of a man in love to resist her pleadings and her witcheries. Presently he spoke, and as he did so his face grew red with a half shame.

"I have no choice," he said. "I do not fear to die if need be, but I should be no man were I to choose death while it is your wish that I should live. Like Ignatio, I say that the gods of this city are to me nothing more than idols, and to deceive that which does not exist is impossible. For the rest, I became a Brother of the Heart not by my own wish, but by accident, therefore on this point my conscience pricks me little. Only, to be a partner in this plot, I must speak or act a lie, and this I have never done before. Still it seems to me that a man may choose life and his love in place of a cruel and secret death, and keep his hands clean, even though he must play a harmless trick as the price of them. Yet, Maya, in this as in every other matter, I will do your wish, and if you think it better that we should die, why let us die and make an end."

"Nay," she answered, with a flash of reckless passion, "I think it better that we should live, far from this unlucky city, and there be happy in each other's love. For your sake my father's curse has fallen on me, and after it all other maledictions of gods or men will be light as feathers. If this be a sin that we are about to work, I do it for the sake of you and of our love; also because I would live awhile in happiness before I go down to the grave. See my father lying there; throughout a long life he has served his god, and behold how his god has served him in the hour of his trouble. Let his prayers answer for us both, for I will have none of such false gods, unless it be to use them for my ends. If this be a sin that we are about to do, and vengeance should tread upon the heels of sin, let it fall upon the heads of my people, who would murder me for no crime; upon the head of Mattai, who tempted me for his own advantage; and, if that be not enough, upon my head also. Little do I care for vengeance to come, if for only one short year I may call you husband."

"Ill-omened words," muttered Mattai, shivering a little, "words that only a woman would utter; but so be it."

As he spoke I thought that I heard a faint groan break from the man upon the couch. I glanced anxiously at Zibalbay, to find that I must have been mistaken, or, at least, that it had not proceeded from his lips, for he lay there rigid and senseless as a corpse.

"The vote is taken," I said sadly. "What next, Mattai?"

"Follow me," he answered, "and I will show you a secret path from this chamber to the Sanctuary beneath. Nay, you need not fear to leave him, for if his life still burns within him, it is fast asleep. But stay, where is the talisman? That will be necessary to us."

"I have one half," I answered, "the other is about Zibalbay's neck."

"Find it," he said, sternly, to the Lady Maya. "Nay, you must!"

Chapter XIX

THE SACRILEGE

Now Maya bent over the form of her father and took the talisman from his neck.

"I feel like one who robs the dead," she said.

"Remember that it is to save the living, and be comforted," answered Mattai. "Come, let us be going, for the night draws on."

"Take a lamp, each of you," he said presently, when we had reached the further end of the great hall, where he unlocked the copper gates with a key from the bunch that hung at his girdle. We passed though, and, turning, he almost closed the gate, but not quite.

"Why do you leave the gates ajar?" I asked.

"Because there are none to follow us," he answered, "and who knows what may happen. Should we be forced to fly the Sanctuary, open doors are easier to pass than those that are shut."

"Who or what could force us to fly the Sanctuary?" I asked.

Mattai shrugged his shoulders and went on without answering. Now we passed down many stairs, along passages, and through secret doors, each of which Mattai left open behind us, till at length we came to a blank wall of marble. On this wall Mattai felt with his thumb, till he found a spot that, being pressed, slid back, revealing a keyhole into which he inserted a small silver key. Then again he pressed upon the marble, and a panel moved that might have been two feet wide by six in height, and we saw that light streamed through the opening. Beckoning to us he walked through the gap in the wall, and one by one we followed him into the Sanctuary of the Nameless god, and stood on the further side of the wall, huddled together and clasping each other's hands, for the place was awesome, and its utter silence and solemnity filled us with fear.

The first thing that caught our eyes, as was natural, for it was built into the wall opposite to us, and through it streamed the light that filled the chamber, was the most wonderful and mystic effigy in the City of the Heart. That effigy was a colossal mask of singular and fearful beauty, fashioned from polished jade, and similar in design to those which are to be found in the ruins of Palenque and other deserted Indian cities, whereof no man knows the age. This huge green mask was placed above the narrow door that gave entrance to the Sanctuary, and had been carved to represent the countenance of a being that, although its features were human, resembled neither man nor woman in its unearthly dignity and its stamp of cruel calm. The thick lips were curved with a contemptuous smile, and between them gleamed teeth made of white enamel; the nose was aquiline, with widespread nostrils that seemed to inhale the incense of worship; and the forehead, in whose center appeared the impress of a woman's hand soaked in some scarlet dye, was broad, low, and retreating. Beneath the solemn and contracted brows were jeweled eyes. Through these eyes, and, indeed, from the entire surface of the mask, streamed light, making the face visible as though it were limned in phosphorus, for the jade was transparent as the thinnest alabaster, and behind it burned two great lamps that were named after the Sun and Moon.

Such was the effigy of the Nameless spirit that we now beheld for the first time, who had face but no form; the spirit, Mouth of the Heart, to whom every lesser god was subject, Utterer of the thoughts of the Heart of Heaven, Lord of power, Dweller in the darkness behind the

Sun, Searcher of the secrets of death. Without pity was this god of theirs, and without wrath, who, clothed in eternal calm, so these people fabled, rested in a home of darkness, watching the shadow of events celestial and terrestrial in his mirror of the moon, and telling of them to the Heart which was his soul. The seal of the woman's blood-stained hand was set upon his brow because woman is a symbol of life renewed, the hand is the sign of purpose and the strength to do it, and by blood and anguish must every purpose be accomplished. But the Nameless one executed no purpose — that was the work of lesser gods. In the beginning the Heart thought and the Mouth blew with his breath, giving life to the earth, and causing it to roll forward among the spheres, and now the Eyes watched, ever smiling, while it and those upon it work out our doom, till at length its primal force grows faint and fails when, so said the priests, Heart and Mouth and Ears will think and speak and search, and at their command a new world shall arise from the corpse of the old, and a new life from the lives of those who dwelt upon it.

Therefore it was, though now faith waned among them with their waning energies, that the people, knowing no better creed, worshipped the threefold Fate without a name, whom they held to be master of gods and men. Therefore, also, long generations since, in this spot which we came to violate — to them the most holy on the earth — they set up effigies of a Heart, a Mouth, and Eyes, as symbols of his attributes.

The roof of the Sanctuary, which was of no great size, was vault-shaped, in imitation of the arching sky, and in it appeared a golden sun, a silver crescent moon, and the stars of heaven. Its walls were lined throughout with polished blocks of the beautiful stone known as Mexican onyx, fretted over to the height of a man with a border of hieroglyphics and effigies of the lesser gods in attitudes of adoration, all of them cast in gold and set flush with the face of the wall. The furniture was very simple, consisting only of stools cut from rich woods heavily gilded in quaint designs, and a small table whereon lay sheets of paper made of bark, together with brushes of reed fiber and pots of pigment, such as were used in the picture-writing of this people. Lastly, at that end by which we had entered the chamber, stood an altar of black marble written around with letters shaped in gold, and upon this altar lay something covered with a silken cloth.

For a minute or more we remained silent, contemplating these wonders; then, with a gesture of impatience, Mattai spoke in a whisper, saying:

"Let that be done which we have come to do, for now the sacrilege is committed and it is too late for doubts."

Speaking thus, he stepped to the altar and lifted the silken cloth that lay over the object which was upon it, revealing the image of a human heart fashioned in bloodstone and veined with arteries of gold. In the center of this heart appeared a small and shallow hole that had been hollowed in its substance.

"This is the tradition," said Mattai, still speaking in a whisper, "that when the two halves of a certain talisman are placed in this hollow, the symbol will open and reveal that which has been set within it since it was fashioned by Cucumatz thousands of years ago, and there is this in favor of the truth of the tale that golden hinges appear upon the sides of the symbol. Now one-half of the talisman has rested here for many generations, till Zibalbay took it with him indeed, when he went out to seek for the other half, and yet the symbol has never opened; still, I am sure that it will open when the whole talisman is set in its place. In this matter, however, there is something more to fear than the vengeance of the gods, for, as I can read well — it is written in those letters that encircle the altar — an ancient tradition tells us that if the symbol be stirred from the place where it has lain for so many ages, the flood-gate will roll back and the waters of the lake will pour in upon the city, destroying it and its inhabitants."

"Yet the flood-gate cannot roll back when it is not shut, nor can the waters flow in during the dry season, when they are not on a level with the walls," answered Maya.

"They cannot, Lady, and yet other things may happen. Why was the Heart set thus? Was it not that in the utmost need of its worshippers they might choose death rather than defeat and slavery? And was this choice given to them in the wet months only? Be sure that if at this moment any despairing or impious hand tore yonder symbol from its altar, either the waters would rush up through the bed of the city, or subterranean fires would break loose and burn it. Still, though there is something, I think that we have little to fear, seeing that the writing says that, in order to bring about so terrible a doom, the symbol must be torn from its altar with might. And now to our task. Stranger, give to the Lady Maya your half of the ancient talisman, that she may set it, together with the half she bears, in the place prepared in the symbol."

Now with a sigh, seeing that it was too late to draw back, I undid the emerald from my neck and gave it to Maya, who laid it side by side with its counterpart upon the palm of her trembling hand, and stepped with it to the altar. Here she stood for a moment, then whispered in a faint voice:

"Terror has taken hold of me, and I fear to do this thing."

"Yet it must be done, and not by me," said Mattai, "or we shall have come on a fool's errand, and go back, some of us, to a fool's death," and he looked towards me.

"I will not do it," I said, answering his look, "not because I fear your gods, but my own conscience I do fear."

"Then I will," said the señor boldly, "for I fear neither. Give me that trinket, Maya."

She obeyed, and presently he had caused the two halves of the talisman to fall into their ancient and appointed bed in the symbol. In the great silence I remember the sound they made, as they tinkled against the stone, struck my ear so sharply that I started.

For some seconds, perhaps twenty, we stood still, watching the altar with eager eyes, but the symbol never stirred. Then I said:

"It seems, Mattai, that you must hide your lying writing elsewhere, since yonder heart will not open, or, if it will, we have not found the key."

"Wait a little," broke in the señor, "perhaps the springs are rusted." And before any of us could interfere to stop him, he placed his thumb upon the halves of the emerald and pressed so hard that the symbol trembled on its marble stand.

"Beware!" cried Mattai, and as the echoes of his voice died away all of us started in astonishment, for lo! the heart was opening like a flower.

Slowly it opened, till the severed talisman fell from it, and its two halves lay back on the marble of the altar, revealing something hidden in its center that shone like an ember in the lamplight. We crept forward and looked, then stood silent and half afraid, for in the hollow of the heart, laid upon a square plate of gold which was covered with picture-writing, glared a red jewel shaped like a human eye, that seemed to answer stare with stare.

"If we stand like this we shall grow frightened," said the señor roughly, glancing round him as he spoke, "there is nothing to fear in a red stone cut like an eye."

"If you think so, White Man," answered Mattai in a voice that shook a little, strive as he would to command it, "lift up the holy thing and give me the writing that is beneath it. Stay, first take this, set it in the symbol, replacing the eye upon it," and he handed him the forged tablet.

The señor obeyed, nor did any wonder come to pass when he lifted that dreadful-looking jewel, and changed the true for the false.

"Read it," said Maya, as the tablet was passed to Mattai, "you have knowledge of the ancient writings."

"Perhaps it were best left unread," he said, doubtfully.

"Nay," she answered, "let us know the worst. Read it, I bid you."

Then he read these strange words in a slow and solemn voice:

"The Eye that has slept and is awakened sees the heart and purpose of the wicked. I say that in the hour of the desolation of my city not all the waters of the Holy Lake shall wash away their sin."

Now the faces of us who heard turned grey in the lamplight, for though the gods of this people were false, we felt that the voice of a true prophet spoke to us from that accusing tablet, and that we had called down upon our heads a vengeance which we could not measure.

"Did I not tell you that it were wiser to leave the writing unread," gasped Mattai, letting the tablet fall from his hand as though it were a snake.

The clatter of it as it struck the marble floor seemed to wake us from our evil dream, for the señor turned on him, and said fiercely:

"What does it matter what the thing says, rogue, seeing that you forged it as you have forged the other?"

"Ah! would that I had," answered Mattai; "but when doom overtakes you and all of us, then shall you learn whether I forged that ancient writing;" and he lifted it from the floor, and, hiding it in his robe, added, "Close the heart, White Man, and give back the severed jewel to those who wear it."

The señor obeyed, replacing the silken cloth over the symbol, so that the altar seemed to be as it had been.

"Now let us be going," said Mattai, "and rejoice, that if yonder eye has seen our wickedness, at least it is hidden from the sight of man. Doubtless the vengeance of the gods is sure, but that of men is swift."

As he spoke we turned to leave the Sanctuary, and of a sudden Maya screamed, and would have fallen had not the señor caught her. Well might she scream, for there in the narrow niche of the secret door by which we had entered, framed in it as a corpse is framed in its coffin, stood a white figure which at first I took to be that of some avenging ghost, so ghostlike were the wrappings, the snowy beard and hair, and the thin, fierce face. Another instant, and I saw that indeed it was a ghost, the ghost of Zibalbay, or rather his body come back from the boundaries of death to spy upon our sacrilege before it crossed them forever.

Yes, it was Zibalbay, for while he had seemed to be unconscious upon the bed in the chamber, his senses were awake, and oh! what must he have suffered when he, the high priest of the Nameless god, heard us plan our fraud upon his Sanctuary. Then, after we had left him, fury and despair unfettered the limbs that had been bound so fast and gave him strength to follow us, though they could not unlock his frozen tongue. He had followed; painfully he had crept down the stairs, along the passages, and through the open door, for the path was known to him even in the dark, till at length he came to the secret entrance of the Sanctuary. Here once more his force deserted him; here, unable to speak or stir, he had leaned against the wall and seen and heard all that was done and said.

Oh! never shall I forget the rage of his quivering face, or the agony and horror of his tormented eyes as they met our own. No course could have been so awful as that look which he let fall upon his daughter, and no outraged deity or demon could have seemed more terrible to the human sight than was the tall figure of this dying man, striving even in death to protect the honor of his gods, which we had violated in their most holy of holies. Never have I seen such a dreadful sight, and I pray that never again may I do so either in this world or the next.

The dying Zibalbay saw our fear, and with a last effort he staggered forward towards his daughter, his clenched hands held above his head. For a moment he stood before her as she lay upon her lover's arm staring up at him like a bird at a snake, while he swayed to and fro above her like the snake about to strike. Then, of a sudden, foam mingled with blood burst from his lips, and he sank down at her feet dead, dying in a silence that was more awful than any sound.

Of all that followed I need not write. Indeed, I cannot do so, for so great was my horror at this scene, and so intense the strain which was put upon my vital force during these hours, that I have little memory of what chanced after Zibalbay's death, till I found myself lying exhausted upon the bed in my prison cell.

Somehow we calmed and silenced Maya; somehow we escaped from that hateful Sanctuary, and by slow degrees brought her and the dead body of her father up the narrow stairs and passages to the hall above, where we laid the corpse upon its bed. Then Mattai left us, and I remember no more till the next morning when nobles and leeches came to watch by the body of the dead *cacique,* and to embalm it in readiness for the tomb.

The next two days went heavily for the three of us, oppressed as we were by the silent gloom of our prison and the memories of that dreadful night. The love between Maya and her father had never been deep, for they were out of tune with each other; still, now that he was dead she mourned him, the more perhaps because he had died hating and cursing her. By degrees she recovered from her superstitious fears, born of the writing in the symbol; but her father's maledictions she never could forget, and though she was willing to earn and to bear these for the sake of her love for the señor, I think that their memory lay between them like a shadow.

"Oh! why did I ever love you?" she would say. "What have you to do with me, whom race and law and fate have set apart from me?" And yet she went on loving him even more dearly.

I, also, was unhappy, for though I put little faith in these omens, or in the vaporings of dead prophets and the tricks of living charlatans, I felt that the ill-luck which had clung to me in the past was with me still. Things had gone cross with me; Zibalbay was dead, and Woman, the inevitable, had drawn away the heart of my friend and dragged me and my plans into the whirlpool of her passion, whence, if at all, they must emerge ruined and shapeless. Still, summoning the patience of my race to my aid, I bore these secret troubles as I might, giving counsel and comfort to the lovers, who, lost in their own doubts and difficulties, thought, as was natural, little of me and my lost ambitions.

At length they carried away the corpse of Zibalbay to be wrapped in its winding-sheet of gold and set with all ancient pomp and ceremony by those of its forefathers in the Hall of the Dead. Maya wept indeed, but I for my part was glad to see the last of him, and so, I think, was the señor, whose spirits had begun to fail him in the presence of so much remorse and grief.

That day — it was the day previous to the night of the Rising of Waters, on which we were to appear before the Council of the Heart in the Sanctuary — Tikal came to visit us. To Maya he bowed low, but on the señor and myself he looked with an angry eye — with the eye, indeed, of one who would have killed us if he dared. First, with many fine words and empty compliments, he offered her his sympathy upon the death of her father. For this she returned her thanks, quoting, however, with a flash of her old spirit, a certain proverb of her own people, of which the meaning is that the death of one man is the breath of another.

"My father was your foe, Tikal," she added, "and now that he is gone you will be able to sleep and reign in peace."

"Not altogether so, Lady," he answered, "seeing that he has left behind him a more dangerous rival to my power, namely, yourself. I will not hide from you, Maya, what you must soon learn, that a large portion of the people, and with them many of the nobles, accusing me of your father's murder, clamor that I should be deposed, and that you should be set in my place as *cacique* of the City of the Heart. Some few days ago I might have stilled their outcry by commanding you to be put to death, but now it is too late, for, since then, Time has fought for you, and doubtless your end would be followed by my own. When last we met, cousin, I asked you a certain question, to which you promised me an answer when your father was dead or recovered, and today I have come to hear that answer. While Zibalbay lived I had much to offer him and you in exchange for your hand, and I offered it freely. So high a value did I place upon it when it seemed lost to me, that I was prepared to lay down my power, to suffer your father to violate the laws, and to incur the eternal hate and active enmity of Mattai, his daughter, and his party. Now I must make you a lower bid: that of equal power for yourself; and for your friends here, whatever they may desire. Should you refuse me, this is the alternative: civil war in the city till one of us is destroyed, and instant death as the portion of these strangers.

"But, Maya, I pray you not to refuse me, for I have something more to offer you — my undying love. From a child I always loved you, Maya, although you have treated me coldly enough, and now day by day I love you more. Indeed I believed that you and your father were dead yonder in the wilderness, for then I had faith in Mattai, whom now I know to be a rogue, and Mattai swore that it was written in the stars. Even so I would not have wed another woman, for my heart bled at the loss of you, had not Mattai made this marriage the price of his support, without which I could not hope to be anointed *cacique*, seeing that I have many jealous enemies. It was ambition that led me to consent, and bitterly have I regretted my folly ever since; for if she who is called my wife loves me, I hate her, and by this means or by that I will be rid of her. Forgive me, then, my sin against you, remembering only that I have loved and served you in the past as I will love and serve you in the future, and that it was you who brought about these troubles because, though I prayed you to stay and did all in my power to prevent you, you determined to accompany your father upon his mad journey into the wilderness. Now I have spoken, and I thank you for the courtesy with which you have listened to me."

"You have spoken, cousin," she answered, "and your words have been gentle; yet, if I understand you right, some few days since you were in doubt as to whether it would not be better to murder me here in this darksome hole where you have placed us."

"If policy put any such thought into my mind, Maya, love drove it out again," he answered, with confusion.

"So you admit that this was so," she said. "Well, a day may come when policy might breed the thought, and love, grown weary, prove not warm enough to wither it. Also it seems that even now you threaten these my companions with death, should I refuse you your desire."

"If you should refuse me my desire, Maya, perhaps it will be for a secret reason of your own" — and he scowled at the señor angrily — "a reason that the death of these men, or of one of them, will remove."

"Be sure of one thing, Tikal," she broke in sharply, "that such a wicked deed would put an end forever to your hopes of making me your wife. Now, listen. I have heard your words, and they have touched me somewhat, for I think that although you have broken your oath to my father, and your troth with me, at heart you are honest in your love. Still, I can give you no answer now, and for this reason, that the answer does not lie with me, but rather with the gods. Tomorrow night we appear before the High Court of the Council of the Heart, and you yourself shall set the severed portions of the talisman that we have traveled so far to seek in the place prepared to receive it, in the symbol that is on the altar of the Sanctuary. Then, as my dead father believed — and he was gifted with wisdom from above — the god shall declare his purpose in this way or in that, showing his servants why all these things have come about, and what they must do to fulfil his will. By that will, cousin, and not by my own, I shall be guided in this and in all other things."

Now, Tikal thought awhile, and answered:

"And if nothing follows this ceremony, and the oracles of the god are silent, what then?

"Then, Tikal," she said softly, "you may ask me again if I will become your wife, and perhaps, if the Council suffers it, I shall not say you nay. Now farewell, for grief still shadows me, and I can talk no more."

Chapter XX

THE COUNCIL OF THE HEART

*N*ow, when Tikal was gone I sat silent, for although it might be necessary to save our lives, and to bring about the fulfillment of Maya's love, all this double-dealing did not please me, and I could not talk of it with a light heart. But the señor said:

"I hope that yonder rogue, Mattai, may not have repented or been overbribed by Tikal, and set some other prophecy in the hollow of the symbol, for then, Maya, you will be taken at your word, and things will be worse than ever they have been."

"I pray not, and it is not likely," she answered, starting, then with a quick burst of passion she added:

"But why do you look at me with such reproach, Ignatio? No, do not answer, for I know why. It is because you think me a cheater and a liar, and are saying in your heart, 'This is a woman's honor. Thus would any woman act in the hour of temptation.' Ignatio, with all your courtesy, you hate and despise us women, looking on us as lower then yourselves, as a snare to your strength and a pitfall for your feet. Well, if so, thus we were made, and can we quarrel with that which made us? Also, in some ways we are greater than you, though you may be pleased to call yourselves more honest. *You* would not have dared for your love what I have dared for mine; *you* would not have offered deadly outrage to the god of your people, to the instinct of your blood, and the teachings of your youth. No, you would have sat still and wrung your hands and seen your lover perish before your face, and then have turned your eyes to the sky and said: 'It cannot be helped, it is well; at least, *I* am clean in the sight of heaven.'

"So be it. I, Maya, am of a different nature, I have dared all these things and I joy in them, even though you watch me ever with your melancholy eyes. Why should I not? Is not my love everything to me, and is it shameful that this should be so? I believe no more in this unknown god; why, then, should I fear to offend him? I will not see my betrothed given up to death, and myself to worse than death; and how can I harm my people by taking a man nobler than themselves to be my husband? Cease, then, to reproach me by your silence; or, rather, learn to pity me, for my strait is sore, and doubtless vengeance dogs my heels. Let it fall, if it will, on me, but not on you, beloved — oh! not on you —" and suddenly her anger left her, and she sank into the señor's arms and lay there weeping bitterly.

Then I went to the further end of the hall and sat there reading the ancient writings of this people, which we had found in the chamber. Indeed, this was my daily occupation, for now I found that these lovers liked to be alone, unless it happened that there were plans to be thought out or counsel to be given. A shadow grew between me and the señor in those days; for, though he said nothing of it, he also was angry because I did not approve of the dark plot to which we were parties, and Maya's outburst spoke his mind with her own. Nor was this wonderful, for now, looking back, I do not blame her or him, or think that they did wrong, and I believe that what I really felt was not indignation at a trick which might well be pardoned, seeing how much hung to it, but superstitious fear lest some force, human or infernal, should visit that trick with vengeance; for, as we know, even the devils have power against us if we give it to them by fighting the world with their own weapons.

On the following day the attendants who set our meals brought with them clean robes for each of us, scented and wonderfully worked, and for Maya certain royal ornaments. In these we arrayed ourselves before evening, and waited. The hours passed, and at length the copper gates were opened, and a band of nobles and guards presented themselves before us, saying that they were commanded to lead us to the Sanctuary. We answered that nothing would please us better, who were heartily weary of living like rats in the dark, and in a few minutes we found ourselves walking up the stairs towards the crest of the pyramid.

We reached it, and saw the stars shining above us, and felt the breath of heaven blowing in our faces, and never have the sight of the stars or the taste of the night air seemed more sweet to me. Leaving the watch-house we walked to the great stair across the lonely summit of the pyramid and began to descend its side. At the foot of the stairway we turned to the right till we came to a double door of copper, beautifully worked, placed in the center of the western face of the pyramid, and guarded by a small body of soldiers, who saluted and admitted us. Beyond the doors was a great hall not unlike that which had served as our prison, lit with lamps, lined with polished marble, and having on either side of its length doorways leading to the apartments that were used as sleeping-places for the officers on duty. At the threshold of this hall we were met by priests clothed in pure white, into whose custody we were given by the company of nobles and soldiers that had escorted us thus far.

Surrounded by the priests, who chanted as they walked, we passed down the hall till we reached another and a smaller door. Beyond this lay a labyrinth of steeply sloping passages, running in every direction deep into the bowels of the rock beneath the pyramid. So intricate and numerous were these tunnels, that, even with the assistance of the lights which the priests carried, it would have been almost impossible for anyone not having their secret, to find a path through them, or even to keep his face in a given direction for more than a few paces.

Along these passages our guides went without faltering, turning now to the right, now to the left, and now seeming to retrace their footsteps, till at length they halted to open a third door, covered over with plates of beaten gold, on the further side of which lay the most sacred spot save one in the City of the Heart, the chamber that served the threefold purpose of a judgment-hall, a church wherein the nobles attended worship, and a burial-place of the departed *caciques* of the city. Here in this vast and awful vault, each of them set in his own niche and companioned by his consort, stood the bodies of every king-priest who had reigned in the holy city, enclosed in coffins of solid gold, fashioned to the shape and likeness of the corpse within, and having the name, age, date of death, and a brief account of the good or evil that the man had done cut in symbols on his breast. There they stood eternally, men and women made in gold, and beneath their brows gleamed false eyes of emeralds. Numerous as were the niches in the chamber, each had its tenants; and in the last recess — that nearest to the entrance — stood a newcomer; for here in his gilded sheath was placed the corpse of Zibalbay, by the side of her who had been his wife and Maya's mother.

For a moment Maya paused to look upon the bodies of her parents, then with a sigh and an obeisance she passed on, saying to me, "See, this Hall of the Dead is full, there is no place left for me or for my descendants, and surely that is an evil omen. Well," she added, with a sigh, "what does it matter where they set us when we are dead? For my part I had sooner sleep in the earth, or beneath the waters, than stand forever cased in gold and glaring with jeweled eyes upon the darkness. Yes, if I might, I should choose the earth that bore me, for it would turn my flesh to flowers."

Then we went on defiling before the silent company of the golden dead, who seemed to watch us as we walked, till, passing round a judgment-seat that was set near the end of the hall, we stood in front of a little door over which burned great lamps. This door was guarded by two priests with drawn swords, which they pointed towards us as a sign that we should halt.

Then the priests who had escorted us so far fell back behind the judgment-seat, and we were left alone.

"Give the sign, keepers of the gate," said Maya.

Thereupon one of the men with the drawn swords uttered a low and peculiar cry like to the wail of a child. When he had made this strange sound thrice at intervals of about half a minute, it was answered from within by another and a louder cry pitched upon the same note. Then of a sudden the door was flung wide, and a stern-looking man with a shaven head came through it.

"Who are you that seek entrance into the Sanctuary?" he asked; "are you gods or devils, men or women?"

"We are two men and a woman," answered Maya, "priests and priestess of the Heart, and we come to take our trial before the Council of the Heart, as is our right."

"Do you know the open signs of the Heart, the signs of Brotherhood, of Unity, and of Love, that you dare to stand upon the threshold of the Sanctuary, to cross which is death to the ignorant?"

"We know them," answered Maya. And one by one we gave those signs.

"Do you know the secret signs of the Heart, that you dare to cross this threshold?" he asked again. "Otherwise get you back and take your trial in the common judgment-hall."

"I know them," answered Maya, "and I vouch for these men who accompany me. Suffer me, then, to enter, and these with me, for I am here by ancient right, and I have knowledge both of the outward signs and the inner mysteries."

Now the man withdrew, and the door was closed behind him. Presently he appeared again and said:

"I have reported to the Council, and it is the will of the Council that you should enter."

"Follow me," said Maya to us, "and when you are spoken to make no answer till I have vouched for you. I will answer for you."

The priests let their swords fall, and, passing through the doors — for there were two of them connected by a short passage — once more we found ourselves standing beneath the mask of the Unknown god in the Sanctuary of the City of the Heart. But now it was no longer empty.

Behind the little altar were three stools, and upon them, clad in wonderful apparel, and adorned with gold and gems, sat Tikal, Mattai, and Nahua, who was the only woman present. In front of the altar was an open space, and beyond its circle, each wearing the orders of his spiritual rank, sat the Brethren of the Heart according to their degree, to the number of thirty-six.

Led by Maya we advanced into the space before the altar, and stood there in silence. None of those present took note of us; indeed, they did not seem to see us, but sat with bent heads and with hands folded crosswise on their breasts. At length one of the Brethren — he who was nearest to the door, and had questioned us without — rose, and, addressing Tikal, said:

"Keeper of the Heart, one who claims to be of our company stands before you, and with her two for whom she vouches, who, although they be strangers, by your command I have proved to be Brethren of the Heart, though what more they may be I know not. Be pleased, then, to prove them also by the voice of their sponsor, that their mouths may be opened and their prayer come to the ears of the Council."

At his words two of the brethren rose and blindfolded the señor and myself, lest we should see the sacred signs, with all of which, indeed, I was well acquainted, but Maya they did not blindfold. Then we heard Tikal asking:

"How are you named who are strange to our eyes?" We made no reply, for a voice in our ears cautioned us to be silent.

"We are named 'the Son of the Sea' and 'Ignatio the Wanderer,'" answered the voice of Maya.

"Son of the Sea, and Ignatio the Wanderer, why come you here," asked Tikal, "through the gate on which is written — 'Death to the Stranger and to the Uninstructed.'"

"Because we have a prayer to utter, an offering to make, and because, although we dwell in a far land, we are the servants of the Heart," answered Maya.

"How come ye here?"

"The Heart led, the Mouth whispered, and we followed the light of the Eyes."

"Show me the sign of the light of the Eyes, or die to this world."

Now there was silence, and, though we could not see it, Maya showed the sign on our behalf.

"Show me the second sign, the sign of the Mouth, or be cursed by the Mouth, and die to this world and the next."

Again there was silence.

"Show me the sign of the Heart, the third and greatest sign, lest the Heart think on you, and ye die to this world, to the next world, and all the worlds that are to be; lest ye be cast out between the Light and Darkness, and lost in the gulf of fire that joins Heaven to Hell."

Now we heard a sound of rustling, as though all the company had risen and were prostrating themselves, and presently the bandages were lifted from our eyes.

"Strangers," said Tikal, "your mouths are opened in the Sanctuary according to the ancient form, and it is lawful for the Council to listen to your prayer. Speak, then, without fear."

Then I spoke, saying:

"Brethren — for so I will dare to call you, seeing that I also, though a stranger, am of the Brotherhood of the Heart, as I can prove to you if need be — aye! and higher in rank than any present here, unless it be you, O Keeper of the Heart: on my own behalf, on behalf of my brother who also is of our company, and on behalf of Maya, Lady of the Heart, daughter of him who ruled you, and heiress to his power, I speak and make my prayer to you. It would seem that we three, together with Zibalbay, who is dead and therefore beyond the execution of your judgment, have violated the laws of this city — we by daring to enter its gates, and Zibalbay and the Lady Maya by leading us to those gates. For this crime we should have been put to death eight days ago upon the pyramid, had not the Lady Maya here claimed a right to have our cause laid before this high tribunal. In her case and in that of her father this was conceded, and I pray now that the same clemency may be extended to me and to my brother."

"Upon what grounds do you claim this, stranger?" asked Tikal.

"Upon the ground that we are Brethren of the inmost circle of the Heart, and therefore have committed no crime in visiting this city, which is free to us by right of our rank and office."

Now there was a murmur of "True" from the Council behind me, and Tikal also said "True," but added, "If you are Brethren from the inmost circle of the Heart, you are free from offence; but first you must prove that this is so, which as yet you have not done. A brother of the inmost circle knows its mysteries and can answer the secret questions. Come, let us put you to the test, but first let the white man be removed from the Sanctuary, for in this matter each must vouch for himself."

Accordingly the señor was led away, and, the doors having been closed and the lamps shaded, the oldest and most instructed of the councilors stood forward and put me to the test with many questions, all of which I answered readily. Then they commanded me to stand before the altar, and, as Keeper of the Heart, to open the Heart in the highest degree. This I did also, though afterwards they told me that my ritual differed in some particulars from their own. After that I took up my parable and questioned them till at length none there could answer me — no, not even the high priest or Mattai; and they confessed humbly that I was more instructed than any one of them, and because of this knowledge from that day forward I was held in veneration in the City of the Heart.

Now I was given a seat among the Brethren — the highest, indeed, after those of the chief priest and the great officers — and the señor was summoned.

He entered with a downcast look, and while Maya and I watched him sadly, his examination began. It was not long. At the second question he became confused, used angry language in Spanish and English, and broke down.

"Brethren," said Tikal — and there was joy in his eye, as he spoke — "it seems that we need not trouble further with this impostor. By daring to enter our city he has earned the penalty of death; moreover he has blackened his crime by claiming to be of our Brotherhood, whereas he scarcely knows the simplest pass-word. Is it your will that he should be taken to his fate? If so, speak the word of doom."

Now Maya rose affrighted, but, motioning to her to be silent, I spoke, saying:

"Hear me before that fatal word is spoken which cannot be recalled! This man is of our inmost Brotherhood, though he has not been formally admitted to the inner circles, and has forgotten those of the mysteries which were taught to him at his initiation. Listen, and I will tell you how he came to join the Order of the Heart" — and I told them that tale of my rescue by the señor, and told them also all the story of our meeting with Zibalbay and of our journey to the City of the Heart, speaking to them for an hour or more while they hearkened earnestly.

When I had done they debated as to the fate of the señor, and — though by only one vote — decided that if I had nothing more to urge on his behalf he must straightway die.

"I have something more to urge before you pass judgment," I said in my need and despair (speaking and acting a lie to save the life of my beloved friend — yes, I who had blamed Maya for this same deed), "though it has to do with the mysteries of your religion rather than with those of our Order. It was the belief of Zibalbay, who is dead, that when the two halves of the ancient talisman — the halves Night and Morning, that together make the perfect Day — are set in their place in the symbol which once they filled before the dividing of peoples, then it shall be made clear what part must be played by each of us wanderers in the fate that is to be. To this end did Zibalbay undertake his journey, and lo! here is that which he went to seek —" and I drew the talisman from my breast. "Take it, Tikal, for I resign it, and lay it with its fellow in the place that is prepared for them, so that we may learn, and all your people may learn, what truth there is in the visions of Zibalbay."

"That is our desire," answered Tikal, taking the severed emerald and its counterpart which Maya gave to him. "Let the white man, Son of the Sea, be placed without the Sanctuary and guarded there awhile, for so at least he will gain time to prepare himself for death. Fear not, lady," he added, noting Maya's anxious face, "no harm shall be done to him till this matter of the prophecy is made clear."

Now for the second time the señor was removed, and when he had gone Tikal spoke, tracing the history of the prophecy so far as it was known, and reciting its substance — that when once more the two halves of the symbol of the Heart were laid side by side in their place on the altar in the Sanctuary, then from that hour the people should grow great again.

"In all this," he said, "I have little faith; still, Zibalbay, who in his way was wise, believed it, and, the story having gone abroad, the people clamor that it should be put to the test. Is this your will also?"

"It is our will," answered the Councilors.

"Good. Then let it be done, and on your heads be it if harm should come of the deed. Mattai, the Council commands you to set these fragments in the hollow of the symbol."

"If such is the order of the Council I have no choice but to obey," said Mattai. "Yet, though none else have done so, I give my voice against it, for I hold that this is childishness, and never did I know any good to spring from prophecies" — and he paused as though waiting for an answer.

"Obey! Obey!" said the Council, for curiosity had got a hold of them, and they craned their necks forward to see what might happen.

"Obey!" repeated Tikal. "But beware how you shake the Heart, lest the legend prove true and we should perish in the doom of waters."

Then Mattai set the two halves of the talisman in their place; and as before, in the midst of an utter silence, lo! the symbol opened like a flower. Leaning forward I saw the eye within its hollow; but it seemed to me that the fire had faded from the heart of the jewel, for now it gleamed coldly, like the eye of a man who is two hours dead. I think that Mattai noted this also, for as the symbol opened he started and his hand shook.

Now, when they saw the marvel, a gasp of wonder rose from the Council, then Tikal spoke, saying:

"It seems that there was wisdom in Zibalbay's madness, for the Heart has opened indeed, and within it is a stone eye resting upon a plate of gold that is covered with writing."

"Read the writing!" they cried.

Displacing the eye, Tikal lifted the plate of gold and scanned it.

"I cannot," he said, shaking his head. "It is written in a character more ancient than any I have learned. Take it, Mattai, for you are instructed in such signs."

Now Mattai took the tablet and studied it long with an anxious face, upon which at length light broke that changed anon to wonder, or rather blank amaze, so that I, watching him, began to think, not knowing all the cleverness of Mattai, that the señor was right, and the tablet had been tampered with since we saw it.

"Read! Read!" cried the Council.

"Brethren," he said, "the words seem clear, and yet so strange is this writing that I fear my learning is at fault, and that I had best give it to others to decipher."

"No; read, read," they cried again, almost angrily.

Then he read:

"This is the voice of the Nameless god that his prophet heard in the year of the building of the Sanctuary, and graved upon a tablet of gold which he set in a secret place in the symbol of the Sanctuary, to be declared in that far-off hour when the lost is found and the signs of the Day and the Night are come together. To thee it speaks, unborn daughter of a chief to be, whose name is the name of a nation. When my people have grown old, and their numbers are lessened, and their heart is faint, then, maiden, take to thyself as a husband a man of the race of the white god, a son of the sea-foam, whom thou shalt lead hither across the desert, for so my people shall once more prosper and grow strong, and the land shall be to thy child and the child of the god, east and west, and north and south, further than my eagles wing between sunrise and set."

Now, as Mattai read, the face of Tikal grew black with rage, and before ever the echoes of his voice had died away, he sprang from his seat crying:

"Whoever it was that wrote this lying prophecy, god or man, let him be accursed. Shall the Lady Maya — for her it must be whose name is the name of a nation — be given in marriage to the white dog who awaits his doom without that door, and shall his son rule over us? First I will see her dead and him with her!"

Then one of the eldest of the Council, a man named Dimas, who, as I learned afterwards, had been foster-brother to Zibalbay, rose and answered wrathily:

"It seems that these things must be so, Tikal, and beware how you utter threats of death lest they should fall upon your own head. We have called upon the god, and the god has spoken in no uncertain voice. The Lady Maya must become wife to the white man, Son of the Sea, and then things shall befall as they are fated."

"What?" answered Tikal. "Is this wandering stranger to be set over me and all of us?"

"That I do not know," said the Councilor, "the writing does not say so; the writing says that his son shall be set over us, and as yet he has no son. But this is certain, that the Lady Maya must be given to him as wife, and in her right he well may rule, seeing that she is the lawful heir to her father, and not you, Tikal, although you have usurped her place."

Now many voices called upon Maya, and she stood forward and spoke, with downcast eyes.

"What shall I say?" she began, "except one thing, that my will is the will of the gods, and if it is fated that I should be given to the white man in marriage, why, so let it be. For many years I was taught to look elsewhere, but he who was to have been my husband —" and she pointed towards Tikal — "chose himself another wife, and now I see that he did this not altogether of his own will, but because it was so decreed. One thing more. I, who am but a woman, have no desire to rule or to take the place that the Lady Nahua holds. The writing says that in a day to come, a far-off day, some child of mine, if indeed I am that 'daughter of a chief whose name is the name of a nation,' shall rule in truth. Let him then come in his hour and take the glories that await him, and meanwhile, Tikal, do you sit in your place and leave me to rest in peace."

"The Lady Maya speaks you fair, Tikal, and my daughter," said Mattai, "and if the people will have it, you may do well to accept her offer, leaving the future to shape itself. She says she is ready to take the white man as a husband, but we have not yet heard whether the white man will take her as a wife. It may be —" he added with a smile — "that he will rather choose to die; but at the least we must have an answer from his lips — that is, if you accept this prophecy as sent from heaven. Say, do you accept it?"

"We accept it," answered the Council almost with one voice.

"Then let the white man, Son of the Sea, be brought before us," said Mattai.

Chapter XXI

THE MARRIAGE OF MAYA

*P*resently the door opened and the señor was led into the Sanctuary, as he thought to his death, for I saw that his teeth were set and that his hand was clenched as though to defend himself. But as he came the most of the Council rose and bowed to him, crying:

"Hail to you! Son of the Sea, Favored of Heaven, Father fore-ordained of the Deliverer to come!"

Then he knew that the plot had succeeded, and he uttered a great sigh of relief.

"Hearken, white lord," said Mattai, for Tikal sat still and scowled on him in silence; "the gods have spoken by their oracle. As Zibalbay thought, so it is, and your feet have been led for a purpose to the gates of the City of the Heart. Listen to the words of the gods" — and, taking the tablet, he read to him the false prophecy. "Now choose, White Man. Will you take the Lady Maya to wife, or will you be put to death in that, having wandered to the City of the Heart, you refuse to obey the command of its gods?"

Now the señor thought and answered:

"The man would be foolish who hesitated between death and so fair and sweet a bride. Still, this is a matter that I cannot decide alone. What says the Lady Maya?"

"She says," answered Maya, "that although this is a marriage for which she did not look, and it is a new thing that a daughter of the Heart should take a stranger of less ancient blood to husband, the will of Heaven is her will, and the lord that Heaven chooses for her shall be her lord" — and she stretched out her hand to the señor.

He took it, and, bending down, kissed her fingers, saying:

"May I be worthy of your choice, Lady."

Now I thought that the ceremonies were finished, and was glad, for I grew weary of assisting at this farce, but the old priest, Zibalbay's foster-brother, rose and said:

"One thing more must be done, Brethren, before we leave this Sanctuary, and it is to swear in these strangers as members of the Council. They have wandered here from far, and here with us they must live and die, seeing that both of them know our secrets, and one of them is predestined to become the father of that great lord for whose arising we have looked for many generations, and therefore, until the child is born, he must be watched and guarded as priests watch a sacred fire."

"Aye! it is well thought of. Let them be sworn, and learn that to break the oath is death," was the answer.

Then Mattai rose, as Keeper of the Sanctuary, and said:

"You, White Man, Son of the Sea, and you, Ignatio, the Wanderer, a Lord of the Heart, do swear upon the holy symbol of the Heart, the oath to break which is to die horribly in this world and to be lost everlastingly in the worlds that are to be. You swear, setting in pledge your souls and bodies for the fulfillment of the oath, that neither by word nor sign nor deed will you reveal aught of the mysteries or the councils of this Brotherhood, whereof you will be the faithful servants till your deaths, holding it supreme above every power upon earth. You swear that you will not possess yourselves of the treasures of the City of the Heart, nor, without the consent of this high Brotherhood, attempt to leave its gates or to bring any stranger within its walls. These things you swear with your hands upon the altar, setting in pledge your souls and bodies for the fulfillment of the oath."

Other clauses there were also which I have forgotten, but this was the substance of the vow that was dictated to us. We looked at each other helplessly, and then, there being no escape, we swore, kneeling before the altar, with our hands resting upon it.

As the solemn words of confirmation passed our lips, we heard a sound of the movement of heavy stones behind us.

"Arise now," said the old priest, "turn, Brethren, and look upon that which lies behind you."

We obeyed, and the next instant shrank back against the altar in alarm, for within six feet of us a massive stone in the floor had been lifted, revealing the mouth of a well, from the deep recesses of which came the distant sound of rushing waters.

"Behold, Brethren," he went on, "and should the oath which you have sworn be broken in a single letter, learn after what fashion you must suffer for your sins. Into that pit you shall be cast, that the water may choke your breath, and the demons of the underworld may prey upon your souls through all eternity. Have you seen, and, seeing, do you understand?"

"We have seen, and we understand," we answered.

"Then let the mouth of the pit be sealed again, and pray you in your hearts that it may never be opened to receive the living body of you or of any of us. Son of the Sea, and you, Ignatio the Wanderer, the oaths have been sworn, and the ceremony is finished. Henceforth till your deaths you are of our number, sharers in our rights and privileges, and to you will be assigned houses, attendants and revenues fitted to your station. Go forth, Brethren, that you may refresh yourselves, and prepare to meet the people upon the summit of the pyramid at dawn; that is, within an hour. Lead them away with you, my Lord Mattai."

So we went, leaving behind us the talisman of the Broken Heart, for the priests refused to return it to me, saying that at length the tokens named Day and Night had come together in their ancient place, and henceforth there they must bide forever. Accompanied by Maya, Mattai, and the escort of priests, we passed through the halls and passages out into the courtyard of the temple, and thence to apartments in the palace, where we refreshed ourselves with food, for we were weary.

*T*he trick had succeeded, the ordeal was past, and for the present at least we were no longer in danger of our lives: more, the power of Mattai was confirmed, and his daughter was assured in her position as the wife of Tikal; and the señor and the Lady Maya were about to attain to the fulness of their desire, and to be declared one in the presence of the people. Yet never did I partake of a sadder meal, or behold faces more oppressed by care and the fear of the future; for, though nothing was said, in our hearts each of us knew that we had become parties to a crime, and that sooner or later, in this way or in that, our evil-doing would find us out. Putting this matter aside, I myself had good reason to mourn, seeing that, whatever the others had gained, I had won nothing; moreover I found myself bound by a solemn oath not even to attempt to leave this city whither I had journeyed with such high hopes. Well, the thing was done, and it was useless to regret it or to think of the future, so, turning to Mattai, I asked him what was to happen on the pyramid.

"There will be a great gathering of the people," he answered, "as is customary at dawn after the night of the Rising of Waters, and there they will be told all that has happened in the Sanctuary, and then, if it is their will, Tikal will be confirmed as *cacique* according to the bargain, and either today or tomorrow the white man here will become the husband of the Lady Maya, in order" — he added with a sneer — "that of their union may be born the Deliverer who is to be. Now, if you are ready, it is time for us to go, for the multitude is gathered, and an escort waits us without."

Leaving the palace we placed ourselves in the center of a party of nobles and guards who were in attendance, and marched across the courtyard and up the steps of the pyramid. The night was growing grey with the breaking of the dawn, and in the pearly light, through which the stars shone faintly, we perceived that bands of priests and nobles, wrapped in their broidered *serapes* — for the morning air was chilly — stood in their appointed places round the altar. In front of them were ranged the dense masses of the people, drawn here to make their prayers upon this feast day, and also by desire to learn the truth as to the death of Zibalbay; the fate of the strangers who had accompanied him from the unknown lands; the decision of the Council as to the successor to the place and power of *cacique*; and lastly, whether or no the oracle of the god had spoken to his priests upon this or any other matter when the lost talisman was set in its place in the Sanctuary.

On reaching the altar, seats were given to us among the nobles of the Heart, those of Maya and the señor being placed in such fashion that they would be visible to the whole multitude.

Then followed a silence, till at length a priest who was stationed upon the roof of the watch-house blew a silver trumpet and proclaimed that the dawn was broken, whereon bands of singers who were in readiness began to chant a very beautiful hymn of which the refrain was caught up by the audience. As they sang, a beam from the rising sun struck upon the fire that burned above the altar, and again the trumpet sounded. Then, in the silence that followed, the priest who stood by the fire, clothed in white robes, prayed in a loud voice, saying:

"O god, our god, let our sins die with the dying year. O god, our god, strengthen us with thy strength, comfort us with thy comfort during the day that is to be. O god, our god, have pity upon us, lift us from the darkness of the past, and give us light in the coming time. Hear us, Heart of Heaven, hear us!"

He ceased, and from the surrounding gloom many voices made response, saying: *"Hear us, Heart of Heaven, hear us!"*

Then for a space the old priest stood still, the firelight flickering on his tall form and rapt countenance as he gazed towards the east. Greyer and more grey grew the gloom, till of a sudden a ray from the unrisen sun shot through the shadows like a spear and fell athwart the summit of the pyramid, paling the holy fire, that seemed to shrink before it. At the coming of the sunbeam the multitude of worshippers — men and women together — rose from the marble pavement whereon they had been kneeling in prayer, and, casting off the dark cloaks which covered their white robes, they turned, extending their arms towards the east, and cried with one accord:

"Hail to thee, O sun! bringer of all good things. Hail to thee, newborn child of god!"

Now the light grew fast, and soon the city appeared, rising white and beautiful from its veil of mist; and, as the glory of the daylight fell upon it, other priests who stood by the altar uttered prayers appointed to be offered upon this day of the beginning of the Rising of Waters. To the People of the Heart the occasion was a great one, seeing that but little rain falls in their country, and thus they depend for a bountiful harvest upon the inundation of the island and of the low shores that lay around the lake by its waters swollen with the melted snow of the great mountains on the mainland. When the waters retreated, then they planted their grain in rich land made fertile by the mud, without labor to themselves, whence, before the lake rose again, they gathered their corn and other crops.

When they had ended their praying, and gifts of fresh flowers had been laid upon the altar by beautiful children chosen for that purpose, Tikal blessed the multitude as high priest, and the simple ceremony came to an end.

Then Mattai rose to speak, telling the people all things that had happened, or so much of them as it was expedient that they should know. He told them of the death of Zibalbay, of the setting of the lost talisman in the symbol, and of the writing which was found therein, which he read aloud to them amidst a dead silence. Then he told them how the Lady Maya and the white man had consented to be married in obedience to the voice of the oracle; and lastly, how she, the Lady Maya, had desired that her cousin Tikal should continue to be *cacique* of the City of the Heart, that she might have more leisure to attend upon her heaven-sent husband, and to be at rest until that child was become a man, whose wisdom and power should make them even greater than their forefathers had been.

When he had finished his address there was much applause and other expressions of joy, and a spokesman from among the people asked when the marriage of the white man, Son of the Sea, to the Lady Maya, would take place.

This question she answered in person, saying modestly that it was her lord's will that it should take place that very night in the banqueting-hall of the palace, and that a great feast should be celebrated in honor of it.

After this the talking came to an end, Tikal having said no word, good or bad, beyond such as the duties of his office required; and according to the custom of the country many people, noble and simple, came forward to congratulate her who was about to be made a bride. Weary of watching them and of hearing their pretty speeches, I took advantage of the escort of a friendly noble and went to see the ceremony of the closing of the flood-gate, a huge block of marble that slid down a groove into a niche prepared to receive it, where it was fastened with great bars of copper and sealed by certain officers, although, so I was told, the rising water would not reach it for another eight or ten days. Even though the flood should prove to be a low one, it was death to break those seals for a space of four full months, and during all this time any who would leave the city must do so by means of ladders reaching from the wall to little wooden jetties, where boats were moored. Afterwards we walked round the walls and through some of the main streets, and I marveled at the greatness of this half-deserted place, for the most of it was in ruins, and at the many strange sights that I saw in it. Indeed, I think that Mexico, in the time of Montezuma, my forefather, was not more powerful or populous than this town must have been in the days of its prosperity.

About midday I returned to the apartments that had been assigned to me in the palace, and, hearing that the señor was still in attendance upon the Lady Maya, I ate my dinner alone with such appetite as I could find, and lay down to sleep awhile.

I was awakened from my rest by the señor, who arrived, looking merry as he used to be before ever Molas came to lead us to the old Indian doctor and his daughter, and full of talk about the preparations for his wedding that night. I listened to all he had to say, and strove earnestly to fall into his mood, but, as I suppose, without effect, for in the end he fell into mine, which was but a sad one, and began to talk regretfully of the past and doubtfully of the future. Now I did my best to cheer him, but with little avail, for he shook his head and said:

"Indian as she is, I love Maya, and no other woman has been or can be so much to me; and yet I am afraid, Ignatio, for this marriage is ill-omened, and I pray that what was begun in trickery may not end in desolation. Also the future is black both for you and for me. You came here from a certain purpose and will desire to leave again to follow your purpose; nor, although I take this lady to wife, do I wish to spend my days in the City of the Heart. And yet it would seem that, unless we can escape, this is what we must do."

"Let us hope that we shall be able to escape," I answered.

"I doubt it," he said, "for already I have discovered that, though we be treated with all honor, yet we shall be closely watched, or at least I shall, for certain reasons. Still, come what may, I trust that this marriage will make no breach in our friendship, Ignatio."

"I do not know, señor," I answered, "though I think that for weeks its shadow has laid between us, and I fear lest that shadow should deepen. Also it has been fated that women and their loves should come between me, my ambitions, and my friends. From the moment that my eyes fell upon the Lady Maya bound to the altar in the chapel of the *hacienda,* I felt that her great beauty would bring trouble upon us, and it would seem that my heart did not lie to me. Now, under her guidance, we have entered upon a dark and doubtful path, whereof no man can see the end."

"Yes," he answered, "but we took that path in order to save our lives."

"She took it, not to save her life, on which I think she sets little store, but to win a husband whom she desires. For my part I hold that it would have been better for us to die, if God so willed it, than to live on with hearts fouled by deceit, seeing that in the end die we must, but no years of added life can wear away that stain. Well, this must seem sad talk to the ears of a bridegroom. Forget it, friend, and rest awhile that you may do credit to the marriage-feast."

Without answering, the señor lay down upon the bed, where he remained — whether sleeping or awake I do not know — till the hour of sunset, when he was aroused by the arrival of several lords and attendants who came to lead him to the bath. On his return other messengers entered, bearing magnificent robes and jewels, the gift of the Lady Maya, to be worn by him and by me at the ceremony. Then, barbers having trimmed and scented his fair hair and beard according to the fashion of this people, he was decked out like a victim for the sacrifice.

So soon as all was prepared, the doors were flung wide, and six officers of the palace came through them, bearing wands of office in their hands, accompanied by a troop of singing-girls chosen for their loveliness, which, to speak truth, was not small. In the midst of these officers and ladies the señor was placed, and, followed by myself, who walked behind with a heavy heart, he set out for the banqueting-hall. As we reached it the doors were thrown open and the singers set up a love song, pretty enough, but so foolish that I have forgotten it. We passed the threshold and found that the great hall was crowded with guests arrayed in their most brilliant attire, whereon the lamplight shone bravely. Through this company we walked till we reached an open space at the far end of the hall, around which in a semicircle sat the members of the Council of the Heart, Tikal and his wife being placed in the center of them, having Mattai on their right, and on their left that old priest Dimas, the foster-brother of Zibalbay, who had administered the oath to us.

As we advanced, with one exception, all the Council rose and bowed to the señor. That exception was Tikal, who stared straight before him and did not move. Scarcely had they resumed their seats when the sound of singing was heard again, mingled with that of music, and far away at the foot of the long hall appeared a band of musicians playing upon pipes of reeds, clad in the royal livery of green, and crowned with oak-leaves. After the musicians marched, or rather danced, a number of young girls robed in white only, and carrying white lilies in their hands, which they threw upon the floor to be trodden by the feet of the bride. Next came Maya herself, a sight of beauty such as stirred even my cold heart, and caused me to think more gently of the señor, who had become party to a trick to win her. She also was arrayed in white, embroidered with gold, and having the symbol of the Heart blazoned on her breast; about her waist and neck were a girdle and collar of priceless emeralds; on her head was set a tiara of perfect pearls taken in past ages from the shell-fish of the lake, and round her wrists and ankles were bangles of

dead gold. Her waving hair hung loose almost to her sandalled feet, and
in her hand, as a token of her rank, she bore a little golden scepter,
having at one end a great pearl, and at the other a heart-shaped emerald.
On she came, or rather floated, her delicate head held high; and so
strange and beautiful was the aspect of her face, that for my part, from
the instant that I beheld it till she stood before me by the bridegroom,
I seemed to see naught else. It was very pale and somewhat set; indeed
at that moment Maya looked more like a white woman than one of
Indian blood, and her curved lips were parted as though they waited for
some forgotten words to pass them. Her deep-blue eyes also were set
wide, and, beneath the shadow of their lashes, seemed full of mystery
and wonder, like the eyes of one who walks in her sleep and beholds
things invisible to the waking sight. Presently they fell upon the eyes of
the señor, and of a sudden grew human, while the red blood mantled
on her breast and arms and brow.

Then for me the spell was broken, and I glanced at Tikal and saw that
on his face was that same look with which he had greeted Maya when,
on the night of his own wedding-feast, he beheld her whom he believed
to be dead, standing before him clothed in life and beauty. Eagerly,
despairingly, he watched her, and I noticed that tears stood in his angry
eyes, and that a gust of jealous rage shook him from head to foot when
he saw her flush with joy at the sight of his white rival. From Tikal my
glance traveled to the dark beauty at his side, Nahua, his wife, and
became aware that in this instant she grew certain of what perhaps before
she only guessed, that in his heart her husband loathed her, as with all
his soul and strength he loved the affianced of his youth who stood
before him the bride of another man. Doubt, fear, rage looked out in
turn from her ominous eyes as the knowledge went home, to be succeeded by a possessing misery, the misery of one who knows that all
which makes life good to her is forever lost. Then, pressing her hands
to her heart for a moment, she turned aside to hide her shame and
wretchedness, and when she looked up again her face was calm as the
face of a statue, but on it was frozen a mask of unchanging hate — hate
of the woman who had robbed her.

Now the bridegroom and the bride stood together in the open space
surrounded by the half circle of the Council of the Heart, among whom
I was given a seat, while behind them were arranged the musicians and
singing-girls, and behind these again pressed the glittering audience of
marriage-guests. When all were in their places a herald rose and cried
out the names and titles of the pair, reciting briefly that they were to be
wed by the direct command of the guardian god of the city, by the wish
of the Council of the Heart, and because of the love that they bore one

another. Next, reading from a written roll, he published the text of the agreement whereby Maya renounced her right as ruler in favor of her cousin Tikal, and I noticed that this agreement was received by the company in cold silence and with some few expressions of disapproval. Lastly, from another roll he read the list of the honors, prerogatives, offices, wealth, houses, and servants which were thereby assigned to the Lady Maya and her consort, and also to myself their friend, for the maintenance of their rank and dignity and of my comfort.

Having finished his task, he asked the señor and Maya whether they had heard all that he had read by command of the Council, and, if so, whether they approved thereof. They bowed their heads in assent, whereupon the herald turned, and, addressing Tikal by all his titles, called upon him, in virtue of his priestly office and of his position as chief of the state, to make these two one in the face of the people, according to the ancient custom of the land.

Tikal heard him and rose from his seat as though to commence the service, then sank down again, saying:

"Seek some other priest, Herald, for this thing I will not do."

Chapter XXII

MATTAI PROPHESIES EVIL

*A*t Tikal's words the company murmured in astonishment, and Mattai, bending forward, began to whisper in his ear. Tikal listened for a moment, then turned upon him fiercely and said aloud, so that all could hear him:

"I tell you, Mattai, that I will be no party to this iniquity. Has such a thing been heard of before, that the Lady of the Heart, the highest lady in the land, should be given in marriage to a stranger who, like some lost dog, has wandered to our gate?"

"The prophecy —" began Mattai.

"The prophecy! I put no faith in prophecies. Why should I obey a prophecy written how, when, or by whom I do not know? This lady was my affianced bride, and now I am asked to unite her to a nameless man who is not even of our blood or faith. Well, I will not."

"Surely, lord, you blaspheme," answered Mattai, growing wrath, "seeing that it is not for the high priest to speak against the oracle of the god. Also," he added, with meaning, "what can it be to you, who are not ten days wed to the lady at your side, that she to whom once you were affianced should choose another as her husband?"

"What is it to me?" said Tikal, furiously. "If you desire to know, I will tell you. It is everything. How did I come to break my troth and to take your daughter as a wife? Through you, Mattai, through you, the liar and the false prophet. Did you not swear to me that Maya was dead yonder in the wilderness? And did you not, to satisfy your own ambitions, force me on to take your daughter to wife? Aye! and is not this marriage between the Lady of the Heart and the white man a plot of yours devised for the furthering of your ends?"

Now, while all stood astonished, of a sudden Nahua, who hitherto had listened in stony silence, rose and said:

"The Lord Tikal, my husband, forgets that common courtesy should protect even an unwelcome wife from public insult." Then she turned and left the hall by the door which was behind her.

Now a murmur of pity for the lady, and indignation at the man, ran through the company, and as it died away Tikal said: "Evil will come of this night's work, and in it I will have no hand. Do what you will, and abide the issue" — and before any could speak in answer, he also had left the hall, followed by his guards.

For a while there was silence, then men began to talk confusedly, and some of the members of the Brotherhood of the Heart, rising from their chairs, took hurried counsel together. At length they reseated themselves, and, holding up his hand to secure silence, Mattai spoke thus:

"Forgive me," he said, addressing the audience, "if my words seem few and rough, but it is hard for me to be calm in face of the open insult which has been put upon my daughter and myself before you all. I will not stoop to answer the charge that the Lord Tikal has brought against me in his rage. Surely some evil power must have afflicted him with madness, that, forgetting his honor as a man, and his duty as a prince and priest, he should dare to utter such calumnies against the god we worship, the white man whom the god has chosen to be a husband to the Lady Maya, and myself, the Keeper of the Sanctuary. There were many among you who held me foolish when, after much prayer and thought, to further what I believed to be the true interests of the whole people, I gave my voice in favor of the lifting up of Tikal to fill the place and honor of *cacique* in room of our late prince, Zibalbay, whom we thought dead with his daughter in the wilderness. Today I see that they were right, and that I was foolish indeed. But enough of regrets and bitter talk, that make ill music at a marriage-feast. Tikal, the head of our hierarchy, has gone, but other priests are left, nor is his will the will of the Council, or of the People of the Heart for whom the Council speaks. Their will it is that this marriage should go forward, and Dimas, my brother, as the oldest among us, I call upon you to celebrate it."

Now the company shouted in applause, for they were set upon this strange union of a white man with their lady, if only because it was a new thing and touched their imagination; and even those of them who were of his party were wrath with Tikal on account of his ill behavior and the cruel affront that he had offered to his new-made wife.

So soon as the tumult had died away, the old priest Dimas rose, and, taking the hands of Maya and the señor, he joined them and said a very touching and beautiful prayer over them, blessing them, and entreating the spirit, Heart of Heaven, and other gods, to give them increase and to make them happy in a mutual love. Lastly, he laid a white silken cloth, which had been prepared, upon their heads as they knelt before him, and, loosing the emerald girdle from about the waist of the bride, he took her right hand and placed it upon the arm of the señor, then he bound the girdle round wrist and arm, buckled it, and in a few solemn words declared these twain to be man and wife in the face of Heaven and earth till death undid them.

Now the cloth was lifted and the girdle loosed, and, standing upon their feet, the new-wed pair kissed each other before the people. A shout of joy went up that shook the paneled roof, and one by one, in order of their rank, the guests pressed forward to wish happiness to the bride and bridegroom, most of them bringing some costly and beautiful gift, which they gave into the charge of the waiting-ladies. Last of all came the old priest Dimas, and said:

"Sweet bride, the gift that I am commanded by the Council to make to you, though of little value in itself, is yet one of the most precious to be found within the walls of this ancient city, being nothing less than the holy symbol of the all-seeing Eye of the Heart of Heaven, which, through you, men behold today for the first time for many generations. Wear it always, lady, and remember that though this jewel has no sight, yet that Eye, whereof it is a token, from hour to hour reads your most secret soul and purpose. Make your thoughts, then, as fair as is your body, and let your breast harbor neither guile nor evil; for of all these things, in a day to come, you must surely give account."

As he spoke he drew from the case that hid it nothing less than that awful Eye which we had seen within the hollow of the Heart, when with unhallowed hands we robbed it, substituting the false for the true. Now it had been set in a band of gold and hung to a golden chain which he placed about the neck of the bride, so that the red and cruel-looking gem lay gleaming on her naked breast. Maya bowed and muttered some words of thanks, but I saw that her spirit failed her at the touch of the ominous thing, for she turned faint and would have fallen had not her husband caught her by the arm.

While the señor and his wife were receiving gifts and listening to pretty speeches, a number of attendants had brought tables laden with every kind of food from behind the pillars where they had been pre-pared, and at a signal the feast began. It was long and joyous, though joy seemed to have faded from the face of Maya, who sat neither eating nor drinking, but from time to time lifting the red eye from her breast as though it scorched her skin. At length she rose, and, accompanied by her husband, walked bowing down the hall to the courtyard, where bearers waited for them with carrying-chairs. In these they seated them-selves, and a procession having been formed, very long and splendid, though I will not stay to describe it, we started to march round the great square to the sound of music and singing, our path being lit by the light of the moon and with hundreds of torches. Here in this square were gathered all the population of the City of the Heart, men, women, and children, to greet the bride, each of them bearing flowers and a flaming torch; and never have I seen any sight more beautiful than this of their welcome.

The circuit of the square being accomplished, the procession halted at the palace gates, and many hands were stretched out to help the bride and bridegroom from their litters. It was at this moment that I, who was standing near, felt a man wrapped in a large feather cloak push past me, and saw that he held something which gleamed like a knife.

By instinct, as it were, I cried, "Beware, my friend!" in Spanish, and in so piercing a voice that it caught the señor's ear. He swung round, for already he was standing on his feet, and, as he turned, the man in the cloak rushed at him and stabbed with the knife. But, being warned, the señor was too quick for him. Springing to one side, with the same movement he dealt his would-be murderer a great buffet, that caused him to drop the dagger and sent him staggering into the dense shadow of the archway.

For some seconds no one seemed to understand what had happened, and when they did and began to search for the man, he was not to be found. Who he was, or why he had attempted this cowardly deed, was never discovered; but for my part I have little doubt that either Tikal himself or some creature of his was wrapped in the dark feather cloak, and sought thus to rid him of his rival. Indeed, as time went on, this belief took firm hold of the mind of the people, and was one of the causes that led to the sapping of Tikal's power and popularity.

Very hastily the señor assured the lords in attendance who crowded round him that he had received no manner of hurt, and then, after speaking a few brief words of thanks, he withdrew into the palace with his wife, and I saw him no more that night.

*T*he day of this marriage was to me the beginning of the longest and most weary year that ever I have spent in a long and weary life. Very soon I understood how it came about that Maya had learned to hate the City of the Heart in which she was born, its people, and its ways, and ardently to desire a new life in new lands. Here there was no change and little work; here, enervated by a cloying luxury, the poor remnant of a great civilization rotted slowly to its fall, and none lifted a hand to save it. Since men must do something, the priests and nobles plotted for place and power indeed, and the common people listlessly followed this trade or that, providing food and raiment for the community — not for themselves — but there was little heart in what they did, and they took no pleasure in it. Basking in the eternal sunshine, they loitered from the cradle to the grave, hoping nothing, suffering nothing, fearing nothing, content to feast amid their crumbling palaces, and, when they were weary, to sleep till it was time to feast again, satisfying their souls the while with the husks of a faith whereof they had lost the meaning. Such were the people of whom Zibalbay hoped to fashion a race of conquerors!

Still, to this life they were born and it became them; indeed, they could have endured no other, for the breath of hardship must have melted them away as my Indian forefathers melted beneath the iron rule of the Spaniard, but to me it was a daily torment. Often I have beheld some wild creature pine and die in its prison, though food was given to it in greater abundance than it could find in its native woods, and like that wild creature was I in this soft City of the Heart.

The wealth I came to seek was round me in abundance, useless and unproductive as the dead hands that had stored it, and yonder in Mexico were men who by aid of that wealth might become free and great: but alas! I could not bring them together. I could not even escape from my jail, for my every movement was watched. Yet I would have tried to do so had it not been for the señor, who, when I spoke of it, said I should be no true friend of his if I went and left him alone in this house of strangers. Indeed his plight was worse than mine, for he too soon grew utterly weary of this dreadful city of eternal summer, and of everything in it except his wife. For whole hours we would sit gazing on the wide waters of the lake, and make plan after plan whereby we might gain the mountains and freedom, only to abandon each in turn. For they were hopeless. Day and night he was watched, since here alone this people forgot to be indolent. They knew that their race was dying and, lifting no hand to save themselves, they preferred to pin their faith upon the prophecy which promised that from this white man should spring a savior. Meanwhile, false though it may have been, the prophecy, or one part of it, was in the way of fulfillment, which in itself was a wonder to this people, among whom the births of children were so rare. At length that child was born — a son — and the rejoicing knew no bounds. Strangely enough, upon the same day Nahua also gave birth to a son, and great was her anger when she learned that it was not on her account or on that of her offspring that the people were so glad.

Within a few days of the señor's marriage we heard that Mattai had been seized with sickness, a kind of palsy, together with a leprous condition of the arms that baffled all skill. For months he lay in his house, growing gradually worse, so said the physicians; but one night — I remember that it was three days previous to the birth of Maya's child — he appeared before Maya, the señor, and myself, as we sat together in the palace looking out upon the moonlit garden. At first we did not know him, for never before had I seen a sight so dreadful. His body was bloated; one arm — his left — was swathed in bandages; his head shook incessantly; and the leprosy had seized his face, which was of a livid hue.

"Do not shrink from me," he began, in a low and quavering voice, as he gazed upon us with his whitening eyes; "surely you should not shrink, seeing that all of you are partners in the crime that has made of me the loathsome thing I am. Aye! deny it if you will, but I know it. The vengeance of the god has fallen upon me, his false servant, and it has fallen justly. Moreover, be assured that on you also shall that vengeance fall, for the Eye has seen, the Mouth has told, and the Heart has thought upon your doom. Look upon me, and learn how rich are the wages of him who works iniquity, and by my sufferings strive to count the measure of your own. Perchance your cup is not yet full; perchance you have still greater sins to work: but vengeance shall come — I tell you that vengeance shall come here and hereafter. I did this thing for my daughter's sake; yes, for love of her, my only child. She was ambitious and she desired this man, and I thought to assure greatness to her and to her children after her.

"But see how her wine has been turned to vinegar, and her pleasant fruits to ashes. Her husband hates her with an ever-growing hate; now they scarcely speak, or speak only to shower bitter words upon each other's head. More — not for long will Tikal be *cacique* of the City of the Heart, for his jealous rage has soured all his mind; his deeds are deeds of oppression and injustice; already he is detested by the people, and even those who loved him turn from him and plot against him. Do you know what they plot? They plot to make that child that shall be born of you, Maya, *cacique* in his room, and to set up you and your outland husband as regents till it shall be of an age to govern. Oh! you have planned cunningly, and things look well for you, but I say that they shall not prosper.

"The curse is on you, Ignatio, Lord of the Heart, for all your high-built hopes shall fall like a rotted roof, and never shall the eagles of that empire you have dreamed of be broidered on your banners. Slaves are the people you have toiled for, and slaves they shall remain, for by the crime to which you gave consent, Ignatio, you have riveted their fetters. The curse is on your child, Maya — never shall it live to become a man: the curse is on your husband — his hair shall not grow grey. But heaviest of all does the curse rest upon you, false Lady of the Heart, you, whose life is one long lie; you, who forsook your faith and broke your oath; you, who turned you from your people and from the law of your high and ancient house, that you might win a wandering white man to your arms. Woman, we shall meet no more; but in the hour of your last misery, and in the long, long ages of the eternal punishment, remember the words that I speak to you today" — and, shaking his withered arm in our faces, Mattai turned and limped from the chamber.

He went, and we sat gazing at each other in horror, for though we none of us had any faith in the god he worshipped, in our hearts we felt that this man spoke truth, and that evil would overtake us. For a moment Maya hid her face in her hands and wept; then she sprang up, and a fire in her eyes had dried her tears.

"So let it be," she cried, "I care nothing. At the least I won you, my love, and for some months, through all our troubles, I have been happy at your side, and, come good, come ill, nothing can rob me of my memories. But for you I fear. Husband, I fear for you —"

Then, her passion past, she flung herself into his arms and again began to weep.

*I*n due course the child was born, a beautiful boy, almost white in color, with his mother's starlike eyes; and on this same night we learned that Mattai had died in much torment, and that Nahua was delivered of a son.

Eighteen days went by, and Maya, new-risen from her bed, was seated with her husband and myself, while behind us stood a waiting-lady holding the sleeping infant in her arms, when it was announced to us that an embassy of the great lords of the Council sought speech with her. Presently they entered, and the spokesman, the Lord Dimas, bowed before her and set out his mission, saying:

"We have come to you, Lady of the Heart, on behalf of the Council and of the people, to rejoice with you in your great happiness, and to lay certain matters of the state before you. For some months the people have grown weary of the oppressions and cruelties of Tikal, who in defiance of the laws of the land has put many to death on suspicion of their being concerned in plots against his power. Further, but yesterday it came to the ears of the Council, through the confession of one whom he had employed to execute his wickedness, that a plan was laid to murder your husband, your child, and the Lord Ignatio here."

"Indeed," said Maya, "and why was my name omitted from this list?"

"Lady, we do not know," he answered, "but it seems that the assassins had orders to take you living, and to hide you away in a secret part of Tikal's house."

Now the señor sprang to his feet and swore a great oath to be avenged upon Tikal.

"Nay, Lord," said Dimas, "his person is holy and must not be touched, nor need you have any further fear of him, for those whom he corrupted await their trial, and he himself is watched day and night. Also, not for long will Tikal remain *cacique* of the City of the Heart; for the Council have met in a secret session to which you were not summoned, and have decreed that he shall be deposed because of his iniquities, and in accordance with the desire of the people."

"Can a *cacique* be deposed?" asked Maya.

"Yes, lady, if he has broken the law, for was not your father to be deposed for this same reason? Also, Tikal holds his place, not by right of birth, but by treaty. You are the true heir to Zibalbay, Lady of the Heart."

"It may be so," she answered coldly, "but I have renounced my claim and I do not desire to go back upon my word."

"If you have renounced it," said Dimas, "there is one to whom it passes" — and he pointed to the sleeping infant. "Yonder is the Child of Prophecy, hope of the people, and he it is whom we purpose to crown as our ruler, setting you and your husband up to act for him till he reaches his full age."

"Nay," said Maya, "for thus shall he become the mark of Tikal's rage and be put to death — openly or in secret, as it may chance."

"Not so, lady, for in that hour when he is proclaimed, Tikal will be taken into safe keeping, where he shall abide for so long as his life lasts."

"And when is this to be," asked the señor.

"Tomorrow, at noon, upon the pyramid, that the child may be solemnly anointed three days hence in the Sanctuary, on the night of the Rising of Waters."

"It is foolish to crown a babe, and neither I nor my husband seek this greatness," said Maya. "If Tikal is to be deposed because of his crimes, let one of the great lords be set in his place until the child is old enough to rule."

"Although you and your husband are to command us in the future," answered Dimas, sternly, "till then you must obey, Lady, for the voice of the Council is supreme, and it carries out the will of its founder and invisible president, the Heart of Heaven. The Council has determined that the heaven-sent child, of whom you are the earthly parents, must take his own."

"As you will," said Maya, with a sigh; and presently they went.

*T*hat evening the señor and I attended a feast at the house of one of the great nobles, whence we returned somewhat late. Having dismissed those who had escorted us, I walked with him as far as the door of his private chambers, purposing to leave him there; but he bade me enter, for he wished to talk with me about the events of the day and this forthcoming ceremony of the anointing of the child. Accordingly I did so, and, passing through the first chamber, we came to the second, beyond which lay his sleeping-rooms. Here we halted by the open window, and I approached a lamp, for I wished to smoke and had no light. As I bent over it, something caught my ear, and I listened, since it seemed to me that through the massive doors of the bedchamber I heard the sound of a woman's voice crying for help. Instantly I flung them open and rushed thither by way of an anteroom, calling to the señor as I went.

I did not arrive too soon, for in the bedchamber itself a strange sight met my eyes. At the foot of the bed stood a cradle, in which lay the child, and near to it two women struggled. One of these — in whom I knew Nahua, the wife of Tikal — held a copper knife in her hand, and the other, Maya, gripped her round the body and arms from behind, so that, strive as she would, she could not free herself to use it. Still, of the two women Nahua was the heavier and the more strong, and, though slowly, she dragged the other closer to the cradle. Indeed, as I reached the room, she wrenched her right arm loose and raised it to strike at the infant with the knife. But here the matter ended, for at that moment I caught her round the waist and threw her back, so that she fell heavily on the floor, letting drop the knife in her effort to save herself. She sprang to her feet and ran towards the door, there to be met by the señor, who seized her and held her fast.

Chapter XXIII

OUR FLIGHT, AND HOW IT ENDED

"*H*ow came this lady here, Maya, and what does she seek!" the señor asked.

"I do not know how she came," gasped his wife. "My waiting-women were gone, and I had begun to prepare myself for sleep, when, looking into yonder mirror, I saw her behind me, having in her hand a naked knife, and searching the room with her eyes. Presently they fell upon the cradle, and, lifting the knife, she took a step towards it. Then I turned and gripped her, holding her as well as I was able; but she was too strong for me and dragged me forward, so that had it not been for Ignatio here, by now she would have made an end of our son."

"Is this true?" said the señor to Nahua.

"It is true, White Man," she answered.

"Why do you desire to kill one so innocent?" he asked again.

"Is it not natural that I should wish to destroy the child who is to supplant my child, and to break the heart of the woman who has broken my heart?" Nahua answered, sullenly. "Amongst many other things, I have learned, White Man, of that ceremony which is to take place tomorrow, whereat my husband is to be deposed and my child dishonored, that they may make room for you and for your child — you, the white-wanderer, and your son, the Heaven-born, the Fore-ordained!"

"What have we to do with these things, O woman with the heart of a puma?" he asked. "If Tikal is to be driven from his place, it is because of his crimes."

"And if you and yours are to be set in it, White Man, without doubt it is because of your virtues; and yet, O black-hearted knave that you are, I tell you that I know all the truth. I know how you forged the writing, setting the false for the true within the holy symbol of the Heart. I know also that my father helped you to the deed, for although he is dead, he wrote down that tale before he died, and gave it to me, together with the ancient prophecy that you dared to steal from the holy Sanctuary. Yes, I have the proofs, and when needful I will show them. I did not come here to do murder, at least not upon the infant; but the sight of it sleeping in its cradle overcame me, and of a sudden I determined to wreak my wrongs upon it and upon its mother. In this I have failed, but when I denounce you to the Council, then I shall not fail; then you will be known for what you are, and die the death that you deserve."

"It comes into my mind, husband," said Maya coldly, "that if we would save our own lives we must rob this woman of hers. Such a doom she has richly earned, nor will any blame us when they learn what was her errand here."

Now when she heard these words, Nahua struggled in the señor's grasp, and opened her mouth as though to scream.

"Be silent," he said, "if you wish to keep your soul in you. Ignatio, close those doors and give me yonder shawl."

I did so, and with the shawl we bound Nahua's arms behind her, fastening it over her mouth so that she could make no sound. Then we took a leather girdle and strapped it about her knees, so that she could not move, but lay helpless on the floor, glaring at us with her fierce eyes.

"Now let us take counsel," I said.

"Yes," answered the señor, "let us take counsel, for we need it. One of two things we must do; kill that woman, or fly the city, for if she leaves this place alive we are certainly doomed to death before the altar, aye! and the child also."

"Fly!" said Maya, "how can we fly when I am still weak and the babe is so young and tender? Should we succeed in escaping from the city and across the lake, certainly we must perish among the snows of the mountains or in the deserts beyond. Also, we should be missed and overtaken."

"Then Nahua must die," said the señor.

"Could we not swear her to silence if we released her?" I asked, for I shrank from such a dreadful deed, however just and necessary it might be.

"Swear her to silence!" said Maya contemptuously, "as easily might you swear a snake not to use its fangs, if one should chance to tread on it. Do you not understand that this woman hates me bitterly, who she thinks has robbed her of her husband's love, that she would gladly die herself, if thereby she could bring about my death and that of those who are dear to me. So soon as she could leave her bed of sickness she came here to taunt me with the doom she had prepared, knowing that I was alone. Then she saw the child, and so great was her desire for revenge that she could not even wait till the law should wreak it for her. No, the issue is plain; if we cannot fly, either she must die or we must. Is it not so, Ignatio?"

"It seems that it is so," I answered sadly, "and yet the thing is awful."

"It is awful, but it must be done," said the señor, "and it falls on me to do it for the sake of my wife and child. Alas! that I was ever born, that I should live to stand face to face with such necessity. Could not another hand be found? No; for then we should confess ourselves as murderers. Give me a knife. Nay, my hands will serve, and this end will seem more natural, for I can say that when I found her in the act of murder, I seized her and killed her suddenly by my strength alone, not meaning it in my wrath."

Now he stepped to where Nahua lay, and knelt beside her, and we two drew away sick at heart and hid our faces in our hands.

Presently he was with us again.

"Is it done?" asked Maya hoarsely.

"No; nor will be by me," he answered, in a fierce voice, "sooner would I choke the breath out of my own body than strangle this defenseless woman, cruel-hearted murderess though she is. If she is to be killed, some other man must do the deed."

"Then it will remain undone," said Maya. "And now, since we have thus determined, let us think of flight, for the night draws on, and in flight is our only hope."

"What, then, is to be done with this woman?" I asked. "We cannot take her with us."

"No; but we can leave her here gagged and bound till they chance to find her," answered the señor. "Hearken, Nahua, we spare you, and to do it go forth to our own deaths. May your fierce heart learn a lesson of mercy from the deed. Farewell."

Two hours had gone by, and three figures, wrapped in rough *serapes,* such as the common people wore, one of whom, a woman, carried an infant in her arms, might have been seen cautiously descending the city wall by means of a wooden ladder that ran from its summit to a jetty built upon piers at the foot of it, which was used as a mooring-place for boats during the months of inundation. As was common at this season of the year, the lake was already rising, and floating in the shallow water at the end of the jetty lay a pleasure-skiff which the señor and I were accustomed to use for the purpose of fishing whenever we could escape for a few hours from our wearisome life in the city.

Into this skiff we entered, and, having hoisted the sail, set our course by the stars, steering for that village whence, a year before, we had embarked for the City of the Heart. The wind being favorable to us, our progress was rapid, and by the first grey light of dawn we caught sight of the village not a mile away. Here, however, we did not dare to land, for we should be seen and recognized; therefore we beached our boat behind the shelter of some dwarf water-palms three furlongs or more below the village, and, having hidden it as well as we were able, set out at once towards the mountains.

Passing round the back of the village without being seen, for as yet folk were scarcely astir, we began our dreadful journey. For a while Maya bore up well, but as the heat of the day increased she showed signs of tiring, which was little to be wondered at, seeing that she carried in her arms a child not three weeks old. At mid-day we halted that she might rest, hiding ourselves beneath a tree by the banks of a brook, and eating of such food as we had brought with us. In the early afternoon we started on again, and for the rest of that dreary day struggled forward as best we could, the señor and I carrying the infant alternately in addition to our other burdens.

At length the evening fell, and we camped for the night, if camping it can be called, to sleep beneath the shadow of a cedar tree without fire and with little food, having no covering except our *serapes.* Towards morning the air grew cold, for already we were at some height above the lake, and the tender infant began to wail piteously — a wail that wrung our hearts. Still we rose with the sun and went on our way, for it seemed that there was nothing else to do. Throughout that day, with ever-wearying footsteps, we journeyed, till at sunset we reached the snow-line, and saw before us the hunter's rest-house where we had slept when first we entered the Country of the Heart.

"Let us go in," said Maya, "and find food and shelter for the night."

Now, our plan had been to avoid this house and gain the pass, where we proposed to stay till daybreak, and then to travel down the mountain slopes into the wilderness.

"If we enter there, Maya, we shall be trapped," said the señor; "our only safety lies in traveling through the pass before we are overtaken, for it is against the law that any of your people should follow us into the wilderness."

"If we do not enter, my child will die in the cold," she answered. "You were too tender to secure our safety by putting that would-be murderess to death; have you, then, the heart, husband, to kill your own child?"

Now at these words I saw the señor's eyes fill with tears, but he said only:

"Be it as you will."

By now, indeed, we understood — all three of us — that if we would save ourselves we must suffer the child to die, and, however great our necessity, this we could not do. So we went up to the house and entered, and there by the fire sat that same man and his wife whom we had found in this room a year ago.

"Who are you?" he cried, springing up. "Pardon, Lady, but in that garb I did not know you."

"It is best that you should not know us," said Maya. "We are wanderers who have lost our way out hunting. Give us food, as you are bound to do."

Then the man and his wife, who were kindly people, made obeisance to us, and set of the best they had before us. We ate, and, after eating, slept, for we were very weary, bidding the man watch and tell us if he saw any stranger approaching the house. Before dawn he woke us, and we rose. A little later he came into my room and told me that a large body of men were in sight of the house. Then I knew that it was finished, and called the others.

"Now, there are three things that we can do," I said: "fly towards the pass; defend this house; or surrender ourselves."

"There is no time to fly," answered the señor, "therefore it is my counsel that we fight."

"It is your counsel that two men armed with bows" (for our firearms had been taken from us on the pyramid, and we had never been able to recover them) "should engage with fifty. Well, friend, we can try it if you wish, and perhaps it will be as good a way of meeting our deaths as any other."

"This is folly," broke in Maya; "there is but one thing to do; yield ourselves and trust to fortune, if, indeed, fortune has any good in store for us. Only I wish that we had done it before we undertook this weary journey."

As she spoke, by the light of the rising sun we saw a great number of men forming a circle round the house. With them were several captains and lords, and among these I recognized Dimas and Tikal.

"Let us put a bold face on it," said Maya. So we opened the door, walked out, and came into the presence of Tikal, Dimas, and the other lords.

"Whom do you seek, that you come with an armed force?" asked Maya.

"Whom should I seek but your fair self, cousin?" answered Tikal — and I saw that his eye was wild, as though with drink. "If Nahua, my wife, had her way, she would have let you go, for she desires to see the last of you; but her will is not my will, nor her desire my desire, and as it chances we have come up with you in time."

Maya turned from him with a scornful gesture, and addressed herself to Dimas, saying:

"Tell us of what we are charged that you follow us as though we were evil-doers."

"Lady," the old priest answered gravely, "it would seem that you have earned this name, you and your companions together. Listen: two days since you were missing, and the Lady Nahua was also missing. Search was made, and at last your private apartments were broken open, and there she was discovered bound and gagged. From her we learned the secret of your flight, and followed after you."

"Did she, then, tell you why we fled?" asked Maya. "Did she tell you that she crept to my chamber like a thief in the night, and there was found in the act of doing murder on my child?"

"No, Lady, she told us nothing of all this. Indeed, her manner was strange; for, so soon as she was recovered somewhat, she took back her words, and said that she knew naught of you or of your plans, and that if you had fled we should do well to let you go before worse things happened. But, knowing that for all this she had reasons easy to be guessed, we followed and found you, and now we arrest you to answer before the Council for your great sins, in that you have broken your solemn oaths by attempting to leave the land without the consent of the Council, and have added to your crimes by taking with you this child, the Heaven-sent deliverer, on whom rest the hopes of our race."

"If we have broken our oaths," said Maya, "we broke them to save our lives. Were we, then, to stop in the city till the knife of the assassin found us out? On the very night of my marriage a murderer was set upon my husband, and perhaps one stands there" — and she pointed to

Tikal — "who could tell us who he was and whence he came. Three days ago another murderer sought the life of our child, and that murderer the wife of the Lord Tikal. Is it, then, a sin that we should take from the land one whose life is not safe within it."

"All these matters you can lay before the Council, lady," answered Dimas, "and if Nahua is what you say, without a doubt she must suffer for her crime. Yet her evil-doing cannot pay for yours, for when you found yourself in danger, you should have claimed protection from those who could give it, and not have betaken yourselves to flight like thieves in terror of the watch. Come, enter the litter that is prepared for you, and let us be going."

"As you will," she said; "but one thing I pray of you, let this man, my cousin, Tikal the *cacique,* be kept away from me, for the sight of him is hateful to me, seeing that, not content with plotting to kill my husband and my child, he puts me to shame continually by the offer of his love."

"It shall be as you wish, Lady. Your husband and your friend can travel by your side, and guards shall surround your litter to see that none molest you."

Then we started. Of our journey back there is nothing to tell, unless it be to say that after its own fashion it was even more wretched than that which we had just accomplished. Then, indeed, we were footsore, hungry, and racked with fears, but at least the hope of freedom shone before us like a guiding-star, whereas now, although we traveled in comfort, it was to find shame, exposure, and death awaiting us at last. For my part, indeed, this thought did not move me very much, seeing that hope had left me, and without hope I no longer wished to live. You, my friend, for whom I write this history, may think my saying strange, but had you stood where I stood that day you would not wonder at it. Even now I sometimes dream that I am back in the City of the Heart, and wake cold with fear as a man wakes from some haunted sleep. True, there I had place and power and luxury, but oh! sooner would I have earned my livelihood herding cattle in the wilderness than fret away my life within that golden cage. What to me were their banquets and their empty pleasures, or their petty strivings for rank and title — to me who all my days had followed the star of my high aim, that star which now was setting. Maya and the señor had each other and their child to console them; but I had nothing except such friendship as they chose to spare me, the memory of my many failures, the clinging bitterness of conscience, the fear of vengeance to be wreaked, and the hope of peace beyond the end. Therefore I, an outworn and disappointed man, was prepared to welcome the doom that awaited me, but how would it be with the others who were still full of love and youth?

Late that night we reached the city and were led, not to the palace where we lived, but towards the enclosure of the pyramid.

"How is this?" asked Maya of the captain of the guard. "Our road lies yonder."

"No, lady," he answered, "my orders are to take you up the stairway of the pyramid."

Now Maya pressed her face against the face of her child and sobbed, for she knew that once more we must inhabit the darksome vault where her father had been taken to die. They led us up the stair and down the narrow way, till we stood in the lamp-lit hall, and heard our prison gates clash behind us. Then they gave us food and left us alone.

Never did I pass a more evil night; for, strive as I would to win it, sleep fled from me, and I tossed upon my couch, wondering where my bed would be on the morrow, after we had stood before the Council in the Sanctuary of the Heart, and Nahua had borne witness against us. I remembered that shaft before the altar, and seemed to hear the murmur of the water in its depths! Well, as I have said, I did not fear to die, for God is merciful to sinners; but oh! it was dreadful to meet this liar's doom, and to remember that it was I who brought the señor here to share it.

As I mused thus, even through the massive walls of the vault I heard a woman scream, and, springing from my bed, I ran into the central hall, where the lamps burned always. Here I met Maya, clad in her night-dress only, and speeding down the hall, her wide eyes filled with terror.

"What has happened?" I said, stopping her; and, as I spoke, the señor came up.

"Oh! I have dreamed," she gasped. "I have dreamed a fearful dream. I dreamed that my father came to me, and — I cannot tell it — the child — the child —" and she broke down utterly, and could say no more.

"This place is full of evil memories, and her strength is shattered," said the señor, when we had calmed her somewhat. "Come back, wife, and sleep."

"Sleep!" she answered. "I do not think that I shall ever sleep again; and yet, unless I sleep, I shall go mad. Oh! that vision! Truly the curse of Mattai has taken hold of me."

*S*ome few hours later we met again in the great hall, but Maya said nothing of her dream, nor did I ask her to tell it, though I could see from her face that it was not forgotten. We ate, or made pretence to eat, and sat for a while in silence, till at length the gates opened, and through them came Dimas and some companion priests. Bidding these to stand back, he advanced alone and greeted us kindly.

"I am grieved," he said, "that you should again be called upon to occupy this gloomy lodging; but I had no choice in the matter, since I am but the servant of the Council, and its commands were strict. It was feared lest the infant might be spirited away, were you left at liberty."

"It will soon be spirited away, indeed, Dimas," said Maya, "if it be kept here in the darkness. Already the child pines — within a week he will be dead."

"Have no fear, lady; your imprisonment is not for long, for this very night, the night of the Rising of Waters, you will all of you be put upon your trial before the Council in the Sanctuary, and charged with the crime of attempting to escape the land."

"Is there no other charge?" asked Maya.

"None, lady, that I have heard of. What other charge should there be?"

"And what will be the verdict of the Council?"

"I cannot say, lady, but I know that none wish to deal harshly with you, and if that charge which you bring against the Lady Nahua can be proved, it will go in your favor. The crime you have attempted is a great one, both in our eyes and still more in the eyes of the people, for now they talk day and night of this Deliverer who has been born to them, and they will not easily forgive those who strove to take him from them. Still, I think that upon certain terms the anger of your judges may be appeased."

"What terms?" asked Maya.

Now Dimas hesitated, and answered:

"By the strict letter of the law, if your offence is proved against you, you are worthy of death, every one, unless you yourself are held inviolate because of your hereditary rank as Lady of the Heart. But it may be that the Council will not exact the extreme penalty. It may be that it will satisfy itself with driving these strangers from our borders instead of driving them from the land of life."

"Yet one of them is my husband, Dimas."

"True, lady, but the child is born!"

"I cannot be parted from my husband. Better that we should die together than that we should be parted. If the people have no need of him, neither have they any need of me; let us bid them farewell and go free together. I am weary of this land, Dimas, for here murder dogs our steps and I am in terror of my life. I desire nothing from my people save liberty to leave them."

"But, Lady, your people desire something from you; they desire the child. Of these strangers they would be rid by death or otherwise, and you — though of this I am not sure — they may allow to accompany them; but with your child they will never part, for he is their heaven-sent king, the Son of prophecy. It comes to this, then, that if the Council should exercise its prerogative of mercy — as it will do if I and my party have sufficient weight — at the best you must choose between the loss of your husband or of your son."

Now the face of Maya became drawn with pain, so that she looked as though age had overtaken her. Then she answered:

"Go, tell those that sent you, Dimas, that these are the words of Maya, Lady of the Heart: My child is dear to me, for he is flesh of my flesh; but my husband is yet dearer, for he is both flesh of my flesh and soul of my soul. Therefore, if I must choose between the two, I choose him who is nearest; for I may have another child, but never another husband."

Chapter XXIV

NAHUA BEARS WITNESS

Some hours passed, and again the gates were opened, and through them came Tikal and a guard of five men. The guard he left by the gates, advancing alone to where we were seated at the far end of the hall.

"What would you of us?" asked Maya. "Can you not leave me in peace even here in my dungeon?"

"I desire to speak with you alone, Maya."

"Then, Tikal, I tell you now what I have told you before, that I will not listen to your words alone. If you have anything to say, say it in the presence of my husband and my friend, or go and leave it unsaid."

"You speak roughly to one who comes here in the hope of saving the lives of all of you," he answered; "still I will bear with you in this as I have borne with you in much else. Listen: all your crimes are known to me, for Nahua, my wife, has revealed them to me. I know how you and that dead rogue, Mattai, on whom the curse of heaven has most justly fallen, forged the prophecy and violated the sanctuary, for I have held the proofs of it in my hand."

"Do you know that we did this to save our lives," asked Maya, "for if we had not done it, Mattai would have murdered us in order that, by removing me, he might assure his daughter in her place?"

"I do not know why you did it, nor do I care, seeing that nothing can lighten such a crime; but I think that you did it in order that you might win yonder white man as a husband. At the least, the thing is done, and vengeance waits you — vengeance from which there is but one escape."

"What escape?" asked Maya quickly, for when she learned that Tikal knew everything, all hope had faded from her heart, as from ours.

"Maya, two people live, and two alone, who know this tale — Nahua my wife, and I myself. Till this morning there was but one, for Nahua only told me of it when she found that you had not escaped, and this she has done that she may be rid of you whom she hates as her rival. Therefore it was that she would have held me back from pursuing you, and therefore it is that she will appear before the Council of the Heart this night, so that her evidence may ensure your instant death in the Pit of Waters. But as it chances, least of anything on the earth do I desire that my eyes should lose sight of you, whom now as ever I love better than anything on the earth."

Now the señor grew white with rage, and he broke in —

"You will do well to keep such words to yourself, Tikal; for of this be sure — if you do not, I will add to my crimes and you shall not leave this place alive. No need to look at your guards. What do I care for your guards, who have but one life to lose. Speak thus again, and, before they reach you, you shall be dead."

"Let him go on, husband," said Maya; "what can a few insults more or less matter to us now. Continue, most noble Tikal; but, for your own sake, restrain yourself, and say nothing that a husband should not hear."

"It is for this reason," he went on, taking no notice of the señor's anger, "that I have come here with a plan to save you all; yes, even this braggart white man who has robbed me of you. If Nahua and I are silent, who will know of your crimes? And if the evidence of them is destroyed before your eyes, who is there that can prove them? Now, I will be silent — at a price. I will even bring the true tablet of the prophecy and the roll of Mattai's confession, and destroy them with fire before you."

"You will be silent," said Maya — "but what of Nahua? Will she be silent also?"

Now Tikal's dark face grew evil with some purpose of his own, though whether it were of murder or of what I do not know.

"Leave Nahua to me," he said. "Withdraw the charge you made against her, of attempting to kill yonder child, and free her thus of the need of appearing this night in the Sanctuary, and I swear to you that no word of her dreadful secret shall ever pass her lips. Then you will be tried upon one issue only — that of having broken your oaths by flying the city — a crime that is not beyond forgiveness."

"You spoke of a price, Tikal; tell us, what is this price that we must pay?"

"The price is yourself, Maya. Nay — hear me out; and you, White Man, keep silent. If you will swear upon the Heart to become my wife within six months from this day, then I, on my part, will swear that the white man — your husband who is not your husband, for he won the consent of the Council to his marriage by a trick — shall be suffered to escape the land unharmed, taking with him his friend and so much of our treasure and things needful for their journey as he may desire. I will swear also — and by this you may see how deep and honest is my love for you — that your son shall not be dispossessed of the place and rank which he holds in the eyes of the people as a Heaven-sent Deliverer whose coming was foretold by prophecy. My child shall give place to yours, Maya. Once before I held out the hand of peace to you, but you refused it and tricked me, and from that refusal has sprung the death of your father and many other sorrows. Do not refuse me again, Maya, lest these sorrows should be increased and multiplied upon you, and upon us all. It is no strange or unnatural thing I ask of you — that you should wed the man to whom for so many years you were affianced, and take your place as the first lady in this city, instead of giving yourself over, with your accomplices, to the most infamous of deaths."

"Yet it is most strange and unnatural, Tikal, that a wife should be asked to part thus from her husband. But stay — it is for him to speak, not me, for he may be glad to buy safety at this cost. First, what do you say, Ignatio? Tell me — though I fear your answer, for it is easy to guess, seeing that Tikal offers all that you can desire, freedom, and treasure to enable you to execute your plans."

"It is true, Lady," I replied, "that he offers me these things — though whether or no he is able to give them I cannot say; and it is true also that I have no wife here whom I must leave, and no prospect save that of a traitor's death. Still, Lady, I remember a certain promise that I made to you yonder in the wilderness, when by your courage you saved your husband's life; and I remember also that it was through me that he, my friend, came to visit this accursed city. Therefore I say, let our fate be one fate."

"Those are very noble words, friend," she said, "such as could have come only from your noble heart. Now, husband, do you speak?"

"I have nothing to say, Maya," replied the señor with a little laugh, "except that I wonder why you waste time, which we might spend happily together, in listening to this fellow's insults. If you bid me to go to save you, perhaps I might think about it; but certainly I will not stir one pace from your side to save myself from any death."

"It seems that I have got my answer," said Tikal. "May none of you regret it tonight when you come to look down into the Pit of Waters. Well, time presses, and I have much to do before we meet again" — and he turned to leave us.

Now, as he went, despair took hold of Maya. For a moment she struggled with it and with herself, then she cried:

"Come back, Tikal!"

He came, and stood before her in cold silence, and she spoke, addressing her husband in a slow voice:

"You are overhasty; *my* answer is not yet spoken, husband. Tikal, I accept your offer. Prevent Nahua from giving testimony against us; destroy the evidences she holds, and set these men safe, with all that they may desire, on the further side of yonder mountain, and within six months I will become your wife."

Now the señor and I stared at each other aghast.

"Are you mad?" he said, "or do you speak so in the hope of saving us?"

"Would it be wonderful, husband," she answered, "if I should wish to save myself and my child? That I have loved you and love you, you know; yet is there any love in the grave? While I live, at least I have my memories; if I die, even these may be taken from me. Go back, husband, go back wealthy to your own people and your old life, and choose some other woman to be your companion. Do not forget me, indeed; but let me become as a dream to you, seeing that for all our sakes this is the best. To you also, Ignatio, I say 'go.' Our fellowship has brought you little luck; may its severing be more fortunate, and may you at last attain your ends. Tikal, give me your hand, and let us swear the oath."

He stepped towards her — his eyes glowing with triumph; but as their fingers touched she glanced sideways and upwards, and saw the doubt and agony written on her husband's face. With a little scream, she sprang to him and threw herself into his arms, saying:

"Forgive me; I have tried my best, but this is more than I can do. Oh! weak and foolish that I am, I cannot part from you, no, not even to save your life. Surely you did not think that I should have fulfilled this oath and given myself to him in marriage. No, no — it is to death that I should have given myself when you were gone. But I cannot part with you — I cannot part with you — though my selfishness is your doom."

"I rejoice to hear it," said the señor. "Listen you, Tikal, if you are a man, give me a sword and let us settle this matter face to face. So shall one of us at least be rid of his doubts and troubles."

"Surely, White Man," answered Tikal, "you must be a fool as well as a rogue, otherwise you would scarcely ask me to risk my life against yours, which is already forfeit to the law. Farewell, Maya; long have you fooled and tormented me; tonight I will repay you all" — and he went.

*I*t might be thought that, after Tikal was gone, we should have spoken together of what had passed, and of the dangers before us. But this was not so. I think we felt — all of us — that there was nothing more to be said. It is useless to fight against Fate, and it is still more useless to be afraid of him, seeing that whatever we do or leave undone, he has his will of us at last. So we sat and chatted on different things — of our life at the mine at Cumarvo, of that night which we spent in the *hacienda* at Santa Cruz, of the death of our brave companion, Molas, and I know not what besides. Presently the child awoke, and its parents occupied themselves with it, finding resemblance to each other in its tiny features, while I walked up and down the hall, counting the lamps, smoking, and wondering where I should be by this time on the morrow.

At length the gates opened, for now it was almost the middle of the night, and there came through them Dimas and a guard of priests. The old man bowed before us and said that the time had come to lead us before the Council in the Sanctuary, but that we were to have no fear, seeing that, from all that he had been able to learn, our offence would be leniently dealt with. Maya asked what was to become of the infant, which could not be left alone, and he replied that she must bring it with her, whereon she began to wrap it in a *serape*.

"Your care is needless," said Dimas. "There is a secret way to the Sanctuary from this place, by which I propose to lead you in order that the child, our lord, shall not be exposed to the raw cold of the night."

Then he took a bunch of keys from his girdle, and, handing them to one who accompanied him — a fellow-priest and a member of the Council — he commanded him to go forward with several of the escort, to open the doors and light lamps in the passages that lay between us and the Sanctuary. The priest went, and, having waited awhile, we followed him, to find him standing by the marble wall which separated the passages from the Sanctuary. On seeing us approach, he gave the signs, which were answered from within; next he opened the false door with a silver key, leaving the key and the bunch to which it was attached fixed in the lock, for Dimas to take as he passed. This, however, the old priest did not do, for he thought that we should all return by this passage, and as we stepped into the Sanctuary he contented himself with closing the door without locking it.

Now once more we stood within the dim and holy place, there to take our trial for offences committed against the laws of the City of the Heart. There was a full gathering of the Council, and Tikal, its high priest and president, sat in his seat behind the altar, but I noted, with a thrill of hope, that Nahua his wife was not by his side, nor was she to be found among the members of the Council. We took seats that had been prepared for us in the open space before the altar, Maya being placed in the center, and the señor and myself on either side of her. Next the Priest of the Records rose and announced that the first business before the Council was the trial of three of its members, namely, Maya, Lady of the Heart, her husband, the white man, Son of the Sea, and Ignatio, the Wanderer, a lord of the Heart from beyond the mountains, upon the charge of having broken their oaths which they took as members of the Council. Having read this formal accusation, the priest set out the case against us clearly but briefly:

"On this very night of the festival of the Rising of Waters, a year ago," he began, "you, strangers, amongst other things swore upon the altar, setting in pledge your souls and bodies for the fulfillment of the oath, that without the consent of this high Brotherhood you would not attempt to leave the gates of the City of the Heart. Yet but the other day you were overtaken and seized in the act of flying across the mountains to the wilderness beyond. Nor is this all your crime, for with you was that infant, born of the white man and the Lady of the Heart, the Heaven-sent Child of prophecy, of whom you wickedly sought to rob us and the people. Say, now, how do you plead to these charges?"

"We plead guilty," answered Maya, "but we ask to be heard in our own defense. Listen, lords: Since that night when we were married by your command, my husband and I myself have been dogged by murder, and yonder, as high priest of the Heart and president of your councils, he sits who would have murdered us. I see among you this night some of those who waited on me upon the day of our escape, having the Lord Dimas at the head of them. What did they tell me? That a plot had been discovered, made by Tikal, my cousin, to murder my husband, my child, and my friend, Ignatio the Wanderer. They told me also that Tikal would be deposed because of this and his other crimes, and that the infant in my arms would tonight be anointed *cacique* of the people of the Heart. Is it not so, Dimas?"

"It is so, lady," he answered, "and learn that you are not the only ones who are on trial this night. Though your case is taken first, that of Tikal the high priest and others will follow; but till then, in virtue of his rank and office, he sits as president of our Council."

Now Tikal sprang from his seat, but Dimas turned upon him and said sternly:

"Keep silent, lord, or speak only to fulfil the duties of your place. Your judging shall be just, but know that there is no hope of escape for you till it is done, seeing that your guards are disarmed, and all the paths are watched."

Tikal seated himself again, and Maya went on:

"On that very night of the coming of the Lord Dimas, when I was alone in my chamber, the Lady Nahua, the wife of Tikal, crept upon me and strove to murder this my child;" and she set out the storytelling how the señor and I, hearing her cries for help, had entered the chamber and seized and bound Nahua. "Then it was, brethren, that sudden terror took us, and we fled, seeking to escape a land where we could not live in safety from one hour to another. This is our sin, and we leave our punishment in your hands. Surely it was better that we should strive to save the child, so that he might live to play his part, whatever that may be, than that he should be kept here to be butchered by those whom you have raised up to rule you."

When Maya had finished her speech, the señor and I addressed the Council in turn, confirming all that she had said, and submitting ourselves to the judgment of the Brotherhood.

Now we were commanded to fall back, and took our stand beneath the mask of the Nameless god, while the Council consulted together, and there we awaited our doom. Presently we were brought forward again, and Tikal spoke to us, saying that our sentence was postponed till the charge against Nahua, the daughter of Mattai, and against himself, Tikal, the *cacique* and high priest of the City of the Heart, had been considered, adding in a slow and triumphant voice:

"Let Nahua, the daughter of Mattai, who waits without, be brought into the presence of the Heart."

We heard, and gathered up our courage to meet the advancing fate, for we knew that death was on us, and that for us there was no more pity or escape.

The door was opened, and Nahua came through it, dressed in the robes of her rank, and wearing the green diadem that could be carried only by the wife or mother of the *cacique*.

"What is your pleasure with me, lords?" she said proudly, after she had made her obeisance to the altar.

Then the Priest of the Records rose and read the charge, namely, that she had attempted with her own hand to do murder upon the body of the infant child of Maya, Lady of the Heart, and her husband, the white man; also that she had aided and abetted Tikal, her husband, in various acts of cruelty and misgovernment that were alleged against him, asking her what she pleaded in answer.

"To the last charge, not guilty," she said. "Let Tikal defend his own sins. To the first, guilty. I did attempt to put an end to yonder brat, but Maya discovered me, and I was caught and bound."

"Surely, brethren," said Dimas, rising, "we need carry this matter no further. We have heard the evidence of the Lady Maya and the others, and now Nahua confesses to her crime. She confesses that she attempted to take the life of him whom she knew to be the sacred child, the hope of the People of the Heart, and for such a sin it seems to me that there is but one punishment, though it is terrible, and she who must suffer it is a woman and of high rank."

"Stay!" broke in Nahua. "You have not heard me out, and I have the right to speak before I am condemned to die. You charge me with having attempted to take the life of 'the sacred child, the hope of the People of the Heart,' and, had I done this, doubtless I should be worthy of your doom, whereas in truth I am worthy of your praise. Lords of the Heart, this child whom you adore, the Heaven-sent Child of prophecy, whom tonight you would anoint as your *cacique*, deposing Tikal, my husband, and who, as you believe, shall be the star to light our race to greatness and to victory, is a living lie, a fraud, and a bastard!"

Now a confusion broke out among the Council, and angry voices called to her to cease her blasphemies; but she won silence, and went on:

"Hear me out, I pray you, for, even if I wished it, I should not dare to speak thus at random, but am prepared with proof of every word I utter. You think that I would have killed this child to wring the heart of my rival, Maya — and indeed I desire to wring it; and that I would set my own son in his place — and indeed I wish to set him there. Yet these were not my reasons for the deed. Lords of the Council, listen to a tale, the strangest that ever you have heard, and judge between me and Tikal, my husband, and Maya, my rival, and her friends. Mattai, my father, was known to you all, seeing that at the time of his death, and, indeed, since Tikal was anointed *cacique,* he stood next to him in place and power among the People of the Heart, holding those offices in the Brotherhood which now are filled by Dimas, and among them that of Keeper of the Sanctuary. Yet, lords, Mattai, my father, was no true man. Alas! that I should have to say it, seeing that it was more for my own sake that he sinned than for his own, since he loved me, and desired my welfare above everything on earth. It was this love of his that ruined him, making him false to his god, to his oaths, and to his country. Thus, in the beginning, he knew that since I was a child I had set my heart upon the Lord Tikal, who was affianced to the Lady Maya; also that I was ambitious and yearned to be great. Therefore it was that he deceived Tikal, pretending that it had been revealed to him by heaven that the Lady Maya and her father were dead in the wilderness. Therefore it was also that when he had persuaded him that she was lost to him forever, he pressed it upon the Lord Tikal that he should marry me in place of Maya, his affianced, who was dead, promising him in return that he would bring it about that he should be anointed *cacique* of the People of the Heart. All these things and others he did, though at that time I knew nothing of them, and thought in my folly that Tikal married me because he loved me, and sought me as the companion of his life and power.

"Then Zibalbay returned on the night of our marriage-feast, and with him came Maya and the strangers; and from that hour my husband began to hate me because I was his wife in place of Maya, whom he loved. More, as I have learned since, he went to Zibalbay while he lay in prison, and offered to resign his place as *cacique* in his favor for so long as he should live, and no more to oppose his schemes, if he would give him Maya in marriage after I had been put away either by death or by divorce. This Zibalbay would have done, and gladly; but, as it chanced, Maya here had her heart set upon the white man during their journeyings together through the wilderness, and refused to be separated from him that she might be palmed off in marriage upon Tikal. Yet he might have won his way, for their case was desperate, and the alternative was death had not Mattai, my father, found a plan whereby they could be saved and I remain the wife of the *cacique.* This was the plan, lords:

that a prophecy should be set in the symbol of the Heart yonder, such as would deceive the Council of the Heart, and bring it about that Maya should be given in marriage to the white man whom she loved. Lords, this was done. At the dead of night they crept to the Sanctuary, and, opening the Heart, they placed within it that tablet which you have seen, the tablet that foreshadowed the birth of a Deliverer. The rest you know."

"It is false," cried many voices. "Such sacrilege is not possible."

"It is not false," answered Nahua, "and I will prove to you that the sacrilege was possible. The Heart was opened, and the false prophecy forged by my father was placed within it, where it was found by you on the night of the festival of the Rising of Waters, this day a year ago. But when the holy Heart was opened, behold! it was not empty, for in it lay another prophecy — a true prophecy — which was removed from it, that the lie which has deceived you might be set in its place."

"Where, then, is that writing?" asked Dimas.

"Here," she answered, drawing the tablet from her breast. "Listen —" and she read:

"The Eye that has slept and is awakened sees the heart and purpose of the wicked. I say that in the hour of the desolation of my city not all the waters of the Holy Lake shall wash away their sin."

"Take it, lords, and see for yourselves," she continued, laying the tablet on the altar. "Now, listen again, and learn how it chanced that this relic came into my keeping. After he had wrought this great sin, the curse of the Nameless god fell upon my father, and, as you know, he was smitten with a sore disease. Then it came about that, when he lay dying, remorse took him, and he wrote a certain paper which he caused to be witnessed and given to me, together with this tablet. In my hand I hold that paper, lords; hear it and judge for yourselves whether I have spoken truth or falsehood" — and she read aloud the confession of Mattai, that set out every detail of our plot and the manner of its execution.

"Now, lords," she added, when the reading was finished and the signatures had been examined, "you will understand how it happened that in my rage at this tidings I strove to kill yonder infant, who has been palmed off upon you as the seed of the god, and I leave it to you to deal with those who planned the fraud."

Chapter XXV

FAREWELL

Nahua ceased and sat down, and so great was the astonishment — or rather the awe — of the Council at the tale that she had told, that for a while none of them spoke. At length Dimas rose, and said:

"Maya, Lady of the Heart, and you strangers, you have heard the awful charge that is brought against you. What do you say in answer to it?"

"We say that it is true," answered Maya calmly. "We were forced to choose between the loss of our lives and the doing of this deed, and we chose to live. It was Mattai who hatched the fraud and executed the forgery, and now it seems that we must suffer for his sin as well as for our own. One word more: Ignatio here did not enter into this plot willingly, but was forced into it by my husband and myself, and chiefly by myself."

Dimas made no answer, but at a sign the two priests who guarded the altar with drawn swords came forward and drove us into the passage that led from the Sanctuary to the Hall of the Dead, where they shut us in between the double doors, leaving us in darkness.

Here, as all was finished, I knelt down to offer my last prayers to Heaven, while Maya wept in her husband's arms, taking farewell of him and of her child, which wailed upon her breast.

"Truly," he said, "you were wise, wife, when you urged us not to enter this Country of the Heart. Still, what is done cannot be undone, and, having been happy together for a little space, let us die together as bravely as we may, hoping that still together we may awake presently in some new world of peace."

While he spoke, the door was opened, and the priests with drawn swords led us back into the Sanctuary. As Maya crossed the threshold first of the three of us, she was met by Tikal, who with a sudden movement, but without roughness, took the child from her arms. Now we saw what was prepared for us, for the stone in front of the altar had been lifted, and at our feet yawned the black shaft from which ascended the sound of waters. They placed us with our backs resting against the altar; but Tikal stood in front, and between him and us lay the mouth of the pit.

"Maya, daughter of Zibalbay the *cacique,* Lady of the Heart; white man, Son of the Sea; Ignatio the Wanderer; and Mattai the priest, whom, being dead in the body, we summon in the spirit," began Dimas in a cold and terrible voice, "you by your own confession are proved guilty of the greatest crimes that can be dreamed of in the wicked brain of man and executed by his impious hands. You have broken your solemn oaths taken in the presence of heaven and your brethren; you have offered insult to the god we worship, and violated his Sanctuary; and you have palmed off as their god-sent prince, upon the people who trusted you, a bastard and a child of sin. For all these and other crimes which you have committed — why we know not — it is not in our power to mete out to you a just reward. That must be measured to you elsewhere, when you have passed our judgment-seat and your names are long forgotten upon the earth.

"This is the sentence of the Council of the Heart, that your name, Mattai, be erased from the list of the officers of the Heart; that your memory be proclaimed accursed; that your dwelling-place be burned with fire, and the site of it strewn with salt; that your corpse be torn from its grave and laid upon the summit of the pyramid till the birds of the air devour it; and that your soul be handed over to the tormentors of the lower world to deal with according to their pleasure forever and for aye.

"This is the sentence of the Council of the Heart upon you, Maya, daughter of Zibalbay the *cacique,* Lady of the Heart; white man, Son of the Sea, and Ignatio the Wanderer: That your names be erased from the roll of the Brethren of the Heart, and proclaimed accursed in the streets of the city; that you be gagged, bound hand and foot, and chained living to the walls of the Sanctuary, and there left before the altar of the god which you have violated, till death from thirst and hunger shall overtake you; that your corpses be laid upon the pyramid as a prey to the birds of the air; and that your souls be handed over to the tormentors of the underworld to deal with according to their pleasure forever and for aye. It is spoken. Let the sentence of the Council be done. But first, since this bastard babe is too young to sin and suffer punishment, let him be handed into the keeping of the god, that the god may deal with him according to his pleasure."

As the words passed his lips, and before we fully understood them, dazed as we were with the horror of our awful doom, Tikal stepped forward and — even now I shudder when I write of it — holding the poor infant, which at this instant began to wail again as though with pain or fear, over the mouth of the pit, suddenly he let it fall into the depths beneath.

The shriek of the agonized mother ran round the walls of the holy place, and before it had died away the señor had leaped forward — leaped like a puma — across the gulf of the open well and gripped Tikal by the throat and waist. He gripped him, and, rage giving him strength, he lifted him high above his head and hurled him down the dreadful place whither the child had gone before.

With a hoarse scream, Tikal vanished, and for a moment there was silence. It was broken by the voice of Maya, crying aloud, in accents of madness and despair —

"Not all the waters of the Holy Lake shall wash away our sin, yet may they serve to avenge us upon you, O you murderers of a helpless child!"

As she spoke, followed by the señor and myself, who I think alone of all the company guessed her dreadful purpose, Maya ran round the altar, and with both her hands grasped the symbol of the Heart which lay upon it.

"Forbear!" cried the voice of Dimas, but she did not heed him. Before he or any of us could reach her, dragging at it with desperate strength, she tore the ancient symbol from its bed, and with a loud and mocking laugh had cast it down upon the marble floor, where it shattered into fragments.

For one second all was still; then from the altar there came a sudden twang as of harp-strings breaking, that was followed instantly by another and more awful sound, the sound of the roar of many waters.

"Fly! fly!" cried a voice, "the floods are loosed and destruction is upon us and upon the People of the Heart!"

Now the Council rushed one and all towards the door of the Sanctuary; but I, Ignatio, by the grace of Heaven, remembered the outer door, the secret door through which we had entered, that the priest had left ajar.

"This way!" I cried in Spanish to the señor, and seizing Maya by the arm I dragged her with me into the passage. When all three of us were through I turned to close the door, and as I did so I saw an awful sight.

Out of the mouth of the pit before the altar sprang a vast column of water, which struck the roof of the Sanctuary with such fearful force that already the massive marble blocks began to rain down upon the crowd of fugitives, who struggled and in vain to open the door and escape into the Hall of the Dead. One other thing I saw; it was the corpse of Tikal, vomited from the depth into which the señor had hurled him, a shapeless mass ascending and descending with the column of water as alternately it struck and rebounded from the roof.

Then, before the flood could reach it, I closed the door, and, possessing myself of the bunch of keys that still hung in the lock, we fled up the passages and stairs till we came to the hall where we had been imprisoned. Here, however, we dared not stay, for already strange gurgling sounds struck upon our ears, and we felt the mighty fabric of the pyramid shake and quiver beneath the blows of the imprisoned waters as they burst their way upward and outward. Seizing lamps, we ran to the copper gates at the head of the hall, and not without trouble found the key that opened them. We had no time to spare, for as we left it the water rushed in at the further end of the chamber, a solid wave that in some few seconds filled it to the depth of six or eight feet. On we fled before the advancing flood, and well was it for us that our course lay upwards, for otherwise we must have been drowned as we searched for the keys to open the different gates and doors. But now fortune, which for so long had been our foe, befriended us, and the end of it was that we reached the summit of the pyramid just as the dawn began to break.

The dawn was breaking and seldom perhaps has the light of day revealed a more wonderful or terrible sight to the eyes of man. Outside the gates of the courtyard of the pyramid were gathered a great multitude of people waiting to be admitted to celebrate the feast that on this day of the year was to be held, according to the custom, upon the summit of the pyramid. Indeed, they should have already been assembled there, but it was the rule that the gates could not be opened until the Council had left the Sanctuary, and this night the Council sat late. As we looked at them a cry of fear and wonder rose from the multitude, and this was the cause of it. Along that street which ran from the landing-place to the great square rushed a vast foam-topped wall of water twenty feet or more in depth by a hundred broad. Now we learned the truth. The symbol on the altar – I know not how – was connected with secret and subterranean sluice-gates which for many generations had protected the City of the Heart from flood. When it was torn from its bed these sluice-gates were opened, and the waters, rushing in, sought their natural level, which at this season of the year was higher than the housetops of the city.

On the summit of the pyramid were two priests who tended the sacred fire and made ready for the service to be celebrated. Seeing us emerge from the watch-house, they ran towards us, wringing their hands, and asking what dreadful thing had come to pass. I replied that we did not know, but that seeing the water gather in our prison we had fled from it. How we had fled they never stopped to ask, but ran down the stairway of the pyramid, only to return again presently, for before they reached its base their escape was cut off.

Meanwhile the terror thickened and the doom began. Everywhere the waters spread and gathered, replenished from the inexhaustible reservoir of the vast lake. Whole streets went down before them, to vanish suddenly beneath their foaming face, while from the crowd below rose one continuous shriek of agony.

Maya heard it, and, casting herself face downward upon the surface of the pyramid, that she might not see her handiwork, she thrust her fingers into her ears to stop them, while the señor and I watched, fascinated. Now the flood struck the people, some thousands of them, who were gathered on the rising ground at the gates of the enclosure of the temple, and lo! in an instant they were gone, borne away as withered leaves are borne before a gale. Ere a man might count ten the most of the population of the City of the Heart had perished!

For a little while some of the more massive houses stood, only to vanish one by one, in silence as it seemed, for now the roar of the advancing waters mastered all other sounds. Before the sun was well up it was finished, and of that ancient and beautiful city, Heart of the World, there remained nothing to be seen except the tops of trees and the upper parts of the pyramids of worship rising above the level of the lake. The Golden City was no more. It was gone, and with it all its hoarded treasures, its learning and its ancient faith, and that which for many generations had been held to be a myth had now become a myth indeed. One short hour had sufficed to sweep out of existence the ripe fruit of the labor of centuries, and with it the dwindling remnant of the last pure race of Indians, who followed the customs and the creeds of my forefathers. Doubtless their day was done, and the Power above us had decreed their fall; still, so vast and sudden a ruin was a thing awful to behold, or even to think upon. What, I wondered, would the founders of this great city and the fashioners of its solemn pyramids and Sanctuary have thought and felt, could they have foreseen the manner of its end? Would they, then, have set the holy symbol so cunningly upon its altar, that the strength of a maddened woman, by tearing it away, could bury altar, temple, town, and all who lived therein, forever beneath the surface of the lake? This they did to protect their homes and fanes against the foe, so that, if need were, they could prefer destruction to dishonor; but they did not foresee — indeed they never dreamed — that this foe might be of their own race, and that the hand of one of her children would bring disaster, utter and irredeemable, upon the proud head of their holy stronghold, the city Heart of the World.

Now foot by foot the waters found their level, filling up the cup in which the town had stood, and the bright sunlight shone upon their placid surface as they rippled round the sides of the pyramid and over the flat roofs of the submerged houses. Here and there floated a mass of wreckage, and here and there a human corpse, over which already the water-eagles began to gather, and that was all.

Presently Maya rose to her knees and looked out from beneath the hollow of her hand, for the light was dazzling there upon the white summit of the pyramid. Then she flung her arms above her head and uttered and great and bitter cry.

"Behold my handiwork," she said, "and the harvest of my sin! Oh! my father, that dream which you sent to haunt my sleep was dreadful, but it did not touch the truth. Oh! my father, the people whom you would have saved are dead; lost is the city that you loved, and it is I who have destroyed them. Oh! my father, my father, your curse has found me out indeed, and I am accursed."

Some such words as these she spoke, then began to laugh, and turning to the señor, she said,

"Where is the child, husband?"

He could not answer her, but she took no note of it, only she bent her arms, rocking them and crooning as though the infant lay upon her breast, then came first to him and next to me, saying —

"Look, is he not a pretty boy? Am I not happy to be the mother of such a boy?"

I made pretence to look, but the sight of her pitiful face and of the empty arms, as she swayed them, was so dreadful that I was forced to turn away to hide my tears. Now I saw the truth. Weariness, sorrow, and shock had turned her brain, and she was mad.

We led her to the watch-house, where there was shelter, and the priests, who had returned, gave us food so soon as we could make them understand that we needed it, for they too were almost mad. Here her last illness seized the Lady Maya. It began with a hardening of the breast, which changed presently to fever. Two days and nights, with breaking hearts, we nursed her there upon the pyramid, striving not to listen to her sick ravings and piteous talk about the child, and at dawn upon the third day she died. Before she died her senses returned to her, and she spoke to her husband beautiful and tender words which seem almost too holy to set down.

"Alas!" she ended, "as my heart foretold me, I have brought you nothing but evil, and now the time has come for me to go away from you. Ignatio was right, and we were wrong — or rather I was wrong. We should have died together a year ago, if that were needful, sooner than commit the sin we worked in the Sanctuary, for then at least our hands would have been clean, nor would the blood of the people have rested on my head. Yet, believe me, husband, that when I did the deed of death, I was mad, for I had seen our child murdered before my eyes and I heard a voice within me bidding me to be avenged. Well, it is done, and I have suffered for it and perhaps shall suffer more, yet I think that I was but the hand or the instrument of Fate predestined to bring destruction upon a race already doomed, and on a faith outworn. That faith I no longer believe in, for you have taught me another worship, therefore I do not fear the vengeance of the god of my people. May my other sins find forgiveness, if they are sins, for it was my love of you that led me to them. Husband, I trust that you may escape from this ill-omened place, and live on for many years in happiness; but most of all I trust that in the land which you will reach at last, you may find us waiting for you, the child and I together. Farewell to you. This is a sad parting, and my life has been short and sorrowful. Yet I am glad to have lived it, since it brought me to your arms, and, however little I may have deserved it, I think that you loved me truly and will love my memory even when I am dead. To you also, Ignatio, farewell. You have been a true friend to me, though I brought you no good luck, and at times I was jealous of you. Think kindly of me if you can, though had it not been for me you might have attained your ends, and, as in the old days before we met, comfort my husband with your friendship."

Then once more she turned to the señor and in a gasping and broken voice prayed of him not to forget her or her child. I heard him answer that this she need not fear, as his happiness died with her, and, even if he should escape, he thought that they would not be parted for very long, nor could any other woman take her place within his heart.

She blessed him and thanked him, caressing his face with her dying hands, and, unable to bear more of such a sight, I left them together.

An hour later the señor came from the watch-house, and though he did not speak, one glance at him was enough to tell me that all was over.

So died Maya, Lady of the Heart, the last of the ancient royal blood of the Indian princes, myself alone excepted, a very sweet and beautiful woman, though at times headstrong, passionate, and capricious.

Now while Maya lay dying we learned that some Indians still lived on the mainland, men and women who had been sent there to tend the crops, for we saw a canoe hovering round what once had been the Island of the Heart. The two priests who were with us on the pyramid tried to signal to it to come to our rescue, but either those in the boat did not see us, or they were terror-stricken and feared to approach the pyramid. Still we kept the body all that day, hoping that help might reach us, so that we could take it ashore for burial. Towards night, however, when none came, we made another plan. On the roof of the watch-house the sacred fire still burned, for the two priests had tended it, more from custom, I think, than for any other reason. Hither we brought some of the gilded stools that were used by the nobles of the Heart on days of festival, and all the fuel that had been stored to replenish the fire, building the whole into a funeral pyre around and above the brazier. Then, as it caught, we carried out the body of Maya, wrapped in her white robes, and laid it upon the pyre and left it.

Presently the great pile was alight and burning so fiercely that it lit up the whole summit of the pyramid and the darkness which surrounded it. All that night we watched it, while the two priests lamented and beat their breasts after their fashion, till at length it flared itself away, and the holy fire that had burned for more than a thousand years died down and was extinguished. It seemed very fitting that the latest office of this ancient and consecrated flame should be to consume the body of the last of the royal race who had tended it for so many generations. Towards dawn a wind sprang up with drizzling rain, and when we approached the place at daybreak it was to find it cold and blackened. No spark remained alight, and no ash or fragment could be seen of her who was once the beautiful and gracious Lady of the Heart.

Now we set ourselves sadly enough to find a means of escape to the mainland, which indeed it was time to do, for the waters, working in its center, were sapping the foundations of the great pyramid, portions of which had already fallen away. Our plan was to form a raft by lashing together some benches that were at hand, and on it to float or paddle ourselves to the shore. This, however, we were spared the pains of doing, for when our task was half completed we saw a large canoe, manned by three Indians, advancing towards us, and signalled to them to paddle round to the steps of the pyramid. They did so, and, taking with us all the food and such few articles of value as were to be found in the watch-house, the four of us embarked, though not without difficulty, for the current ran so strongly round the crumbling edges of the pyramid that it was hard to bring the canoe up to the stairs.

From the Indians we learned that those on shore were so overwhelmed with horror at the catastrophe which had fallen upon their holy city, that they did not dare to approach the place where it had stood. But when on the previous night they saw the great flame of Maya's funeral pyre, they knew that men still lived upon the pyramid, who, as they thought, were signalling to them for help, and ventured out to save them. They asked us how it came about that the waters had overwhelmed the city which had stood among them safely from the beginning of time. We replied that we did not know, and the priests with us, now that they had escaped with their lives, seemed too prostrated to tell our deliverers that we had been imprisoned in the hollow of the pyramid, even if they knew that this was so.

On reaching the shore we found a little gathering of awe-stricken Indians — perhaps there may have been a hundred and fifty of them — the sole survivors of the People of the Heart, unless indeed a few still lived on the high land of those portions of the island of the Heart that as yet had not been submerged. Open-mouthed and almost without comment they listened to the terrible tale of the sudden and utter destruction of their city. When it was done, one among them suggested that the white man should be killed, as without doubt he had brought misfortune and the vengeance of heaven upon their race, but this proposal seemed to find no favor with the rest of them. Indeed, had they known the part which we played in the disaster, I doubt if they would have found the spirit to make an end of us.

On the other hand, they gave us what food and clothing we required, and even weapons, such as *machetes,* bows and arrows, and blow-pipes, and left us to go our way. Often I have wondered what became of them, and if any of their number, or of their children, still survive.

So we turned our faces to the mountains, and on the second day we crossed them safely, for Maya had told us the secret of the passage through the rocks, which, under her guidance, we had passed blind-folded.

Thus, at length, having looked our last upon the blue waters of the Holy Lake, sparkling in the sunshine above the palaces of the city and the bones of its inhabitants, did we leave that accursed Country of the Heart, where so much loss and evil had befallen us.

Envoi

My friend, now I, Ignatio, have finished writing that story of how I came to visit the Golden City of the Indians, which so many have believed to be fabulous, and that today exists no more. It is a strange story, and I trust that it may interest you to read it when I am dead and buried.

Perhaps you would like to know the details of our homeward journey, but in truth I have neither the strength nor the patience to set them down. It was a terrible journey, and once we both of us fell ill with fever from which I thought that we should not recover; but recover we did by the help of some wandering Indians who nursed us, and at length reached this place from which we had fled for our lives nearly two years before. We found the *hacienda* deserted, for it had the reputation of being haunted, though some of the Indian dependents, or rather slaves, of that great villain, Don Pedro Moreno, still worked patches of the land. Well, the señor took a fancy to stay in the place, for it was here that he had first seen his wife, and so we sold that girdle of emeralds which Maya took from the chest of ornaments and gave to me when we were imprisoned for the first time in the hall of the pyramid (do not lose the clasp, friend, for it is the only remaining relic of the People of the Heart), and with the proceeds we bought at a cheap rate from the government of the day, who had entered into possession of them, this house and the wide lands round it, that I have cultivated ever since. For, my friend, now my ambitions were finished. I had played my last card and it had failed me, and, albeit with a sorrowful mind, I abandoned my hopes for the regeneration of the Indians which I had no longer the means or the health and vigor to attempt. Also, I was no more Lord of the Heart, for with its counterpart it was lost in the Sanctuary yonder beneath the waters of the Holy Lake, and with the ancient symbol went much of my power.

For five years the señor and I lived here together, but I think that during all this time he was dying. He, who used to be so strong in body and merry in mind, never regained his health or spirits from that hour when Maya passed upon the pyramid, and though he seldom spoke of her, I know that night and day she was always present in his thoughts. Twice in the spring seasons he suffered from *calenturas,* as we call the fever of the country, which left him sallow in face and shrunken in body; and when the spring came round for the third time, I begged him to go to Mexico for change, returning to the *hacienda* in the summer. In vain; he would not do it, indeed I do not think that he cared whether he lived or died. So the end of it was that the *calentura* took him again, and die he did in my arms, happily as a child that falls asleep.

Now my days are accomplished also, and, having failed in all things and known much sorrow and disappointment, I go to join him. My friend, farewell. Perhaps you will think of me from time to time, and, though you are a heretic, send up a prayer to heaven for the welfare of the soul of the old Indian —

Ignatio

www.ingramcontent.com/pod-product-compliance
Lightning Source LLC
Chambersburg PA
CBHW060346030726
47497CB00003B/611